THE LIGHT OF THE NORTH SAGA · VOLUME 1

A SONG ·OF· STEEL

· J. C. DUNCAN ·

First edition March 2021

Cover design by Damonza.com
Photography by Studio Zahora
Illustration by James Nathaniel
Maps by Red geographics

ISBN 978-1-8383522-0-2 (paperback)
ISBN 978-1-8383522-1-9 (ebook)

www.jcduncan.co.uk

PREFACE

ONE OF THE most interesting and overlooked periods of European history in fictional literature is the period between the great Viking adventures of the ninth and tenth centuries and the wars following the Norman invasion of Britain in 1066. The empire that would eventually become Germany was just expanding into the lands on the southern Baltic coast. France was coalescing out of the chaotic mess of successor states that followed the reign of the mighty Charlemagne. The Papacy was flexing its relatively new-found strength, warring with the Holy Roman emperors for power and influence across the Christian world. The Norse tribes were shaking out into nation states. This was the period in which modern western and northern Europe was first starting to become recognisable to someone with a current map. A thousand years on, roughly the same nations still exist in roughly the same places. It was the age when modern Europe was seeded, if not founded. The time of the Roman Empire creating nations around Europe and wiping others out, the time of the Huns and Goths and Vandals and Franks burning and conquering their way across Europe as they migrated, was over forever.

Then, at the end of this fascinating period, which is named after them, the Vikings seemed to simply drop out of popular history. Their power appeared to dissipate, and their legendary raids ceased. Their last significant contribution to mainstream history seemed to be their role in the conquest of England in 1066 when the king of Norway, Harald Hardrada, was killed at Stamford Bridge at the head of an army of Vikings. The Franks took over the nation of England on the back of his costly defeat, arguably settling the demographic status of western Europe forever and bringing an end to the Viking age.

The Norse, or 'Vikings', as they are euphemistically and mostly incorrectly known, were degenerating from the peak of their power abroad even as they grew as nations at home. But their disappearance from historical interest was primarily a factor of their successes, not their failures. It seems that most people think the end of the Vikings was equivalent to a defeat, but it was not. It was due to their maturing as nations. The Viking raids were mostly a reaction to fairly tough conditions at home and constant warring between factions that left a very experienced and active group of warriors looking for new and better lands to plunder or conquer. This was driven by a culture of violence and low-level warfare – or was the cause of it. Both viewpoints are valid, I think. You could argue that the widespread nature of their raids and settlement was a symptom of calamity, a similar phenomenon to that of the Vandals, who conquered Rome because they were flee-ing other enemies across Europe, or the Saxons, who conquered England because they were fleeing enemies in what is now north-ern Germany.

The Viking raids actually stopped not because the Vikings were defeated but because their situation at home drastically changed. The warring factions coalesced into three nations: the Norse kingdoms of Sweden, Denmark and Norway that survive to this day, relatively unchanged in border or name. As these nations solidified and slowly stopped infighting, they prospered, and their people stopped looking outwards so desperately for conquest and plunder. Trade supplemented and then replaced raiding. Wars became formalised and were about the power of nations, not the wealth of local leaders and warlords. Surplus warriors became famous mercenaries and settlers, not raiders. It is much more profitable and less draining to trade than to plunder when you have a web of trade routes extending further than any other on earth at the time. The Norse trade network at the end of the Viking age encompassed the entirety of Europe from Iceland to near the Ural Mountains and extended deep into Central Asia.

Another significant factor that influenced the end of the Viking raids was the coming of Christianity. Christianity was known to the Norse for hundreds of years before they converted, of course. They encountered it, and Islam and other Asian religions, on their travels and raids, but they only started converting in large numbers in the tenth century. Harald Bluetooth, the king of Denmark, declared Denmark a Christian country in AD 975. From this point, it took two hundred years for the three Norse Scandinavian nations to be mostly converted to Christianity and to become accepted into the Christian European family of nations like any other. Their families intermarried, and they traded and conducted diplomacy as unified Christian nations. Sigurd I Magnusson, the king of Norway, went on crusade to the holy land, the first king of any Christian nation to go on a crusade. Eric 1, king of Denmark was the first Christian king to go on pilgrimage to the holy land after the First Crusade, (although he died on the journey). The Viking Norse nations had become as Christianised as any nation in Europe and actively participated in European efforts while remaining entirely independent. This was not the behaviour of beaten and downtrodden people.

It was a fascinating time with a slightly anti-climactic ending from a storytelling point of view. The age of the Vikings ended not with the clashing of swords and the shattering of shields but with unification, advances in farming techniques and the chant of prayer (a gross simplification, perhaps, but not totally unjustified).

The Norse culture was largely eroded in Scandinavia by the spread of Christianity and the laws, culture and ways of living that came with it, which were immiscible with the old ways. Their fascinating former way of life – their religion, storytelling, art, laws, honour code and society structure – was mostly subsumed. Most people outside of Scandinavia know very little of those aspects of Norse life, preferring to remember the Norse as raiders and conquerors, which is a grievous injustice to their history. Given that the Scandinavian Norse left little in the way of written works compared to many of their contemporary cultures, it is an injustice that has been hard to fight. Their brethren in Iceland left a rich history of written works, poetry, laws, sagas and other records that help keep their history much more alive and well known.

However, what if it hadn't played out that way? What if the Norse had refused to peacefully accept Christianity? What if that single decision by Harald Bluetooth to convert had been instead to ban Christianity? What if they had not gone quietly into the Christian brotherhood of nations? What difference would it have made to Europe then and now, from that one decision on that one day in history? That series of questions is one that fascinates me and is the central premise of this series. In this alternate reality, The Norse remain unconverted at the dawn of the twelfth century, and the Viking raids and conquests have continued to haunt Europe's shores from northern France to southern Italy.

I have sought to tell this story in the most appropriate way I can think of, in the context of a fictional Norse saga (or legendary story), seen both through the lens of its creation and through modern eyes. The Norse tradition of storytelling and oral history is both fascinating and misunderstood. I am excited to shine a little light on it with my own take on a Norse saga and its creation story. Welcome to the saga of *Ljós a Norðan*, (*The Light of the North*) set during an alternate history of what becomes the nation of Nordland and the Northern Crusades that create it.

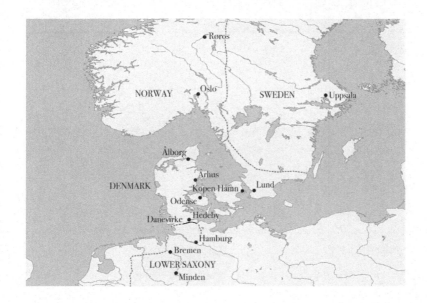

The world of Ljós a Norðan in AD 1100 with major locations and towns

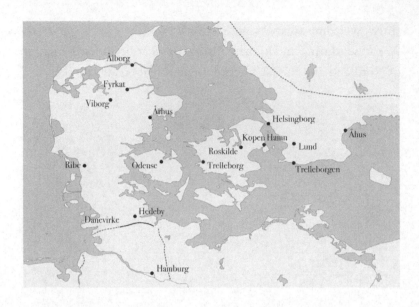

The named locations from the Kingdom of Denmark

Bright blade flowed smoke
Through arrow-stricken air
The Aesir kin awoke
To find their worthy heir
Sword and spear were turned aside
Shields were rent and broke
No mortal could defy
The fate that Odin spoke

The heart of a fallen star
Entwines the lives it takes
Flames eating at their souls
Bright steel slicing fates
Into the ranks of hel-formed foe
The hopes of victory strode
With him did our bravest go
Stout hearts with no fear showed

As victory spread her wings
And all the world seemed saved
A final foe descended
His pact with chaos made
Loki slipped into the fray
And clouds blew in his wake
He struck the mighty Gjaldir down
And turned our hopes to ash

Battle Poem of the sword Ljós a Norðan
Norse – 12th century

CHAPTER 1

THE FISH AND THE FUMBLE

Bjørsjøen lake, Nordland
August 2015

T HE LATE SUMMER sunlight, dancing off ripples on the water, was giving Ingrid sore eyes. Her father, Aurick, had told her to bring sunglasses, but she had ignored him and was too proud to admit that mistake. So she stared at her line and stubbornly pretended that all was well. The pain in her eyes did somewhat distract her from the pain in her backside from sitting for too long on the narrow wooden bench, and the pain in her forearms from leaning on the side of the small boat that her father loved so much. Her neck was aching from staring down at the line too. *Why was fishing so uncomfortable?* It was utterly beyond Ingrid how her father could love fishing so much, but her mother had insisted she go on the trip with him this year, so here she was, trying to pretend to be enjoying herself and failing miserably.

Aurick smiled to himself as he watched his daughter impatiently fuming. He had told her to feel the line, not stare at it, to relax and sit back to enjoy the time. She had always been such a wilful child; it was part of the reason why he loved her so much. His own father used to own the small cabin beside Bjørsjøen lake and he, Aurick, had spent many a happy summer weekend there as a child, fishing, swimming and enjoying adventures in the woods. He had hoped his daughter would take to the outdoor life as he once had, but he had known it was unlikely.

As with her generation in general, she was far too focused on achieving rather than doing. She didn't yet understand that fishing was about more than just acquiring fish. She also didn't understand that continually fussing with the line the way she was would extend that process, not shorten it.

'Ingrid,' he said, leaning in to put a hand on her hunched shoulder. 'You can't see the fish, and you can't catch them by force of will. Relax, enjoy the lake and let the fish come as they will.'

'How can it be this hard?' she replied, gesticulating with her free hand. 'Why haven't we caught more fish?' She sat up and looked at her father with squinting eyes and furrowed brow.

'If fish were easy to catch, there wouldn't be very many of them left, would there? And, anyway, we're here to do some fishing, not just to catch fish.'

Ingrid opened her mouth and stared dumbfounded at her father, as if she had just noticed that he was mad. 'That's the dumbest thing I've ever heard. What's the point of fishing if it's not to catch fish?'

Aurick leaned back and laughed heartily. Ingrid shrugged off her father's hand and returned to sulking over her line. Aurick regained his composure after a time and looked around the small lake, the centre of which they gently drifted in, near a small island of rocks, turning on their anchor in the gentle wind. The rocks looked like a crouched wolf from this side, lying on the surface in wait for prey in the sunlight, waiting through the ages, weathered and moss stained. He loved this lake. His was one of only three cabins here on the lake's shore in this remote corner of the mountains. The bigger and more popular lakes down towards the lowlands were often crowded in summer, but this was almost his own private haven. The mountains behind him soared into the sky, snow-capped the year round. The rolling forest surrounded the lake and swept unseen into the broad valley below.

He was just working out how he would phrase this in a way to gain his daughter's attention when he felt a chill breeze and heard a sound like the rustling of leaves or feathers, perhaps the flapping of wings, faint and out of place on the lake on that warm summer's day. Aurick looked around puzzled but saw no birds. He forgot about it as his daughter suddenly perked up.

'I've got something!' she shouted, so loudly and suddenly that he nearly dropped his rod. He would really have to teach her more about fishing etiquette – if he could ever get her in the boat again, that is.

'What is it?' he asked.

'The line is pulling against me!'

'Great, start pulling it in. Not too hard!'

Aurick looked at the line. It was definitely taut, but there was no vibration or jerking. This was probably not a fish. Shame. His daughter would not take that news well.

'Ingrid, it's probably not a fish. It might be caught on some weed.'

'Don't be stupid. Of course it's a fish. It suddenly moved away from me.'

'The boat is moving, not the line.'

Ingrid scowled and looked at the line. 'Well, I felt something. Something tugged. It pulled away from me – maybe it's just a slow fish.'

Aurick chuckled. 'How slow do you think you would be with a hook in your mouth? Pull the line in, and let's see what it's stuck on. Perhaps it needs re-baiting.'

Ingrid muttered to herself. She couldn't decide which was dumber: her father or fishing. She started winding the line in. At first, it would not come in despite her straining at the reel, then there was a dull twang and the line was light again as it rushed in.

As the hook came to the surface, there was a weed-covered lump of mud and detritus covering it.

'Swing it over here,' Aurick told her. 'Careful. Okay. Let's get this rubbish off and reset it.'

The muck and weed was stripped off by careful fingers, avoiding the barbed double hook and the remains of the worm attached to it. The worm had indeed been nibbled and worried at by something. The fish were outsmarting him as usual, but that was okay. One would make a mistake soon and become dinner. Fishing is more about patience than it is about technique – that's what his father had always said.

The last of the mud and weed came free and revealed a congealed and rusty mesh of metal tangled on the other barb of the hook. Aurick snapped a rusty ring off the hook, and the whole mess fell into the bottom of the boat.

He reached out and held the shaft of the hook in one hand and carefully slipped another worm onto the twin barbs. He then swung the hook back around the end of the boat and whipped the rod forward again, casting the hooks back into the lake twenty metres to the side of the boat. Keeping his eye on where the hook splashed, he shifted the rod to his left hand and proffered it to his daughter. When she didn't take it after a few seconds, he glanced to his left and saw Ingrid holding the rusty mess in her hand and peering at it. She held it up to the light and turned it around in her fingers, a thoughtful expression on her face.

'What is this, Father?'

'Hmm? Oh, I don't know, some old rubbish. Old fishing gear, something off a fishing trap. Don't know. Leave it before you cut yourself and get an infection. You don't know what's in there, could be hooks or sharp edges. Here, I'll drop it over the side, and you take the rod.'

Left arm still outstretched to offer Ingrid the rod, he leaned forward with his right hand open, palm up.

'No, I want to know what it is. It looks interesting.' Ingrid leaned away out of the reach of Aurick's awkwardly crossed arms. She lowered the congealed mess carefully into the water and waved it around, little pieces of mud and rust and weed breaking free and drifting away, turning the clear water brown around her hand.

She brought the mass back into the boat, water running gently through her fingers and dripping onto her legs, but she either didn't notice or didn't care. Her eyes were wide.

'Father, look!'

Aurick returned his eyes from the bobbing float out in the lake with an eye roll and a sigh. 'What? What is it?' What she was holding in her hand quite clearly was not fishing gear.

'I think it's chain mail!' she exclaimed, thrusting the rusty mass towards his face with excited eyes. 'Remember the chain mail we saw at the museum in Røros? This looks like that, don't you think?'

Aurick leaned in and squinted. Sure enough, the pattern of links, although rusted, congealed and still infused with lake mud, was fairly pronounced. Shifting internally from frustration to curiosity, he put the rod down in the boat, setting its shaft on the side.

'Here, let me see.' He smiled and reached out his hand once more. Ingrid suddenly furrowed her brow and snapped her hand back.

'You'd better not be tricking me. Don't you dare throw it away just so we can fish again!'

Aurick chuckled. 'Oh come on, I'm not that mean.'

Gingerly, she leaned back over the tackle box between them

and laid the rusty mess in her father's hand, brows furrowed, eyes watching him like a hawk for a hint of betrayal.

But there was no betrayal. Turning the mass over in his fingers, picking at the dirt and trying to free some of the metal for closer inspection, Aurick hummed to himself and wondered. Suddenly the fragile mass gave way in the middle and broke apart. The metal links in the centre, reduced to almost nothing but rust, disintegrated and scattered flakes of reddish metal and globs of brown mud all over his lap.

'Hey!' Ingrid shouted, lunging for the pieces. 'Why did you do that? What is wrong with you?'

The boat tipped alarmingly as she clambered over the box between them and grabbed at Aurick's left hand with its rusty contents. There was a moment, as Ingrid shouted and grappled with her father's arm and Aurick laughed and tried to placate her, when the boat seemed on the verge of capsizing.

Of course, this was when the fish bit.

Just as Aurick managed to get his daughter's wild grabbing under control and began to explain that he didn't mean to break her discovery, the line suddenly went tight. Unattended, with the reel lock on and the boat already leaning, the rod simply slid over the side with a splash.

'Damn!' Aurick exclaimed. He lunged for the rod, rusty links still digging into his palm. And that was when capsizing went from being a possibility, to being a reality.

A couple of hours later, back ashore and next to a line of sodden clothes drying around a fire, peace was finally made between father and daughter. Aurick sat with his blanket around his shoulders, palms out to the fire and thinking over the afternoon's events. Once the boat had capsized, he had been in a state of near panic until he found his daughter, safe and gasping in the cold water on the other side of the upturned hull. Bits of equipment, a beer can, the cool box and spare clothes were spread out around them on the lake like the aftermath of a shipwreck. Somehow, the rod had caught in the anchor rope of the boat, an unseen fish still futilely pulling away at it.

He had tied the rod on securely to save it, righted the boat and started to splash about, returning all the floating detritus to the boat, daughter first. Once everything in sight was recovered, he had started to reel in the line. The fish, which had come close enough for him to see that it was a superb specimen, had slipped the hook just three metres short of the boat. It was just one of those days.

After paddling to shore as a very soggy, cold and grumpy duo, Aurick had tallied up their equipment to see what was missing. Casualties of the capsize included the boat's spare anchor, his box of fishing tackle, his sunglasses and one of his shoes. The shoe and sunglasses he could live without, and the anchor was cheaply replaceable, but the box of fishing tackle had been collected over twenty years, and he was irritated to have lost it. It would be hard to replace the contents.

Setting that aside as the next day's problem, he spent his time trying to rescue the situation with his daughter. He felt disappointed to have this weekend so utterly ruined and hoped that this would not be his last chance to bring her up here. He had always dreamed of bringing his children up here and teaching them to fish and hike in the mountains as he had done. Now it was all in jeopardy, and he felt foolish for allowing it to happen. He should have known better than to lunge for the escaping rod.

Fortunately, Ingrid was also feeling sheepish. Wrapped in three blankets and sitting cross-legged by the fire, like a tiny tipi with just her head poking out, she feared her father's disappointment and anger over his lost equipment and was trying to think of how to apologise. The evening sun was still bathing the firepit in its gentle glow when the human tipi finally unravelled and shuffled around the fire to sit next to her father.

They looked at each other for a moment before the silence was broken.

'Father?'

'Yes, daughter?'

'Fishing sucks.'

There was a pause before they both burst out laughing, and the tension drained from the air like the water had drained from the beached and overturned boat. Aurick leaned down and lifted his daughter onto his lap to embrace her.

'I'm sorry I lost your chain mail. I do think that is what it was.'

'It's okay. It was more exciting than catching a fish.'

'Well, tomorrow I need to go out diving to see if I can find my tackle box, so you'll be glad to know there will be no fishing, at least for the morning.'

She smiled and leaned her head into his chest as they watched the sun slowly dropping behind the mountains in front of them.

The next morning, the sun was blazing once again, and the lake was calm and beautiful. Aurick was standing in the shallows on the shore, wet suited from neck to toe, wearing a hood and face mask and with his mask and snorkel snugly fitted to his head. The boat was too small to get in and out of easily without risking it tipping over again, so it was easier to wade and swim a hundred metres out into the shallow lake to the area of the capsize to look for the box. It should be easy to see in the crystal-clear waters, as they didn't get more than three metres deep in the centre of the lake.

Aurick pulled his mask down over his face and worked the rim of his hood over the seal. He turned briefly to wave at his daughter, perched on the step of the cabin with instructions to watch for trouble and to stay out of it herself.

As the water came up to his waist, he gently slipped into the water. He could walk all or most of the way out, but walking along the bottom would kick up dirt, making the water too cloudy.

After a couple of minutes of swimming along the surface, Aurick stopped and rotated upright in the water. Gently turning himself round, he decided he was roughly in the right place and started swimming around in a lazy circle, looking for the green box on the weed-covered bottom.

For a while, he didn't see anything other than a single, startled fish that bolted from the weeds when he swam over it. Just as Aurick was starting to get cold and annoyed, an irregular shape caught his eye in the weeds. He took a deep breath and duck-dived down to look. To his disappointment, it clearly wasn't the box, just a rock, slightly protruding from the mud of the lake bed. Just as he was about to return to the surface, he noticed the rock looked odd and weeds appeared to be growing in it. Going up for air, he puzzled over the find and dived down again for a closer look. He dropped right down to the lake bed next to the lump and put his hands on it. He couldn't see much at all. Mud from his landing had exploded in the water like smoke.

Aurick searched through the weed with his hands. Underneath a thin layer of mud, there was the flat, uneven surface of something harder than the mud, but not the solid surface of a rock. In places, it moved or cracked a bit. It seemed to be about a metre square. It definitely wasn't his box, but his interest was piqued.

Having found the edges of the mass, and running out of breath, Aurick tried to lift it from the bottom of the lake. It shifted and moved, but the weight of it and the clinging mud stopped him from lifting it further. As he tugged, the left edge broke off in his hand. He kicked for the surface in annoyance, and once he got there and drew in a deep sputtering breath, he brought the mass to his face and held it up to his mask.

Chain mail.

He knew it the second he saw it. This was the same stuff his daughter had brought up on the hook. He felt excitement grip him and, forgetting the encroaching cold, dived back down into the murky water, clinging to the mass in one hand. Now completely blind, he probed through the mud, trying to find the big mass again, but the water clouded up into the colour of tea and Aurick lost track of where he had and had not searched. His scrabbling hand found another lump, a large ring of some sort. He grabbed it and flew back up to the surface. He examined his new muddy prize with bubbling excitement – it was a dull black metal ring, some sort of jewellery. He took a moment to calm himself and get his breathing under control. For a moment, he considered swimming back to shore; he was cold and tired and one of his hands was full. But he worried about finding the spot again and decided to make one more dive.

His searching hand found another metal object under the thin layer of mud, some sort of bar. He wrapped his fingers around it and gently pulled it free of the cloying mud. It was long, and he had grabbed it at one end. He pushed again for the surface and, spitting his snorkel out, swirled the bar around to clear the clumps of mud off it. He let out a childish cry of excitement.

It was a sword.

It was black with corrosion, pitted and rough, and it was covered in smears of sticky mud, but Aurick felt himself utterly captivated by the sight of it. Waving at his confused daughter and awkwardly paddling back to shore with his hands full, he managed to breathe in half a mouthful of water and arrive, still spluttering and coughing, at the shore where Ingrid was waiting.

'It's a sword! I found a sword!' he said with glee, entirely unnecessarily, as his daughter was staring at the soggy, wheezing, mud-smeared spectre than had crawled out of the lake with an ancient sword in hand. 'I found it with some chain mail – must be the one that got stuck on your hook.'

'So, *we* found a sword,' said Ingrid with a pointed glare.

Aurick looked taken aback for a moment but then nodded fervently. 'Yes, quite right, a team effort.'

'Good,' said Ingrid with a smug smile. 'So, uh… what do we do with it?'

Aurick looked at her in surprise. He hadn't thought about that in his excitement.

'Uh, I know who we can start with. In Røros – the museum there. The owner will know what to do.'

'Røros Museum of Norse History and Mythology' was written on the gable end of the pitched roof of Halfar's little museum in block wooden letters. He could see it from near the bottom of the main street as he was walking up the steep incline. It always brought a smile to his face to see it there: his own little slice of history. It wasn't a grand building, and it wasn't even built for the purpose. It had been his neighbour's house, which Halfar had bought and converted. But that didn't matter to him. It was his, and he loved it.

Halfar Asleson was a diminutive seventy-three-year-old who was visually unremarkable from other men of his age. But to those who met him or saw him in his beloved museum, there was fire in his eyes and a spring in his step. Something of an eccentric local celebrity in this quaint old mining town in the mountains, the ex-history professor had got bored three days into his retirement thirteen years ago. He had, within a few weeks, decided to make his lifelong passion of learning about and collecting Norse history into a small museum in his home town.

The small collection, initially in his own front room, had expanded to take up the entire ground floor, and then the second floor, of the converted house next door. His rather lofty goal was to educate and reinvigorate the locals about Norse history and help them regain a pride in their roots. This goal was met, as Halfar frequently and cheerfully put it, with a 'surprising lack of success'. That small downside was not the sort of thing to dissuade the ever-positive Halfar, however, who would also often say that history is fast in the making and slow in the learning.

Røros was an early industrial-period mining town, but it was known that there had been ancient Norse settlements in this area, some of the last Norse settlements in existence in Scandinavia. Despite officially being part of the dominion that became Nordland in the late 1100s, in practice, the locals were isolated and ignored at the time, and Christianity had not firmly taken root in this area until the High Middle Ages. It is possible that the last people to worship the old Norse gods had lived in the valleys surrounding this broad plain, hidden deep in the mountains.

The simple fact was that most of the country regarded its Norse history and the events that ended it as a footnote to its more recent Christian Germanic past.

He had hoped, of course, that the government would support his efforts, and those of revival historians around the country, to really bring the knowledge of Norse life back into the national awareness, but the government was disinterested, even hostile, and the population at large still cared much more for their country's Germanic, rather than Norse, roots.

However, some serious academics, archaeologists and researchers did make the pilgrimage to his little museum. He was well known in that small community for his excellent collection and his rather unique displays on Norse legends and mythology, and he often had conversations with them long into the night on this or that aspect or interpretation of a certain legend, which was something he enjoyed above all things.

Halfar reached the door of the museum and went in, flipping the sign in the window to read 'open' as he closed it behind him. As he sat down at the counter by the front door, he set about the tedious task of replying to a TV producer who had asked a long series of questions about the use of Viking axes, making it clear he had no idea what Vikings or their war axes were like at all. As he was tapping his fingers in frustration on the side of his keyboard, the door clanked open, and a man and a young girl hurried in with much more bustle and excitement that people usually entered his museum. The man was carrying a long package of wrapped newspaper, and both were breathless and wearing nervous smiles.

'Hello, can I help you?' he said.

'Yes, we found something we want you to look at. We called, but there was no answer, so we decided to come anyway. It's important.' The man placed the long package gingerly on the front desk and started peeling the layers of newspaper away.

'What is this?' Halfar said, as the layers, some damp, came away. The shape of the bundle was starting to kindle his excitement.

'You'll see, then you can tell us.'

The last layers came away, and a sword was revealed. Halfar made a quiet exclamation and straightened up. The sword was glistening with moisture, and wet mud and bits of green weed were still clinging to it. Halfar could see straight away that it was ancient, and with a squeak of excitement, he saw that the cross guard was bronze and decorated with runes under the embedded mud. *A Norse sword!*

'I would say it's a tenth- or eleventh-century Norse sword. Wow, this is a spectacular artefact, incredibly rare! Where did you find it?'

'At the bottom of Bjørsjøen lake, but there's more – here.'

With a dramatic flourish, the man put another small parcel on the table, this one clearly oozing muddy water, and then one more.

Halfar unwrapped each parcel in turn. The first was heavily congealed and covered in dirt but unmistakably chain mail. Then, a near-perfectly intact, albeit deeply tarnished, silver arm ring.

'Oh my God!' Halfar exclaimed, turning the arm ring in his hands. 'Is this everything? This is an incredible find!'

'No, these are just a few items I scraped off the surface! I found all this stuff together, and the chain mail came off a lump that was on the bottom. There is a huge mass of it and…'

'You broke it off?' Halfar exploded. He stood up straight and took a step forward. Suddenly, Aurick felt like a rabbit facing down a bull.

'You found some ancient chain mail and you *broke some off* to show me? Do you have the mind of an infant?'

'No, it's not like that,' Aurick said, hands out in front of him, placating the tiny and suddenly terrifying museum custodian. 'I didn't know what it was. I was trying to free it. I stopped when I realised what it was.'

Halfar took a deep breath and contained his outrage, noting the shock and amusement on the young girl's face and inwardly rebuking himself for losing his temper in front of her.

'Hmm, well don't touch it again, any of it. You shouldn't have even taken it out of the water.' He gestured wildly with his arms in consternation, as if it should have been obvious. 'Fortunately I have been processing some bog finds this week, and I have a tank next door for preserving them. Let's get these in there straight away.' He paused, the normal courtesies slipping his mind in the excitement. 'I am Halfar, by the way. Thank you for bringing this to me. What is your name?' he asked, smiling disarmingly at the girl as he spoke.

'I am Ingrid, and the infant is my father, Aurick.' The girl gave a broad smile as her father rolled his eyes. 'And I am the one who discovered the chain mail.'

'Did you now?' said Halfar, flicking his eyes up to Aurick.

'Yes, my father just went out to collect it.'

Aurick did not protest, but he gave the curator a raised eyebrow and got a knowing wink in response.

'I see. Well, this is a very significant discovery. Congratulations! Come, let's get this into the preserving solution. I'll show you how it works.'

A few minutes later, with the father and daughter gaping in amazement at the wonders hidden in Halfar's back room – his 'work in progress/personal' collection – Halfar turned to them again.

'Okay, so tell me everything from the start, and then we need to record the finds with the authorities and find someone to do an excavation. Oh, and don't tell anyone, not until this find has been properly explored. You understand me?' The diminutive professor spoke with a firm smile and a tone honed over four decades of dealing with students.

'Yes,' said Aurick, nodding meekly. The two described their find as Halfar carefully unwrapped and cleaned the artefacts. He occasionally interrupted to ask a question or shake his head at the cascade of mishandling that had happened.

Finally, after washing most of the half-dissolved newspaper, weed and mud from the sword, and biting his lip in concentration, he gently swirled the sword in the distilled water and then, when most of the detritus was gone, transferred it to the preserving tank. As he lowered the blade into the tank, the light rippling through the solution reflected on some lines on the surface of the sword.

Halfar furrowed his brow and squinted down, trying to see again what had caught his eye as he held the sword there. Then he saw them, faint but unmistakable on the surface of the core of the blade: engraved lines. He leaned even closer in, blanking out what Aurick was saying, trying to decipher the markings. They were shallow and irregular, half-filled with mud. He could see they were Norse runes, but he couldn't make out more than one or two letters. Frustrated, he laid the sword gently on the bottom of the tank.

'What is it?' asked Aurick.

'Hmm?' said Halfar, finally becoming aware again of the room outside the tub.

'What were you looking at so closely?'

'Oh, there is an engraving on the blade, but I can't make it out.'

'An inscription?'

'Yes, it is not common, but sometimes a sword would be inscribed with the maker's name, a chosen phrase or even the name of the sword. I can't tell which this one is. It will need proper investigation.'

'Oh.' Aurick nodded vaguely, staring at the tank. 'Well, what now?'

Halfar thought for a moment. 'I am going to make some calls, and you should return home. Nothing will happen quickly. I will give you a call when I have news, okay?'

Aurick looked disappointed, but he nodded. Halfar smiled and thanked the two again and shuffled them out as fast as he could without being overtly rude. Ingrid had been starting to get bored and wander around the room touching things, and he hated it when people did that.

When they were gone, he cleaned up the workbench and found himself again staring into the tank, deep in thought. He looked around, almost guiltily, before reaching in and bringing the sword to the surface again, balancing the hilt on the rim so he could gently rub away the mud that still clung to the engraved runes with a small brush.

He managed to get a few of the less corroded runes cleaned, and he stared at them in puzzlement. He could not make out more than two characters and, overcoming his frustration, lowered the sword back to the bottom. He washed up and reached for the phone, dialling a number from memory.

'Good morning. Lundjen History Department. How may I help?'

'Hello, yes. I'm calling for Professor Hallsson, dean of archaeology. I need his help with a sword.' He sat staring at the sword as he was put on hold, burning with curiosity about the artefact's past.

What's your story? How did you end up in a lake?

CHAPTER 2

RAIDS AND REAVERS

Off the coast of Francia
Spring 1112

EVERYONE ON THE northern European coast feared the longships. In the Slavic kingdoms of the southern Baltic, driven ever eastwards as they were by the German princes, the people still lived in terror of the death that came from the Cold Sea. In the rich Frankish provinces, the coastal settlements still felt the sting of the raids despite their power and wealth. Their fathers had always kept one eye on the sea, their fathers' fathers before them. For as long as anyone could remember, death came from the waves on wings of wool and riding ships of riveted planks. Like foul birds of prey, they would swoop in and snatch their victims and fly away across the squall-lashed sea before the hunters could raise a hand against them.

The longships. For three hundred years, their wretched sails had cast a shadow over these coasts every spring and summer. And this day was no different. Six ships. Six beasts of carrion come to strip the land of its lives and riches. Violent, uncaring, unafraid of revenge. Longboats full of hard men in furs and leather and iron. Men carrying misery on the edges of their bright steel blades. Men who were, at this moment, at least in the lead boat, pissing themselves with laughter.

Ragnvald hadn't heard the joke, but he grinned anyway as he stood at the prow of his ship *Sedemonr*, the *Sea Demon*. Why shouldn't his men be merry? They were out on the open sea, the whale road, hunting their prey and celebrating the victory they would surely soon earn. It would be a foul leader who castigated them to sullen silence at such a time. The silence, the concentration, the discipline: these could wait for the coast where their quarry was waiting. No, for now, he let his men relax and enjoy the ride south-west, a strong north-west wind driving them down towards the unsuspecting Frankish shore.

Ragnvald was a Swedish warlord, a *jarl* going Viking in the tradition of his forebears, a sword Svear of the old ways. Not many still followed the old ways. Many had fallen to the temptation of easier lives: trading, farming, becoming fat off the land and its products. But enough still earned their keep the old way, with the edge of their blades and the skill of their arms. Enough to keep the fear in the people of the coast he headed towards, enough to keep the warrior skill alive in his people.

Ragnvald was a tall man with light brown hair, just starting to show a tinge of silver and swept back into a leather tie to keep his face clear in the stiff breeze. His beard was tied into tight braids. He was no longer a young man but still strong and restless, the energy of youth not quite gone from his aging body. This was his first raid in two years, the yearning for another trip balanced by the difficulty of organising a successful one in these troubled times. Single crews were no use at a time when every town and village had a watch and coastguards, where every port had small, fast boats sitting ready to hunt marauding ships.

Jarl Birkir, a stocky, dour man from the north of Svealand, with significant lands and a solid crew of fighting men, was in the next ship and also owned the one that followed it. Four of the ships were Ragnvald's men, the best fighting men of his large dominion, two hundred men of violence and steel.

As Ragnvald stood, contentedly watching the waves, a cry from afar snatched his attention. He looked and, following an outstretched arm on the prow of the next ship, swept his eyes across the horizon to see what had caught that man's eye. White sails, low on the horizon, were headed straight for them, just a single ship. His bearded face cracked a smile. It was time for these predators to feast.

The ship had been a fat merchant, heading out of Hamburg with a full cargo, round belly full of fine cloth and linen bound for England. It had wallowed helplessly as the sea reavers fell upon it, sails thrashing as if in horror as its crew panicked and lost control when the screaming demons swarmed up its sides and onto the deck.

The guards, such as they were, had died, and the fat merchants had been cast overboard to gurgle and struggle as their fine, heavy clothes dragged them down. The unarmed crew, young, fit, hardened sailors, had been condemned to slavery and forced at sword point to sail the ship back to the Northlands with a dozen scowling Vikings to ensure their compliance.

The ship and its cargo had made this entire raid a success already. The cargo would fetch a good price in the markets of Sweden and Norway. The ship itself would be beached and stripped of its valuable timbers and iron. A ship that size would have enough iron nails, fittings and other components to make a hundred spearheads, or a dozen swords. Iron was scarce in the north. It collected in bogs or fell from the sky, but mostly it was smuggled or stolen from the southerners who always had it in such abundance.

Ragnvald smiled broadly as his men returned to his longship. They were laughing and jesting at those who would have to return with the ship and miss the rest of the raid. To his surprise, a prisoner was bundled into the ship by his men. Ragnvald raised an eyebrow as the terrified man, a slim and weak-looking German with curly black hair, slumped to the deck at his feet.

'What the fuck is this?' he asked Fenrir, one of his *huscarls*, his elite household guard, who had brought the whimpering German aboard, while he pointed at the prisoner. 'This doesn't look fit to pull a plough, and it doesn't seem to have any wealth about it. Why do I want it?'

'He speaks our tongue,' said Fenrir as he jumped down into the boat. 'Well, he begged for his life in our language anyway. Thought you might be interested.'

Ragnvald regarded the mewling man in a new light. 'Speaks our words, eh? Yes, that might be useful.' He kicked the pathetic-looking bundle with the toe of his boot, and the man squeaked and tried to retreat across the deck. 'You understand me, boy?' he asked, following the prisoner. He got no reply beyond more mewling. 'You are talking out of your arse, Fenrir. Perhaps he knows a few words, enough to beg for his life, not enough to be useful. Over the side with him.'

Fenrir shrugged and picked the man up under each arm, moved to throw him overboard.

'No!' the man screamed in panic. 'It's true! I do speak your language. I do, very well! I understand everything you say. Yes, everything.'

Fenrir dropped him to the deck again and gave Ragnvald a smug look. 'As I said.'

'Fine. For once you are more useful than you look.' He grinned at his huscarl and laughed at the mock offence the smaller man returned. 'Now, you. What is your name?' Ragnvald frowned at the new slave and lifted the man's chin with the haft of an axe.

'Otto,' the man squeaked out, eyes fixed on the length of spruce that was digging painfully into his jaw.

'Otto, you are now my slave. You are a thin little wisp of a man, so your only value to me is turning my words into your people's and theirs into mine. Understand?'

Otto cried out in protest, eyes swinging wildly around him, looking for a way out he knew didn't exist.

'If you do what I command, you will live a fine life. If you don't… well, I only need you for your mouth. The rest of you is unnecessary.' Otto was barely listening, his eyes wide and glazed with terror.

'Don't think he understands,' said Fenrir nonchalantly.

'Doesn't seem that way, does it? Let's take a finger and see if that helps him.'

Fenrir grabbed a hand and pinned it to the side of the boat, splaying the fingers and holding them down with the back of his *seax*.

'No, I understand, I do. I understand!' wailed Otto.

'Are you sure?' asked Ragnvald, leaning down so that his beard was almost touching the chin of the desperate man. 'Because, if you ever become unsure, I will take fingers until you get sure again. Then, if you run out of fingers before you get sure, I will take other protruding parts until you are sure because, remember, all I need is your mouth.'

That mouth gaped in horror, and the eyes widened even further, but Otto said nothing, his voice snatched by the violence of the threat.

'Still don't think he gets it,' said Fenrir.

'He'll learn real quick,' said Ragnvald and brought the axe

down on the side of the boat, a hair's breadth from the outstretched fingers. Otto's eyes rolled up, and he passed out and slumped, voiding his bowels in the bottom of the boat.

'Bugger,' said Ragnvald.

'What a total streak of piss,' said Fenrir in disgust. Do we have to keep it?'

'He might be useful yet, when we get home. If not?' He shrugged and turned away without another word. Fenrir knew what he meant and smiled wolfishly.

Later that day, the small fleet pulled into sight of the coast. Ragnvald knew which town he wanted to raid. They had seen it several years ago on the way past, a mid-sized coastal town, protected on the land by a wall and from the sea by broad mud flats and impassable marsh. The only weak point was the channel leading to the harbour. The harbour had a guard boat and a small sea wall, but not enough to keep his six ships out. Or so he hoped. It was not possible to permanently guard every town for years on end against three hundred trained warriors coming with no warning. Or so he hoped.

The ships dropped their sails, men hauling in the yards of thick material and dumping the wrapped sail and boom into the bottom of the boat. Half the men slid oars out into the cold water, and the other half started putting on their war gear. Maille *byrnies* or thick woollen shirts went over their tunics; thick felt hats or iron helmets went on their heads. Those men with swords strapped the scabbards to their belts; those with axes tucked them away close to hand. Spears were stacked next to the benches, and the two halves of the crew swapped. When the ships reached the dock, every man would be ready to leap into a fight from the benches in a moment.

The jokes and the laughter were stilled now. The pre-battle quiet was upon them. It was not total silence – it never was. Some men muttered nervously to themselves, others invoked their favoured god and some reassured each other or pointed out good omens. Every man in the boat was afraid. Only a fool could not be afraid in the long wait before the battle song started, and no fools lived long in Ragnvald's crew, his *hird* of seasoned warriors.

'Steady now,' Ragnvald called to the helmsman and rowers. They were rowing steadily, speed building as they came into view of the harbour. They would be seen at any moment – perhaps they had already been. Perhaps unseen men in that town were rushing into their own armour, shouting orders and gathering weapons to repel them. Perhaps they were already at the sea wall, spears gripped in trembling fingers, waiting for the terror that swept down the channel in six snarling, beast-prowed ships.

The sea demon head, snarling and spitting painted wooden fire, was carved into the prow next to Ragnvald, its mad white eyes ever looking forward, seething with rage at whatever enemy was put in front of it, striking terror into their hearts. Or that was the idea anyway. Ragnvald thought it looked more comical than fearsome, but that errant thought was swept away by the tolling of a bell from the town, still half a mile ahead of them.

'We are seen. They will be coming for us, lads. Let's not disappoint them. Not too fast,' he said as he grinned and looked down at his men. 'Save some breath for the killing.'

One of the men, Sebbi, an experienced man and one of Ragnvald's ten huscarls, started up a chant, as was his habit when the ships were going into battle, each line sung out between strokes. They all knew it well. It was hardly the work of a skald, a skilled song weaver, but the familiar words and the defiant energy it brought them lifted the whole crew, took their minds off the fear and suspense, got the battle rage boiling.

Sea demon
Stroke
Wave rider
Stroke
Carry us
Stroke
Here we come

The oars were crashing into the water, beating it into white froth. Backs strained as the oars pulled through the water.

Thor, Lord of Thunder
Stroke
Hear our fury
Stroke
See our rage
Stroke
Here we come

The hull was humming beneath Ragnvald's feet now.

Odin, Spear Master
Stroke
Guide our arms
Stroke
Watch our shields
Stroke
Here we come

Each chant was building in volume, men working themselves up into a nerve-driven fury.

Ran, Queen of Waves
Stroke

Carry us
Stroke
Speed our journey
Stroke
Here we come

The shore was only a hundred paces away. Ragnvald could see men running to and fro along the wall behind, others milling on the docks in apparent confusion.

Men of Svealand
Stroke
Gird your wrath
Stroke
Wear it round you
Stroke
Here we come

The chant was building into a crescendo now, the dock only a dozen strokes away.

Shield of courage
Stroke
Spear of vengeance
Stroke
Sword of wrath
Stroke
Here we come

Ragnvald snarled, gripping his axe. His sword *Bjóðr* –'Giver' – was sheathed at his side, safe from the lashing salt spray. It would stay there, waiting, until he was safely ashore. The crew burned their lungs with the strain of the rowing and the volume of their battle song.

Foemen, face us!
Stroke
See our steel
Stroke
We are death
Stroke
Here we are!

The crew was roaring now, the chant done and lost in a crashing wave of noise that washed over the waiting townsfolk and reverberated back at the oncoming ships. All six crews were screaming themselves hoarse as they shipped their oars and picked up their shields and weapons, leaving the momentum of the boats to carry them into the docks.

Alongside, another ship was going to reach the dock just before Ragnvald. Ragnvald saw Jarl Birkir in the prow, helmetless, waving his long axe at the waiting locals and screaming curses at them. The ship hit the dock, and Birkir leaped from the prow, scything his axe at the terrified defenders who scuttled back out of range, allowing room for the rest of the crew to begin pouring onto the dock behind their wild jarl.

Ragnvald was so engrossed watching that he almost lost his footing as his own ship hit the dock. He gathered himself and leaped down onto the empty stretch of planking, hearing his men following, and started running down the dock towards the melee that had gathered nearer the shore.

The town guard had finally found enough courage to stand and were desperately fending off Birkir's crew at the gap in the sea wall that led to the docks. The crumbling wall was only five feet high and didn't even have a gate. Rusted hinges showed where one used to stand, the salt air and crashing storm waves having hewn it off long ago. How the town would rue not having replaced it.

Ragnvald looked around for a way past that chaotic crush and saw that the wall on the right was barely defended and cracks and ledges covered the uneven stonework. He turned along the dock that ran along the face of the wall and found a good spot.

'Up!' he roared at the men who followed him. He wasted no time and launched himself at the wall, gaining the top after a single bound from a ledge halfway up, his tough leather shoes finding ample purchase on the rough, weathered stone. He was vulnerable at the top as he stood, but the only man facing him on the raised path behind the wall was a terrified boy in ill-fitting maille armour, who simply dropped his old spear and ran.

A wave of snarling, armoured Northmen poured over the wall behind him as he surveyed the scene. Beyond the wall was a broad path, ten paces across, that ran down the whole front of the harbour along the sea wall. Behind that were buildings, storage sheds and fish-drying racks. To his left, down the path, a crowd of perhaps fifty armed men were pushing and shoving at the entrance to the docks, the sound of that fight still roaring in his ears. To the right, there was the sound of shouting and running men from deeper in the town.

For a moment, he couldn't decide if he should run left and attack the defenders of the dock gate or right and intercept the oncoming but unseen enemy. At the dock gates, he could see a bloodied axe rise and fall into the crowd, a high scream cutting through the rest of the sounds of combat. Then a Norse helmet appeared in the throng, then another, and the whole mass of defenders visibly quivered and retreated a step as the huscarls and axemen of Birkir's crews pushed through the gate in a fury of chopping axes and stabbing swords. The best armoured men, the most experienced, the hardened edge of the Norse warband, were cutting through the hapless guardsmen. Birkir didn't need his help.

'Shield wall!' he roared, pointing his sword to the right where the sound of running men was growing louder. His men stretched out across the road, those with helmets, maille and short axes and swords going to the front two ranks. Men with spears and long axes filled the third and fourth ranks. The shields of the front rank crashed together to form a single solid wall of wood topped with peering eyes, steel weapons and iron helmets.

Not a moment too soon either. A large force of well armed and armoured men appeared from a path between two buildings and hastily formed into a mass opposite them, over a hundred, perhaps even three times his own number.

The enemy held their shields together in a makeshift wall of their own and nervously watched the silent Norse, a slab of foreboding enemies blocking them from the massacre of their comrades, who were being torn apart as their defence of the dock gate failed.

'Forward!' shouted Ragnvald from his place in the second rank. Sebbi was on his left, long hair flowing from the back of his helmet. Fenrir was on his right, Leif beyond him and others behind him. The huscarls formed a block in the second and third ranks where the best warriors always stood. The front rank was filled with younger men, eager to prove themselves in battle, willing to stand the risk of being at the front of the wall.

Ragnvald smiled wickedly at the thought of the coming battle with men such as these beside him. His men were more than a match for the citizens of any fat Frankish town. He always had ten huscarls. Some lords had more, some less, but Ragnvald always had ten, the cream of his warriors, honoured men who would fight at his side in battle, could be entrusted with small groups to command and who would sleep, eat and drink in his own hall when they were in Uppsala. When a huscarl died or grew old and hung up his shield over his door with honour, one man would be selected to replace him, and so there would be ten again.

Bjóðr was in his hand now, patterned steel shining brightly in the spring noon sun. It had been his father's sword, a sword that had given death to many warriors over many seasons, and now he would use it to give death to his enemy. Now he raised it in his fist and pumped it with a shout, giving the order to advance. The Viking shield wall stamped forward on the hard-packed earth, warriors snarling and shouting curses and insults at their enemy, straining to get their weapons into the enemy ranks but maintaining the line of the wall. Anyone who broke the first rank to charge would never be trusted to stand in it again. A wall with holes in it, as every Norseman learned when he trained for battle, is a shitty wall. Norsemen don't waste complicated words on simple concepts.

The enemy wall was pretty shitty by that standard. It had gaps, holes and a great kink in the middle where a few men were shrinking away from the oncoming Svearmen. Some of the shields were different types and sizes; some men in the front had spears and others had swords; some had no helmets. Some were old or terrified and clearly not fighters; others were steady-looking soldiers. But a *skjaldborg* is only as strong as the weakest man, and the Norse front rank was filled with hard men, Vikings of the old ways. Killers.

The Viking wall hit the ragged line of defenders with a sickening crash and simply *consumed* it. Axes flashed over the line at the heads and shoulders of those who did not hold their shields high enough. Swords stabbed up at those who held their shields too high. Spears licked out to catch the unprotected faces of those in the second rank who were gawping at the oncoming violence. A dozen defenders fell in the first clash, and their wall degenerated into a mass of desperate and wounded men fighting for their lives, all cohesion lost, with men giving way or dying before they could re-form the wall. Ragnvald felt the man in front of him stagger back and heard his cry as an unseen spear punched through the

Norseman's thick woollen shirt, even as his killer was cut down. But he was one of only two Norse that fell in those moments of unleashed violence, as the discipline and experience of the Vikings made them wolves among sheep.

Into the mass of terrified men, a new horror arrived. Over the wall on the enemy's left, a new wave of screaming demons appeared and jumped down into the flank of the townsfolk's compressed ranks, spreading terror and death. Another of Ragnvald's ship's crews had arrived.

Ragnvald felt the pressure at his front ease as the enemy died or tried to face the new threat, and he smiled. 'Break!' he shouted, giving the signal that all his men loved to hear. The wall dissolved and charged, each man rushing into the enemy mass in a fury of violence that shocked the already demoralised enemy to the point of failure. The hammer strike of the Norse warriors, contrasted with the anvil of the skjaldborg. One moment there was a fight, and the next, Ragnvald was chasing a herd of broken and fleeing men. Sebbi howled with glee and lunged forward, putting his spear into the side of a man who was trying to turn and flee. Fenrir surged past the dying man and ducked a desperate sword swing, putting his axe into the back of the knee of his opponent as he passed, splitting the leg and bringing his opponent down with a piercing scream, quickly silenced by the man that followed. Ragnvald followed his huscarls as they ran forward, seeking their next victims.

There was no mercy as the Vikings surged through the town. Anyone with a weapon or armour was killed. Anyone the right age to carry them was killed. Anyone who got in the way was killed. Most of the town's population had fled into the fields and woods outside the walls; those who stayed died or hid from the victorious, rampaging raiders.

Ragnvald and most of his crew headed for the stone church,

the tallest building in the town and the one they knew would hold the greatest riches. As they broke down the door, a clutch of terrified citizens and priests screamed and tried to retreat from them, cowering into the corners. A single-armed man yelled in outrage and terror and then died with a choking cry as Fenrir rammed his sword into his guts.

Why do they always hide in the church? It's the one place we always search. Idiots! Go hide in the shit pits and you would be fine. His ironic thought was interrupted by an old man in the robes of a priest who tottered towards him, yelling and swinging a large, ornate cross as a weapon. Ragnvald caught the cross in one hand, wincing at the weight of the blow, and calmly ran his sword through the old man's chest. The priest's eyes widened in shock, and he dropped to his knees, cries of pure horror coming from those huddled against the back wall of the church.

Ragnvald withdrew his sword and dropped the dying priest casually on the steps leading up to the altar. The altar itself was bare, he noted with a grimace. 'Where is that new slave, the one who speaks our words?'

Fenrir went to the back of the group and pulled the slim man to the front, dumping him to the floor in front of Ragnvald.

'Ask these people where the riches are.'

'What?' Otto gasped, recoiling in horror from the spreading pool of blood emanating from the now-dead priest.

Ragnvald snarled and grabbed a handful of Otto's hair. 'Ask them where the church's riches are. All churches have riches. If they give them to me, they live. If you don't ask them, you remember what I said I would do.'

'But these are people sheltering in the house of God! That man you killed is a priest – have you no shame?' Otto's horror overcame his fear for a moment.

Ragnvald nodded at Fenrir, and the huscarl stepped forward,

grabbed Otto's hand in a grip of iron and separated his fingers, holding the hand out for Ragnvald. 'No, I have no shame. This is not my god, and this is no longer your hand. Believe me, I will have no shame a long time after you have no fingers.'

He grabbed the proffered finger and sliced it off with a single pass of the base of his sword.

Otto struggled and wailed again, but the grip on his arm was resolute.

Ragnvald placed his sword against the second finger. 'Ask them.'

Otto turned his head to the cowering people and stammered out a string of unintelligible words. One of the still-living priests shook his head and pointed out of the door.

Otto turned his wide, bloodshot eyes to Ragnvald. 'They aren't here. The other priests fled with the silver.'

Ragnvald glared at the huddled mass, thinking for a moment as disappointment gripped him. 'I don't believe them. There are three priests here. Are you telling me there were others enough in this one church to flee carrying all its riches?'

'I... I don't know,' spluttered Otto, still vainly wrestling for control of his arm.

'I'm not asking you, idiot. I'm asking them. You ask them. That's your job, or do you need another reminder?'

Otto turned again to the priests and gabbled more of their strange language. Ragnvald was surveying the group and saw that, at the back, one priest was silent, pressed against the wall and looking nervous while the other one was at the front of the crowd, trying to protect the worshippers.

Otto turned again to him and shook his head. 'They say the same thing. Please, the treasures are gone!'

'Fenrir, take this useless shit away.' He let go of the sobbing slave and stood up, eyes on the priest at the back. 'You see how the priests are trying to protect their people? I have always found this with priests. They put themselves between what they seek to protect and me.'

'What of it?' replied Fenrir.

'That priest at the back – what is he protecting?'

Fenrir's eyes narrowed, and his mouth twisted into a smile. He strode forward, clearing the terrified people out of his way with the flat of his sword. The priest in the corner paled and started to wave his hands in front of him as if to ward the Viking off.

Fenrir swung at the man, his sword cutting right through an outstretched arm and deep into the priest's face. The man gurgled and thrashed as Fenrir flung him aside into the lap of an old woman who seemed not to be aware of what was happening around her.

Under where the priest had been crouched, an area of the floor was exposed, but nothing else was there. Fenrir looked at it in confusion. Bare stone walls met wooden floorboards with no indication of a hiding place. Ragnvald stepped past with a sigh – *Fenrir really was nothing more than a killer* – and he dug his sword between the floorboards and levered one up. It popped up with no resistance, and the next ones too. Five boards came up before the hiding place beneath the floor was fully exposed.

Ragnvald smiled broadly. *This is a rich church.*

Ragnvald was walking back down towards the docks with his men when he found Jarl Birkir. The man was bleeding freely from a wound on the side of his head, but he appeared not to notice. He beamed broadly when he saw Ragnvald and swept his arms wide to embrace him.

'Ha, brother! What a day! By the gods, I have missed this.' He fell into step with Ragnvald, glancing back at the heavily laden men who followed. 'Thor's balls, you did well. Some great lord's hall?'

Ragnvald smiled at the shorter man. 'You have never raided a Christian town before?'

'No, just Danes, or more recently the tribes along the shore of the Cold Sea. In fact, I've not raided for six years, not since my feud with Jarl Forkir ended. Damn, I missed having excuses to go raiding.'

'Well,' Ragnvald said with a smug smile, 'the key thing to understand about Christians is they keep all their wealth in their churches. Most of it anyway.'

'In their churches?' Birkir said, looking around them down the narrow streets of the town. 'How do you know which ones are the churches?'

'Simple. They are the biggest, and they are full of bald men who dress like women.'

Birkir looked at him in pure disbelief and then roared with laughter. 'What a fine load of horse bollocks that is, Ragnvald.'

'No, I am serious. That is the truth.'

'Fine. If you want to keep your secrets but I am no spring mare who would believe such amusing nonsense. My men have plenty of loot, and I don't envy you your success. This was your raid. You keep your loot and your secrets.' He thumped Ragnvald on the back.

Ragnvald laughed with him and protested. 'Birkir, really, it is the truth. Go up the hill and see for yourself. In any case, you will have a share of the church treasure for your help with this raid.'

Birkir grinned from ear to ear and turned to those of his men who followed him. 'You hear that, lads? Jarl Ragnvald will share his treasure with us!' His men gave a heartfelt cheer and shouted out their thanks.

'And I will share my food and mead with you, Jarl Ragnvald, if you ever come to visit my hall.'

'And I would be honoured to visit your home. We will arrange it.'

How the gods laugh at the intentions of men.

'But now I say we leave this husk of a town behind us before someone comes to take it from us.'

'You think its wealth is done? I submit to your greater experience,' said Birkir, still beaming from the generous promise of wealth shared.

'On the subject of greater experience, perhaps you should wear a helmet next time. It helps when someone tries to make a hole in your head.' Ragnvald ribbed the shorter man gently.

'Bah, this scratch? It's nothing. Didn't know it was there until the blood was pissing into my eye.'

Ragnvald shrugged. 'Your choice.'

'I don't like helmets. Make my head hurt. Anyway, I have a reputation now. Putting one on will make me look bad.'

Ragnvald suppressed a laugh as he looked at the dishevelled and slightly rotund northern jarl, clotting blood caking his hair and beard on one side of his head, a slice the length of a finger in his scalp. 'I don't think you could look any worse.' He dodged away as Birkir aimed a hearty punch at his ribs, receiving only a glancing blow.

'Careful now, Ragnvald. Wouldn't want me to embarrass you in front of your men.' His smile betrayed the lack of heat in his words. 'Wouldn't want us to end up fighting, eh?'

The two men chatted and laughed away the nervous energy of the fighting as they walked back to their ships with their crews, oblivious to the fate their actions had brought.

In the desecrated church in that devastated town, lying dead with one arm severed, was the nephew and personal chaplain of Pope Paschal II. The pope had sent him on a goodwill tour of the German clergy to quietly muster support for his beloved pontiff during the period of conflict between Church and State in the Holy Roman Empire.

Paschal never had children, his brother was long dead, and he had looked on his loyal young chaplain as his own son. Europe would shake from the scale of his rage and the depth of his revenge.

Ragnvald had started a fire that would threaten to consume his world.

CHAPTER 3

THE SMITH AND THE SON

Minden, Lower Saxony
Autumn 1115

*T*HANK GOD THAT'S *finished. I fucking hate polish-*
ing. Ordulf was rubbing the final oily blemishes off the
highly polished finished blade in his hands with a clean
linen patch. Four days of hard, repetitive work finally behind him.
He hated finishing the top-quality blades for that reason – an ordi-
nary blade required no real polishing, just grinding and a bit of
smoothing with stones. Well, he didn't hate all of it. He did love
finishing a good blade; he loved the look and feel of the surface
and the satisfaction of producing a quality piece of work. He just
really hated the process. A whole week of running increasingly fine
stones back and forth along the bevels, of knowing one mistake
could set him back a day or two, of having aching, sodden fingers
and a cramped and sore back. He had been in this side room for
four straight days working this blade, and now it was done, the
relief was almost physical.

As a journeyman smith, it shouldn't really have been his job, but he regarded the apprentices as useless, so he just did important blades himself. His master scolded him and said it was a boy's work, but the apprentices really were worse than usual at the moment.

A tall and broad young man of seventeen years, he had been an apprentice himself until two years ago, when his vast strength and particular skill with the hammer had seen him selected to become a journeyman, despite his young age. For his journeyman piece, he had made a fine arming sword from scratch. Blade nearly as long as his arm; straight and true fuller perfectly set in the spine; cross guard, hilt and pommel designed in the demure, geometric style of all the fashionable Christian knights. It was a sword he had been overtly proud of.

His master, Herman, a stern and barrel-chested smith with a stormy temper and a fine eye for forging, had given him an appreciative grunt and allowed him a day off and five silver coins to enjoy it with. He was taken to the guild house and given a forged steel miniature of a sword to pin to his apron. That was his only badge of rank, such as it was.

But that appreciative grunt and that miniature sword made him a journeyman of the Bremen Cutlers' Guild and he was now a 'someone'. No longer a lickspittle apprentice with no station, he had envisaged a new life of respect and reward. But now he was polishing swords again and, well, he really hated polishing swords.

With the sword done and the sun setting, he shrugged off his apron and stretched his aching back, trying to loosen the painful knots that a hard day hunched over the sword had created. He needed to loosen up, and he would be doing what most of the young men of the town did on the last evening of the week. They were going to the patch.

He put his tools and apron away – he would receive a verbal or perhaps even physical thrashing for leaving his equipment carelessly discarded – and headed out of the forge compound doors, grunting to the man who would stay behind and watch the place that night. He would be back. An orphan since his ninth year with no other home to go to, he lived in the forge that he had joined as a floor sweeper a decade ago. But this evening he was set on a purpose. He couldn't resist a smile as he strode down the gently sloping dirt path, skirting the edge of the main part of town. He was looking forward to tonight.

The patch was really just that. An area of flat, beaten earth between a washhouse and the back of a cheap alehouse on the outskirts of town, an uneven shape about thirty paces long and twenty wide with a huge rock the size of a horse in one corner. Once a week, when the sun had set, the town's youth would gather there to drink and fight by firelight. The weekly patch fight was older than any of the participants, but the reason it had started was still known to them. The previous alehouse owner had been sick of the constant fights in his alehouse and one night banished the participants to the waste ground behind the alehouse to finish and cool off. What started as a punishment became a habit and then a tradition.

The fights were a chance to let off steam, to establish dominance and settle scores, perhaps to impress a girl when they were there. The rules were simple: no weapons, no breaking legs or arms, no dangerous blows to the eyes, throat or balls, no carrying on when one person yielded. The rules were enforced by the whacker, who wielded a long, rusty iron rod that someone had stolen from somewhere years ago. The rules were not broken often; getting hit by the whacker was not worth it.

Ordulf arrived at the patch and perked up when he saw there was a large crowd tonight, drinking cheap ale and eating bread and the stringy meat stew that the alehouse served in wooden bowls. There were at least a dozen nervous, hyped-up boys and young men there, posturing and trying to look tough. Ordulf could always tell who was there to fight and who just to watch, and he started sizing up his potential opponents.

He strolled into the crowd and was met with the usual mix of displeasure and wariness from the other participants and the usual excitement from the watchers. He was almost always the biggest man there, and he almost never lost. He was fun to watch and horrible to fight. Sometimes no one would even agree to take him on.

'You fighting tonight, Ordulf?' asked the baker's son with a wide smile. Arnold was not a fighter. He spent a little too much time eating his own products to fight anything other than the waistband of his trousers.

'Well, I didn't come for the food or your company, Arnold,' Ordulf replied lightly, getting a chitter of laughter from the group, which parted to let him through. Ordulf didn't see Arnold's hurt reaction or much care – he had spotted a newcomer. The young man was a beast, perhaps as big as him, not as tall but wider, older, bristling with aggression. Perhaps that was why no one was in the patch yet. If you wanted to fight, you entered the patch. And then anyone could join you. If you refused to fight whoever came out to you, you would be jeered out of the patch and couldn't enter it again that night. A few had refused Ordulf, but not many, and he was a genial enough man if he wasn't throwing you to the ground. This lad opposite him, though, had an air about him that exuded malice. The designated whacker for the evening was standing by the rock, nervously fiddling with the bar and eyeing the newcomer.

'Who is he, then?' asked Ordulf to a group standing next to him and watching the man. He had seen Ordulf now and was eyeballing him while he stripped off his tunic so that he stood only in his trousers, the mark of a fighter. Clothes could be used as a weapon against you by an opponent who could grip them and seek to control you with them.

'A farmhand. Came for the market from a fair few miles away,

I think. Never seen him before. You gonna fight him? No one else dares.' Said one of the boys.

'I might if a proper challenger doesn't show up. I didn't know we let oxen fight.' Ordulf was making sure he could be heard across the small patch, and the farmhand snorted in anger and slapped his hand into his fist. He strode into the centre of the patch, muscles popping under his unusually hairy torso and sun-browned arms. Ordulf eyed him with unaccustomed nerves. *This one might be difficult.*

'Any of you lazy town girls got enough balls to come and face me?' The brute was talking loud enough for everyone to hear, but his eyes were fixed on Ordulf. 'I heard about your little fights. I was expecting it to be between men, not a bunch of frightened washerwomen.'

All eyes in the group were now on Ordulf and the farmhand. Ordulf smiled and stepped out into the patch, guts knotted with excitement and fear, casually flexing his arms, trying to hide the stiffness and discomfort across his back from a long day hunched over steel.

'Easy, friend. We aren't scared of you – we just aren't used to wrestling farm animals here. Has anyone got a halter I can put on this thing?' He looked around at the crowd behind him quizzically, putting out an ease he did not feel, trying to goad his massive opponent into a rage that would cloud his judgement. It was one of the fundamentals of the patch that you learned with time. Stay cool. Make your opponent angry. Angry people make mistakes. Not many people in the crowd laughed; the atmosphere was foreboding. *Well, it was worth a try.*

The farmhand bristled with anger at the insult but did not react. *Guess I will have to do this the hard way.*

'Has the whacker told you the rules yet?' he asked the farmhand, gesturing at the nervous lad holding the iron bar.

'Rules?' said the farmhand with contempt. 'You little girls have *rules?*' He looked round at the whacker and his bar. 'What are the rules, pup?'

The whacker swallowed nervously and listed the rules.

'I see. Don't want me to hurt your lover's precious face, is that it? And what if I break the rules and his face?' said the brute with scorn in his voice.

The whacker looked around dumbly, as if searching for support, while Ordulf sighed to himself at the display. *For God's sake, look like you mean it. Who let this guy be the whacker?*

'Um…' The whacker looked at the bar sheepishly and hefted it a bit before letting his hand sag back down, shrugging slightly, almost apologetically.

The farmhand roared with laughter. 'You gonna hit me with that little stick?' He slapped his hand on his stomach in mirth. 'Kid, if you hit me with that twig, I will take it from you and take your maidenhead with it. You understand me?' He smiled a vicious smile at the whacker, who was half his size, and the poor kid just nodded and backed away, bumping into the rock and dropping the rod in nervous surprise. Ordulf sighed and closed his eyes at the embarrassment of the situation. This was not how it usually went. Yes, often the fights got out of hand or became vicious, but they never usually included someone this aggressive. No one in the crowd was jeering or cheering; everyone could feel the tension and the potential for serious violence.

The farmhand turned his vicious grin back to Ordulf. 'You finished throwing words, little man? Or do you need a while longer to find your courage? I can wait.'

Ordulf had lost the game of words, he knew that, and he pressed his lips together and nodded. He could already tell this was going to be awful, but he wasn't about to back down.

Ordulf reflected, as he was slammed to the ground for the third time, that he had been wrong in thinking it would be an awful fight. It was horrendous. The farmhand was at least as strong as him, and heavier, bigger in the chest. Ordulf had longer arms and a powerful punch that was *mostly* saving him from taking too many nasty blows from those rocks of fists, but any time they got too close, he was just overpowered.

He had tried all his usual tricks: he had gone for the man's legs, tried to bait him into a charge so that he could trip or roll him, tried to feint for the eyes to unbalance him so he could get a solid punch to the gut. Nothing was working well enough. When he did get a solid blow to the man's cheek, he simply shook it off. Even Ordulf's fist screamed in pain; it was like punching a tree.

He gazed up from the ground, trying to decide if he really wanted to get up again. The first time he had gone down, he had expected a hail of blows, or for the man to kneel on him and force him to yield. But the brute had just stood there, watching and smiling, waiting for Ordulf to get up. This time, he came over and proffered a hand and a wicked grin. 'You need some help or are you done, little man?'

Who the fuck are you calling little man, you dressed-up donkey? Ordulf was always the biggest, always the strongest. This was grating hard on his pride. No one here had ever seen him beaten like this. No one *had* ever beaten him like this. He was angry and humiliated, completely unaware that this was how he usually made others feel. He growled at the offered hand, refusing to take it. The brute shrugged and backed up a step as Ordulf tried to spring up and get a surprise punch in, but he was too tired and too slow, and the big lad simply took a step back to avoid it completely. Then he mimicked a yawn. That was too much. Ordulf snapped and charged, swinging wildly.

The sheer aggression of the charge, and the farmhand's

play-acting, caught him off guard and slowed his response, so Ordulf landed a handful of heavy blows with his fists and knee; he heard and felt the other man grunt in pain. But Ordulf was angry and out of control, and the farmhand absorbed the blows, covering and retreating, forcing Ordulf to follow, unbalanced and tiring. As Ordulf threw a huge, arcing fist at the other man, the brute ducked with astonishing grace and returned a straight punch that Ordulf barely had time to see, let alone block.

Oh shit.

Ordulf woke to a splash of cold water that smacked him in the face. He spluttered and grabbed in front of him, trying to find his attacker. His hands closed on empty air. He opened his eyes and wiped the water from them, confused. He could see stars. He tried closing his eyes and shaking his head to clear his vision and opened his eyes again. *Oh, those are actual stars.* He looked around and found he was on the ground in the middle of the patch. Off to his left, the farmhand was getting thumps on the back and laughs from his companions, and the rest of the crowd were looking on in shock or talked excitedly among themselves.

'What… Who?' Ordulf's mind was fuzzy, and he tried to focus on the dark figure above him. It resolved as the whacker, rod long abandoned. 'Uh, you lost,' the boy said lamely. And then reached down to help him up. Ordulf levered himself to his feet, a wave of nausea washing over him suddenly, and he vomited, helplessly, onto the dusty ground.

'Woah there, you alright?' Ordulf looked up to find the farm-hand walking over and smiling. 'Sorry about putting you down so hard, but you hurt me, and I really needed you to stop.' The brute had entirely lost his air of malice, and even the smile was friendly, no longer laced with a sneer. He now just looked like a big, genial man. A huge, muscular, hairy ox of a man but with a look about as threatening as a puppy.

Ordulf felt even more sick. 'You tricked me?'

'I did.'

'The whole thing was an act.'

'Yup, did it to scare you? You are a big fucker, and I needed the advantage. Did it work?' The man seemed earnest, even a little nervous.

Ordulf was stunned. He always thought he had the measure of his opponent. He had got this one completely wrong. 'Uh, yes. I guess it did.'

'Excellent!' The man came over and offered a hand to the unsteady Ordulf. 'My name is Leuter. Good to meet you, Ordulf. Great fight – you hit like a horse. And I would know!' Ordulf's new companion guffawed and led the dumbfounded, stumbling smith out of the patch for some well-earned ale.

There were a few more fights that evening now that the two biggest men were finished. One fight per person per night, that was the system. It was a system made to stop Ordulf or any other winning fighter occupying the patch all night and simply thumping everyone in turn. Ordulf barely watched; the audience barely watched. No one had got over the shock and excitement of the big farmhand, Leuter, and his fight with Ordulf. Ordulf sat on a rough plank bench against the back wall of the alehouse and chatted to the farmhands. It turned out they were all the sons and nephews of a single farmer. Ordulf couldn't remember who was who, but they were all very friendly, increasingly drunk and talked much too much. He got the impression they didn't meet new people often.

Ordulf's thoughts were still fuzzy, and his head hurt like hell – something the cheap ale was making worse – but something else was bothering him. He finally worked out what it was. He turned to Leuter. 'You knew my name.'

'Uh, what?'

'When you came to help me up, you introduced yourself, and you knew my name. How did you know my name?'

The big man looked sheepish. 'Oh, yes. Well, at the market today I talked to the trader we were delivering to. Said we were sleeping the night and asked if there was anything fun to do.' Ordulf frowned at the long-winded explanation. 'He asked if any of us were fighters and, if so, to go to the patch and try and beat Ordulf. He said you were the big one, the one to beat.'

Ordulf was shocked. 'So you came here tonight just to beat me?'

'Yeah. My pa, he is a fighter, and he trains me sometimes. He told me the best way to learn is always to try and fight the best, not someone easy to beat. Makes sense to me.' Leuter smiled and shrugged.

Ordulf nodded and chewed this over. Leuter seemed like a simple enough lad, but he had made Ordulf feel stupid twice now in a night. It bothered him. 'Yeah, makes sense. Why is your dad a fighter?'

Leuter visibly glowed with pride as he answered. 'He's a soldier, a man in the lord's guard, a chosen man, goes with him on all his campaigns. A great fighter, so everyone says.' He poked himself in the chest. 'I'm to join the guard myself when I'm not working on the farm. I'm going to go on the great crusade next year with the lord. So I'm getting as much practice as I can.'

Ordulf looked at him, confused. 'But you will be fighting with weapons, not fists. Why does this help?'

'Pa says that fighting with weapons is much the same as without. You learn to do one, you can learn to do the other pretty quick. Fast hands are fast hands; a good eye is a good eye. Let your enemy make a mistake and then hit him. Same as fist fighting. Makes sense to me.'

Ordulf felt stupid for the third time that night. 'Wise man, your pa,' he said, smiling back at his new friend.

'He is that, my pa. A smart man.'

The next morning, Ordulf shook his still-aching body awake and prepared for the day's work. He felt pretty bad, but today was an important day. The customer would come to inspect the sword. Important as it was, it was not what Ordulf loved, fussing around with the finished work. Ordulf lived to swing a hammer, long arms burning with the effort, huge shoulders straining with the rhythm of the swing. He lived to feel the heat of the forge, to see the sparks fly and feel the steel move beneath his hand. The wind of the bellows was his music, the strike of the hammer his heartbeat.

Being a journeyman made him the lead hammer in the hammer team and more responsible for shaping the blades. The two or three apprentices helping just followed his strokes, all under the careful gaze of the master, who held the blade steady in tongs and called the directions and pace with an odd series of grunts, whistles and foot taps. For lesser blades or finishing work that only required a single smith, Ordulf was now allowed to work alone and forge his own work from scratch, sometimes even with an apprentice to assist.

Ordulf didn't just have huge strength and stamina. He was gifted with the eye. The eye that could pick out just the right colour in the steel being heated in the forge. The eye that could read the lumps and bulges in rough forged steel and know exactly where to place a blow to shape it, to move the glowing metal into place, to spot potential weaknesses and correct them, to look down a line and spot the tiniest inconsistency.

God, did he love forging. Almost as much as he hated polishing.

He returned to the room to inspect the blade, to check for any imperfections he might have missed. He found none. Setting the now-finished blade aside for the moment, Ordulf gently rested it in a notch in the cradle made specifically for that purpose. He arched his back in a broad stretch, still trying to remove the tension of the day and the night before, and stood up. The customer should be here, or would be arriving soon, and he went out to check with the master if anything else needed doing. He ducked his tall frame out of the door from the back room where he had been working all week and stepped out into the forge yard.

On his left, the forge itself was half-open to the central yard, with a broad, sloped roof over it and walls on three sides, which were covered in racks of tools and materials. More equipment hung from the rafters. The open side of the forge had two sets of huge folding doors that swung closed at night and could be locked with massive iron bolts. The apprentices took it in turns to sleep in the forge, hammers at hand, to deter thieves. The outer yard doors were secured with huge bolts of their own smithing, but you could never be too careful.

Across from the forge was the main building where the master lived and kept his shop, which was open to the main street beyond it. To his right was the bunkhouse where Ordulf slept, the storerooms and a low, open structure with the grinding wheels and workbenches. It was overall a mid-sized smithy, but for a town the size of Minden it was impressive, the largest for a day's ride in any direction.

The master was indeed in the main room of the shop area with the customer, the son of a great local lord sent to get his first proper sword. He was younger than Ordulf, perhaps fifteen, just old enough to have a full-sized sword for training. He exuded an air of arrogance, from his bizarre and uncomfortable stance, one leg thrust forward as if he were about to make a speech to a crowd, to his casual holding of his current undersized and scabbarded sword's hilt. He was standing with it ready to hand, as if an enemy might appear and strike him at any moment.

Ordulf thought the young man looked like a total joke, his tunic and hose absurdly over-elaborate for the small country town of Minden. It was the sort of clothing he had seen in Bremen on market day or during his few trips up to Hamburg with his master. Clothing chosen to impress, but there was no one here worth impressing. *Just sheer vanity and pride, then.*

Regardless, Ordulf had been well schooled by his master in the requirements of his rich customers, and so he stood quietly at the back of the room to wait on his master's convenience, trying as hard as possible to seem not to exist. The young lord's eyes wandered around the room, passing through Ordulf as if he were not there, confirming that he was doing his job correctly. The room was the main place of business for the forge. Comfortable seats were arranged around a small table in one corner, and a counter ran along the back of the room upon which the wares could be examined. On the walls were examples and patterns of various types of weapons available to order. It was a tidy and presentable space, if a little dark and small compared to the more prestigious smithies in Bremen or Hamburg.

His master was behaving in that special, uncharacteristically obsequious way that he reserved for the higher gentry. It was all Ordulf could do not to laugh and he managed to merely breathe more loudly than strictly necessary.

'Do you require any more adjustments to the belt or scabbard?' his master intoned, bowing in front of the young man half his size and spreading his palms outwards, a concerned and quizzical look on his face. 'If so, I will send it straight for such changes, as you require.'

'I am sure it is quite fine,' the young lord replied, not looking at the master or indeed the scabbard or belt, which he had briefly and disinterestedly tried on.

'Superb, Master Hartung. Then I shall have the blade finished and the scabbard fitted to it by matins the day after tomorrow.' He bowed deeply. 'Is there anything else you require?'

The young boy simply turned around and left with a half flick of his fingers to indicate that the meeting was over. Ordulf let out a surpressed chuckle, to be met with instant hot rage from his master. The burly master smith closed the distance to him in half a heartbeat and, despite being shorter, seemed to stare down at the cowering seventeen-year-old journeyman.

'Think that's funny, boy?' He emphasised 'boy' as if it was a vulgarity. 'That's your food just walked out that door. That's your bed, your roof, your very reason for existing and not being returned to the filthy milkmaid from whose belly you gushed forth. Do you understand me?'

Master Herman was a force of nature both in form and personality. Thick arms protruded from his massive chest, perched atop ludicrously short legs. The only man Ordulf knew with arms as strong as his own, he was a powerhouse of a smith who could swing the heavy hammer from dawn to dusk, day after day. A thick, wild beard was paired with a nearly bald head. His moods ranged from blazing fury to cold indifference, and unlike any other man Ordulf had met, he could switch between the two in a heartbeat. He was truly a unique man in Ordulf's limited experience.

Herman had lived in Minden all his life and been at this smithy since joining as a boy of six years to sweep the forge floor at night. He had eventually risen through the ranks to buy it from the previous master when the old man could no longer swing a hammer. Now, in his mid-forties, Herman had built this smithy up into the envy of the whole county with his smithing skill and his ferocious management of his workers.

The master smith turned around, leaving the questions unanswered, as they were intended to be. Instantly cool again, he said, 'Now bring me the sword, and we will set the fittings before we peen it together tomorrow.'

Ordulf slunk out of the room and returned to the forge. On his way through the central courtyard, he passed Henrick, one of the particularly useless apprentices they had that year. The boy was red-faced but Ordulf thought nothing of it. The boy was overweight and lazy and was always red-faced.

Ordulf went to the cradle and the sword. Something was wrong. It was the other way around to how it had been left, tip facing away. Brows furrowed, he picked it up and inspected it. That bloody halfwit Henrick had probably been playing with it. He hoped the boy hadn't dropped it or hit something. He desperately searched the blade, checking for marks or scratches.

His heart sank like a stone. He ran his eyes to the very tip and saw that it was bent and chipped. He cursed out loud. That couldn't just be straightened or polished out. It would ruin the entire profile of the tip. The whole point would have to be reground and profiled and then repolished back up the entire length of the blade to get a consistent finish. That bumbling moron had set him back five days' work, at least. Oh God, they only had two days to finish it. His mind raced. They could not fail to deliver; this was their most important customer.

By God, he would have that apprentice flayed to the edge of his life. Just as he turned to run to his master, a huge, meaty hand slammed down on his shoulder and whipped him around. He was presented with his master's boiling red face an inch in front of, and a foot below, his own.

'Henrick says he heard a clatter and saw you picking up the sword from the ground!' He shook the big journeyman. 'What did you do, boy?' Spittle flew from his lips up onto Ordulf's chin. 'Show it to me *now!*'

Ordulf opened and closed his mouth like a landed fish, speechless at the betrayal and shocked into silence. The moment to protest came and went as the master found the damaged tip and exploded into incandescent rage.

The world seemed to slow down and blur. Orders were shouted, but he didn't hear them. Rough hands grabbed his wrists as the other journeymen took him in their grip, dragged him into the smithy and held him down over an anvil. A whir and blur of noise and anger surrounded him. He heard everything and nothing. He was in total shock over the suddenness of the events. In front of his nose, the forge scale left on the anvil vibrated and moved with the movement of his breath and the pounding of feet around the forge. His whole world narrowed and shrank to that chattering forge scale flake.

As his eyes regained their focus and his hearing came back, leather was thrust into his mouth. The sudden realisation of what was happening hit him like a rush of wind the second before the knotted leather thong hit his bare backside like a chain of lightning bolts. He roared and struggled to throw off his fellow journeymen. Despite his own huge size and strength, the three of them held him down as the blows rained like the fire of God on his exposed rear. Ten strokes, twelve? He wasn't sure. Suddenly the blows stopped, and he lay there, panting, across the anvil. He opened his eyes and struggled to focus them as he sank to his knees beside the forge.

For a long moment, he hung there before the agony really kicked in: a dull ache followed by burning fire. He groaned and, as he opened his eyes once more, saw Henrick, eyes pinned wide and legs quivering, standing in the background. Henrick looked back, seeing nothing in the quivering, pain-filled face but the promise of revenge. Henrick gurgled and ran back to the bunkhouse, blabbering incoherently.

The master's lecture was almost as painful as the whipping. One month's pay deducted and his status reduced to lowest journeyman, Ordulf would work under supervision until he was trusted again. He would prostrate himself in front of the customer and beg forgiveness for his stupidity. How could a journeyman not know better than to play with a sword? He wasn't a knight; he was a peasant whose usefulness only extended to his skills in the forge. If he lost his master's trust in that again, he would be thrown out into the world as nothing, to be a labourer or a beast of burden on a farm.

With the mental whipping concluded, he was thrown into the bunk room and told not to reappear for two days until the lordling returned.

For two days, unable to sit down or lie comfortably, Ordulf raged and sulked in his room. He plotted his revenge, he planned great speeches pleading his innocence and he lived in utter terror of losing his position as a smith. He thought himself a superb smith, not just for his age but in absolute terms. He had a lot to learn, but he felt he could *see* the hot metal. He could see inside it: its twists, its imperfections, its structure. He felt he could plan his hammer strokes in real time to caress or stretch or bludgeon the steel into shape as required.

His blades warped less, and required less finishing, than any other smith's he had seen in this smithy, or indeed in the forges he had visited in Bremen. Sure, he was guilty of great pride, but was it not deserved? For two days with no food, he worried and sweated and slept fitfully. On the second day, the door burst open and his master's scowling face appeared in advance of his massive chest.

'You fucking stink. Go and wash your filth off and be ready

to see the lordling. If he demands your punishment or objects to the delay, you had better be ready to hand me the hammer that I will crush your balls with, you little shit. Do you understand me?'

The master smith turned on his heel and stormed out. Shaken and crestfallen, Ordulf dragged himself to the kitchen and got a pail of water to wash himself with. Changing into his least-worst working clothes, he slunk to the main room like a man being dragged to the gallows.

He stood in the centre of that room for what felt like an eternity, but was probably only as long as it takes a priest to say Mass, when the door opened and the lordling's servant came in. He walked up to the master smith, ignoring Ordulf, and performed a perfunctory bow.

'My lord regrets that he is unable to attend today. He will visit you at noon in three days to collect his sword. I assume all is well with it.'

Stunned at this turn of fortune, the master babbled, 'Of course. Convey my assurance that we will be ready and waiting for him at whatever time is convenient to him.'

'Excellent.' And with that the attendant swept out of the room.

Ordulf let out the breath he hadn't realised he had been holding and nearly sank to the floor. His master was giving him a wry grin. 'Someone up there loves you, boy,' he intoned, waving vaguely at the ceiling. 'Now go finish the fucking sword. You have two days, and if it isn't perfect, I'm going to wear your ears for jewellery, since you clearly don't need them for listening. You got me, boy?'

'I've got you, Master.'

'Don't fucking stand here flapping your mouth at me. I pay you to work, not talk. Now get going. You've got two days to do three days' work, and you ain't even managed three days' work in three days before now, not in your whole, miserable life.' The language was as harsh as ever, but the master had a barely suppressed grin on his face, and he gave Ordulf a hearty pat on the back as he walked out of the door. Ever the mercurial character, his master would run hotter than hell if things were going wrong, but as long as all was well, he was a reasonable man.

Ordulf practically ran to the back room. The sword point was being carefully recreated by a worried-looking journeyman. He looked up as Ordulf ran in.

'Master says I'm to finish the sword,' Ordulf blurted out.

'Lord Fancy Pants didn't kill you, then? Thank fuck for that. I hate polishing,' replied the other smith, standing up from the workbench before he farted, grunted and left to go about his other work.

CHAPTER 4

A CLATTER OF SWORDS

WHEN THE LORDLING did arrive in the forge yard, he unexpectedly came with his father, who was the lord of the neighbouring province and a great and powerful man. After furiously bowing and begging his lord's forgiveness for the state of himself, his forge and his unkempt workers, the master smith invited the lord and his retinue to meet in the main room, even as he worriedly eyed the number of them and wondered how they would all fit in.

'No need, good man. It's a fine day, and I would rather conduct this affair outside in the air,' said the lord. One of his footmen promptly appeared with a folding chair and set it out for his lord to sit in the shade under the edge of the sloped forge roof. 'Conclude your business with my son, and then I will talk to you on another matter.'

'Certainly, my lord. Thank you, my lord.' The master bowed and retreated from the seated noble.

The lordling stood, much less assuredly this time under the gaze of his father, as a table and a tightly bound roll of reeds on a stand was brought out into the yard. Journeymen and apprentices lurked in the shadows and peered through windows, keen to watch the proceedings. Ordulf, who was standing behind his master with the carefully wrapped and scabbarded sword, looked everywhere for Henrick but didn't see him. He hadn't seen him in the last four days. He had done nothing but sleep and refinish the sword, cooped up in the back room.

He was still furious about the whole episode, but he acknowledged that the adversity and the desperation to be perfect had brought out his best work. The sword was, quite simply, gorgeous. The finish on the blade was as smooth as a lake on a calm spring morning. The guard and pommel shone like the sun out in the daylight, and the hilt was fitted to perfection. This was the best-finished sword he had ever made.

When his master indicated to him, he came forward to the table and handed it over, keeping his head down, trying not to exist. The master laid the sword on the table and uncovered it with a small flourish.

He stepped back and, with his open palms, invited the lordling to examine the sword. Along with its fittings and scabbard, it had cost enough to rent a small farm for a decade, so even for the great lord, it was a serious expenditure.

The sword was in its scabbard and belt. The belt was of rich black, tanned leather, decorated with gilded fittings, buckles and bronze rivets. The lord's coat of arms was engraved into the fitting above the sword itself and replicated on the outside of the scabbard. The scabbard was covered in the same rich black leather, banded underneath with iron over a double-leaf wooden core. The sword fitted inside snugly, requiring a sharp tug to free it from the throat so it would not rattle or fall out. The top of the scabbard was covered with a gilded cap with the cross emblazoned on the outside.

The lordling stepped forward and ran his hands over the leather and fittings. Even the lord himself perked up and craned his neck to see the details. An attendant helped the son to fit the belt, and he walked around in a small circle, testing the weight and feel of the belt with the sword mounted to it. All his earlier hesitancy and arrogance were gone. He was, after all, a man who had been training for swordplay since he was half his current age. He turned to face the reed bundle and dropped into a fighting stance, front foot forward, knee bent, back foot opening out. He took a step away. He grasped the hilt and drew the sword in a wide flashing arc before bringing it down to inspect it, left hand lightly holding it near the tip.

He spun and swung it a few times to test the weight and balance, circling with his feet. Then he abruptly turned, leaving the sword trailing behind his shoulder, and swung down with a vicious cut from a high guard at the roll of reeds on the stick. There was a thunk, and the top of the reed bundle toppled without moving sideways more than a handspan. The lord and his men applauded the little display, and the master smith beamed. The lord leaped from his chair to examine the sword himself and twirled it and rolled it in his hands.

'Master smith, this is a magnificent sword. How dare you make my son a better one than I myself carry?' he intoned, casting a grim look at the smith.

The master's face fell and drained of colour. 'My lord, I… I beg your forgiveness for my thoughtlessness.'

The lord chucked and broke into a smile. 'I jest with you, master swordsmith. I expected nothing less from a smith of your reputation. The one in my own town is good for nothing but horse tack and watchmen's spears.'

The master stammered and nodded his head vigorously in relief. Ordulf had forgotten not to exist and was beaming broadly off to one side. Suddenly the lord's eyes turned and locked with his. Ordulf froze. He then panicked, lost the smile and returned his eyes to the ground, cap in clenched hands in front of him. His mind raced; he had never made eye contact with a great noble before. Oh God, had he caused offence? He knew he couldn't afford to create another round of trouble.

There was a moment of silence that seemed like an age but was probably no longer than it takes a horse to swat at a fly. He wondered what was going on. Surely the lord had simply moved on and was looking elsewhere? He risked a quick glance up. Oh God! The lord was still staring at him, except he was now only half the distance away and closing in purposeful strides.

Ordulf opened his mouth to apologise before remembering that you never speak first to a noble and slammed it shut again. He could feel himself sweating profusely. The sweat was making the healing wounds on his backside itch like the devil but, by God, he couldn't scratch them now.

Oh, sweet mother of Jesus! The lord had arrived in front of him. What should he do now? The lord was only slightly shorter than Ordulf, who was usually a giant among men. The lord stopped and addressed him.

'You there, young lad. I saw the pride of craftsmanship in your eyes as I praised this blade. Is this your work?'

Ordulf opened his mouth, and some incoherent stammers leaked out before he slammed it shut once more and bowed his head.

The lord turned to the master smith with an amused grin on his face. 'Is he simple, or is he just encountering his first great lord?'

'His first great lord, m'lord,' the smith replied, wringing his hands as he watched the scene, desperately hoping his wayward journeyman wouldn't cause some great offence.

'Ah, I see. Look up at me, lad. It's allowed, I won't punish you for looking at me. I'm really just a man like you, except smaller and with more important parents.'

'My lord!' the lord's chamberlain protested quietly from

behind him. Ordulf let out a shocked squeak and suppressed a laugh, but the tension was broken. He met the lord's gaze and inclined his head awkwardly.

'Ah, there we are. You have returned to us. Don't mind my chamberlain over there. He is overly obsessed with protocol and will harangue me at great length for talking to someone so far below my station so candidly. You see, I am supposed to give orders and occasionally dish out punishment to someone like you, nothing more. In fact, I am probably supposed to have someone else do even that for me.' He smiled warmly and brought the sword up for inspection. 'But this is your work, isn't it? I saw your pride as you handed it over.'

'My master designed and directed its forging, my lord,' Ordulf spluttered, 'and the whole company did parts of work on it, too, if that pleases your lord.'

'Your lordship.'

Ordulf looked at him blankly.

'When you say "your lord" to me, it sounds like you mean *my* lord, the Duke of Saxony, who probably isn't all that pleased by that answer – in fact, he probably cares not one jot. What you meant to say was "your lordship",' the lord said, an amused expression on his face.

'Yes, my lordship. S-s-s-sorry, m'lordship.'

The lord chuckled and continued. 'So you honourably note the contributions of all the other members of your fine company of smiths, but I ask again: Who really put their soul into this blade? Who made this blade whole and beautiful? I feel a great love of craft sunk into this sword; the detailing is perfect, the lines and joins immaculate. I have owned many swords in my lifetime, seen many more, swung a few in battle. And this, young lad, is an exceptional-looking sword. Tell me, is it as good as it looks?' The lord became stern, his eyes narrowing, his voice taking on a rough edge. The air suddenly felt colder, like a winter's morning despite the sun.

'This sword will bear responsibility for guarding the life of my firstborn son, my heir, the entire future of my family line and my legacy. If it looks pretty and doesn't work properly, it counts for nothing. Nothing!' The lord barked the last word and stood in front of the shaking young smith, sword between them, eyes boring holes into Ordulf's very soul.

'It's a strong sword, m'lord, well forged and ready for battle,' Ordulf managed to force out through quivering lips.

'The boy speaks out of turn, but he speaks the truth, m'lord,' the master interjected with a bizarrely high-pitched voice, the amount of hand-wringing he was doing having reached the level at which it could now be heard as a sweaty squeaking.

'You certain of that fact, lad? You willing to bet my son's life on it?'

'I, uh… Well, yes, my lord.'

'That's all very well, as it's not your life to bet. How about your own life? Would you stake your own life, which probably means as much to you as my son's does to me, on this sword, that it is as good as it looks? That like a drunken sot at a dance you didn't forget inner quality in the search for outer beauty?'

There was a stony silence around the yard. Ordulf breathed hard and then, calmly and quietly, replied, 'Yes, m'lord. I would stake my life on the quality of that sword.'

'Excellent,' said the lord, turning and striding towards the table that the sword had been laid on. 'Let's take you up on that immediately, with a better test than some reeds.'

The table was a simple, portable thing, with boards as thick as a thumb laid side by side on some crosspieces.

Sweeping the stuttering master out of the way, the lord violently turned the table onto its side with a thrust of his boot. He swung the bright blade over his head with all his strength and down into the edge of the boards. There was a resounding crack that echoed around the packed yard and startled the tethered horses as the first board split to half its width and jagged splinters flew out.

The lord kicked the blade free of the cloying wood, raised the blade again and hammered it down into the damaged board, which split in half and parted. Again, the sword rose. Again, the lord roared and brought it flashing down into the ruined table. And again, and again, cutting chunks out until the last board had split and the end of the sword had buried itself in the dirt of the yard, the table completely split asunder.

The lord let go of the hilt, leaving the sword swaying, embedded in the earth. Straightening, he shook the splinters out of his dark-green hose. He plucked an errant one from his thumb, and bright blood showed. There was a shocked silence after the sudden violence of the last few moments.

'Son,' the lord called.

'Yes, Father?' The lordling stepped towards his father, regaining his composure.

'Inspect that blade and hilt, and if it is damaged or unacceptably affected or loosened in any way, kill the boy with it. He gave his word.'

Gasps and whispers circled the yard. Master Herman rushed forward. 'M'lord,' he called to the retreating green-clad back as the son pulled the sword free of the dirt. 'M'lord, please, I beg you, don't commit violence here! The boy is arrogant and doesn't know his skill yet. The blade he made may not be perfect, but he is a good lad, and he is learning well.'

The lord turned abruptly, causing the smith to nearly crash into him. 'Master smith, do you believe that blade to be anything less than perfect? If so, how dare you sell it to me for my son? Say nothing more or I will assume you were knowingly selling me substandard weapons. Your reputation, and the life of your lad, rests on the quality of your work now. You should hope your confidence in the blade is deserved.'

As the lord returned to his seat, he smiled to himself. He loved acting the great lord and doing outrageous things. It really was one of the highlights of his life. People would speak of this event in reverential whispers for miles around, adding to his already fearsome reputation. Craftsmen would put extra effort into work done for him; swindlers would think twice before looking his way. The boy was in no danger. The lord had known from the feel of cutting those boards that the sword was solid and undamaged – he was merely making a show of it.

He accepted the cup of wine that his attendant had somehow provided. The lord swept his gaze over his son, who was alternating between swinging the sword and holding it up to the light, inspecting it, and then he fixed his stare on the lad whose life hung in the balance.

He found a steady gaze fixed back on him. He found himself to be mildly disappointed. The lad clearly also knew the sword to be fine. He went from feeling disappointed to feeling highly impressed when Ordulf inclined his head in a subtle bow. The lad was thinking ahead; he also knew how this would benefit his reputation. The lord laughed to himself as he realised the big, cocky bastard was actually grateful.

'Father,' his son's annoyingly high-pitched voice called out. 'The blade is fine, and the hilt solid. There is no serious damage beyond a small notch in the edge and some scratching across the middle of the blade from it. You must have hit a nail. Yes, I see the two halves of it here.' He pointed to the ground beneath the ruin of the table.

The lord smiled and turned his head to the young smith. 'Lad, what is your name?'

'Ordulf, my lord.'

'Ordulf, I congratulate you on your work. I am Adolf, Count of Schauenburg and lord of Holstein and Stormarn.' He rose to his feet and clicked his fingers at his attendant, who produced a small number of silver coins as if by magic.

'Ordulf, I would consider it a signal favour to me if you would take this token of my appreciation and repair the scratches on that blade. Two days should do it?'

Normally, Ordulf would have groaned inwardly at the thought of another two days of polishing. But he found himself longing for more of this great man's praise and leaped to the task like a hound off the leash. 'Of course, my lord. It would be a pleasure,' he replied, bowing deeply.

'Excellent. Master smith, I am most pleased by your service. Now we must retire inside to discuss another job I would have you do for me, if you would be so kind as to lead the way?'

The master bowed sharply, relief worn like a mask across his features. 'Thank you, my lord. Of course, my lord. Please, this way.'

In the back room of the forge that had become his virtual prison for days, Ordulf was selecting the stones and leather he would use to clean up the light marking on the blade. He couldn't help but smile and whistle a happy tune. He had been awed and seduced by the power Count Adolf exuded, breathless at the way he had controlled the attention of everyone present, thrilled by the praise that had been publicly bestowed on him so soon after his whipping and humiliation. He felt vindicated and appreciated, a feeling so rare under the harsh eye of Master Herman. He suddenly realised that for the right man, he fucking loved polishing.

CHAPTER 5

THE COUNTRY COUNT

C OUNT ADOLF SETTLED into his chair in the centre
of the main room. Somehow, the chair that he had stood
up from in the courtyard had moved there before he
arrived. He did not concern himself with how his chamberlain
achieved these things, but the man really was excellent, if a bit
haughty and fussy.

The master smith, much more comfortable now the drama was
over and his customer was not only happy but offering more business, stood in front of him by the counter, waiting to be addressed.

'So, to the main business of the day. Are you aware of the preparations for the crusade?' the count asked.

'Yes m'lord. I have been preparing a few items for men partici-
pating in this great campaign,' the smith replied.

'Good. Are you also aware that I spent ten years clearing the
lands to the north-east of the Elbe, between Hamburg and the lands
of Denmark, under the instruction of Lothair, our duke?'

'I did not know that, m'lord. Apologies. I am aware of the

campaign, of course, and I made my reputation supplying weapons to men headed to that war.'

'War! Ha!' the count guffawed. 'That was no war. It was like clearing mice from a barn: long and tedious and with much killing of inferior creatures. But, regardless, that has put me in a position of much demand for this crusade, given my experience in the area. Now, between you and me, I had thought to stay and manage my lands here for a while, but my duke calls me, and I must answer.'

He waved a hand airily. 'I digress. The point is that I must summon my vassals and commit a large force to the coming crusade. I intend my force to be the best contingent and thus be allocated the best positions and tasks. Part of this will be ensuring my men are well armed and armoured.' He slapped his hand on his thigh with each of the final words for emphasis.

'Now, I already have every low smithy and armourer between here and Hamburg making horse tack, maille, shields and spears. What I need is someone who can make a batch of arming swords of simple design and high quality. Nothing flashy, mind you; these are swords for war.'

The smith bowed low and excitedly babbled, 'M'lord, I would be honoured to complete such an order for you.'

'Of course you would. It would make you a small fortune.'

The smith raised his hands, and his eyes widened in protest. 'M'lord, I would give you an excellent price; my taking would be very modest, I assure you.'

'Yes, you will give me an excellent price. But, still, it is a large order and, of course, you will do well by it. Now, to the requirements. My noble vassals, of course, provide their own equipment and have their own swords. However, my men-at-arms of lower rank may not have good swords or even swords at all. In addition, swords break and are lost in combat.'

Herman nodded sagely in understanding.

'So, for my contingent of four hundred and fifty men-at-arms, I would like one hundred spare swords. Made to a simple pattern, ready for battle, no extravagances other than my coat of arms upon the pommel. I will need them when we leave Hamburg in the spring in four months' time. Can you do this?'

The master smith's mind raced. He had never made such a large batch of swords before. Normally, such orders would be completed by the big workshops in Hamburg where teams of workers would make batches of simple swords fit for a lower-born man-at-arms or a household guard.

His company, with himself as master, four journeymen and eight apprentices working on their three forges, usually made between three and four swords a week during busy times. Twelve weeks would be, at most, fifty swords. But that was for custom pieces with varying decoration and individual design. Could they make a single, simple pattern twice as fast? He thought they could.

'Yes m'lord, such an order is possible.' He nodded his head fervently.

'Excellent. If you say you can, then I expect nothing short of success. Do you understand me? You have seen today how seriously I take such claims, yes?'

The smith gulped nervously. 'I understand, m'lord.'

'I offer one hundred and fifty silver pieces per sword. I trust that will be sufficient?'

The smith hesitated briefly. One hundred and fifty silver pieces was a low price for a sword. Normally, his work started at two hundred and went as high as the masterwork for a thousand silver pieces that he had just sold to the count's son. However, having a consistent pattern with no embellishments would save a lot of time and cost and, in any case, fifteen thousand silver pieces was more money than he had ever seen in his life.

'I accept that price, m'lord,' he said with a deep bow.

'Excellent. There are a couple of other things I need. A new sword for myself in the latest style. It is to be a battle sword, but also take care to make it impressive – I have a reputation to uphold.'

'Certainly, m'lord. It would be a great honour to make a new sword for you. I will make it myself.' The smith beamed.

'No, actually, I want the young lad to make it. I want you to focus on the supervising of the hundred blades – that is the more important job. I have many swords. I want to test the young lad's capabilities because, you see, the last thing I require of you is him.'

'You want the lad, m'lord?' the smith asked, puzzled. 'But for what reason would you require a journeyman smith? He is a crucial part of the operation here, though I would never tell him that. Without him, I don't know if we can make the hundred blades.'

'As to your first question, I want to take a smith with me on crusade. Experience has shown me that having a competent smith with your party is a huge advantage. Weapons get damaged, break and go missing. I need someone who can repair them, maintain them and possibly make new ones if we find a suitable smithy. I am assured that the Norse have a smithy in every village. As to why that lad? I see something in him that I like. A certain toughness and self-assurance. He will need that on campaign.'

The smithy started the hand-wringing and babbling again. The count raised a hand to cut him off.

'Don't worry, master smith. I only need to rent him for the duration, and he will not be involved in the fighting. He will be quite safe and return to you at the end of the crusade. I am sure he will also learn and develop his skills and perhaps be even more useful upon his return. Also, I won't need him until we leave, so you may send him along with the swords when they are ready.'

The smith could see that he had no refusal open to him, so he sighed and assented with a nod. 'As you say, m'lord.'

'Now, what do you pay him?'

'Two silver pieces a week, m'lord. Three extra when he completes a job.'

'Two! My, that is affordable. I will pay you three a week for the duration of his absence, to cover his cost to you and the cost of replacing him.'

This news perked the master up again. 'That is most kind, m'lord. I will be able to hire a good man from Bremen to cover his absence.'

'Excellent. Then we are all agreed? Good. My man here will stay and deal with the particulars. I have to be away to deal with other matters of preparation.'

The lord stood and raised his arm so that his attendant could attach his cloak. Everyone in the room bowed, and he turned to leave, shouting for his horse. His horse was already there and ready, of course, but he liked shouting for things. It was one of the perks of his station in life. He threw himself up into the saddle, eschewing the proffered stool that was placed for him. He felt alive and was basking in the sunlight and the feeling of power that came with organising his own army.

For five years, he had managed his estates and watched his son grow, settled minor disputes and attended on his lord, the duke. It had been five years since his last campaign against the northern tribes that had finished with his triumph and his being raised to the title of count. In the northern campaign, he had been the commander of an army and the conqueror of new lands, receiving praise and jealousy in equal measure from his peers and his superiors. He had never been satisfied by anything since.

He could barely suppress his delight at being sent to war again. He laid his spurs into his horse, surprising the poor beast as much as his followers, and set off down the road that would lead home, trailing dust and panicked attendants in his wake.

Hartung was the first of his people to catch him up on the road outside Minden that led back to his own estates and to his fortified manor that sat on the hillside just over ten miles away. The boy loved to ride and was a talented horseman. Despite his many flaws in temperament and discipline, his physical skill on a horse and burgeoning talent as a swordsman gave Adolf hope that his only son would make a great man of himself, and a worthy successor.

The count slowed his childish flight and smiled warmly at his son, who gave him a clipped smirk in response, and the two men settled their mounts into a walk as they followed the broad road home. Soon, his mounted page arrived in a flurry of dust and apologies, then a while later harried footmen and attendants appeared, riding or leading horses, some weighed down with other purchases they had made in the town. They were flustered and sweating and casting resentful looks at the back of their master's broad frame, looks that he could not see but felt nonetheless.

Adolf felt a small prick of guilt for the trouble he had put them through, but it was quickly quashed. It was a fine day, and he was simply enjoying life too much to care for the problems and petty grievances of his retinue. He had worried for years that his time of glory was over, that he would grow old and obscure, strangled of the opportunity for further military success or renown. But now he was shortly to ride to war, on a crusade no less, the highest expression of honour.

As a young man, refused the opportunity to go by his father, a country knight of no great significance. He had watched with intense jealousy as the great crusader lords had returned from the east to acclaim and near-worship from their peers. Men his age had gone out to the Holy Land as squires of no name and returned as celebrated knights. The missed opportunity galled him. When his father had finally coughed himself to death in 1100, he had thrown himself into the service of the old Duke of Saxony, earning a name as a skilled knight and loyal follower, befriending and serving his son, Lothair. When the old duke had died and Lothair had succeeded the duchy, he made his loyal friend Adolf the lord of the new county of Schauenburg, a good sized rural county seated at his family manor, and the two ambitious young men had set about building their reputations and holdings.

North of Saxony lay the Elbe River and beyond that the lands of the Wagrians that sat at the base of the Jutland peninsula. The Empire had long wished to tame those wild tribes of Wagria, and Lothair raised his forces to attempt the task. Lothair was no military man, but he was a cunning politician. He had given command of first a large detachment, and then his army, to his friend, the lord of Schauenburg.

As they followed the rutted track Adolf saw a leafy stem of one of the roadside bushes leaning out over the path ahead of them. He reined his horse to a halt and looked at Hartung. 'You see that hanging plant? It is your enemy. Do you think you can part that stem, at a gallop, without either half touching you or your horse?'

The boy looked up and appraised the odd challenge. His father was prone to eccentric tests. 'I believe so.'

'Good. How would you do it?'

The boy thought again for a moment. 'I would slice it with a rising cut from the left,' he said, somewhat uncertainly.

'A rising cut over your horse's head? Be sure not to slice off an ear. It won't thank you for it; I've seen that before.'

Hartung looked at the stalk again uncertainly. 'Well then, perhaps...'

'No, you have made your decision. There is rarely time to change your mind. Now execute the attack with skill and ensure the right result. Go, now!'

Hartung stuttered but then nodded, drawing his old arming sword and putting his boots into the sides of his horse. It was only a riding horse, but it was trained for the charge and barely protested as the boy forced it into a gallop within just a few strides, hooves gripping well on the firm surface of the earthen road. Hartung let the reins go loose in his left hand, guiding the horse with his knees, and crossed his sword over, dropping it down on his left side, point facing forward, as if to threaten his imaginary foe with a thrust to the face. He judged the distance to the stem, and at the last moment, he flicked his wrist and swept the point of the sword up, almost kissing the left ear of his horse. The front of the blade sliced through the stem, and the flicking motion of the blade carried the cut half beyond him, falling to the right. The remaining half of the stem, suddenly unburdened by the hanging weight, sprang back, and horse and rider passed into the gap between the two.

Adolf let out a whoop of delight as his son reigned in and returned. The movement had been near perfect. His son even blushed as the count and his footmen applauded the display.

Hartung gave a curt nod of acknowledgement and fell back into step alongside his father.

'Well cut, my boy. Well cut.'

'Thank you, Father.'

'Do you understand how that cut could be used?'

Hartung nodded. 'I imagined that perhaps I was representing a thrust to the face, drawing my enemy to parry and strike me to the chest. But that flick would push his blade high and give me an opening to cut with the back edge.'

'No, you would be going too fast, and you would be past him before you countered.'

'Oh.' Hartung sounded disappointed.

'But you are rarely alone in a mounted fight. The man behind you would have had an easy strike on an unbalanced enemy, and your sword would have been perfectly positioned for a new attack on your second enemy. How would you have attacked the second enemy from that position?'

Hartung nodded in understanding. 'My hand was high and my point downwards, so I would have thrust for his chest and been able to parry, if needed, by turning my wrist.'

'Excellent!' exclaimed Adolf. 'You get it entirely. Now remember that lesson. You do not have to strike an enemy to defeat him. Rely on your fellows and deliver to them easy kills, but also remember your enemy's fellows and be guarded against them.' Adolf smiled broadly, proud of his clever lesson and the skill his son had showed. The little cortege continued its slow way back to Schauenburg.

Castle Schauenburg was a fortified manor, nestled on the hill above the villages and pastures of the broad river valley below like a bird of prey above a flock. The views from its upper floors were magnificent, and from his bedchamber Adolf could, and often did, gaze out over his first domain. When he and Lothair had driven the Slavic tribes from the lands north of the Elbe and secured the entire base of the Jutland peninsula, Lothair had made him Count of Holstein, as the newly conquered lands were known by the Empire, and also lord of Stormarn, the county that included the prosperous city of Hamburg.

The gift was enormous. Adolf had, in ten short years, transformed himself from an obscure knight to one of the most powerful counts in all of Saxony, and the lands he held in Lothair's name, particularly Hamburg, made him rich beyond his wildest dreams. But yet he still chose to live in the house his father had built, in the least significant of his holdings. It was called a castle but was a parody of the name; it was merely a largish manor house, which he had greatly expanded, with a wall and small gatehouse. But it was his home, and he eschewed finding or building a great castle that befitted his station and that would be far less comfortable and practical to live in.

It was also the home where he had raised his son. Adolf had

married Hildewa when he was a young knight of no fame and she the daughter of an old knight of no renown. Their son Hartung had been born before he set out on his great adventures, and he was loath to uproot them from this quiet country town, where he was the most important man for miles around, and move them to Hamburg, where the powerful moved like smoke through rushes and politics governed everything. His wife had no experience of the ways of the court in the big cities. She was a wonderful wife and mother, and a superb administrator of his affairs when he was away, but like him had no interest in fine society and the politics of the big cities.

So in his birthplace Adolf remained, and he was content to visit his other holdings periodically to scare his stwerards and pore over their accounts.

And yet his idle hands yearned for more, for a return to glory, and as he trained his son to the life of a knight, he envied him his adventures yet to come.

The party finally passed through the wooded lane that led to the gates of the castle, and Adolf tried to hide his stiffness as he dismounted, cursing his body, which felt every one of its nearly forty years after a long day in the saddle. He kept a broad smile fixed on his face as his weary party dismounted and set about dealing with the horses and their cargo.

Leaving the work in the yard to others, he strode to his private quarters with only one thing on his mind: getting someone to fill the bath.

As he was lying back in the broad, round tub, relaxing in the cooling water, Hildewa came into the room. It wasn't usual for her to come into the bathhouse when he was using it, and for a moment his interest was stirred, and he smiled at her coyly. But her expression poured cold water on that intent and made it clear that was not the purpose of her visit.

'I have just spoken to Hartung who seems very excited about the prospect of going on the crusade with his new sword and his father.' Her tone poured ice water on any desire he had remaining.

'Ah,' Adolf replied awkwardly.

'Why would you say he was going with you?'

Adolf raised his hands in defence. 'I did not tell him he was coming.'

'But did you tell him he was not?'

Adolf paused, and his defence deflated. 'I did not.'

'You took him on a trip to gather equipment for the crusade, to buy him a magnificent new sword, and you did not tell him he was not to be joining you?'

'No.' Adolf looked away, embarrassed. He had been so focused on his own dreams of glory that he had forgotten his son might have them.

'Well, now he thinks he is going, and he is telling everyone he is going.'

'Damn. Well, now he has told everyone, and he is so intent, perhaps I should take him.'

'Husband, you cannot take him. He is but fourteen years old!' Her stern demeanour cracked, and she sounded plaintive.

'Many men his age will be going as pages, squires even.'

'And how many of them will return?' his wife half shouted, pointing a thin finger at his eyes.

'We cannot keep him here forever, Hildewa. One day he will have my title, and he must have earned the respect of his peers. He must prove himself, as I did.'

'You were nineteen when you went to war. He is not ready!' She grabbed his hand and squeezed it. 'Please, husband, do not take my boy to war – I cannot bear it. I thought you were done with campaigning. I would not waste my breath stopping you this time... but not my son.'

Adolf looked into his wife's eyes and relented, gently squeezing her hand in return. 'You are right. I will tell Hartung, and he will hate me for it.'

'He will forgive you, and he will be alive.'

'One day soon you will have to let him make his own way, Hildewa,' Adolf said, smiling up at her sadly as she perched on the edge of the tub.

She let go of his hand and got up. 'Not today.'

Adolf could still feel the damp in his hair as he went out to the court-yard. He sighed as he found Hartung fencing with practice swords with the old guard master who often trained with him when Adolf was not at home. He watched for a while. He had to admit, the boy was good. Quick, and with a keen eye. Nevertheless, the guard master was far too wily and soon disarmed the boy with a neat reverse and a pommel strike to the forearm. Hartung yelped in pain and dropped his sword, shaking his hand and trying to massage the feeling back into his numbed fingers. He looked up and saw his father and went red in the face, humiliated.

'You fight well, son,' said Adolf with rare affection. The surly boy mumbled something without looking up at him, still gently massaging his wrist and ignoring the sword that the guard master was proffering him.

'I will be ready when we leave for crusade, Father, I promise,' he said defiantly, and Adolf's heart sank. Adolf dismissed the guard with a subtle nod, and the man bowed and left with the swords.

'Hartung, there is something we must speak of. Come, we will have dinner and speak about your future.' Adolf immediately regretted his neutral choice of words as his son's face perked up and he smiled at his father excitedly.

Damn.

Adolf, Count of Schauenburg and lord of Holstein and Stormarn

CHAPTER 6

FORGING A FUTURE

I N THE FORGE in Minden, the rest of that autumn and the winter that followed passed to the beat of hammer strokes. The forge was a bustling hive of activity throughout the short days, beginning at dawn and continuing well into the evenings, lit by the fires of the forges and extra torches set up through the yard.

The steel for the swords arrived in rough bars or rods from the smeltery. The master smith supervised the selection of suitable pairs and then the forging of these onto the sides of bars of wrought iron to form a sword billet. The blade that could then be hammered from that billet would have strong, hard edges and a soft centre that could flex and absorb blows.

The billets were then hammered into the basic shape of the sword, teams of apprentices and journeymen working the sledgehammers as the master smith directed them in the glow of the forge. Then, when the blade was finished, they would harden and temper it. Ordulf loved this part. This was the dark art of swordsmithing. It was always conducted at night with just the light of the forge and a torch by the anvil. The temperature of the blade in the forge had to be just perfect, and the only way to judge was experience. The master smith taught this skill carefully and through much repetition.

For the count's new sword, Herman let Ordulf do the process himself without aid for the first time, the master watching like a hawk. At his direction, the bellows were pumped more slowly and steadily than for forging, the forge fire lower and more subdued than normal.

Ordulf sawed a blade back and forth through the fire, carefully watching the colour of the blade and the way the sparks flew from the coals. When he judged the moment was right, he pulled the sword from the fire with the tongs and held it, smoking and glowing, in the cool night air. As the glow receded, a ripple of darkness spread out across the metal. The wave of darkness spread through the whole of the blade until it was gone and the blade had cooled to black.

Chasing out the shadows, the master called it. And with the shadows gone, the blade would be ready for hardening. It was truly a beautiful moment, in the dark of the evening and the quiet of the usually bustling forge. Ordulf liked to think that those shadows being forced out let some light or soul into the sword.

Once the blade was cool, Ordulf once again heated it rapidly in the forge until it was glowing like a sunset on a clear day, then whipped it from the coals and plunged it into a barrel of water to instantly cool. One blade in about five or ten would crack or shatter at this stage and some others would fail to harden. The steel they received varied, and that was the nature of the craft. Those that survived might still not be suitable for finishing. But as the steaming blade emerged from the water, it was intact, and he laid it aside to cool. Herman grunted at him gruffly, a distinct mark of approval.

Ordulf picked up the now cooled and hardened blade from

the bench in front of him. He tapped it with a small bronze hammer, and it rang like a bell. Then he ran a handsaw blade over the edge. The smith, carefully listening, looked at him and nodded. The pitch was right. The note was high and clear, and the saw blade screeched and did not mark the blade. The blade was hard and uncracked internally. It would be suitable for Count Adolf's new weapon.

The blade would have to be carefully tempered overnight by the apprentices, gently baking it in a brick oven built for the purpose. The blade had to sit in the brick oven for half the night at a temperature just high enough to make meat gently sizzle, then be removed to cool and left until morning. With the first blade done, and Herman satisfied, the forge was extinguished, raked and left to cool for the night.

Once the grinding of a blade was finished, a process that took nearly two days per blade, the final edge was applied by hand with sharpening stones. The master inspected and tested each blade by cutting scrap leather and then sent it for the fitting of the cross guard, handle and pommel, a simple job of fitting pre-made parts done by the apprentices. The cross guards were of the simple bar pattern, with a slight incline towards the blade starting from the centre. The handle was wooden, ribbed in shape and wrapped in leather. The pommel was a hollow rounded block of iron, impressed with the shape of the cross on one side and the count's coat of arms on the other, which the smith had stamped into them as they lay red hot on the anvil. The sword's tang, the sliver of steel than ran from the blade up through the handle, protruded through the pommel and was carefully hammered flat, peened into a dome, sealing the pommel and handle tightly in place.

The swords were elegant and simple, made to the latest designs and fashions. They were austere, as befitted a crusader, but also decorated subtly to show their quality.

By the third week of the first month of the year 1116, the swords were completed, a full month ahead of schedule. The smith paid his exhausted staff an extra ten silver pieces a man for the apprentices and twenty for the journeymen and gave them the week off. He was worried that one or two might not return. They had become highly skilled over the winter with so much practice, and the money might tempt them to go elsewhere looking for new adventures. He supposed it mattered not. He could hire anyone he liked now with his money and reputation.

He opened his strongbox; there were only five hundred silver pieces left, but the other half of the payment was now due. Once that was paid and he had settled his remaining debts with all the various suppliers, he would be left with around four thousand silver pieces. An unimaginable profit from a single winter's work. He was a man utterly at peace with the world. He could sell the smithy and buy a nice plot of farmland with a house on it to retire to and spend his days managing tenant farmers on his own land if he was so inclined. But he was not. He was a man born to the fire of the forge and would never leave it while he had strength in his arms.

He supervised the preparation of the shipment of swords. He and Ordulf shepherded some day labourers as they went down to the town docks and packed the boxes of swords onto the barge they had hired for the journey downriver to Bremen. There, they would hand over the consignment to the count's people who would take it overland to Hamburg under escort. The journey down the River Weser was about seventy miles and would take three days, with overnight stops in two small towns along the way. A couple of dozy-looking guards in ancient maille shirts and carrying rusty spears would be their escorts, but the river and the area was very safe, especially with so many armed crusaders passing through, and

Herman didn't want to waste coin on lots of guards who would be more likely to draw attention than provide real security.

Ordulf carried a scant few possessions for his great trip on the crusade. He carried his core tools including his favourite hammer and tongs, spare clothes, a new and fine warm woollen cloak he had bought with his bonus, spare boots with long tops for marching and some other assorted gear he thought he might need. He also carried all his money for buying whatever else he needed, which was thirteen silver pieces and a small purse full of coppers. Hardly a fortune but more money than a simple peasant might own at one time in his life. He also carried a long knife of his own forging, with a blade as long as his hand and a single curved edge leading up to a straight spine. It had a small iron guard at the base of the blade, a wooden handle and a small iron pommel peened to the tang. A simple but strong construction, it was suitable for eating and general use but also, if it came to it, for defending himself and the contents of his purse.

Of course, Ordulf knew nothing about fighting with knives, but his arrogance and sense of invincibility due to his size, strength and youth prevented him from thinking this through. The barge moved off from the dock, and the lively late winter current swept them swiftly along as they huddled and shivered on deck.

The journey passed uneventfully at first. Two stops in small, quiet riverside inns along the way were pleasant and allowed the smiths to talk openly away from the strictures of the forge. Ordulf had come to appreciate the generous and caring side of his employer away from the pressure of work, even while he remembered with a shudder the full strength of his rage and the sting of his whip.

On the second night, the master shocked him as they ate some stringy mutton broth and some surprisingly fine bread. 'I knew it wasn't you who damaged that sword.'

Ordulf gagged and spluttered out his mouthful.

'But you whipped me for it!'

'Yes. You needed a right good whipping – not for the sword, but to jolt you out of complacency. That sword, once you re-did it, was the best work you have ever produced.'

Ordulf sat there, red-faced in outrage, while the master continued calmly spooning the broth into his bearded mouth.

'But... you *whipped* me!' Ordulf cried, raising his voice another level. 'Was that little shit Henrick ever even punished?'

'In a manner of speaking, yes,' the master intoned, wiping drips from his beard. 'He's dead.'

That brought Ordulf back down to earth with a thud. 'He's what? Did you kill him?'

'No, don't be absurd. He ran away after your whipping. I sent two apprentices to bring him back. He tried to evade them by jumping into the river to swim across. He drowned.'

The master sighed and continued, 'The boy was a waste of space. I knew from his guilty face that it was him, but everyone heard him accuse you and they all wanted to believe it. They all hate you, partly for being so good and partly for being so much bigger and stronger, but mostly for constantly rubbing their faces in it. I could have argued that the boy was lying and punished him, but they would all have cried foul and favouritism. Perhaps some of them would have lied and claimed to have also seen you damage the sword.'

He sat back, bowl finished, and munched on the last corner of his bread. 'So, I could either risk open revolt, or I could end it by punishing you. In the process, I would get to hammer some sense and humility into you. You were drifting along, not using all your skill. Jesus, the arrogance of youth.' Herman shook his head in exasperation. 'What do you even want from your life, boy? Do you ever even think about it? Do you have any ambition beyond getting by with the least effort you can manage?'

'I work hard!' protested Ordulf stridently, angrily even. 'I've always worked hard for you!'

'With your arms? Yes,' replied Herman. 'But up here' – he tapped his forehead – 'you do as little as possible. I've never met anyone with so much skill, so much arrogance about it and such little ambition to use it.'

Ordulf sat, thunderstruck. The truth of the smith's level words hurt almost more than the whipping had. It was true. He had always behaved as if he was better and, at the same time, neglected to put his full effort into his work. He had often deliberately annoyed the other smiths. He cringed at the childishness and arrogance of his past, for the first time laid so bare before him.

'Now listen here, boy, and listen good,' the master said, pointing at Ordulf with a mutton bone he had been chewing the last vestiges of meat from.

'You are the best damn journeyman smith I have ever seen. One day soon you will be better than me.'

Ordulf tried to get out a mealy-mouthed protest.

'No, don't protest, no false modesty. You have believed it yourself for a while.'

Ordulf slammed his mouth shut. It was true he believed that, although he often doubted it when confronted with the sheer arrogance of the thought.

'So here's my advice to you, my lad. Don't come back.'

The master smith gazed sadly across the table at him. Ordulf's face fell, and he gaped at Herman. 'What do you mean? You don't want me back? I promise, I will be less trouble. I will work with the others better. Master, don't abandon me, I beg you.'

'No, boy, you mistake me. I would have you back – hell, I

would make money off your work for a decade and retire a fat and happy old man.' He sighed and leaned back. 'No, I'm saying you are too big for my country forge, in skill and body. You need to make your own way in the world. You need to find your own path. Find a real master swordsmith in one of the big cities – there are some superb swordsmiths in Hamburg who would love to have a talented journeyman like you. You could make your name there and be someone. Your future at my forge wouldn't even be half as bright as that.'

Ordulf sat and stared at his bowl long enough for the broth to go cold. He had never considered a life outside Minden. He realised with a jolt that he had been content simply to continue, letting others decide his fate, never even considering trying to control it himself. He felt foolish and small.

Finally bringing his gaze up to the older smith, he nodded. 'I understand. I was happy at the forge, and that was enough.'

The master snorted in derision. 'I didn't work as hard as I did to get to where I am to then watch you bumble through a copy of my life with such lazy ease.' He reached into his vest and brought out a small purse, which he dropped onto the table with a meaty thunk of coins.

'I'll be going back with the barge the day after tomorrow and like as not I won't see you again. Here is a bonus for securing that sword deal with the count, a thank-you from me. Use it to start a new life when you get back from this damn fool crusade.'

'A bonus? I didn't do anything for that.'

'The lord hired you as much as he hired me. Now, that's a purse of one hundred silver coins, and if the last advice I ever give you is to never say no to fair money, then it will be great advice. Now take the damn purse before I change my mind.'

Ordulf's eyes bulged in his head. One hundred silver coins! That was a king's ransom for a low-born peasant. He stammered out a string of thank-yous, and Herman waved it off. 'I'm a rich man now, lad, and I don't mind sharing it with those that helped me.'

The two men sat in silence as Ordulf stared in shock at the purse of silver, sticking his fingers in and stirring the coins around as if to check they were real. Herman sat awkwardly and looked around the dark room before clicking his fingers at Ordulf to get his attention.

'Now, one last bit of advice, and then I'm going to bed. That lovely young alehouse girl over there has been giving you the eye all evening. Whatever you do or don't do about that, guard that purse most carefully. She will strip you of that silver much faster than she would strip you of anything else, you understand me?'

Ordulf went bright red and ruefully nodded his head. Pausing, he reached into his belt bag and proffered the purse to the master smith, who chuckled. 'You want me to keep this safe until tomorrow, eh? Smart lad. That's the first good decision you have made in a while. Now, I'm off to bed. I know you've made a lot of swords, but I doubt you ever had much time to use your own on someone, eh? Well, that's one area you will have to learn about without my help!' The master roared with laughter, slapping the embarrassed smith's shoulder, and then walked away, calling out to the smiling girl as he passed.

'He's all yours, lass! I need him bright and early tomorrow, though, so don't you ruin him.'

The girl sheepishly sidled over to the door to the back rooms, trying to avoid the gaze of the few remaining patrons but keeping her smile and wide eyes firmly locked on Ordulf.

With a lack of confidence he hadn't felt in a long time, Ordulf gingerly slipped out of his seat and followed the disappearing girl into the darkened depths of the building.

The morning arrived, and the master was sitting impatiently on the barge when Ordulf came hurrying down the steps with his cloak in one hand and assorted possessions in the other.

'Ah lad, good of you to join us,' the smith intoned with mock seriousness. The guards chuckled as they stepped aboard and poled away from the bank.

The flustered Ordulf, refusing eye contact and looking straight ahead, sat down on the box next to his employer and tried to behave as though everything was normal. His desperately strained face caused the smith to burst into fits of laughter until tears ran down his cheeks and froze in his beard in the freezing morning air.

'My God, lad, that good, eh? No wonder you were late.'

Ordulf pulled his cloak tighter around himself and quipped, 'Sorry, I… um. She realised we still had business to attend to this morning. I… lost track of time.'

'Oh, hear that, lads,' the smithy laughed, gesturing at the guards. 'He's had one little sword fight with a girl and he thinks he's a man who knows about business! Here,' he said, handing over the purse to the red-faced young man. 'I hope you didn't lose too much of the contents of your own purse last night.'

'A small number of copper pieces maybe,' Ordulf replied. 'But I checked my purse was still on my belt this morning before… well, you know, before she, um…'

Suddenly he froze, and his eyes went wide. He tore aside his cloak and slapped his hands to his belt. There was no purse on it. Standing and turning a circle, looking desperately at the deck, he shouted a great curse and looked back along the river to the receding shape of the dock disappearing into the mist.

'God damn her!' he shouted. The master smith roared with laughter and held his hands across his belly, laughing so hard that when Ordulf angrily shoved him, he fell to the deck and rolled around in mock submission, hands still clutching his belly as he struggled to draw breath.

Ordulf stood on the deck boiling with rage. 'There were three damn silver pieces in that purse! And a handful of coppers.' He cursed again and sat on the box trying to ignore the hysterical laughter and jibes of the other men while they continued their slow course downriver.

'You can't trust a girl whose head and hands are both busy at your waistline, boy,' the master smith said as he finally got control of his breath. 'A man doesn't have the wits to keep track of the activities of all those parts of her. Didn't anyone ever teach you that?' The smith fought back tears from his position flat on his back as the wizened navigator cackled from the tiller position behind them.

Ordulf sat back down and said nothing, but he scowled with anger and embarrassment. He prepared himself for more pearls of wisdom from his hysterical companions. Maintaining his stony stare downriver into the mist, he pulled his cloak around him and brooded.

It was going to be a long day.

CHAPTER 7

THE DRUMS OF WAR

Bremen
February 1116

B REMEN WAS A bustling market town in the spring
and summer months, but even now in the last vestiges
of winter, with ice floating on the river that bordered it
and crops yet to be planted, the town was heaving with life. As
the barge pulled up to the docks late that afternoon with the day-
long jests of his companions still burning his ears, Ordulf gazed in
wonder at the hive of activity.

Outside the walls, vast fields and temporary stables teemed
with huge warhorses and herds of smaller riding and pack animals.
The docks were crammed with boats unloading supplies. As they
finally found a spot to unload and the captain shouted into the
chaos, trying to hire some men to unship the cargo, Ordulf leaped
ashore and was promptly spun around by a pair of men carrying a
huge crate between them.

Dodging both them and their curses, he stood gazing in won-
derment at the very visible sinews of war gathering here in the

central town square. A major contingent of the Frankish crusaders was using Bremen as a staging area, while the Saxons and other Germans mostly gathered at Hamburg, three days' ride to the north-east.

Hassled dockworkers were paid a few coins to help unload the barge, and the precious boxes of swords were carried up onto the docks. The count's men were there to meet them. They opened and checked the crates, counted the swords and checked their condition. The leader of the group, a grizzled Saxon veteran called Henry, whistled in appreciation at the blades, running his fingers down their flats and testing their edges with a fingernail. The bargemen were desperate to leave; they were being harangued by the next boats trying to get alongside. The master smith received his note of payment, which he would present to the count's representative back in Minden for remittance, and shook hands with the soldier.

He walked towards Ordulf and put one meaty hand on his shoulder, clasped the other to his elbow and gave him a firm squeeze and a broad smile.

No words passed between them. Ordulf was lost for what to say. For a moment, he contemplated all manner of niceties but couldn't decide which one to use. The master smith smiled knowingly, patted him on the back and released his grip. He set off, walking past him towards the barge, and was gone into the crowd. Ordulf felt very lost and confused on the edge of that bustling street, the petty concerns of the day's taunting forgotten by the seismic change of the moment. He had nothing but the clothes on his back, his equipment and the money in his purse. He had no friends, acquaintances or family ahead of him. He was suddenly and utterly alone. The weight of it was crushing.

His new employer strode over to him. Henry had a black, wiry beard and was wearing a no-shit-taken expression. Ordulf tried to look unaffected and missed his mark.

'So you're the smith?'

'Yes, sir.'

'Don't call me sir – I'm not a fucking knight. I'm Henry or just "mister" to you. Put your bag on that wagon. I assume you can't ride a horse, so you get to be baggage for four days on that wagon, or you can jog alongside us when you fancy. Up to you. Just don't slow the group down or you will get my boot so far up your arse you will be able to taste the dust on it.'

And that was Ordulf's introduction to campaigning. He immediately missed the warmth and familiarity of the forge and his harsh but inspirational master more keenly than he thought possible. He also missed the already forgiven girl from last night. No one had ever smiled or looked at him that way. He missed her touch, and he missed the softness of her... well, the less he thought about that the better, he supposed. He thought he was unlikely to see the likes of her again on campaign.

He strode by the wagon for the short but slow trip through the town. He wanted to bounce around in that unsprung wagon as little as possible over the coming days. Henry had with him five other armed men, all mounted, and a wagon driver with a lad to help him manage his team of four horses. It was a large wagon, but even so, one hundred swords in boxes of ten took up much of the space. The rest of the wagon was full of other crates and equipment they must have collected from Bremen. There was just enough space left for him to perch on the back on a box next to his bag of possessions. As the wagon finally pulled out of the town gates through the throng, which parted to let the armed men through, he jumped up onto the wagon. He would see how fast they went before risking a jog alongside.

He needn't have worried. The roads were thick with travellers going both ways and progress was slow. Henry cursed and shouted and moved people out of the way, but most of the time walking pace was all they could manage. The four-day trip took seven, and Ordulf walked as much as he could, trying to get used to the distances and his boots. His feet were sore and blistered in camp every night. There were few inns with space to rent, and the party just camped in fields most nights, the fires of other travellers dotting the roadside.

This didn't seem to bother the soldiers. The escort were all old veterans, and they could make or break camp in less time than a pot takes to boil over a fire. They shared their rations with him, and he responded by buying items of food or skins of ale from roadside sellers when they found some, the only times the men showed him anything other than disdain.

Ordulf hardened up a lot on that journey. The cold, the foot-soreness, the utter lack of empathy from his companions. He got a first taste of what campaigning would be like. By the time they reached Hamburg, he was striding alongside the wagon all day, keeping pace and earning some guarded respect from his surly companions.

They arrived from the south-west to a slight rise overlooking the great city. Hamburg was on the far side of the Elbe, a mighty torrent, swollen by winter rain and crossed by two large, wooden bridges. The whole city was packed onto several large islands near the far bank and was totally surrounded by water. Thick stone walls surrounded it, and a citadel loomed squat over the town to the east. It was truly a magnificent sight.

As at Bremen, but on a larger scale, the fields and barns around the city were full of camps, equipment, horses and livestock as far as the eye could see. It seemed to Ordulf that all the world was in arms and arriving here. It was as great a host as he could imagine existed. But his unimpressed companions assured him it was at most a mid-sized force.

'Remember that army we marched into Mecklenburg with?' said one of the soldiers to Henry.

'Aye, now that was a proper army. Lad, you wait until we move to the border in a couple of months. Then you will see a real army.'

'In a couple of months? What? I thought we were leaving in three weeks!'

The soldiers all laughed together. 'Shit, son,' said one, 'there has never been an army born, especially one composed of this many contingents, that has done anything when it said it would or gone anywhere when it expected to. No, the fat lords won't move this circus one inch until every last opportunity for delay or self-promotion is over with.'

'I thought the count was one of the leaders? He seemed like a man of action,' said Ordulf.

'Aye, he is, one of the better ones is our lord, thank the Blessed Virgin, but he isn't in charge. His lord, the Duke of Saxony, isn't even in charge. No, Henry is in charge.'

'Oh, very funny,' sighed Ordulf, not understanding the soldiers' odd humour.

'Not me, you white-arsed muppet, Emperor Henry. Rumour has it he is coming down from his palace to lead this shit show himself. Which will make our lord count the third tier, barely even at the table when it comes to decisions. Which is a right shame – he'd sort this mess out in a hurry.'

Ordulf shook his head, bemused. He has always thought of armies as well-organised and disciplined groups. But then he knew less of armies than he knew of women.

When the carts rolled into the Lower Saxon camp area on the near side of the river, Ordulf could see that most of the contingent was not there yet. There were neat rows and clusters of tents mostly standing empty around cold, bare firepits. Horse lines set up behind the camp stood mostly empty. The cart's escort swiftly unloaded the boxes into a storage area, under the eye of a man Ordulf would come to know as the camp master, and then simply walked away. No instructions, no advice.

He stood there like a lost lamb in the middle of the quiet camp, just looking around him for any inspiration as to what he should do. He could see, from what he had witnessed of the other camps they had passed so far, that this was one of the most organised and disciplined, but he realised he had no idea what to do, and no idea who to report to. In his mind, he had imagined being greeted by the count. But now he realised that that was impossibly naïve. The count would be off somewhere conducting important business, he was sure. Ordulf simply wandered over to the side of what he didn't know was the training square and sat on a box.

'Move,' said a gruff voice a short while later.

He jumped to his feet and skittered to the side. The fat, greying man he had seen supervising the unloading of the cart opened the box and rummaged around in it. Finding what he was looking for, he noted it on a parchment with a list of something on it.

'Who are you, anyway?' he asked, without looking up.

'I'm Ordulf, the swordsmith the count requested.'

The man scanned down his parchment and then grunted, 'You aren't on the list.'

He turned to walk away.

'What?'

'You deaf? I said, you aren't on my list, so you aren't supposed to be here, so fuck off.'

'What? But I travelled for over a week to get here, on the request of the count!' Ordulf protested.

'I don't give a shit. You aren't on my list, so you aren't my problem, so fuck off out of my camp,' the man said over his shoulder as he waddled away.

Ordulf stood there, dumbstruck. There was no one else around except soldiers, no one else to ask. He shouted at the receding camp master, 'I'm not a sodding box of carrots – of course I'm not on your list!'

The distant figure stopped, his shoulders visibly clenched. The figure turned around to start waddling back. With more purpose this time.

Oh shit, thought Ordulf. *I'm here for less than a turn of the glass, and I've just pissed off the guy in charge of the food. The guy in charge of eating the food, too, it looks like!* The self-amusement of that internal joke failed to overcome the sense of dread bearing down on him.

'Now look here, boy… '

'That will be enough, Orbert. Thank you,' came a voice above and behind Ordulf.

'But sir!' the fat camp master whined, 'this lad is interloping into my camp, and he has a rotten mouth on him and all!'

Ordulf turned around to see a well-dressed knight on a horse arriving behind him.

'This lad is sorry for upsetting you, aren't you, lad?' the knight said, fixing Ordulf with a pointed stare.

'Uh, yes sir. Of course, sir.' He turned. 'I'm sorry, Mister Orbert.'

Orbert resumed his waddling, whinging overly loudly to himself.

The knight whistled to a stable boy, who came running to take his horse while he dismounted. He turned to face Ordulf. 'I'm Sir Hans Metel of Oldenburg, one of the count's vassals and, I believe, a near neighbour of your own home town. You are Ordulf the smith, from Minden, are you not?'

'Yes, sir.' Ordulf bowed his head deeply.

'Good lad. Now don't mind Orbert over there. He is a very strange man and not right in the head, but he is the best camp master in Christendom for all that. You probably noticed this is the most orderly camp in the city.'

'I did, sir.'

'Well, that is mostly Orbert's doing. His only drawback is his inflexibility over his lists. I will make sure you are put on it or you won't eat. The men are fiercely loyal to him, perhaps second only to the count. That's because Orbert is the one who feeds them and keeps them warm. Now, I know you are new to campaigning, but there is only one thing a soldier cares about more than food and warmth, and that's money. Orbert is in charge of distributing all three. So don't get on Orbert's bad side, you hear?'

Ordulf nodded rapidly.

'Excellent. Now, the army has set up a smithy down by the river.' Sir Hans pointed down the slope where Ordulf could now see smoke rising from behind some trees. 'It's been arranged for you to share that space, so grab your tools and I will show you where. Do you have everything you need?'

'Yes, sir.'

'Excellent. Come now and bring everything with you. Anything you leave unattended in a military camp is as good as gone – into Orbert's lists or someone else's bags.'

Sir Hans led him down the slope to the sprawling, makeshift smithy. A dozen forges were set up along the flat meadow bordering the river under a jumble of temporary, interconnected shingled roofs. There were grinding stones of all descriptions, workbenches, boxes and boxes of materials and shelves, and racks and all manner of other equipment. Ordulf had never seen anything quite like it. He could see dozens of smiths and workers there, forging, grinding, making leather fittings, repairing kit. It was ten times the size of his forge in Minden.

The whole thing was set up in the shadow of the main bridge into Hamburg. The bridge was long, and broad enough for two carts to pass each other and leave space for those on foot either side. The roadway was formed by wooden planks the thickness of Ordulf's leg laid on huge, square trestles formed from a single trunk each. It was an impressive and dominating structure. Sir Hans took him to the end of the sprawling forge area that sat in the bridge's shadow and gestured to a big smith who was inspecting a rack of spearheads. The man nodded and walked over.

'This is Ordulf, the smith for the Lower Saxon contingent. Please show him the facilities and let him have what he needs.'

'Right you are, m'lord,' said the smith, wiping his hands on a rag.

Sir Hans turned to Ordulf and smiled thinly. 'When we have repairs that need doing or new weapons that need making, someone will come and let you know. Until then, practice your art, help the master smith here and make yourself useful.'

'Yes, Sir Hans.' Ordulf returned the smile and made his awkward half bow. Sir Hans strode off and left him there with the burly master smith, who had folded his arms and was looking Ordulf up and down.'

'Yer a damn young 'un. You an apprentice?'

Ordulf bristled and then realised his journeyman smith badge was in his bag. 'Journeyman of the Bremen Cutlers' Guild,' he said with no attempt to conceal his pride.

'Oh, a journeyman, eh? Of Bremen? Oh, my apologies, young man,' the smith said with a pained expression and a barely suppressed giggle. 'I'm Master Gunther, of the Bavarian Swordsmiths.' Ordulf's eyebrows perked up. Even he knew the Bavarian Swordsmiths were said to be the best in all Christendom.

'Pleased to meet you, Gunther,' he said evenly.

'*Master* Gunther,' said the big smith, all trace of amusement gone.

Ordulf paused for a moment, trying to control his annoyance. 'Yes, Master Gunther. Sorry.'

'Good lad, you'll learn. Now I see you've got your own tools, but if you need more the racks are down there. I'm making a batch of spearheads – you made spearheads before?'

'Yes, but...' Ordulf started, not wanting to get roped into other work immediately.

'Great, you can help me out. Let's see if you know yer business.' The smith tossed Ordulf a set of bowed tongs that were used to grip the hollow shaft of a spearhead, and he had to drop half his kit just to catch it. Gunther walked towards the forge whistling and yanked a big dog's head hammer from a rack as he went, snapping at a boy to start working the bellows. He shoved a blank spearhead billet into the fire and then looked at Ordulf, who was still standing there dumbly, tongs in one hand and toolbelt hanging from the other.

'Fuck ye waiting for?' said the master. 'Come on.'

Ordulf sighed and dropped the toolbelt and went over to join the big smith, muttering under his breath.

A couple of weeks later, Ordulf hadn't heard from anyone beyond a few Saxon men-at-arms who turned up with weapons that needed sharpening or repairing. He went up to the camp every day for food, but there was nothing else to do there, so he spent all his time at the forge or the tent in the field behind that he shared with some of the other smiths.

He had initially resented the Bavarian smith, Gunther, but he quickly realised, much to his annoyance, that the man was much more skilled than Herman had been and undoubtedly much more skilled than he was, and he found himself learning rapidly by helping the man work. Gunther was also cheerful and didn't mind Ordulf questioning everything he did or even suggesting alternatives.

They shared ideas and different designs and techniques. Ordulf found himself learning about forging barbed arrowheads and curved, eastern-style swords, and he was shown how to turn a sheet of iron into a shield boss using a wet leather bag of sand to make the deep bowl shape. When Gunther was busy or didn't need his help, he experimented with the new techniques on his own or played with different tools and materials.

In the evenings, the smiths sat around a fire and joked and told dirty stories and drank watered ale under the stars. Ordulf's life was a pleasant cycle of forging, chatting, drinking and sleeping, and he had never known a better time.

It wasn't until early spring had really broken that the crusader army seemed to finally buzz with purpose. The rest of the contingents had started arriving, and the alehouses were filled to bursting, with more seating laid up outside, until the local militia had to try and evict the hundreds of drunken soldiers in an event that became known as the Battle of the Five Taverns by the soldiers gleefully recalling the great rout of the town militia the next day. This caused something of a crisis with the crusade leadership, who relied on the town's good favour to be able to remain.

For a whole week, all common soldiers were banned from the town by order of the duke. The soldiers were doing what bored soldiers do: getting restless. Everyone was wondering why the crusade hadn't started. But behind the scenes, the cogs of war were turning and plans were taking shape.

It was on one of the slow days, when Ordulf had finished his day at the forge and was starting to run out of ideas, that Sir Hans arrived in the smithy without warning.

'Have the forge facilities been useful and sufficient?' Sir Hans said by way of greeting.

'Oh, yes, m'lord, quite sufficient,' Ordulf said politely.

'I have damaged my sword while sparring. I need you to repair it or make me a replacement.'

Sir Hans drew the damaged weapon and laid the sword on a nearby workbench. Ordulf picked up the blade and examined it. The blade was bent about three finger widths off line at the tip, and there were several notches in the edge on one side, as well as heavy scratches on both flats. He screwed up his eyes and looked down the length of the blade to try and identify the exact point of the bend. It was about one-fourth of the way inwards from the tip.

'Well, can it be repaired?' Sir Hans sounded irritated.

'No, I do not think so, sir. The damage is too deep, and the weapon left behind would be weak.'

'Damn,' said the knight, looking bitterly disappointed. Breaking a sword was an expensive mistake, even for a wealthy knight. 'Could you make a replacement blade?'

'Yes, sir, I could. Would you like me to copy this one? Or I could make a newer style. Master Gunther is adamant that newer, more tapered swords are superior.'

'A thrusting sword, eh? A maille breaker. Hmm, yes, I have seen some of those here with other knights. An excellent idea, as I would like to try one. Do that for me, will you? The master will provide whatever you need.'

Ordulf bowed and stood back as the knight left. He then picked up the damaged blade and clamped it in a vice. He filed the peened pommel cap off and then stripped the guard and pommel from the damaged sword. The steel of the blade would be remade into something else, probably knives or spears, and he would reuse the guard and pommel on the new sword to save time. Nothing would be wasted.

The Bavarian smith helped him forge the new blade in exchange for helping in the man's hammer team. It was the first time he had forged the different, more tapered blade style, but Gunther was adamant that this design was the future.

When the work was finished, Gunther passed an appraising eye up and down the sword, turning it in his hand and examining every feature while Ordulf waited in nervous excitement.

'That's a damn fine job, young 'un,' the smith finally said, putting the sword carefully down on the table beside them. 'Would 'a been better with a new pommel – balance is a bit wrong – but you did well with the time and materials ye had.'

Ordulf smiled broadly and blushed, mumbling his thanks.

The master smith looked at him inquisitively for a moment. 'You got plans for when you finish with this crusade?'

'Uh… no. No, I don't really,' he said with a hint of embarrassment.

'You not going back to your old forge?'

'No, I don't think so.'

'Oh yeah, why not?'

'I… uh.' Ordulf tried to work out a way of saying it that didn't make him look bad. He could hardly say Master Herman didn't want him to return. 'It's a bit… small.'

The bladesmith laughed his slow, hearty laugh. 'Too small for you, eh? Yeah, I can see that in you. You got ambitions, then? Aspirations of something bigger?' The tone was slightly mocking, and Ordulf bridled.

'Yes, what of it?'

The smith raised his meaty palms in a placating gesture. 'Nothing wrong with it, lad. You got the skill – you just need to learn more.' Ordulf grunted non-committally. The smith picked up an oily rag and carefully wiped his fingermarks from the blade. 'Look, when you get back, I reckon I could use a lad like you. You got rough edges, and your design is a few years out of date, but that isn't surprising for a country smith.'

Ordulf looked away in irritation at the continued insults, his pride pricked but his vanity listening intently to the offer he could feel coming. 'When you get back, come with the Bavarian lot down to Regensburg and look for me. Ask for me at the Cutlers' Guild, tell them I invited you, show them your badge and they will bring you to me.'

Ordulf nodded brusquely, trying to hide his excitement. The Cutlers' Guild at Regensburg was reputed to be perhaps the finest in all Christendom.

'You got nothing to say to that? Fuck me, lad, half the boys here would cut an arm off to get that invite!' The big master laughed his hearty laugh again. 'The pride in you, lad, it's quite something. We'll soon forge that out of you. It's the last thing between you and being a great smith.' The master chuckled and walked away, back to his own work. Ordulf stood there, filled with excitement and annoyance in equal measure. The opportunity to work at the guild in Regensburg might give him the future he wanted, but Gunther thought he would change him? *Nonsense. There is nothing wrong with me.*

He received a summons from Sir Hans to come to the camp training square with the swords. He took the new sword and went back across the fields and up the slight hill to the Saxon camp. When he arrived, he saw that the count was in the central training square, sparring with Sir Hans with practice swords. Both men were stripped to a simple tunic and hose. Nearby, a wooden cross was dressed in what looked like a sack of straw covered with a gambeson, an old, padded jacket of the type he had seen the soldiers wearing, with a maille shirt over the top.

'Ah, young Ordulf. Good lad. Come and join us.' Sir Hans stopped and waved his hand for a drink of water. He was sweating profusely in the warm spring sun.

Ordulf jogged over, holding the wrapped sword in both hands. He proffered the hilt to the knight, and Hans brandished it in the light. He looked down its edges and then took a few swings, rolling it in his wrists and judging the weight.

'Sir Hans told me you were making him a new sword, to a new design,' said the count, coming over to join them. 'I was interested to see him judge this new creation of yours. Perhaps I will want one too?' He smiled affably at Ordulf, who nodded politely and tried to make himself invisible, the habit of a lifetime being hard to overcome.

Sir Hans was looking at the blade quizzically. 'Well, it's certainly interesting. Its balance is definitely nearer the hilt than I am used to. It is light and easy in the hand. But I don't feel any great cutting power in the swing. However, I can feel that it would be steady and easy to direct in the thrust, and that point looks wicked. I bet it will go through maille like a spearhead.'

He flipped the sword over and proffered it to the count, who took it and repeated the actions of judging and checking it. 'My God, it does feel different. And I can't get past how odd it looks. I do wonder if this will be too light and narrow. Could you parry with it?'

Sir Hans thought about this, scratching a small cut on his chin. 'I think it could be overpowered in a hard parry to a sweeping cut, or at least be forced aside. But if you are fighting in the line, with limited space either side, it would be fast in the strike and very effective against armour, I think. Let's test it on the maille. Your prerogative, my lord?'

'No, you test it first. I want to judge it by watching a more skilled hand wield it.'

Sir Hans moved over to face the straw-filled dummy.

Ordulf watched eagerly as Sir Hans settled into a fighting stance. He did not drop low and flat as the count's son had done; instead, he put his left arm forward, as if holding an imaginary shield, and drew his right hand back until it was nestled in his hip, blade flat and pointing forward, his weight on his front leg.

He snapped his arm forward from that position like an arrow leaving the bow. The tip of the sword hit the target on the right side. It burst through the maille with a thump and a rattle, went through the gambeson and buried itself halfway to the hilt with a screech of steel on steel.

Sir Hans let go his grip and gave a low whistle. He moved around to the far side and found that the sword was holding the back of the maille out from the gambeson like a steel tent. 'Well that was certainly effective.'

The count nodded in agreement. 'Ordulf, excellent work, lad. I am pleased we brought you with us.' He beckoned at the smiling young smith.

'You have proven a wise investment already. Come, sit with me while I rest. Hans has run me ragged.'

Ordulf shuffled over, perched on the end of the bench and tried to sit in a dignified way, although he really had no idea what that entailed. The count sat for a moment watching Sir Hans discuss the sword with another knight over by the maille-clad target. The count spoke to Ordulf without looking away. 'Are you pleased you came on the crusade, Ordulf?' Ordulf was tongue-tied for a moment, trying to concoct the correct response.

'Yes, m'lord. I am honoured to be coming on this great crusade,' he replied. The count rolled his eyes at the deadpan reply.

'Really? Do you even know why we are going on crusade? Speak the truth, boy.'

Ordulf nodded and thought for a moment before sheepishly replying, 'If I am honest, I don't, m'lord. Going to fight the pagans?'

'Well, I think a man going on crusade has a right to know why he is going, so I will explain it to you.'

'That's very generous of you, m'lord,' Ordulf replied, bowing his head in the sitting position, which made him look utterly ridiculous.

The count chuckled at the sight. *By the Lord, this boy is odd. Skilled, but undoubtedly simple.*

'For the last three hundred years, the Norse have been raiding good Christian lands all over northern and western Europe. You know this much, yes? Good. From then until recently, there was really no power in northern Europe that could challenge them in their homeland and thus stop the raids. The place is just too damn far away and inaccessible, the lands between full of pagan Slavic tribes.

'In the year of our Lord 970, a Christian priest was sent to the great Norse king, Harald Bluetooth. His aim was to try to achieve some degree of peace by showing the king the light of Christ. Somehow he deeply offended the Danish king, and Harald killed him and his companions and banned Christians from his lands forever. Every Norse king since then has upheld this rule, which, of course, has earned the ire of the Papacy and every emperor since.' Ordulf listened intently as the count explained. He had almost no knowledge of history, and 970 seemed impossibly long ago.

'Now, our current emperor is on a mission, supported vociferously by the Holy Father, to cleanse the entire north of the pagan religions and ways. My lord, the Duke of Saxony, and I have been conducting a campaign on and off for fifteen years to clear the northern lands up to the border with the Danes and with the sea that carries them. I hear the pope is suddenly very keenly focused on converting the northern pagans, and I am very willing to help him!' The count smiled smugly and leaned back to stare at the sky.

'I won't bore you with politics, lad, but my successful fighting in God's name has taken me from being the owner of some farmland in Saxony to being the lord of Holstein and Stormarn. It's given my lord the Duke of Saxony double the lands and wealth and a real shot at being the next emperor. It's given the emperor the favour of the pope and ended the simmering conflict between Papacy and Crown that was threatening to tear the Empire apart. Shit, it's even given you a new job.'

He leaned back with a content smile on his face and, spreading his arms, declared, 'Everyone is benefitting from this.'

'Well, everyone except the pagans,' Ordulf said, instantly regretting opening his mouth and trying to be clever.

The count was unfazed. 'I don't have any sympathy for the Norse. They have been raiding our people for three hundred years, raping, murdering, stealing. They have earned this war a hundred times over. You should have no sympathy for them either, lad. War is their life, and they live to die in battle. We merely intend to help them with that.' He stood suddenly when he noticed Sir Hans walking over towards them and added, 'So you are wrong, lad. The Norse are benefitting. We will give them the deaths they seek!' He walked away across the square, chuckling merrily as he went, leaving the young smith on the bench in the sunlight.

Ordulf was left in deep consternation by the admission of the count that his motives for going on crusade were not due to a belief in the cause. While he was not particularly fervent in his religious practices, he did not like the idea of the crusade being so mercenary in nature. He had wanted to believe that it had a purer intent. But then, Ordulf was still a very naïve young man.

The next day, news reached the forge that the crusader army was finally leaving to start the campaign six days later. The rest of the week passed in a whirlwind of confusion and activity. Ordulf was commandeered to helped pack the contingent's baggage train, and the rest of the time he tried to stay out of the way. He had bought, over the months in Hamburg, a number of extra items for the campaign. Better clothes, camping gear, a better pack, better boots and a number of other items to make his life easier. Despite the expense of living in Hamburg for all that time, he still had, secreted around his person and gear, just under one hundred silver pieces, something that would endanger his life if the wrong people found out.

In the fourth week of the fourth month of the year 1116, the crusade set out for the Norselands in Denmark. The great column was so long that the vanguard containing the Saxon contingent was making camp for the evening fifteen miles to the north-east before the last contingent of Austrians could even cross the bridge to march through the city. The first obstacle for the crusade would be the Danevirke, the line of fortifications across the narrow stretch of land between the Cold Sea and the River Treene. This formidable line of fortifications was over four hundred years old but had been constantly upgraded and repaired over the centuries. It had been built for one purpose and one purpose only: to keep southern enemies out of Denmark. In the centuries it had stood, it had never been breached. Now would come its greatest test.

CHAPTER 8

THE HUNTERS AND THE HUNTED

Uppsala
Spring 1116

THE WINTER SNOWS were receding, brown bare earth appearing from beneath four months' worth of hard-packed drifts. The roads were passable and the rivers swelling with meltwaters that could accommodate longships. So the great lords of Sweden were gathering in Uppsala for the Thing of all Swedes, and the preceding Dísablót festival. Everyone had heard the rumours of the Christian invasion aimed at Denmark. There was not supposed to be trade or contact with the Christian European nations, but there were so many smugglers that news spread fast of the army gathering and preparing to march north. King Eric Silverfist had called the great assembly of the Thing of all Swedes to decide the campaigns and raids and other matters of state for the year, and all anyone cared about was if they would march south to meet the Christian invasion in battle.

'Ragnvald!' Ragnvald turned to look over his shoulder and found a beaming Jarl Birkir bearing down on him, arms outstretched. He grinned wholeheartedly as the heavy-set man barrelled into him and nearly knocked him off his feet.

'Birkir, you great sow,' said Ragnvald as the overexcited embrace ended. 'I didn't know you were here, and you are even rounder than last we met.' Ragnvald playfully tapped Birkir in his considerable paunch as the man let out a grunt of protest and slapped his hand away.

'Hah! A rich and happy man eats well, and I eat very, very well. And I could still best you, old goat. Is the sun too bright, or is your hair even whiter than I remember? No wonder you always wear that fancy helmet.'

Some of the other men who were gathered around looked on with curiosity or wariness, lest jest lead to insult and drawn swords, but neither man lost his warm smile as Ragnvald patted the shorter man on the shoulder. 'It is good to see you here in these troubled times, my friend.'

'Well, I wasn't going to miss the chance of a scrap. I haven't had a proper scrap since that fun we had four summers ago. The odd bandit, some troublesome farmers, but nothing like a proper fight.'

'Well, I think you have come to the right place.'

'So I hear. And what have you heard? Is it true?'

Ragnvald indicated the loose group who stood around him outside the hall of the king. 'We were just discussing it. The Christians are raising a great army south of Denmark and intend to bring it north. That much we know. Exactly what they will do, or when, we cannot be sure.'

'Hmm, I have heard the same, everyone has, but nothing more. So what will the king decide? Will we go out to face them, the men of Svealand sailing as one once again?'

Ragnvald looked uneasily around the group. Birkir's question had caused eyes to drop to the ground, brows to furrow. Birkir saw the reaction and frowned, his humour instantly retreating. 'What is the problem?'

'The Danes have requested our aid, but there is disagreement over whether we should give it,' said Ragnvald wearily.

'What? What disagreement?' said Birkir incredulously.

Another of the jarls grunted and spoke up. 'The Danes have been our enemies. Not seven seasons ago I was fighting them in Scania, after they raided land. We lost a lot of people, a lot of good men. Now they call for our aid?' The man spat on the ground. 'Let them fight the Christians. Let our enemies weaken each other.'

Birkir shook his head. 'Seven seasons ago? We may have squabbled, but they are our kin. We must stand with them against the Christians whatever our differences, surely?'

'Squabbled?' The man squared up to face Birkir. 'They are no kin of mine. My son died defending his home from them. You live in the north – you never faced their raids. It's simple for you to forgive and call them kin, to sail south to help them. You have no grievance to lay aside, northerner!' The man pointed at Birkir with a snarl.

'Stay yourselves, brothers. We do not need to go down this path again,' said Ragnvald. The man huffed and turned to walk away, several others following him.

Ragnvald gave Birkir an irritated look. 'We had only just finished that particular argument, for the second time today. The split runs deep here. In any case, we must wait to see what King Eric decides, whether we go to war or not. We will find out soon enough.'

'You have no influence with the king? I thought you were close?'

'There was a time,' Ragnvald said slowly, bitterness in his voice, 'before... bah, before a great many things.'

Birkir nodded thoughtfully and chewed his lip. 'I see. I will be more careful,' he conceded. He looked up at the man who remained at Ragnvald's side. 'We have not met. I am Jarl Birkir. My hall is at Fljótsode, on the river east of Ulfhafen.'

'I have heard of you, Jarl Birkir of Fljótsode, and of your escapades with my brother-in-law,' the man said with a wry smile. 'I am Jarl Frode of Tiderhóll, south of here across the water from Sigtuna.'

'Ah, excellent. A brother of Ragnvald is a brother of mine.' Birkir extended his arm and gave Frode's an enthusiastic pump, his humour restored as quickly as the argument had drained it. 'So, brothers, what are we to do until the Thing begins?'

'Tomorrow the king is taking us on a great hunt. The next day we will feast and the festival will start.'

'Excellent. So I have not missed the feast, but I missed most of the arguing?' Birkir looked hopeful.

'No, my round friend,' said Ragnvald darkly. 'I fear the arguing has only just begun.'

Ragnvald padded as carefully as he could through the low forest, trying to keep the noise from his soft leather shoes to a minimum in the heavy pine litter, even as he felt overwhelmingly that it was all a pretence. They were far too close to Uppsala for good hunting, and it was too early in the season. The deer would not be moving through this area yet, and most of the moose had moved north with the retreating snow. Perhaps a few boar might be around, as they often stayed close to the city, scavenging scraps and farmers' crops. But the king had not wanted to travel far, and Ragnvald had found out to his great disgust that a few dozen deer had been captured and would be released and driven into the path of the hunting party.

It was a mockery of the whole process, just another thing that the king had made a mockery of as his years progressed. Ragnvald was riled by the thought. When Eric had risen to the throne he had been an adequate king, securing the crown through his network of allies, not his prowess as a leader or his fame as a warrior. His rich lands and trading hub of Visby in his native Gotland had allowed him to buy favour with the poorer inland jarls and secure his position when the previous king had died childless. His name Silverfist was both a mark of respect and an insult. A nod to his power but also a jest that he wielded it with a fist of silver, not iron.

As he had grown old on the throne, his silver had sustained him, but his vigour had fled. Sweden had fought a pitiful campaign against the Danes, a half-hearted attempt designed to appease the southern jarls who suffered at the hands of the Danish raiders and demanded their king support their revenge. A short and desultory war had followed. The Swedish forces burned some villages, sank a few ships and took some captives, but they made no serious attempt to reach the great Danish cities of Lund or Roskilde and risk a real battle. Winter had ended the war and it had never restarted, the raids dying off only when Denmark became involved in another war of conquest in the vast islands of Britain to their west, distracting them from the more dangerous and less lucrative raids against their Norse brethren.

Ragnvald had watched for over a decade as the Silverfist was content merely to maintain his position, never adding to the kingdom he bought, never risking anything to improve its future. He merely kept the seat warm and ruled over lands of increasing discontent. Now, old and childless, he was going through the motions of kingship, pretending to hunt, pretending to consider a war with the Christians. Ragnvald felt sick of it all. Powerful as he was, he had never had the power or the allies to challenge the Silverfist, and the man simply refused to die of his own accord.

As Ragnvald was brooding, he heard Frode whistle softly. He

froze on the spot and grasped the shaft of his ash spear tightly, shifting his eyes right to where Frode was eyeing the low trees and sparse undergrowth ahead of them. Then he heard it too: a soft crack, something walking. He nodded to Frode, who was carefully nocking a heavy, broad-bladed arrow onto his hunting bow. They had often hunted in a pair like this in their younger years, spear and bow a versatile combination against most prey. A pair of bows would not bring down a boar or a bear easily, making them dangerous at close range, but two spears were useless for deer.

The soft crunch happened again. It sounded too heavy for a deer, too careful for a boar. It could be an early spring bear. Frode slowly drew his bow, breath misting as he carefully exhaled. The low branches of the trees at their front slowly rustled, and then two forms stepped into the clearing. Frode pointed his bow at the ground and muttered a quiet curse. It was another two of the hunters, somehow ahead of them and crossing their path. A less experienced hunter might have feathered them as the branch moved.

'Apologies, Jarl Ragnvald,' the lead man whispered as he lowered his own spear. Both men carried them. They were a little short, more war spear than boar spear, but it was not unusual for common men to only own one, and these were no jarls. They were simply dressed in woollen caps and unadorned tunics. They must be huscarls of one of the other lords, probably a southern jarl from their accent, which marked them as Geats, not Svearmen. But this was not the time or place to have a discussion. Ragnvald angrily flicked his eyes back as he signalled the men to get behind the line of the hunt. They nodded and moved to go behind him.

Ragnvald eyed them with irritation. The leader of the two, the man who had spoken, had an irritatingly easy smile, almost mocking. Words would be had with his jarl after the hunt for his indiscipline and his disrespect.

'There is a boar ahead. We were tracking it,' the man said with a strange smile and in too loud a voice as he approached. He jerked his head in the direction they had come from, but his impertinent eyes never moved from Ragnvald.

Ragnvald hissed at the man to quiet him. They were terrible hunters, and he cursed his luck at being so close to them. The man was speaking too loudly, moving too quickly, and his spear was all wrong, held wrong. These were perhaps coastal men, far removed from the forests and the craft of walking and hunting in the deep woods.

The man stepped sideways and held out his free hand, indicating the way forward, where he said the boar had been seen. Beyond him, the other man moved to follow Frode, who Ragnvald could see was equally annoyed. Then a hair prickled on Ragnvald's neck as the man shifted even closer and to his side, his disarming smile still pasted on his face. He flicked his eyes up and down the approaching Geat, looking for anything that was out of place, and he found it.

'That's enough,' he said with a low growl, turning to face the man, who looked taken aback. Ragnvald was trying to get Frode's attention, but his friend was still occupied with his irritation at the man following him.

'What?' asked the man loudly. *Much too loudly.* Frode looked around in utter anger, and Ragnvald caught his eye, flicking his to the man following Frode, who tensed and looked back in confusion.

'Brother,' said Ragnvald, shifting his grip on his spear as he brought it across his body. 'Your peace bands are undone.' The man looked down. His scabbarded sword was at his side, but the leather thongs that should be tied around the hilt, thongs that stopped the sword being drawn quickly and traditionally proved that a man had no hidden hostile intent, were hanging loosely from the scabbard's throat.

'Oh, yes. I used the sword to cut through some bushes earlier.' The lie died in his throat, and his whole posture stiffened as the tableau of four men froze in place in nervous expectation. Frode's hand slipped unseen from his bowstring down to his seax at his waist. For the timespan of an eagle's wingbeat – slow, deliberate, unhurried – no one moved.

There is a moment, before violence occurs, when all men used to violence can sense its approach like a shadow passing over the sun. A stillness of the breath, a tensing of muscles and flexing of fingers, a flicking of eyes as they judge distances and evaluate possibilities. All four men in that clearing were men of violence.

The stillness exploded into movement as all of them made their first move. Ragnvald swept his spear sideways, scything at the man who was too close to his front, forcing him to step back and give Ragnvald room, even as his own spear lanced out at Ragnvald's face. *Fuck, he is quick.* Ragnvald whipped his head back so late that he felt the tip pass his chin, swishing through his beard. The man had a shorter, lighter spear, and Ragnvald's heavy boar spear felt leaden by comparison.

Behind the man, Ragnvald saw Frode turn and fling his bow at his opponent's face, drawing his seax with the other hand, no time to untie and draw his own sword. Seax against spear – a bad matching. Frode did the only thing he could. He slapped the spear shaft aside and charged into his distracted opponent.

Ragnvald's eyes snapped back to his own enemy. His only advantage over the man was reach. He brought the point of his heavy spear down into line, shuffling back as his opponent danced and weaved with his own spear, tapping it at Ragnvald's waving tip, trying to find purchase to force it aside. The man darted and half lunged, trying to lure Ragnvald into a counter lunge that would leave him unbalanced. Ragnvald cursed his own sword's worn leather fittings. His own peace bands were firmly tied, and he would never get the sword out in time. He had not expected a fight. No one brought violence to the sacred Disting or to a king's hunt.

A false lunge nearly caught him off guard as his opponent ducked and brought his own spear up, held across his body in both hands. He lifted Ragnvald's up, rushing forward, faster than Ragnvald could back up, and pushed his spear further up into the air where it pointed uselessly at the sky. As the man moved to rotate and thrust his spear, Ragnvald let his shaft move with the pressure and spun the butt upwards, catching his enemy a thumping blow to the ribs that knocked him to the side and spoiled his attack. But it did little damage.

The man grinned and reset, predatory eyes fixed on the jarl as he pushed him backwards again. Off to his side there was a sharp cry, and Ragnvald recognised Frode's voice cursing. The man facing him laughed. If Frode was down, Ragnvald was a dead man. His heart raced as he tried to work out a plan, but nothing came. He went with his instinct, the only thing he believed you could do when hard pressed and unsure. He attacked.

He switched from a pace back to a leap forward, almost catching the enemy off guard as his heavy spear point lanced forward. The man skipped back with a shout of animalistic delight and snapped back with his own spear, catching Ragnvald's left arm and leaving a red line in his tunic sleeve, but he barely felt it. The man was taunting him now, circling, as Ragnvald attacked again and again, breathing heavily and gasping with the effort of wielding the heavy spear, desperation born of fear for what was happening behind him to his friend driving him on.

He jabbed once more at his enemy, who slapped the blow aside and mocked him, begging him to attack again. Ragnvald knew what was happening. The man was wearing him out and would then counter one of his attacks and finish him off. It was what he would have done as a younger, fitter man. Sweat was pouring from his brow now, despite the cold, as his arms burned and his spear slowed. He felt his death coming and felt real, primal fear. Then the man cried out and stumbled, his foot turned in some hole or on some stump in the pine litter, and he went down heavily on his arse.

He was not badly hurt, and with alarm in his eyes, he tried to use his free arm to rise, even as he swept his spear in front with the other hand, trying to keep Ragnvald back with his short, poxy and insufficient little war spear. Ragnvald didn't even have to stretch or dodge as he put the point of his spear through the horrified man's stomach.

He left his spear embedded in the wailing man and turned back with deep foreboding to see what had become of Frode. He saw Frode on the ground, bleeding from an ugly gash on his forehead as he wrestled with the man who was kneeling on top of him. They were both fighting over Frode's seax, the bloodied spear discarded.

Ragnvald stumbled into a jog as his fingers worked the straps free from the hilt of Bjóðr, and then he drew it, whispering in the cold air, from its scabbard. The man furiously fighting for control of the seax looked up at the last moment. His jaw fell and his whole body slumped as he saw Ragnvald coming. Ragnvald put the meat of his palm behind the pommel of his sword and shoved it through the chest of the beleaguered man while Frode held on to his hands. The man sighed and collapsed around the blade, barely making a noise as he died.

Ragnvald wiped the sweat from his eyes and reached his hand down to Frode who took it and then pulled it in to give Ragnvald a ferocious hug. 'Ten more moments and I was dead, brother.'

He pulled away a fraction and pressed his bloodied forehead to Ragnvald's in unspoken thanks.

Ragnvald nodded. 'A rabbit saved us both.'

'What?'

'I'll explain later. Let us find out who these men are while one still breathes.' They walked back over to the man with the spear in his gut, but to his disgust, they found the man had slit his own throat rather than face his fatal wound, or their questions.

'Fuck!' shouted Ragnvald, kicking the corpse repeatedly until his toes blazed with pain.

'Calm. Leave it, brother. It's done.' Frode pulled him away from the cooling body.

'Who sent them? Who dared do this?'

'Not now. We must leave; there may be more.'

Ragnvald stopped and nodded. 'I hadn't considered that.'

He left his spear in one body and retrieved his sword from the other. They started to move west, through the trees towards the centre of the widely spread hunting line, when they found men running through the trees towards them. Their initial alarm was short-lived. It was a local jarl Ragnvald knew well, Bjornsson, and two of his men, looking too confused to be part of the plot.

'Jarl Ragnvald, we heard cries…' The man spotted the blood on Ragnvald's hand and arm. 'Ah! You have made a kill. Excellent.'

'Two, in fact,' said Ragnvald wearily.

'Two! Superb. Do you need help carrying them? Where are they? What was it, deer?'

'See for yourself.' He pointed back past the trees behind them.

Bjornsson jogged through the trees, and there was a cry of surprise. Ragnvald and Frode exchanged looks and turned back again to follow the men. He was sure they could be trusted, and five men would surely repel any further attack.

'By the gods, what happened? Ragnvald, who are these?'

Bjornsson was gaping at the boar spear standing at a drunken angle from the belly of the dead man.

'We don't know. They attacked us. We killed them.' Ragnvald shrugged as if it was nothing. He left out the desperation of the short fight.

'Henson, go. Send word to the others.' Bjornsson raised his hand to cancel the order. 'Wait. Ragnvald, is that what you wish? Should we alert the others or…' He paused uncomfortably. 'Do you need to leave? We could wait a while.' Bjornsson was giving them a chance, if they needed it, to slink away.

Ragnvald shook his head. 'It is fine. We have nothing to fear – we were the aggrieved party. Let as many see this crime as possible while the blood is still fresh. We will stand and explain it as the law demands.' He turned to Henson. 'Bring them all.'

Men started trickling into the small clearing with its bloodied bodies. One after another they expressed their shock. One after another Ragnvald carefully assessed their reaction. He had come to the conclusion that the true attacker had to be with the hunting party. He had enemies, like any powerful lord, but nearly all of them would be here. And those who were not could barely arrange such an act while absent. But he saw nothing that gave anyone away. The king was one of the last to arrive. Eric walked into the clearing with his huscarls leading the way and looked with disdain at the bodies.

'Ragnvald, explain yourself. Why was this hunt sullied with killing and violence?' he said, without looking Ragnvald in the eye.

'Lord Eric, we were attacked by these two men, who did not name themselves or their grievance with us but attacked without warning. We were wounded by them, and then we killed them in our own defence.' He gestured to his arm and Frode's head. His wording was careful. He was making sure everyone heard it and that it was known his actions were lawful and correct. He would not allow the king to make an issue of them or twist this event for his advantage.

'And there were no other witnesses to this attack?'

Ragnvald tried to keep himself as calm as the pointed question. 'There were not. But these are men of no consequence. Jarl Frode and I would not have killed such vermin if they had not given us cause.'

'Whose men are they?' the king asked, looking around the circle. No one answered. Come now, everyone on this hunt is here by my invitation. Who recognises these men? Who did they arrive with? The men in the clearing looked around in confusion as still no one spoke. 'No one knows?' The king sounded angry now. 'Did you not question them before you slaughtered them?' the king asked derisively, pointing at the man with the slit throat.

'He did that to himself to avoid our questions,' retorted Ragnvald, trying to keep himself calm.

'He slit his own throat?' asked the king incredulously. 'I find that hard to believe.' He paused as the gravity of that accusation sank in to the stunned group. 'But I see no reason not to.' Ragnvald let go a breath he had been holding in his shock and rage. The king had danced with accusing him of lying about a crime, something that would have led to more blood on the damp forest floor, his and others, most likely. Even a king has limits on what he can say. Coming so close to accusing a man of lying with no evidence… It was a very deliberate provocation.

'As lord of these lands and king of this nation, I pronounce this killing lawful,' the king said with a perfunctory, almost bored tone. 'The matter is closed. Their possessions belong to the victims of their crime. Leave the bodies for the crows.' He turned and left the clearing as a babble of voices broke out. Ragnvald stood there fuming with anger at the public questioning and humiliation. He looked up as Frode strode over with a worried expression.

'Calm yourself, brother. You look like a man about to make a mistake.'

Ragnvald's hooded eyes flicked up to where the king was walking off with some of his kinsmen, and they held nothing but malice. 'A man is his *wyrd* and his word. Our fate was not to die in this clearing, but the king questions my honesty in front of every-one?' He kicked the damp leaf litter and ground his teeth in anger, attracting glances from the few men left in the clearing.

Frode moved to put a hand on his arm. 'It was a transparent ploy. Everyone knows your reputation, and this will not affect it.'

Ragnvald growled like a wounded animal, and indeed the wound was deep. He would rather have been marked with the spear than be marked with the stain of suspected dishonesty. 'Even if men do not believe it, my enemies have been given an excuse to say it of me.'

Frode nodded sympathetically. There was nothing he could do to salve that injury. 'Did you see anything?' he said, trying to change the focus.

Ragnvald shook his head. 'Not now, not here.' Let's search them and return to the city. We will talk later,' he said stiffly, unable to meet Frode's eye in his anger.

The bodies yielded almost nothing but Ragnvald's spear, finally retrieved. They carried only their weapons and some supplies of food. Ragnvald was disappointed; there was nothing to say who they were. 'Geats, from their accents,' said Frode, as they left the scene to walk back home, Jarl Bjornsson and some other men of theirs following them, keeping close enough to watch them and far enough away to stay out of earshot.

Ragnvald nodded his agreement. 'That may mean nothing.'

'And they came for you. They knew your name.'

'One of my enemies. That does not narrow it down much.'

'And you saw nothing, no reaction that gave anyone away?'

'Nothing.'

'Me neither. I saw no one who wasn't surprised. Except for the king, and he was merely angry.'

'Angry that it had happened, or angry that it had failed?' Ragnvald said carefully.

Frode sighed. 'I had come to the same conclusion. His questions seemed intended not to reveal the truth but to check if it had been revealed. As soon as he was sure we had not questioned the men, he no longer cared at all.'

'Indeed.'

'But really, on his own hunt?'

'Who else would dare?'

'And why would he?' added Frode.

'I am a threat to him, always have been. The older and weaker he gets, the more of a threat I become.'

'But his men are not Geats.'

'The Silverfist can have any men he wants. And who knew better the plan for the hunt, how to get two men into the party, where to find us in the woods?'

'It is troubling,' agreed Frode. 'What will you do?'

'I can do nothing except be careful. We have nothing but our own words and thoughts as evidence. It is possible he merely saw an opportunity to humiliate me and had nothing to do with the planning. I will take my men with me from now on, even when among friends in my own lands. It was stupid not to bring some with us this time.'

Frode shook his head. 'We could not have known.'

'No, but we won't have that excuse next time.'

The men walked in silence for a while before Frode turned to him with a quizzical expression. 'Can you explain to me how I was saved by a rabbit?'

Ragnvald snorted with mirth. 'Yes, but promise that you won't think less of me?'

The feast that ended the assembly of the lords of Sweden in the hall of the king was mediocre. The Silverfist provided the food, so it was thinly spread, and the ale was weak, just enough to prevent outright complaint. Ragnvald infuriated the king by sending to his own home, just fifty paces away, for enough good ale for the entire assembly, who roared their appreciation for him as he presented it to the king as a gift with an effusive toast.

The insult was calculated and deadly, but the men were so happy to have good ale that they either didn't notice or didn't care and spent the rest of the feast smacking Ragnvald on the back and toasting their thanks while the king fumed. The gift had emptied Ragnvald's storeroom, but as he sat there smiling at the king, he realised it was worth every drop.

Frode chided him for his childishness, but he didn't care. It was easier to know the king was his enemy than to merely suspect it. At the end of the feast, the king stood to give his orders for the season to come. The moment everyone had come here for. Silence fell on the packed hall as the king's huscarls hammered their spear butts on the wooden floor of the dais.

The king was as sparse with his words as he was with the food. 'The lords of Denmark report that a huge army of Christians will invade their country, seeking to conquer it, impose their nailed god on their lands and throw their people into slavery.' He looked around as his words sank in to the ale-fuddled crowd, the assembled lords of Sweden.

'I have heard of those of you who wish to help them and those who wish to either ignore their plight or even profit from it.'

There were grumbles of discontent, which the king irritably waved away. 'The Danes are no friends of our people, but their enemy is our enemy, and if the Christians control Jutland, they control the Skagerrak and will cut off our raiding and our trading and suffocate us in our homes.' There were shouts of agreement and dismay, and the king waited for silence with an irritated expression. 'There is no reason why we cannot achieve the aims of both parties here tonight. I have made an agreement with the lords of Denmark. If we come to their aid, they will send us a tenth part of their income for ten years, and the town and area surrounding Åhus on the border between our lands.' The king raised his hands in triumph, a smug grin on his face. 'Men of Sweden, gather the men of the *leidang*, caulk your ships, sharpen your steel, shine your maille and sound the horns of battle to gather the Valkyr host around us. We go to war against our enemies, and our enemies will pay us to do it!'

There was a fairly unanimous roar of approval from the crowd. Even Ragnvald had to admit it was a clever manoeuvre. In one stroke, the king had united those who wished to profit from Denmark's woes, those who wanted to fight and perhaps even some of those who wished to have nothing to do with it. As he looked around the hall, he could see that the matter was settled. Only a few glum faces were visible, and men were now even standing and pumping their fists or horns of ale into the air. Ragnvald looked at Frode and shrugged with a wry smile. It was the outcome he wanted, but he felt a deep sense of foreboding. For the first time in a decade, the men of Sweden were sailing to war.

Chapter 9

The Danevirke

WHATEVER ORDULF THOUGHT being on crusade and being in an army on the march would be like, this wasn't it. The first shock was being given to the camp master as spare labour for the wagon train.

'I'm what?'

'You are on the list as one of my labourers,' said the agitated Orbert.

'But I'm a smith!' protested Ordulf. 'I'm here at the request of the count himself.'

'Oh, are you, Your Highness? Let me just check my list of the count's butt boys. Oh, wait. I don't have a list of those!' Orbert screamed up at Ordulf's face from about a foot below him. 'Now, if you are a smith, where is your forge, eh?'

Ordulf opened his mouth to explain, but he could see where this was going. 'I don't have one.'

'So what use is a smith without a forge? Hmm, no clever answer, eh? You are a big strong lad with fuck-all to do and no way to earn your keep. So someone smarter than you has put your name on my list of labourers.' Orbert smiled smugly, waving the parchment up at Ordulf's face. So, much as I would rather have a fucking box of carrots, I've got you. It's written right there. See?'

Ordulf stared blankly at the hovering parchment and its list of names.

Orbert narrowed his eyes and then rolled them and pulled the list away. 'You can't even read your own name, can you, boy? And that, you ham-fisted moron, is why you are now a labourer. And you will continue to be one until someone finds you something to hit with that stupid little hammer.' With that, Orbert waddled off, shouting at a cart team who were having trouble controlling their horses.

Ordulf's life for the next week as the army crawled north fell instantly into a dreary and exhausting routine. In the morning, he helped break down the camp and pack it into the carts. He was merely a set of useful arms attached to a set of useful legs, and everything else was superfluous. People pointed at crates and bundles and then at a cart. He picked up the indicated item with the arms and moved said crate to said cart with the legs. Then another item would be indicated, and he would repeat. After a day's marching, the soldiers would stop in a location the scouts had marked for them with coloured flags and start clearing the ground. Then the baggage train would arrive, and the soldiers would recover their tents – if they had them – cooking equipment, rations and other gear.

Ordulf would help unload and set up the required company gear from the wagon train. Horse lines, officers' tents, tables, cooking equipment, all of it stuff he had loaded that very morning, came back off and was set up in the same pattern. Soon he didn't need anyone to point at things, as it was the exact same, day in, day out. It was monotonous and exhausting. He was either marching, working or sleeping, and little of the latter. He slept in one of the empty carts under a tarpaulin. It was one of the only perks of the job working the wagons: staying high and dry if it rained and away from the ants and insects on the ground.

After a week of marching through first rich and then increasingly sparse and overgrown farmland north-east of Hamburg, they entered the lands near the old border with the pagan Wagrians to the east and the Danes to the north. These lands had been too dangerous to settle unprotected and too far from Hamburg for protection. The carefully kept fields and villages near Hamburg had given way to rough wildlands and forest with sparse, walled communities of German settlers. Husks of burnt villages on the trail marked where the conquests had torn through the lands a few years ago.

The army's progress slowed as the road became winding forest tracks, newly hacked clear by the men preparing the route. The army made barely five miles a day. The column of march was over five miles long on the narrow track, from vanguard to rearguard, so the army didn't even cover its own length on most days. Proper camps became harder and harder to set up each night until, finally, the order was given to the Saxon baggage train to pull off the road and wait. For a whole day, they and the other wagon trains of the other contingents waited as the majority of the army passed.

'What is happening?' Ordulf asked Orbert, who ignored him.

'We are in enemy lands once we pass this forest,' said Henry, one of the old soldiers who drove the wagons. 'The army closes up and we move slower; the baggage train sticks together for protection behind the main body and before the rearguard.' He leaned over and spat over the side of his cart while his tethered horses rummaged in the undergrowth around the trees. Ordulf went back to staring dumbly at the passing army.

Eventually, no more men were passing them on the road, but the light was waning, so they made a makeshift camp there in the woods. In the morning, the army moved on again on a war footing.

The Saxon company was in the vanguard, too far from the baggage train on that narrow forest path to use their camping equipment. Like most of the army, they carried only their basic cooking gear and bedrolls as they marched in the new order. They slept on the ground, and their tents lay unused in the wagons.

This was a blissful change for Ordulf. Making and breaking camp each evening and morning became a fraction of the work. The wagons were pushed off the road, they cooked and ate, the horses were seen to and then he slept under a wagon. Food for the next day was delivered to the vanguard by wagon each night, but Ordulf wasn't often needed for that.

The days marching, however, were a different story. There were fifteen thousand men and four thousand horses on the rough and narrow road ahead of Ordulf's place in the baggage train. He spent his days wading through the detritus of an entire city on the march. The smell was hard to describe, like walking through a tannery mixed with a latrine pit. His good boots were caked in the layer of filth that coated the road, the leavings of horses and mules churned to a dusty paste by thousands of boots and hundreds of wheels. The roadside was littered with broken and discarded equipment and possessions, the odd dead animal and the occasional sick or lame soldier sitting forlornly by the hedges or lying motionless in the undergrowth.

Earlier in the march, in the open fields, soldiers had simply walked out of the line of march to do their business in the fields. Here, in this rough country, there was little opportunity to leave the column and danger in doing so. As a result, many men simply relieved themselves as they marched.

Ordulf turned to Henry, who had seen too many winters to

stand in the battle line but who knew no other life and so was retained as a baggage guard. The man was whistling a cheery tune. He was actually happy. Ordulf was horrified.

'How can you stand this?' he asked. 'We are walking through a mix of piss and horse shit. There are men lying on the roadside dying. How can you whistle and ignore this? Is this normal?'

'Normal?' The man stopped whistling to himself and looked at Ordulf wide-eyed. 'Lad, this isn't normal! This is a nice walk in the country. So what if there is horse shit on the road? This is a healthy army who has fought no battles marching in fine weather.' He shook his head in disbelief. 'Lad, you wait until we are walking in high summer where that shit turns to choking dust that fills your mouth. You wait until we are walking in heavy rains where the mud and shit is knee deep or until the army has the stomach sickness and the shit isn't just from the horses. When we have marched behind fifteen thousand men with stomach fever, then you might hear me complain. Until then?' The old soldier grunted and looked back to the road. 'How many men have we passed in the ditch today? Ten? Twenty? Half of those will be picked up by the straggler carts at the back and returned to the line in a few days. The other half will be sent home with the next convoy of empty wagons or be buried by the road like decent men.

You wait until a retreat after a battle where the wounded fall like flies and you have to step through guts that have been trampled by a thousand men and crushed by wagons. Where falling out of the march means death, and injured men beg you from the roadside to help them or just kill them to save them from the scavengers, both human and beast, that will follow us.' The old man shook his head at the young smith. 'Lad, this is the best march I have been on in ten years. So shut up and be grateful in your ignorance.' The old veteran returned to his whistling. Ordulf returned to his horrified silence. But then he was a very naïve young man.

Later that day, they heard the first sounds of battle: the muffled and distant sound of shouting and clash of steel on steel and wood. Ordulf looked around nervously, hand on his belt knife. Henry sat behind him and laughed at the smith's nervousness. The train didn't stop or slow; most men didn't even look up from their march.

'Easy, lad. It's just our scouts playing with their scouts on the flank. Nothing will happen back here.'

Ordulf tried to appear relaxed and carried on. They didn't see any evidence of the fight, and the skirmishes and distant sounds of battle became closer and more frequent as the day wore on. But the army didn't slow, and nothing was visibly different other than a stronger guard being set that night. A job Ordulf was blissfully not trained to be allocated.

Then, the next day, and very abruptly, they crossed a low rise and the whole army was laid out in the fields a mile or so in front of them. Beyond them, on a low ridge, was a brown scar along the horizon, topped visibly in some places with palisades and low towers.

The Danevirke. It looked… smaller than Ordulf had expected. Ordulf was almost disappointed. But then, as they got closer, he realised those palisades were made from whole logs and the brown scar was just the lip of a deep and wide ditch before a fifteen-foot wall of grassy earth. It looked a formidable obstacle, and the wall stretched in both directions as far as he could see across the grassy plain.

The army was making camp in the low ground before the wall. Hives of activity were visible everywhere. A mounted man rode along the column wearing the count's colours, looking for the Saxon baggage train. Spotting Orbert, he slowed and turned his horse, chased white with sweat and splattered with mud. 'Camp master!' he called. 'Our site is down to the right behind the next hedge, one mile. Look for the green flags.' Orbert waved his assent, and then the man spurred his horse and was gone.

The wagons trundled into the allotted area of rough grass, and a stream of orders were given. Orbert stood in the centre of a storm of activity directing the erection of a more permanent camp, similar to the one at Hamburg. All the rest of the day and through the next morning, they worked until it was complete. Ordulf saw the count and his officers arrive and enter the command tent. The flap was closed behind them.

'Water carriers!' cried Orbert. Ordulf sighed. He had no doubt that meant him. He trudged over to the gathering line of wagon attendants and other men. He took a bundle of canteens and followed the directions to the watering site. Two miles there and two miles back. They would do this twice every day until the wagons became properly organised to distribute supplies. Those wagons were still unloading siege equipment in front of the wall, or so the man in front of him said. Ordulf put his head down and re-settled the load on his shoulders. He was filthy, tired, footsore and regretting his life choices. He'd lost a wrap of paper containing ten silver pieces that had been hidden in his boot. Whether it had fallen out on the march or been stolen, he didn't know.

He cursed inwardly for agreeing to go on this crusade, as if he had been given the choice. It wasn't likely to get any better any time soon. He was pretty sure it could still get worse. Once the day's chores ended, he collapsed into his tent to meet with a fitful sleep, the noise of the army dying down around him.

'Blacksmiths!'

Ordulf cracked his eyes open under his blanket. He rubbed his face. Did he really hear that?

'Blacksmiths! Over here.' Yes, that was a real voice. He

struggled to get up just as Orbert's huge face thrust itself through the flap of his makeshift tent.

'Oi, you, boy. Someone wants blacksmiths. Any chance you are a smith, eh, son?' he said with a sarcastic grin. 'Get up and go report to the shouting man so he goes away and stops shouting in my camp. This is my camp, and I'm the one who's supposed to be shouting here.'

Ordulf groaned and levered himself to a sitting position. 'Actually, I'm not a blacksmith, I'm a –'

'I don't care. You are going over there to report to the man shouting for blacksmiths.'

Ordulf had learned that arguing with Orbert was pointless, so he ruffled himself to full awakeness, grabbed his toolbelt and trudged after the man shouting for smiths. It turned out they wanted help putting together siege engines and making huge ladders.

It was just basic work: heating iron in braziers and hammering it to shape on flat rocks. He was making huge, crude hinges and forcing them into shape around a rounded log, then working plates to hold ladders and crosspieces together, but the simplicity of the work didn't bother him. It was better than carrying water, and the things they were building were awe-inspiring.

The siege engine being constructed in front of him was like nothing he had seen before. A great wooden frame, like a bed frame for a giant, was laid on rollers on a flattened patch of earth. On each side, near the front part, were two squared tree trunks standing vertically at least thirty feet high. Smaller timbers stretched down from the uprights, holding them strongly in place. Workers were busy at the top of the two vertical pillars installing the giant hinge system and the horizontal rounded log.

As the day progressed, a long arm, short at the front and long and tapering towards the back, at least fifty feet long in total, was mounted securely to a joint in the middle of that rounded log. As the engine was finished, a bundle of thick hemp ropes was hung from the short end at the front. The long end rested on a cradle above a wooden rack at the back of the frame.

One of the siege engineers saw Ordulf staring at it in openmouthed amazement. He was from the northern shores of old Francia, or so his accent suggested.

'You are strong. You want to help cast stones?' he asked, looking up at Ordulf while he cleaned his hands on a rag.

'Cast stones?' Ordulf asked, puzzled by the man's stuttering attempt at the German language.

'The engine, it throws stone at wall, wall fall over,' he said, emphasising the actions with his hands. 'Men, big strong men, they pull down the ropes, stone is cast.' He motioned with his hands again, pointing at the two ends of the engine and the dangling ropes.

'Yes, I can do that,' said Ordulf, with absolutely no idea what he had just let himself in for. But the engine was standing a thousand feet from the wall, well out of range of the defenders. *Must be better than carrying water.*

Happy in his ignorance, he had not learned lesson one of soldiering: never, ever volunteer for anything.

Two days later, the line of six engines was complete, the ladders were ready and the ground in front of the wall had been flattened and cleared by work parties in the dead of night, scurrying around while defenders and crusader archers exchanged arrows and curses.

The army was starting to take casualties. Ordulf saw them while he was working on the engines: bodies out in the area in front of the wall, arrows sticking out of them like tiny flagpoles, wounded men lying on pallets in the giant area behind the engines that was reserved for treating casualties and where orderlies changed bandages and priests accepted confession and gave last rites.

When he told Orbert that he had agreed to help run the siege engines, Orbert alternated wildly between laughter and anger. 'You are on my list. Who said you could go on another list, eh? What if they lose you?'

'Lose me?' Ordulf was confused. 'I will come back. I can't get lost,' he said, starting to feel the first pangs of worry. Orbert just shrugged and walked off, muttering to himself about stupid boys.

He reported to the engine site at dawn the next day. It would be the first assault. In the mustering area just out of bowshot of the walls, groups of maille-clad soldiers waited in hushed silence with shields, helmets and swords at the ready. Bales of straw, bundles of wood and long ladders lay alongside them. Piles of huge wood-and-hide shields lay in rows in front with the archers who were fussing with their fletchings and conducting last checks on their bows.

The engine had moved. It was at least six hundred feet closer to the walls than where it had been constructed, at long bowshot range. It must have been moved overnight. Orbert felt sick; he hadn't expected to be that close to the wall. He nervously asked one of the siege engineers why it was so close.

'Close? Lad, the first thing we have to do is move it a lot closer before we can use it.'

Ordulf's heart sank into his boots. He looked out over the field in front of the walls. He looked back; it was too late to change his mind now. He was being shepherded into a group with eighty other men, all lightly dressed, all looking nervous. *God, things were happening fast.*

Then, a single horn sounded from behind the line. Without much more than a combined exhale of breath, groups of men surged forward, led by their commanders. The first line was the archers. Each archer had a man to carry his huge shield, and they jogged forward into positions about a hundred and fifty feet in front of the wall, hunched down behind their shields. As soon as they were in range, a mighty cheer sounded from the ramparts above them, flags and banners were raised and a storm of arrows started to fall. One moment, the crusader archers were scanning for targets, and the next, they were sheltering from an iron-tipped hail of death.

'Amateurs,' said the man next to him, smiling for the first time.

'What?' Ordulf snapped back. His throat was dry, his limbs shaking. He had a desperate urge to piss. He could see other men around him stepping to the side to do so themselves. Should he? No, they would think him weak or afraid. He thought his heart would burst. His head was swimming.

'They are wasting their arrows on our archers' shields. Look, the main attackers are going forward, and they aren't even being shot at. The defenders are amateurs. Everyone who has defended a wall knows the archers are just a distraction – it's the foot soldiers you have to stop.' The man grinned at him. 'Let's hope they are that stupid when it's our turn.'

Either side of them, groups of armoured men ran back and forth, carrying their loads of wood and straw. Each man held his bundle in one hand, his shield in the other, above and in front.

The defenders on the wall noticed the new threat and some shifted their aim, but with shields and bundles held in front, the attacking men were well protected. Nevertheless, arrows found gaps. Men started to fall.

'Go!' shouted their siege engineer from behind the group of men Ordulf was part of. They started sprinting down the field towards the engine. Ordulf was caught off guard by the sudden command but ran along with them, his feet pounding the earth down that gentle slope. His ears were buzzing; everything seemed muffled and quiet. He looked up at the backs of the men in front. His foot hit a rock and he nearly tripped, but he steadied himself with flailing arms and kept going. His toes hurt like hell, but he ignored them. Other men were running alongside, breaths loud and ragged. The need to piss had become all consuming. *Why was it so far to the engine?* He kept going.

One hundred feet to go until they reached the engine. The world was still silent. He looked ahead. Soldiers were throwing their bundles into the ditch in front of the wall. In their vulnerable moment, they were being hammered with arrows and stones from above. Men twisted and fell. Ordulf saw one man hit with a stone on the back of his helmet so hard that the helmet flew off and his head shattered like an egg. Then his body crumpled and rolled into the ditch. His mates simply threw a pile of sticks in on top of him and ran back, shields held over their shoulders, covering their backs.

All this time, the crusader archers worked their bows. As Ordulf ran, keeping his head down and eyes up, they loosed arrows and crossbow bolts up at the defenders on the wall, ducking into cover between shots.

Ordulf was slowing, lungs burning despite the short run. The engine was right in front of them. Just as they were about to reach it, the back of the neck of the man in front of him, the one who had called the defenders amateurs, suddenly sprouted an arrowhead in a shower of dark red blood. The man gasped, stumbled and fell, twisting to the side and rolling as he hit the ground.

Wide, shocked eyes met with Ordulf's for a fleeting moment and then he was past, leaping over the gasping, prone man to avoid tangling with him and then stumbling to a halt as he reached the engine. The first twenty or so men were already pushing it across the field. As the logs appeared behind it, other men were grabbing them and hauling them around the front to lay them down.

About thirty feet of logs were already laid in front. The engine was moving as fast as a man might walk to market on a nice day, impossibly slow for the situation despite the feverish speed of the men driving it onwards. Ordulf joined the queue of men waiting for a log, looking nervously around him. Arrows still flitted past. Several were sticking into the uprights of the engine. He stumbled on something and fell. The thing squished and moaned. *Oh God.* He realised it was an injured man. He suppressed the sudden desire to vomit, pure fear flowing through him and turning his insides to water.

The man cursed and tried to throw the huge smith off him. He had an arrow through his thigh. Ordulf mumbled some profuse apologies, the absurdity of the situation snapping him back into the moment.

He stood and ran forward; the end of a log appeared in front of him, and he grabbed it with six other men. They ran around the side of the engine and towards the front. An arrow hit the log beside Ordulf at a shallow angle, scoring a gouge and skipping off in a shower of splinters. It took the man on the other side of the log in the open mouth. The man went down with a horrifying gurgle and was gone. They reached the front of the roller path and dumped their log before scrambling back. Arrows thunked into the soft dirt around them.

Ordulf suddenly lost his fight to contain his bladder. He ran to one side and pissed; it was all he could do not to let it go in his trousers. As he finished, rough hands shoved him back towards the line while he was fumbling at his belt.

'Not now, moron! Move yourself, lads. We get to the front or we die here. Move!' Ordulf was propelled back towards the line of men, trying to both put himself away and secure his trousers with hands that shook and flapped almost as wildly as his still-exposed parts while he half jogged and half stumbled back into the line. As he wrestled with what suddenly seemed an impossible task, all he could worry about was a stray arrow hitting him before he could get his trousers tied up again. The irrational thought would not leave his head. *Please don't let me die with my prick out.*

He finally managed to tie some sort of knot and was back in the log line, running back to the front with a log. Men fell. More men came.

'That's enough. Halt!' the engineer roared.

More men arrived with fascines of sticks and some of those huge shields, which they rapidly set up to the sides and in front of the engine. Ordulf and the other runners gratefully threw themselves down behind the cover and heaved air into their lungs. They lay there, shaking and gasping, while the engineers prepared the engine. Stones the size of a man's chest were brought up on a cart and laid in the rack on the back of the engine.

Ordulf couldn't see in front of the barrier, but he could hear men still shouting and screaming out there, the sound of bows twanging, arrows thudding, feet pounding.

'Right, boys, up and on the ropes!' the engineer shouted. The men flinched and peered out of cover before the whole mass erupted like a kicked beehive. There were a dozen thick hemp ropes hanging from the front of the engine and trailing between the uprights. Ordulf saw the men in front of him rush forward and take up position, about six men to a rope, the first man reaching as high as he could, taking the rope as it hung seven feet above the ground, the others spreading themselves along behind him.

'You! You are the tallest – front, go!' someone said to Ordulf as they shoved him to the front. He reached up and grabbed the rope, higher than anyone else around him could reach, and spread out from the other ropes. He and the team had practiced this only a few times yesterday and he hadn't been put on the front and there hadn't been a stone on the arm. For about five breaths, he stood there waiting. Those five breaths felt like the longest of his life. He felt sure every Norseman in Denmark must be aiming at his exposed ribs. He expected the thump of an arrow at any moment. *What would it feel like?*

'And… pull!' the engineer roared.

Seventy men pulled down on the ropes with all their strength and dug their heels into the ground to start running, pulling towards the back of the engine. The front end of the beam above them jerked down on the ropes, the back end whipping up through the air with its stone in a short sling at the end.

The men stopped at the marked position on the bed, some crashing into each other and falling in a heap. Ordulf looked up to watch the stone – it sailed towards the wall and then over the other side.

'Long!' shouted the engineer. 'Heavier stone, reset!'

They shuffled back to the front of the engine, the barricade of baskets and shields providing protection until they needed to reach up to the ropes again.

'Ready!' the engineer shouted, and they jumped up into their positions on the ropes. Faster this time. 'And… *pull!*' Ordulf heaved down and started running forward, the taut rope from the men in front almost carrying him along. The sling whipped; the stone sailed.

Crack. The stone hit the palisade wall near the top. Three logs snapped, and a six-foot section of walkway behind was cleared of men in a shower of broken limbs and flying wood.

The engineer looked on, his mouth wide with joy. He saw a couple of other stones from other machines hit the earth bank and then another hit the palisade, low down near the base. The stone crunched into the upright logs and snapped them like toothpicks. *Wood backed with earth shouldn't break like that*, Ordulf thought.

'By God, it's rotten! Ha!' The engineer threw his cap in the air with a triumphant shout. 'Come on boys, reset! We will bring this wall down in a single day!'

Along two hundred feet of wall, the hail of arrows and stones fell among the defenders. In some places, the wall was strong and resisted. In others, rotten logs burst apart and fell. Sections of walkway collapsed, forming breaches. The number of arrows coming back trickled to a halt as the defenders died, hid or ran out of arrows.

Ordulf felt his spirit soar as a horn sounded and waves of ladder teams rushed forward. They ran over the filled-in ditch and slammed their ladders into the earth in front of the undamaged wall sections and other men started scaling the breaches.

Some brave defenders did contest the top. Stones were dropped, axes were hacked at ladders and swords were thrust into screaming crusaders, but the defenders broke as quickly as their wall. After about as much time as it took to cross the bridge into Hamburg, the banner of the golden cross of Christ on its red field was raised triumphantly over the parapet. A crescendo wave of cheers rolled across the whole field. Ordulf pumped his fist in the air and shouted his lungs hoarse. Around him, men hugged and clasped hands or sat, head in hands, mourning a lost friend or just in shock.

Ordulf was exhausted. The beaming siege engineer let the lot of them go back to camp with warm words and pats on the back. 'You did a fine job, lads. Be proud,' he said as Ordulf passed, exhausted and struggling to trudge through the muddy, churned ground.

New waves of men came forward, going past him the other way to start clearing the field. The injured were helped to the rear. Ordulf looked down as he passed and saw the man who had called the Danes amateurs lying dead on his side, arrow buried in his neck, mouth open, eyes glazed and staring into the distance.

He stopped, feeling queasy, and then he suddenly doubled over and turned to vomit into a bush. All the fear, buzz, excitement and horror emptied itself out of him, and he fell to his knees, retching into the undergrowth until it hurt.

He slept like the dead when he returned to camp. The army had expected to be there for a week or more to break the wall and now would be moving in just three days after the equipment was repacked, the men rested and the injured either treated, placed in the dirt or sent home on wagons. Around the cookfire, he heard some of the soldiers who had been in the assault talking about the fight. The top had been sparsely defended, and there was no army waiting behind it as expected. No more than five hundred Danes, mostly bowmen, had been on the wall, and more than half of them had run to safety when the first crusaders had hit the top, leaving their dead and a handful of brave men to slow the enemy down. Two hundred men of the crusader army had died taking the wall, and another hundred were so badly injured they would yet die or never fight again. Even more had less serious wounds and would take time to return to the ranks.

The men seemed happy with the result. The legendary Danevirke was breached, and it had cost very little Christian blood. But that's not how Ordulf saw it. He couldn't shake the image of that man in front of him suddenly growing an arrowhead near his spine and collapsing. His wide eyes, his shocked expression. A life taken in front of him in the passing of a moment. If the unlucky man had been one step to either side, the arrow would have passed him and hit Ordulf. His whole life had hung on such a small fact, and it horrified him. Henry came and sat next to him, a pair of steaming pots in his hands. He proffered one to Ordulf, who took it gratefully.

'I hear you went forward to work the engines, lad,' he said, looking respectful for the first time since they had met.

'I did,' said Ordulf, spooning the hot and delicious broth into his mouth.

'Good on you, lad. Mostly the men on those ropes are there as punishment or because they are good for fuck-all else. It's not often a good man volunteers to do it. I only ever did it once, and that's because I was caught arse up, tits down with a priest's daughter,' he said, grinning like a loon. 'What made you go? Wanted to test your mettle, huh? Get out of being just a baggage bitch?'

Ordulf giggled manically and looked at the old soldier. 'I went because I thought I would be safe at the back pulling ropes. I wanted to see the battle from a distance. I had no fucking idea what it involved.' He burst out laughing at the old soldier's amazed expression, laughter that just wouldn't stop. He spilt some of the steaming broth on his leg, swore and carried on eating, giggling uncontrollably between mouthfuls.

The old soldier shook his head in bemusement and stood to go back and join his friends. He chuckled to himself at the ignorance of the young these days. The giggles of the mad young smith receded into the background as he went back to his fire.

CHAPTER 10

THE VALLEY OF BLOOD

FOR NEARLY A week after crossing the Danevirke, the army steadily continued north in a tight column along the road, without deploying again. The rumour mill in the baggage train was running full speed. The scouts often came back to collect replacement gear or food, and the wagoners pumped them for information. They were almost as well informed as the commanders of the army.

The picture they painted, which Ordulf gleaned about third hand, was that the army was driving the Danes before them with almost no fighting. The enemy was not strong enough to face them, and so they abandoned their settlements along the road and fled with whatever they could carry. Some bands were caught by Christian cavalry in skirmishes in the open and were obliterated, but most escaped.

The abandoned settlements part was true, at least. The baggage train passed through and by many of them, burned or just empty. For a whole week, Ordulf didn't see a Dane, dead or alive. Apparently, they were passing the town of Hedeby heading to the

Danish capital Aarhus, although Ordulf didn't know where that was or how far away. It was north along this road, and they would get there when they got there. That was what Orbert deigned to tell him anyway.

On the seventh day, horsemen were suddenly riding up and down the column shouting orders. The wagons and pack animals were unceremoniously driven off the path and into abandoned fields. The army's spare warhorses were led to the front in strings. The greater portion of the rearguard followed them shortly after at a jog.

Ordulf was nervous. Even the wagoners were twitchy. There was tension in the air everywhere. 'What do you think is happening?' he asked Henry.

'Scouts say the Norse army is formed on a ridge blocking our path ahead. There is going to be a battle, lad,' the old man said, fiddling with his belt.

'Why are you looking nervous now?'

'Because the scout said their army is fucking huge.'

Ordulf shuffled on the spot, craning his head as though he could see the three miles through low hills and woods to the army in question. Eyes wide, he turned back to Henry.

'So, what if we lose?'

'You'd best be ready to leave, and in a fucking hurry.'

'But we won't lose, right? Our army is vast.'

'Our army is medium at best, and it's from four states and speaks half a dozen different languages. It's been marching for nearly a month, the men are tired and anything can happen in battle,' Henry intoned, keeping his voice low. 'We can lose. If it goes badly, anyone can lose. But yes, I reckon it's likely we'll win,' he added, trying to look convincing.

Count Adolf sat on his horse chewing his lip and studying the enemy position as the crusader army moved into position to attack. The Norse had cut the road with a ditch and spiked it with wooden stakes all along its length. Their army was smaller than the crusaders' but significant and well positioned, with several thousand well-equipped men lining the ditch in the centre and a larger militia guarding the flanks. The hedges and woods on each side would help prevent a flanking assault.

For the third time, Adolf came to the same conclusion. They would be forced to assault straight up the ridge and earn the top through sheer force. The cavalry would not be able to charge up that slope and over the prepared positions. But he had an idea – a hope more than an idea – and he knew the man for the task.

'Hans.' The knight rode over to the count's side.

'Yes, my lord?'

'I need you to take a message to the duke. His orders are for the cavalry to wait here as reserve, but I doubt they will be needed or useful. I have a different idea, and I want you to go back to the command group and present it. I will remain here with the main body.'

Hans nodded, controlling his horse with his knees as the big stallion shifted restlessly and nipped at the count's riding mare. 'Yes, my lord.'

Hans cantered off up the hill with the message as Adolf watched the army deploy. The Saxons, including his men, were on the left flank with some small French contingents. Units of Italians, Bavarians, and other Germans made up the centre. The Bohemians made up the right flank with the Austrians and other small contingents, out of his view in the low ground on the right of the road.

Adolf waited nervously as the army settled into position, sending runners to adjust the deployment and ensure he was level with the centre as it formed up. Sir Hans had not returned, so he assumed that the request had been granted, but he cast it from his mind. His business now was with the ground and the enemy in front of his own men.

The sound of hoofbeats drew his attention behind him, a group of messengers riding hard along the back of the army, stopping to talk to the commanders of each contingent. One pulled up near him, horse's legs splayed, nostrils flaring, damp earth spraying. An unnecessary but impressive display of horsemanship. The armoured knight dipped his head to the count as he relayed his message.

'I bring the regards of the duke. He asks that you advance your men when the horn sounds thrice. It will be soon.'

The man didn't stay to receive a return message, and he pirouetted his horse and was gone in a spray of earth to the next contingent in line.

Adolf dismounted, untied his helmet from the side of his saddle and jammed it onto his maille-clad head. He fumbled with the strap until it was tied securely under his chin. He left the flap of leather and maille that would tie across his lower face open; he couldn't give clear orders with it up. He handed the reins to his page. This battle would be no place for a horse, especially his fine riding mare.

No sooner had he checked his sword and mumbled a quick prayer than a horn sounded from behind the line. Adolf nodded to the men around him and his own horn was blown, the tuneless sound melding with a dozen others along the line. The formation in front of him set off at a walk.

There was no complex plan for the attack. The first line would advance to the foot of the rise and then assault the ditch line under cover of archery. If the attack faltered or failed, a second line would assault. The third line, which Adolf himself stood with, would be the final resort.

The left wing moved steadily over the open ground and then assaulted the hill, shields up. Adolf watched as the archers stopped to loft their arrows up the gentle rise, then as the first line made their assault in tight groups, bravely cheering and waving banners as they marched up to the enemy force.

Adolf fidgeted with his sword as he watched helplessly from the third line. Initially, the assault appeared to be going well. The defenders' missiles did not slow the advancing crusaders, and they reached the ditch line. But the assaulting formations had to break up to navigate the ditch, the stakes and obstacles. The Norse unleashed a wave of spears, axes and arrows into the attackers while they were vulnerable. Even from two hundred paces back, Adolf could hear the thunder of the impacts and the screams of the wounded.

Yet enough attackers kept pushing forward, kept their feet, for the assault to push through the obstacles, ragged though it now was. Adolf could see commanders dragging and shoving men back into line, urging them forward through the stakes even as the deadly hail rained down upon them. Men fell. More men kept going forward. The attacking soldiers finally reached the defenders behind the stakes, but not as one surging mass, only in smaller groups. The Norse shield wall held firm as they started trading blows with the Christians. Adolf could see that they would not be able to break through. Too many men were dead, injured or simply not moving forward. The attack had stalled.

He looked to his left and right. The same thing was happening on his left, the first line broken up and not fully engaged. On his right, the situation was worse. The central units had broken against the steel of the best enemy warriors, who were jeering and shouting at the crusaders as they retreated down the slope in disarray, leaving their dead behind them.

Adolf shouted at his signaller; he wasn't going to wait for orders. The man blew his horn and the second wave started advancing from their position a hundred paces back from the fighting. On his left and right, the line moved to go with his contingent, the other commanders coming to the same conclusion or simply following his example.

The second line marched up the slope almost unmolested and pushed into the ditch. They filtered into the gaps the first line had left and added their numbers to the areas where the fighting was fiercest. Soon, the entire line of defenders was heavily engaged. For a while, the lines were locked together at the line of stakes, the defenders using the advantage of the slope and defences to keep the more heavily armed Christians at bay, long axes flashing in the sun as they hacked at the struggling, desperate crusaders.

Then, just as Adolf was considering leading the third line in, the enemy facing them started to be pushed back past the ditch under the intense pressure as they became tired and their lesser armour started to tell. The Saxon line pushed through the ditch and the stakes behind, and the whole right wing of the Norse army started to sag. In the centre, he could see the second wave had also faltered, although it had not yet broken. They were unable to push through the ditch, and a ditch choked with bodies was evidence of their failure. In the centre, the horns blew again, and the final line moved forward, the Duke of Saxony throwing his last men into the bloody fray in the hope of turning the tide.

Adolf stared at the carnage in the centre and worried. Then he saw that on his flank the advance was also slowing. The combined first and second waves were tiring and grinding into a bloody stalemate further up the slope. Adolf set his face into a grimace and turned to his signaller. Drawing his sword, he set off with the men of Saxony and Francia up the hill into the jaws of the slaughter.

Sir Hans cursed as his horse half stumbled on the rough track. He ducked low under a branch and felt the trailing leaves and twigs run over the back of his hauberk. The meeting with the duke had been brief. He had already been contemplating the same plan Adolf had put forward and approved it quickly. There had been a lot of high concepts and fine words bandied about, but essentially the plan was as simple as it was desperate. Send the cavalry around the flank and hope it could find and force its way through the rough countryside and the locals to reach the rear or flank of the enemy.

Successive scouting parties the previous day had either not found a suitable route, been seen off by heavy bands of Norse or simply not returned, lost or fallen to some ambush. But now, with the way along the road blocked, half a dozen parties of knights were trying to find a way around the flank by brute force. And it was not going well, not where Hans was anyway. He could neither see nor hear the other groups. The road that the Norse army had cut followed the route of the dry land, but marsh, woods and streams covered the flanks. The right was utterly impassable: a broad marsh that could, and did, swallow a horse and rider to the haunches. The left flank, thickly wooded and broken, offered at least some hope. That was the idea, anyway, not that anyone had told the land that, and it resisted them as tenaciously as any Norse warband.

But yet the Norse patrolled it heavily. They must be guarding something. *Surely a way through existed for a body of horsemen?* The path he and his men were hacking their way through was ancient, unused and overgrown. Hans alternated between scanning the dense undergrowth for ambush and battering his way through the low boughs and trailing branches, hacking at them with his sword in anger and frustration. In his attempts to hack off a stubborn branch, he didn't hear the first bowstring twang or the first arrow thud home, but he did hear his horse scream and then feel it start to bolt. In a moment of indecision, he tried to decide if he should kick clear of the saddle or try and duck the branch ahead.

He managed neither in time. The stallion bolted, and the branch swept him unceremoniously from the saddle and dumped him in a painful heap on the track. There was chaos around and above him as men reacted to the small fusillade of arrows that sliced into the column. Hans desperately shuffled about on the path, trying to avoid the turning horses and flying hooves, each a much more deadly threat than the desultory ambush. Two knights managed to force their way past the tree and spurred their horses into the undergrowth. There were whoops of joy, and the arrows stopped as fast as they had started. Hans never even saw the enemy.

A short time later, one of the men returned with a bloodied sword and leading Hans' horse. It was whinnying, eyes wide and afraid. Hans calmed the big stallion and searched for the arrow. It was high, in the top of the rump, snapped off against something during the horse's panicked flight. He examined the wound while the other man held the horse. The arrow was not deeply embedded, just stuck under the skin at a shallow angle. Hans could feed the tip under the skin, up near the top of the big leg muscle. The horse was not badly hurt, just scared and in pain. He took a firm hold of the arrow and yanked sharply on it. It came free easily, and the horse snorted in anger and twisted away from him, half tugging the man holding him from the ground. The horse stared at him as if in reproach. Hans inspected the arrowhead. It was a simple iron point, not barbed. The horse would be fine. He muttered to it, stroking its mane and trying to calm it down.

As he calmed and then remounted the horse, cursing again the lost time, a man shouted from the front of the column, which continued around the gnarled tree. Hans forced his twitchy horse to the front and found a gaggle of men standing in the open in a large clearing, all looking in the same direction, off to their right. Hans trotted over to them, maille whispering and rustling as he went.

'What is it – a way through?' The question died in his throat as he emerged from the trees and looked along the line of their stares. A gap between the trees revealed, across some boggy, impassable low ground, the battlefield. The two armies were heavily engaged. Even as Hans watched, a distant horn note blew, and he saw a second line of crusaders surge across the open ground, beginning the advance. His heart sank. They were already late.

'Stop watching – move! We must find a way through to them.' He spurred his reluctant horse on, the men turning to follow, and they pounded across the clearing and into the woods on the other side.

A short time later, after hacking their way through the forest for another few hundred paces, they came abruptly upon a large force of knights moving across them from the left. Hans stopped in confusion.

'You there! What lord do you serve?' a knight stopped to ask.

'Count Adolf of Schauenburg,' he replied.

'The Saxons? Good. Send for your men. We have found a path through the woods, and we are forming up behind their army.

Hans looked to the right in confusion. 'And the enemy don't try and stop us?'

The knight shrugged, difficult in full maille. 'They tried, but it didn't do them much good.' He kicked his horse into a trot and continued with the column.

Hans thought for a moment and turned to the man next to him. 'Follow this path back to our main body. Ignore the way we came – I'm sure this will be quicker. Bring the rest as fast as you can, or we will miss the battle.' Hans had never been in a large battle, and the thought of missing it because his men were lost in the woods churned his stomach.

The ragged column continued to pass, different units mixed in with each other, some cantering to catch up, commanders shouting for their banners to re-form. It was chaos. Hans chewed his lip impatiently, unwilling to continue without his men, hating being unable to see what was going on. The battle must be well progressed by now. *Come on, damn it. Where are you?*

Adolf staggered as a spearhead struck his shield and twisted it around with the impact. He hacked ineffectually at the shaft as it was withdrawn by the warrior behind the wall. He saw the man's wild eyes beneath his thick woollen hat, the battered and splintered round shield still up in the wall of its fellows. Bloodied but unbroken.

The attack had stalled completely. Both sides were exhausted, but no matter how far the Christians pushed the Norse up the slope, step by bloody step, the enemy just retreated over their dead and held the line. The crusaders still had a large number of men, but they were disorganised, tired and not able to mount a decisive attack against the steadfast wall. Instead, tired men fell out of the line, and those who had grabbed a precious few moments of rest replaced them. Adolf knew they were winning. The bodies they stepped over were far more often Norse than crusader, but still he had passed dozens of dead crusaders. The toll the battle of attrition was taking was horrific, and he did not believe the Norse would break before the attackers finally lost heart.

Adolf struggled to put a foot forward, breath rattling out of him in huge shudders. He was not as fit as he once was, and fighting in full armour, even for a short time, was shattering. Someone grabbed his arm and dragged him back out of the fight, and he didn't resist, grateful for the opportunity.

He bent over double, sticking his sword into the earth and leaning on it. Next to him, a dying Norse warrior mumbled and pawed weakly at his speared guts. Adolf frowned but ignored the man. There would be hundreds more before the day was done. As he turned his eyes away from the dying man, he heard a commotion from the soldiers around him, those waiting for their turn at the front. The ripple of surprise turned into a ragged chorus of cheers and waving weapons.

Behind the Norse line, just visible over the crest of the ridge, a line of banners was flying in the crisp spring sky, a riot of coloured streamers flying behind a forest of spearheads – dozens at first and then hundreds. The Norse saw this too, the line suddenly wavering, men at the back turning to look at the new threat. Large numbers of the Norsemen, those waiting behind the line for their turn to fight and those in the rear ranks of the shield wall, turned around in groups and individually, trying to form a new line facing the rear and failing in their haste and confusion.

Then, as Adolf watched, the spearheads and banners stopped spreading out along the skyline and, for a moment, just hung there like a crown of thorns on the ridge.

Then a muffled horn blew and the spearheads fell and disappeared. The Norse looked around in confusion, the Christian soldiers so transfixed by the sight that they barely took advantage of the distraction. Not many seemed to understand why the spears had disappeared as suddenly as they had appeared.

But Adolf understood. He grinned wolfishly to himself and placed his hand on the hilt of the sword, its tip still buried in the earth. He felt it start to tremble, weakly at first, and then so much he could see it and feel the thrumming in his feet. The pounding of thousands of hooves.

The skyline was broken again, this time by a line of helmeted riders, then horses underneath them, stretched out at a gallop, spearheads down and pointed at the rear of the Norse line.

'Fall back!' Adolf roared, shouting at the men in front of him, some of whom obeyed, some of whom just stood there dumb-struck. Down the line, other men understood the command and repeated it. Within moments, most of the left wing of the crusader army disengaged from the stunned Norse and pulled back down the slope, leaving their enemy in disarray and confusion.

Some in their lines understood the doom that swept down upon them, but not enough. Men desperately shoved other war-riors into line, shouted at them to get their shields up. But it was too little, too late. The tide, the rushing wave of armoured knights going downhill at a full gallop, perhaps a thousand of the finest knights in all Christendom and half the nobility of Saxony, Bavaria and a dozen other smaller states, smashed through the first ragged line of Norse like a bull going through a wicker fence. The Norse warriors on the hill above Adolf were swept away, the knights and their rampaging horses running them down, spearing them, slashing at necks and arms and splitting skulls.

In twenty heartbeats, the defiant enemy's right flank became a mob of desperately fleeing men, trapped between the waiting crusader foot soldiers and the knights who had so cruelly broken them. The horsemen swept through the fleeing crowd like deer through a field of wheat, cutting them down in swathes. Adolf and the survivors of the three attacking lines cheered themselves hoarse and cut down those fool enough, or panicked enough, to run into their ranks.

Adolf saw that the total victory on his flank had not been mir-rored in the centre. There, the prime of the enemy warriors, on a slightly higher piece of ground, had managed to form a solid wall to face the new threat. There, where the men were better armoured, more experienced, the cream of the enemy fighting men, they held firm against the torrent like a rock in a flood. The knights of the crusade and their big horses, for all their power, would not charge into a solid wall of shields and spears.

The charge, its fury spent, died out, and the horsemen and weary foot soldiers of the crusader army were scattered across the flank of the ridge, hunting down survivors or simply resting where they stood, the shock and relief of that earth-shattering charge washing over them.

But not Adolf. He looked at the surrounded and defiant body of warriors on the hill with mounting dismay. There were perhaps a thousand, well-formed and still fighting, occupying the very peak of the ridge. They would take a heavy toll on the tired army to dislodge, and his flank of that army was now scattered and victorious. Nothing saps a man's strength like believing his fighting is done.

Hans was furious. The main body of his men still had not arrived, and he stood impotently on the path as he waited. All the other contingents had now passed, yet the path remained stubbornly empty of his own men. Just as he considered leaving them and taking the few men he had to the battle, there was a crashing from the woods behind them.

'Ware! Ware rear!' a man shouted, and the band lowered their spears and turned their horses to face the unknown threat. They eyed the woods suspiciously and waited to see what emerged.

A ragged line of horsemen appeared in the trees, and the trickle became a flood. His missing men. Hans was relieved and angry in equal measure. 'Why did you come that way?' he shouted at the first man to emerge. 'I sent word to follow the main body.'

The man stopped, and his mouth opened in confusion. 'We

never received any orders. I waited for a time and decided to ride to the sound of the battle. I'm sorry, I thought it was the right thing.'

Hans cursed to himself for the man's disobedience but pushed it to the back of his mind. 'Never mind. We ride to the battle. It may already be too late. Pray it is not.' He turned his horse and cantered off down the churned-up path, his men streaming out of the wood to follow him. For several hundred paces they rode, until finally the ground opened up and he saw the ravaged remains of the Norse camp spread out to his left, a few crusader horsemen picking over the wreckage. To the right, over the ridge, the battle could clearly be heard.

Hans spurred his horse towards the crest and pulled up at the top. The scene that spread out below him on the gentle slope took his breath away. To his right, the shattered wing of the Norse army was spread out across a thousand paces of open ground, hundreds of horsemen riding about, hunting down the fleeing enemy. Beyond, he could see Christian foot soldiers in groups, reforming or simply sitting on the ground. The scene repeated itself on his left.

However, in the centre, level with where he stood, a fierce battle was still raging. A crescent of Norse warriors, in a dense shield wall, was still facing downhill, hotly engaged with crusader forces. A thinner line guarded their rear, fending off the few brave knights who dared an attack. As yet, no formed body of soldiers had reached them to surround them and envelop that defiant bubble.

All this he took in in a few moments as he tried to decide what to do. A knight rode up the hill to him, muddy and bloodied, filth flying from his horse's hooves. The man reined in and greeted him with a broad smile. 'Missed the attack?' Hans frowned in return, and the man ignored him and continued. 'It's down to the levies now. We tried charging that group in the centre, but they formed a tight wall and we couldn't press home. Damn spears!' The man laughed. 'Never mind. We played our part. Should have seen it – we crushed them! Crushed them!' The excitement dripped off him, and his eyes were wide.

Hans bridled at the man's enthusiasm. *He was one of the leading knights of the crusade, and he had missed the battle?* No, that would not do. It was not over. He eyed the remaining fight with a fierce stare. He made up his mind.

He looked behind him and raised his spear, angling it out to his left. 'Form line!' he shouted. 'Close formation!' The knight in front of him looked on in confusion. 'What are you doing? You can't mean to... Our battle is over, man. Leave the levies to finish it off.'

Hans untied his helmet from his saddle and jammed it onto his head, not even bothering to tie it on. He turned the steel faceplate to the knight and stared at him through the slits. 'Sir, I would get out of the way.'

The man looked around at the lines of fresh knights that were forming to the left and right of the man with the steel face and backed his horse up. 'You're mad.' But then he turned and galloped off to the side.

Hans turned to his left and shouted down the line. 'Close up! Knee to knee! We go in as one line. Don't let your horse turn and don't stop. We go through them. Our men are dying down there, and I won't stand here and watch it!'

The men shuffled their horses together and formed a straight line, wrestling their excitable horses into place. The horses could smell the blood, hear the battle. Ears were pinned back and nostrils flared. But they had practised this, the close formation, the line breaker. Few of them had ever done it in battle, but Hans sensed the moment, felt the weight of it on him. He was sure this was the right time. *His time.*

'Forward!' he roared. Not into a gallop, just a walk. When the line was moving together, he shouted again, and they sped up into a trot, men jostling to keep their horses in place, in line, together. They sped up again and moved down the hill at a canter, eating the distance between them and the enemy. The enemy had seen the threat now. Men were repositioning from the front line to the rear, urged on by dozens of commanders. The shield wall shuffled into place, spears out and level, axes waiting behind the line.

Hans was sweating profusely under his helmet. The line looked solid, unbreakable, the snarling faces and bloodied steel of the men in it getting bigger by the moment. There was still time to break off the attack. Still time to turn around or to the side. No one would blame him.

He took a deep breath and held it for a moment, judging the right time to call for the gallop, the charge that would take them over the last fifty paces, letting them arrive in a single armoured wave, at a full gallop, irresistible and deadly. The horse on his right missed a step and lurched into him, crushing his leg between the two beasts. He cursed and lost his breath with the scale of the pain.

But the distance was still closing, the wall looming large. There was no time. He drew in a quick breath and shouted again, dropping his spear into the crouch. All along the small line, a hundred spears dropped down in near unison, and two hundred spurs dug into the flanks of terrified horses. A single arrow could have toppled half their line, they were so closely packed, but the Norse had none left to spend. So tightly constrained, the superbly trained horses couldn't turn aside, couldn't slow down. Hans felt his horse's steps through the seat of his saddle, felt the smooth wood of the shaft of his spear tightly gripped in his hand, smelled the blood in the air that rushed under the rim of his faceplate. He leaned forward in the saddle, watching the onrushing enemy line through the slits in his helmet, judging his moment. His horse pinned its ears back, turned its head, desperate to stop, but Hans urged it on with his knees, forcing the terrified beast to continue. On towards the line of battered men that waited for them with narrow eyes and broad blades.

The horses did what horses won't do: they ran into the shield wall at a gallop. The spears, swords and horses hit the shield wall with a thunder that was heard around the field and simply *crushed* it. Hans nearly lost his seat, his spear ripped from his hand as it hammered through a shield and the owner behind it, and he clung desperately to his horse's neck, trying to get upright to draw his sword. Some horses went down. Knights were thrown and broke bones and necks. Some were catapulted into the Norse ranks ahead and died under a flurry of axe blows. But most held their seats or regained their feet once thrown, slashing at the shocked Norse warriors around them. Hans blocked an axe swing with his shield and countered with an overhand swing of his sword that cut the axeman's hand from his arm. Then he spurred forward again, his horse sluggish and swaying under him, and he stabbed down at a man who was trying to stab his leg with a broad knife, the blade bouncing ineffectually off the maille chausses he wore. He sank the tip of his sword down into the frenzied man's shoulder, who fell with a weak cry.

Hans' horse was staggering drunkenly now, and Hans cried out in alarm and tried to steady it, but then the horse's front legs buckled, and Hans was pitched over its neck, rolling and sprawling, jumping to get back to his feet. He looked back at his horse in confusion only to see a spear shaft snapped off in its chest. Blood was frothing in the brave beast's nose as its lungs filled. Hans felt a pang of pride and pity as his horse finally collapsed onto its side. He tore his eyes away and looked around him for danger, but there was none.

His horse had carried him just long enough. As he looked

around, the circle collapsed into a rout. The victorious Christian infantry surged through the gaps and swarmed over the last defenders. No quarter given. The victory was absolute. Hans staggered over and gave his dying horse's long nose a gentle caress, whispering into its ear as it gently whinnied and its struggles died down.

For Ordulf, it was a long day standing in the field. Much as he had hated being in a battle, waiting for one had almost been worse. The baggage train was mobilised to move to the battlefield to help with the wounded, clear the dead and prepare camp for the army. They set off down the road. As the battlefield came into view, Ordulf was shocked at the scale of the carnage. He had imagined neat lines of men lying on the grass. What he saw was chaos and horror. Hundreds and hundreds of bodies were strewn about the field with dozens of dead horses. Some were alone, some in clumps, some in piles two to three deep along the centre. The whole field on both sides of the road was churned to mud. A narrow ditch filled with spikes marked the main line of defence and was where the bodies started lying thickly. The carnage was thickest above and beyond the ditch, and then, beyond that, it thinned out again. Blood was actually running down the hill and collecting in the ditch in such quantity that it was overspilling the lower end and flowing down the hill in a small stream. All this Ordulf could see from the rise. What he couldn't yet do was smell the stink of death or hear the pleas of the injured or the moans of the dying. Not yet.

It was a vision of hell. He crossed himself instinctively.

Men were moving through the carnage, killing wounded horses and Norsemen alike, finding injured Christians and helping them back down the hill, stripping the dead of gear and wealth. Ordulf had been told the Norse wore their wealth into battle as a sign of their confidence and prowess and a mark of their standing. Much good it had done them. The Christians were removing arm rings and other decorative items, dragging off choice pieces of armour and rifling through clothes for coins with no one appearing to stop them.

'Nothing worse than the field after a battle, lad,' said his veteran comrade Henry sombrely, walking alongside the wagon next to him. They stopped the wagon at the base of the rise, below where the fighting had taken place. Clumps of injured men sat around or lay on the ground. The men of the baggage train spread out to help, handing out water or cloth for bandaging wounds or helping carry men back. The old veterans with the baggage train came into their own, a lifetime of binding wounds and cutting arrows from violated flesh.

Ordulf followed Henry around, helping him as the day wore into evening and the shadows lengthened and finally disappeared. They helped wounded men, Ordulf in a sickened daze doing as the veteran directed him before finally making a fire by their wagon and collapsing down beside it with a group of soldiers who had stripped their armour and were sitting with their backs against the wagon wheels, eating cold meat and talking in low voices.

'So, lads. Tell me what happened,' Henry said, once they were all settled around the fire, a scene being repeated hundreds of times across the valley, relieved survivors eating what food they could get and swapping tales of their battle.

One of the men, an archer who had seen the whole battle unfold from behind the Saxon lines, spoke up. He told them of the struggle for the ditch and the rise beyond. Of the crushing cavalry charge on the wings. 'You should have seen it, boys. It was fucking spectacular,' the archer said, gesturing with a stub of bread, eyes staring off into the distance as he remembered the view of the charge. 'Our lot had been slogging up that hill for so long I ran out of arrows. Me and the lads were just being sent up to join the fight with our knives and axes, the situation was that desperate. Then we heard the horns and saw the horsemen charging down that hill. I'll never whinge about those pampered knights again, I swear it,' the archer solemnly intoned, jabbing his finger for emphasis. 'They crushed the fight right out of the Northmen we were about to face. Saved a lot of our lives they did, and they lost of a few of their own to do it too.' He nodded grimly at the memory and shook his head in wonder. 'Never saw nothing like it. 'Honestly, lads, long as I live, I'll never forget seeing that.'

Ordulf and the other men with him listened in wonder and fascination as darkness fell and men wandered off or slept where they sat, dead tired. Ordulf thought of the true dead men cooling out on the field or still dying in the hospital lines. He could hear their soft moans and cries. Even now in the darkness, men were still dying out on that bloody ditch line, curled up undiscovered among the bodies, too weak to call out or crawl back, losing their last grip on life.

He shivered despite the fading fire and succumbed to a fitful sleep. He dreamed of the man who had died on the run to the engine at Danevirke, eyes open, mouth gaping, the shadow of death chasing him off that fearful field of shattered bodies and into his very dreams. He woke shivering and with tears flowing down his cheek, which he angrily cuffed away.

In the morning, the army wearily dragged itself into activity. There were graves to dig, equipment to repair and clean, and water canteens to fill and carry. The army had lost nearly a thousand men. Thirteen of Sir Hans' hundred mounted knights and men-at-arms were dead, thirty-six of Adolf's levy foot soldiers. Double that would never fight again, cursed to live as cripples if they survived the coming nights. Ordulf knew this because Orbert had read them the casualty list.

Ordulf was delighted to come across Leuter, the ox of a

farmhand who had beaten him on the patch, helping carry recovered weapons and equipment down from the hill. Ordulf tried not to think about their previous owners.

'Leuter! You great oaf!' He strode over and slapped the big man on the back as he dumped a pile of chain maille onto a wagon.

'Ordulf, I'll be damned. What's a smith doing here? You didn't join the levy, I'd ha' seen you.' He looked at Ordulf quizzically.

'No, I got asked to come here as a smith, to fix stuff, you know, things like that…' Ordulf trailed off, aware how trivial it sounded to a man who had just fought in a great battle.

'Oh, yeah, makes sense. Lotsa stuff to fix, eh?' Leuter said, glancing at the wagons of gear they were collecting.

Ordulf winced. He hadn't thought of that. The quantity of damaged weapons this battle would have produced was beyond reckoning. He looked into his future and saw a lifetime of sword repairs that needed to be done. He shook the thought aside and clapped his friend on the back as the man returned to work with a cheery wave. He watched them trudge back up the hill past the bodies, which they ignored as they swept the field for things more valuable than the dead.

It seemed everything was more valuable than the dead. Forty-nine men of Lower Saxony had died for their lord's ambition. The thought churned inside him, competing with his admiration for the count. He had expected to find honour and glory on this campaign. That was always what he had heard described back home in Minden, old soldiers sitting in the alehouse telling tales of magnificent victories and daring deeds of arms. He had seen only terror and death. Churned, body-strewn mud and a river of blood.

CHAPTER 11

A GATHERING OF CROWNS

Aarhus, kingdom of Denmark
Mid-May 1116

SEDEMONR CARRIED JARL Ragnvald into Aarhus on a
fresh southerly breeze and into a world of chaos. As soon as
they landed, they were aghast to find that the bulk of the
Danish army, and most of the lords of Jutland, had been utterly
defeated three days before, twenty miles to the south. Few men
had survived the battle to report back to the city of the carnage, of
the terror, of the Christian knights.

King Magnus 'Barefoot' Olafsson of Norway was in Aarhus
too. He and his small army had landed in the north of Jutland
a few days before at Aalborg and marched south. The king of
Denmark had survived the battle by the simple mechanism of not
being present and staying in the city. He was old and half-mad,
and his sons, who had died on the field, had been ruling for him
for a decade.

It was chaos. The few Danish scouts still alive and doing their
jobs reported that the Christian army was just a day away from the

city, inciting further panic into an already disintegrating population. Into this maelstrom arrived the Swedish fleet. A hundred ships, five thousand men, all that could be brought at such short notice, and yet it seemed they were too late. All three kings of the Norse nations were gathered in one place for the first time in a generation, but none had control of the situation.

King Eric called his leading jarls together, to his credit laying their dispute aside and including Ragnvald, and went to meet the Norwegians and those of the Danish lords who had survived. The party hurried to the hall of the king in Aarhus and found King Magnus was there with many of his lords and the remaining Danes of note. The Danish king was not present, and no one cared to ask or explain why.

'King Eric, I am pleased to see you here, come to join us as brothers.' Magnus embraced his fellow king warmly, and Eric returned the gesture stiffly. He put his hand to his mouth and coughed sharply, waving Magnus away when he showed concern.

'It seems our arrival is too late. Why did the Danes march to battle without us?' he asked with a scowl as the cough receded.

'Why?' shouted a Danish jarl. 'We marched because you were not here!'

'We came as soon as we could. Our lands are vast, and it takes time to gather our forces,' snapped the king.

'And yet you took so long and arrived with so few,' sneered another jarl.

'Yet here we are,' boomed Magnus.

'And you, with even fewer. How many men did you bring? Four thousand?'

'We came to our enemies' lands to help you defend yourselves, and you question us?' roared Eric, raising his voice for once.

'I know the price you extracted for your ill-timed aid,

Silverfist,' the man spat, turning his back on the king, who was roiling with anger.

'And why did you march without us? With nine thousand more men, would you not have won? Were you too proud to have help? Did you, in your pride and foolishness, hope to avoid paying my price by winning before we could help? Your foolishness has cost you your country.'

'Enough!' shouted Magnus above the rising tension in the room. 'What happened before does not matter. We are here now, and we must act with what we have. Denmark is not lost, and we have a fine army here, with fresh men, and the Christians are tired and worn from marching and battle.'

'You think we can carry on the fight?' a Danish jarl asked incredulously. 'If you had seen their army, seen them fight, you would not be talking of facing them in battle.'

'Then tell us how they fight, and tell us how to beat them,' said Magnus in a placating tone.

'Beat them? We will beat them by leaving this place. Their engines will tear these walls down like angry sows going through a reed fence. Their knights go through a shield wall like a scythe through hay.' The man shuddered. 'The best men of our nation died on the field against them. We had the hill, we had the defences and we had the numbers. They destroyed us. Utterly.'

'If the best men of your nation died there, what are you doing here wasting my time with your weasel words?' sneered King Eric, putting his hand to his mouth as he coughed again. Magnus saw with alarm that as the king's hand came back down, there were flecks of blood on it. The king deftly wiped them on his brown cloak.

The Danish man blanched and spat a string of curses. 'I hope you face them and all destroy each other. My folk and I are going north. There are strong fortresses there, and marsh and woodland no army can pass. We will survive this catastrophe, wait until it passes and the Christians leave, then rebuild our people. We will not die to salve the pride of those who were too late to join the fight.'

A Norwegian jarl made to step forward and draw his sword to avenge the insult to his king, but Magnus grabbed him and shoved him back.

'Enough. Let him go. Men such as those who run from battles are of no use to us.' He straightened his neat beard and turned to the Danes who yet remained in the hall. 'And what do you say?'

The men looked at each other uneasily. 'We are sworn to the king. We will stay here to defend his hall.'

'Good man, and we will help you.'

'Is that the best course?' asked Eric, breaking Magnus' stride.

'What?' The Norwegian king looked concerned.

'Is fighting here, tomorrow, the day after we arrived and in this defenceless town, the best use of our forces? Perhaps we should move north and gather more men, have time to plan and decide a course of action,' he said evenly.

'A course of action? We cannot run from this battle, leaving Aarhus to the enemy, just to have time to talk. Who would follow us? What men would we gather? We make our stand here. We have the walls at our front and our brothers at our side. This is where we can fight. No knight can charge a ten-foot wall of wood and earth,' Magnus replied.

'Then we would be trapped here, under siege, while the enemy cuts us off from the rest of Jutland. And what would we have gained? Saved a city and lost a country. How long would we hold? A week, a month? We have the ships for only half the men here, and half the army would die in this city.'

Magnus bristled. 'You speak as if we have already lost! What is this madness? The enemy won just one battle, and everyone speaks of nothing but giving up! Where are the men of the Northlands, the men who will face any foe? Are we afraid? Have we no honour? I said I would come here and fight with the Danes, and I will fight with them. Here is their king, and here I stand with him!'

'Then you may stand alone,' said Eric sadly. 'We march north together, or we part ways here. I did not come to be the victim of a siege. I am not a young man with vain dreams of glory, and neither are you. We must be smart, not rash.'

'This is outrageous!' shouted Magnus, the tension in the room between the old king of Norway and the even older king of Sweden rising like the tide on a full moon.

'My lord!' shouted a new voice from the back of the hall, as the owner of the voice shoved his way through the packed room. 'My lord king!' The man got to the front and came to a halt in front of Magnus. 'They are here.'

'Who are here?'

'The Christians. They are marching just beyond the hill to the south, four miles, no more.'

'What? But they were a day away! You must be mistaken. Perhaps it is just a scouting force.'

'No, a column of men, as far as the eye can see, thousands upon thousands. I saw it myself. They must have marched through the night.' The man shook his head sorrowfully.

'That settles it. Magnus, I implore you, take your men north. We can meet at Aalborg, and we can fight again or retreat from Jutland to defend the islands or our homes. Do not throw your men away here. We cannot organise a defence in the time we have. We must leave now or remain here till the death.'

Magnus shook his head in anger. 'Never! I have never run from an enemy or left a friend behind, and I will not start now. I will not be hunted up the northern road or run into the ground like a wounded sow. No, leave if you must, and consider us never to be brothers again if you do, in this life or the next.' Magnus turned away with a last bitter look and gathered his men in one corner of the hall, near enough for Ragnvald to hear him speak to them in urgent tones. 'My son, Øystein, take the bulk of the army and march north for Aalborg. Take your brother Sigurd and continue the fight. If all is lost, take the ships home.

'Nonsense. We will stay here with you.'

'You will do as I command! The future of our country lies with you, and you will make a fine king. Do not fuss over an old man. We will hold them here and win you time to get away. There is no time to argue. Go now.' The king pulled his son into a tight embrace, so raw that Ragnvald felt awkward watching despite there being another fifty men also watching the scene.

'Ragnvald, we are leaving. Now!' Ragnvald turned to see King Eric walking to the door and Frode urgently signalling to him. With one last look at the legendary Magnus Barefoot, he turned and hurried from the hall in shame. Leaving was the right thing to do, but it tore at his soul. He hurried past Frode on the way down the street to the docks and caught up with the king, who was struggling and wheezing. As he drew level, the king was racked with a cough, and bright blood speckled his hand, which he immediately tried to hide. He turned and saw Ragnvald looking at it, and he snarled. 'Walk with me, Ragnvald.'

Ragnvald looked nervously around at the men of the king's huscarls who walked with them. He suddenly felt surrounded by his enemies, and he was defenceless against them. They reached the dock very quickly, where men were piling into their ships, leaving the dock so others could be swung in to receive their own. Ragnvald signalled at Fenrir and Ulf, his shipmaster, to get their ships loaded and ready, and the men nodded and ran off.

'We have little time, and what I say is important.'

'How long have you been coughing blood, King Eric?'

'Long enough to know what is coming for me,' the king said gruffly.

'I see. What is it you wish to say?'

'We have never been like-minded, you and I, but I always respected your honour, your judgement. Now I must ask you something that you will not agree with.'

Ragnvald looked at the man suspiciously and saw with shock how sunken his eyes were, how stretched his skin. He had not been this close to the man for years. The shock suppressed his anger. 'What is it?'

'I have always been a practical man, you a man of the code, the old ways. You may not believe it, but I have always acted in the best interests of our people. I know you would too. We just disagree on the method.'

'I don't think you are famous for acting in the interests of others, King Eric.'

The king laughed and coughed again, painful racks that sounded awful. 'Fortunately, my interests and the people's are often the same. When I avoided battle with the Danes, did we not secure an end to their raids? Did the people not all return home alive and with plunder? We did not engage in some vainglorious battle, but the people returned home to their families. Has the nation not grown stronger and more secure under my rule?'

Ragnvald grunted begrudgingly. What the man said was broadly true. 'But your lack of action made you hated.'

'Are you a child? A good king is always hated. It is his task to rule the people, not befriend them.'

Ragnvald tensed his fist and took a half step away. 'Is that all you wish to say to me? I have a ship to return to.'

'Stay, Ragnvald. Curb your pride. This is why we must speak. Always your pride leads you and your honour. That is not what the people need now. They need a pragmatic leader, one who is not afraid to do the wrong thing for the right outcome, not afraid to be unpopular. Not afraid of the hard choices. They don't need another Magnus, a beloved champion of skald song. That would lead them to ruin. We have never faced a threat like this before.' Eric grabbed Ragnvald with surprisingly strong fingers and pulled their faces together, sunken eyes imploring him. 'When I die, there can be no squabble for the throne, no squabble with the Norwegian king. The people must be united. I hoped to arrange it myself... but the Norns have other plans.' The king looked desperate, destitute.

'You have always believed you would be a better king, and you will seek the throne after I am gone, will you not?'

Ragnvald felt embarrassed. 'I had not considered it.'

'Liar,' the king croaked with a suppressed laugh. 'Ragnvald, you cannot be king. No Swede can be king. We can only weather this storm as one people. I am leaving instructions to offer the crown to Øystein, to unify our countries under the son of Magnus.' He let go of Ragnvald's collar with a sad whimper.

Ragnvald was shocked into silence. 'You mean to give our nation away? To a Norwegian king?'

'I mean our nation to survive me! And I will do anything to achieve it. I knew you would oppose it. I need you to swear to me. Swear to me, Ragnvald. I know you will never break your damn word, you proud fool. This is my command as your king. Swear to me you will complete it!'

Ragnvald's stomach churned as the words sunk in. 'You would do anything?'

'Yes.'

'The forest, the men on the hunting party...' Ragnvald's voice was slow, deathly.

The king dropped his eyes. 'Yes,' he said, sadly.

Ragnvald breathed in deeply and felt his anger flowing through his body, the buzz of potential violence in his fingers.

'You tried to kill me to stop me from letting you commit treason by giving our nation away to a foreign king, and now you want me to help you do it.' He grated the words out, one by one, like ripping stitches from an old wound.

'Yes.'

'And you wonder why we never agreed,' Ragnvald said with a bitter laugh.

'Swear it!' the king implored, nothing in his eyes but desperation. 'They will all look to you when I am gone. Swear that you will think of nothing but the survival of our people. Forget me; forget my commands. Tell me that you will leave your vanity and pride, your belief in a code that cannot be broken. Tell me you will put it aside and do…' The king wheezed and stopped to catch his breath. 'Tell me you will do what is *needed*.'

Ragnvald felt the anger flow out of him as the sick old man, the man who had been his enemy for so many pointless years, begged him on the dockside. 'My lord!' shouted one of Eric's huscarls. 'We must leave.' The king waved him away with irritation.

Ragnvald gazed down into the dying eyes and felt the foolishness of his ambition, of his petty hatred of the man who had led them to this place. 'I swear it.'

A look of pure relief swept over the king, and he half crumpled. 'Thank you, Lord Ragnvald. Thank you.' The old man clasped his hand and smiled wanly before letting go and turning to leave.

'There is one thing, my king, that would help.'

'What is it?' said the king, turning with a concerned look on his face.

'You say you will do anything to help? Leave your silver to the next king. He will need it to fight the war. Your famous riches don't need to go into the ground with you.'

The king smiled sadly. 'You want my riches?' He peeled a gold arm ring from his wrist and unhooked the fabulous gold necklace from around his head, passing them to Ragnvald. 'There. You have my riches.' Ragnvald looked at the intricate gold jewellery with a perplexed frown.

'What of the rest?'

'It doesn't exist except in words, Lord Ragnvald. I am not stingy at feasts because it pleases me but because I have no more silver.'

'But… But the tithes from Visby. You bought your way on to the throne. Where is the money?'

The king laughed wryly. 'I spent every coin and bit of hack-silver I owned convincing everyone I was rich, buying the throne and then maintaining that image. Visby is not the port it once was – the trade has been dying for many years. I have been selling my old swords, digging up my father's grave goods, scraping every bit of silver I can find to stay in control.' He shrugged his shoulders. 'I'm sorry, Ragnvald. As I said, whatever it takes.' He nodded to himself and walked away, leaving the stunned Ragnvald standing there with the fabulous heavy gold chain, and the even heavier legacy of the truth of King Eric's rule.

Ragnvald stood in the stern of his ship as they left the dock, mind awash with his muddled thoughts and revelations.

'We really going home without a fight?' asked Fenrir from behind him. Ragnvald turned to find the man also gazing back at the receding shape of Aarhus. He shook his head.

'No, I don't believe we will. I need to see these Christians for myself, get a taste of how they fight. We will go north, see if we can help the Norwegians if possible. There is a man I would like to meet.'

'Who?'

'Hard to explain that, hard to explain,' said Ragnvald, who

had only ever seen Øystein once in the hall at Aarhus that day as he was sent away by his father.

Fenrir shrugged. 'If it gets us into a fight, I'm happy, and I'm sure the rest will be too.'

Ragnvald nodded and called to the shipmaster. 'Ulf, turn us north. We are leaving the fleet. We have a little work of our own to do before we return home. Signal to Leif – his ship needs to come with us too.'

'North? Right you are, my lord,' said Ulf, leaning into the steering oar and shouting at men to adjust the sail and set it square across the boat to catch the wind that still flowed steadily from the south on that fine spring day. Leif's ship didn't need signalling; it turned to follow them like a loyal hound. And how like hounds they were, Ragnvald mused to himself, and the hunt was where they were headed.

Ordulf sat with the rest of the wagon train on the hill overlooking Aarhus and watched the battle for the city unfold. The crusader army was deployed to cut the road, too late to stop a large column of armed men and refugees that spewed from the gates as the army formed up. Then they advanced, ladders carried with them, towards the old city with its short, wooden palisade. The crusader formations reached the wall and set their ladders, swarming up the walls and fighting their way inside the city. The defenders held out for perhaps an hour, then the gate was opened from the inside, and the cheering crusaders flooded through, swarming into the wooden city in a delighted rush.

Soldiers like nothing more than sacking a city after a siege, explained Henry, watching the scene with him. Every sin you ever wanted to commit, every transgression, was possible during a sack, and there was rarely a consequence. It was a reward, he opined, for the terror and danger of scaling an enemy-held wall. A man could rape and kill and steal and drink and burn and gorge himself on whatever pleasure of the flesh he wanted. Every dark corner of desire could be explored.

Ordulf felt ill as Henry gleefully described what would be happening in the city. He felt nauseous as he watched its capture and then watched it burn. The crusade had changed him. He was sick of the idea of adventure and war. He longed for the simple life of home, or even the bustle of Hamburg. He longed for his forge most of all. Watching the great city of Aarhus burn in the name of Christ, in an unstoppable orgy of killing and destruction, robbed him of the last vestiges of his dedication to the cause. As Henry and the other wagoners chuckled and bantered about their jealousy of being left out of the sack, Ordulf dreamed of returning south, of finding the Bavarian master smith, of escaping the war forever.

CHAPTER 12

THE FALL AT THE FORD

THE DAY AFTER the fall of Aarhus, Sir Hans was waiting with a few other knights outside the command tent for the meeting inside to finish, in the fields outside the smoking ruin of the Danish city. The crusade commander, the Duke of Saxony, had called a meeting of the contingent leaders to discuss the next steps of the campaign, and Hans was waiting to hear from Count Adolf what his orders would be. He was wearing his battle-marked armour. His squire was injured, and he had not had the time or energy to clean his maille himself the night before.

This bothered him. Sir Hans had particularly magnificent maille armour, something he was very fastidious about. He had visited half a dozen armourers before the crusade and talked to a number of veterans of previous campaigns to try and decide on the best equipment. His hauberk was long – it hung down nearly to the knees – and was split in the middle to allow riding with maille chausses and sturdy leather shoes. The maille chausses were only just becoming common among the richer knights, but Hans regarded them as essential for a mounted man. They were suspended from his hips by a belt and tied under the soles of his shoes, extending his protection from thigh to ankle. His hauberk had a built-in maille head covering, which right now was unlaced and hanging down behind his head. It was too hot and heavy to wear all the time. He had left the tight linen cap that usually sat under his maille on. Thus his armour covered him from the tip of his head to both wrist and ankle. Hans had experimented with gloves, but they were cumbersome and impeded his use of the sword, so he went barehanded in combat.

He was wearing a green surcoat over his armour. This was a new fashion, brought back to Europe by the knights of the First Crusade, who had started wearing them to protect their armour from the blazing heat of the sun, but it also offered extra protection and made the wearer more visible and distinguishable. The most unique part of his armour was his helm. It was a single beaten dome, common to most knights, but it had a curved faceplate riveted to it with two eye slits. A few breathing holes were the only features.

There was a sudden bustle of voices and swishing chain maille that preceded a stream of lords emerging from the entrance to the tent. Many of the great men of northern and western Europe were in that little gaggle, perhaps the most significant gathering of power anywhere in the world at that moment. Count Adolf detached himself from the group and came over to Sir Hans. He did not look happy, red in the face and eyes narrowed. Hans wondered what the cause could be so soon after the defeat of the Northmen. It didn't take long to find out.

'Walk with me,' snapped the count, without breaking his stride as he walked past Sir Hans towards the Lower Saxon camp. Sir Hans knew better than to ask questions when the count was in this mood, so he followed his lord at a fast walk, almost jogging to keep up with the taller man.

'They fucking declared victory. They ended the crusade! Can you imagine?' The count did not look round as he spoke, pounding his hand into the pommel of his sword. Sir Hans was perplexed. Victory didn't seem like such a bad thing, but he was wiser than to say so.

'The enemy is on the run – we have them by the neck – and the commander has declared the crusade successful and that it is a great victory. The damn Norsemen will have time to escape and regroup. It's fucking madness.' The count was fuming, voice rising in volume as they left earshot of the other lords.

'When you clear a barn of mice, do you stop after you find the first nest? No, you damn well search every corner until the last one is dead. We have barely scratched the surface of the Norselands. We merely taught them how we fight and how big a threat we are. Now, with their kings dead and their army in disarray and retreat, we decide to stop?' Count Adolf slammed to a stop and turned on his heel, Sir Hans almost crashing into him. The enraged count raised his hands to the sky as if beseeching God for intervention.

'It's not even midsummer. It's perfect campaigning weather, and we have a fine army assembled here ready to continue, a gathering that took a year to organise. We should be taking this army, clearing the peninsula, crossing the Cold Sea, sweeping up the islands in the middle, with all the rich farmland and sup-plies that will surely be there, and pushing into the Northlands before winter. Nothing would stand in our way. Instead, they have declared that there will be a new crusade next year to do that. A year!' he shouted, nearly losing control of himself. 'We will give them *a year* to reorganise and prepare to face us. Thousands of our men will die because of this. It's madness.'

There was a silence while the count stared at his boots and shook his head, deflated. 'Why do you think it has been done then?' asked Sir Hans hesitantly.

The count sighed and answered, 'The emperor promised a quick victory to the pope, so he told the duke to declare it as soon as possible. He didn't want to wait for a real conclusion. The duke cares above all else about remaining in the favour of the emperor so as to bolster his chances of succeeding him. It's just bloody politics. Most of the lords in there believe we will have an easy time next year, so it doesn't matter if we wait. Fools.' He spat the last word out as if it had an unpleasant taste.

'So we are to go home, then?' asked Sir Hans, hope and disappointment mixed in his voice.

'No. The one smart concession Duke Lothair managed to allow was that I be appointed governor of this province as his vassal, tasked with clearing it of remaining resistance. It is not to be regarded as part of a crusade, only as clearing rebels from what is now our province.'

'Well, that is good news. So we can continue the campaign under a different guise?'

'No, not entirely. We are not to be given any ships – we cannot cross the sea and carry this fight to the islands. We are only to clear this peninsula. Which the enemy is fleeing anyway.' The count shook his head bitterly and started walking again.

The two men walked in an uncomfortable silence until they reached the count's tent. They sat down at the low table, and an attendant brought wine, which the count snappily waved away. He tapped his fingers on the table and was deep in thought for a good while. Sir Hans waited, either for orders or dismissal, trying to ignore the heat and the sweat under his armour, which he longed to remove.

Finally, the count spoke. 'Here is what we will do. Most of the army is leaving, including all the great lords. None of them are willing to stay and fight rebels under my command; they feel it is beneath them.' Sir Hans nodded in silent understanding.

'What is left to us is our men, contingents from various German minor lords still hoping for more glory, fame or favour and some of the other troops from Duke Lothair's lands. Oh, and some Englishmen, although they are near enough Norse themselves. Their leader styles himself a Christian, but he dresses and acts like a pagan.' Hans smiled faintly to himself.

Adolf paused, still deep in thought. 'We must try and catch the enemy who left to go north before they can escape. There was a significant force, and apparently the son of the king of Norway commands them. They are headed for the Fyrkat fortress and beyond that probably the port of Aalborg. It's the only port left they can escape from in those numbers.'

'Aalborg?' asked Sir Hans. 'I've never heard of it. Where is it?'

'No idea. We will get a local guide to explain. All I know from the reports from interrogated prisoners is that it is where they will head. We must get there first, and the enemy have a day's lead on us. I will take the main contingent to follow the enemy force to Fyrkat, this Danish fortress somewhere to the north. Hopefully, we will capture it swiftly and perhaps trap much of the enemy there. I want you to take three hundred of our men, travel light and fast and follow the coast. Bypass this fortress and try to reach Aalborg first. Deny them the chance to leave, if you can, and trap them against the main force.'

Sir Hans nodded. 'Can the fortress be bypassed along the coast?'

'I hear so. The fortress is at the head of a river, and the river can be forded. Although it may not be easy, it will give you a shorter route and might let you get there first. Perhaps not. Only one way to find out.'

'Yes, my lord. It will be done if it can be. I will need a local guide and some time to gather the men. I will leave before sundown.'

'Good. Get to it.' The count stood and then raised his hand to stop Sir Hans before he turned to leave. 'One more thing. Duke Lothair will be leaving, but he wants regular reports. I, in turn, need regular reports from you. So send me word of your movements and keep me informed. Take some scouts on fast horses with you to act as messengers.'

'Of course.' Sir Hans bowed and turned to leave the tent. Removing the armour would have to wait for another day.

So, less than a day after the massacre at Aarhus and barely rested, the Saxons set off for the march north. They travelled light, leaving most of the baggage train behind. They travelled only with a contingent of cavalry, packhorses and light wagons. They would have to cross the small river east of the fortress at a ford that a conscripted local guide promised he could show them.

Sir Hans came up to Ordulf as he was watching Orbert and an assistant organise the split in the baggage. Splitting his inventory was causing Orbert an unprecedented level of stress. He would not be going with the party north and was desperately trying to explain to his near-illiterate assistant how to use the new lists he had made.

'Ordulf,' Sir Hans shouted, gesturing at him. Ordulf jogged over and bowed awkwardly. 'The army will use Aalborg as a major staging base for the later invasion of the northern lands. We want to set up workshops and forges there to supply the army. You are to come with us along the coast road to scout out the existing facilities and work out what we need to set up a proper smithy there.' Sir Hans put his hand on the smith's brawny shoulder as he spoke. 'I hear you have conducted yourself well on this crusade. I am pleased we brought you along. Hopefully now we will actually use your skills to more purpose. Then, when it is done, you can return home to Minden with us.'

'Oh, actually I think I will be going to Bavaria,' said Ordulf with an excited smile. 'I have been offered a job there with Master Gunther.'

'Ah, well, good for you, Ordulf, good for you.' Sir Hans said in a tone that made his disinterest clear, and he clapped Ordulf awkwardly on the shoulder. 'Now, be off and collect your things.'

'Thank you, Sir Hans.' Ordulf bowed his head again and left to collect his gear.

The small force moved like the wind compared to the army they had been a part of – they covered twenty miles or more a day, walking fast alongside the horses and wagons. Two months on the road had hardened Ordulf, and he found the march so much easier for it. On only the second day, the force of three hundred men reached the river ford. The water was high, waist deep for the men, up to the bellies of the horses and running fast.

The leading troop of cavalry and foot soldiers pushed across, losing one man who tripped and disappeared into the current, never to surface again, his maille carrying him to the bottom in the torrent. It was a dire warning for those who followed. The majority of the remaining cavalry and foot soldiers crossed next, manhandling and guiding the frightened packhorses. The rear-guard of about fifteen footmen and five mounted men waited until the wagons were nearly clear. A few of the civilians who did not have wagons or packhorses to manage were still waiting to cross behind the wagons, Ordulf among them.

The last wagons were being wrestled into the ford, so Ordulf and his fellows were just walking down the slope to cross behind them when one of the men-at-arms behind them shouted in alarm and pointed off to their left.

'Norsemen!'

Heads whipped round. Sir Hans stood in his stirrups to follow the outstretched hand. He looked again at the river. The last wagons were nearly halfway across, so they would be safe. His other men were already forming on the far side; they had seen the threat too. They could hold the narrow crossing against any foe. The only men in danger were his small rearguard and the civilians waiting to start crossing.

He looked back towards the bank overlooking the road, just thirty paces away.

A line of shields appeared at the top, forty men. No, more. Sixty.

The river was fifty paces away.

They wouldn't make it. The Saxon foot soldiers were backing away and forming into a tight line, nervously looking around them and eyeing the river. No one broke and ran. Despite the desperation of their situation, their discipline held. They couldn't cross with the Norse at their backs. Their forces on the other bank couldn't come back to help them. They were trapped, a stone's throw from safety.

Sir Hans took all this in. He could take his four mounted men to safety. The horses would give them an edge in the flight and could swim the river. He would escape cleanly if he left the men on foot behind now. If he left most of his men and the unarmed civilians to die.

Sir Hans pulled his faceless helm down onto his head and drew his sword as he turned his horse to face the enemy. He put his spurs into his horse and lowered his sword like a spear. 'Run!' he shouted as his war cry as he launched his horse past the men on foot.

His mounted men followed him like hounds on the hunt, unhesitating. The foot soldiers turned and ran for the river in one disciplined group, the civilians running in terror in front of them. Ordulf pounded along as fast as he could, fear in his throat stealing his breath. He dumped his pack, after stupidly holding it for a dozen paces while he worried about the fifty silver pieces hidden inside. His toolbelt bounced around his waist where he had secured it for the crossing, the hammer painfully digging into his side. But stopping to release it would slow him down. As he ran, fear gripping his heart like a cold hand, he felt a chill run through his whole body, like a cold wind was consuming him. He heard, as if far away, the shrill caw of a raven, the feeling of wings beating the air, and then the feeling was gone. His knife fell from his belt and clattered to the ground; he cursed his stupidity for not holding it but couldn't stop to retrieve it. How had it fallen out? He was sure he had tucked it in securely. He cast the thought from his mind and sped up, legs pumping and lungs working desperately.

Sir Hans and his mounted men burst through the now-charging Norsemen, cutting several down. But most of them ignored his few riders and ran to cut off the fleeing foot soldiers. The Norse won the race to the river. Some of the civilians, swift of foot and unencumbered with armour, made it, splashing into the ford just before the leading Norse arrived. Then a handful of the enemy came between the Christians and the river, turning to block their escape. The leader of the foot soldiers held his sword up and charged into them with a few of his men; the rest formed a line ten abreast and set their feet to face the rest of the oncoming Norsemen and buy time to clear the ford.

Ordulf and the three other trapped civilians splashed into the shallows and stopped, looking desperately from side to side, unarmed and helpless as they cowered in the ankle-deep water with the sound of swords and spears ringing in front of and behind them, enveloped by the desperate fight. The horse groom next to Ordulf went down with a thrown spear through the groin, another chose swimming rather than death by the sword and jumped into the deep water of the ford, desperately striking out to reach the other side and failing almost immediately. Ordulf considered following, but the current was strong, and he couldn't swim. All this passed in about ten pounding beats of his heart. Then the main force of Norsemen hit the fragile Saxon shield wall.

The Saxon soldiers were superbly equipped, they were well trained, and they were brave. But ten men can't fight thirty in the open.

Their armour, shields and sword skills kept them alive only long enough to make a fight of it. Then the shield wall broke apart and each man was fighting alone or in a pair against two or three opponents. Some of the snarling Norsemen claimed a victim and fought their chosen man one-on-one while their fellows cheered them on. A couple of them even died at the edge of a Saxon sword. But most of the Saxons were taken down, weapons finding the gaps in their heavy maille or spears simply punching through it.

The Saxon leader put his opponent down into the river with a thrust to the leg, and the way to escape was briefly clear, at least for him. He shunned the chance to run. Instead he turned and plunged back into the melee, trying to get to the handful of his men still on their feet, shouting at them to retreat.

Behind them, unseen by Ordulf, two of Hans' horsemen had been dragged down or speared off their horses. Hans and his two remaining companions turned and spurred their horses down to the ford, crashing into the fighting there in a shower of spray, desperately trying to free the few remaining men.

Hans' sword rose and fell, trailing red water in arcs that glittered in the sun. His horse twirled, kicking and thrashing and clearing his rear. The last of the Saxon foot soldiers were being felled despite his desperate efforts. A dozen Norsemen were between Hans and Ordulf now. Ordulf reached for his knife and, remembering it was gone, pulled his hammer from his belt. His heart felt as if it was bursting in his chest. The Saxon leader splashed down lifeless into the river in front of him like a felled tree, a spear in his face. Ordulf gagged at the horror of the wound and the depth of the fear he felt, fear that rooted him to the spot.

Sir Hans desperately fended off a spear thrust and turned his helmeted head until it was facing directly at Ordulf. For a fleeting moment in the chaos, Ordulf's wide eyes locked with that helmet's dark slits across twenty feet of water and a dozen enemies. The path in front of Hans' horse was almost clear, and his last mounted companion was shouting at him from his other side, urging him to run for the ford. The third horse was dying and thrashing in the shallows, drowning its wounded rider, but its flailing hooves were momentarily holding the Norsemen at bay.

Those emotionless dark slits held Ordulf's gaze for the time it took the water drops from Hans' sword to fall and splash into the bloodstained waters. It seemed an eternity.

They both knew that Ordulf was about to die. They both knew Hans could survive if he ran right that moment and no later. Ordulf's whole being soundlessly implored the knight to turn, to cut his way to him. He imagined grabbing hold of the saddle and being carried to safety. His eyes pleaded with the steel face, begged for salvation. He started to gesture, to wave for the man's attention.

Sir Hans held Ordulf's gaze for another beat, then he turned his head and spurred his horse. He and his companion burst past the last Norseman between them and freedom and surged into the river. Ordulf wailed quietly as the knight fled in a shower of cold spray. He had believed for a moment that salvation was his, imagined that his deliverance had lain in that steel gaze, and that brief hope flying from grasp crushed him. The green knight, the hero of Blood River Ridge, had left him to die. Watching the man abandon him and turn to flee ripped a chunk of his heart out of his chest.

Ordulf's attention snapped back to the horrifying full speed of reality after that drawn-out moment of shattered hope. A Norse warrior was charging towards him ten paces away, sword raised, shield forward, death in his eyes.

Ordulf shuddered and raised his hammer and, trying to muster strength he did not feel, set his feet into the firm sand beneath him. He could see the water pouring from the oncoming man's clothes, see the blood running down from his raised sword. Ordulf stepped forward and, with a great shout, swung his hammer in an arc over his head towards the oncoming man, seeing the sword lance out towards him, fast as an eel, mocking his leaden hammer strike. His death had arrived.

There was a blur of motion in his peripheral vision. Another warrior had shoulder-charged the oncoming one out of Ordulf's path from the side. Both men tumbled down into the shallows in a bundle of furs and clattering gear. Ordulf's hammer did nothing but glance off the rim of a shield. The sword missed Ordulf entirely. Someone standing on the bank was shouting at the men, gesturing at Ordulf.

The first man got up, angrily shaking off the second, who ignored him and advanced on Ordulf, discarding his sword, shield up and in front. Then he lunged with his empty sword hand for Ordulf's left arm as he covered his move with his shield. Ordulf brought his hammer down with all his strength onto the upraised shield. It hit the boss with a clang that shook his arm up to the shoulder. Ordulf braced his feet and levered the warrior's right arm with his left.

His enemy was a big man, and strong, but Ordulf was stronger. He raised and brought his hammer down again with all his strength, strength built over seven years of swinging hammers such as this. The hammer hit with a loud crack this time and the central board of the shield splintered near the boss. The combination of the hammer blows, Ordulf's twisting away of his arm and the pressure from his planted feet overwhelmed the warrior. His eyes turned from predatory to surprised as he was rolled over to his right and fell into the water.

Ordulf raised his hammer and roared as he brought it down again. The Norseman released Ordulf's left arm and held his shield over his face and upper body with both hands. The hammer hit the boss and nearly turned it inside out; the cracked wood around it split further. He swung the hammer again, and the warrior desperately pushed his shield into the blow. It split in half, leaving him with half a shield dangling from the ruined boss, held together by the rim, and a shocked expression on his now-exposed face.

Ordulf roared down at the prostrate and defenceless Norseman and raised his arm again. Before he could swing it, strong hands grabbed him from behind and a thick, maille-clad arm wrapped around his throat. Ordulf bellowed like a bull as he twisted and rolled his shoulder, years of instinct built from fighting on the patch taking over. The surprised Norseman who had been holding Ordulf's arm appeared over his shoulder and landed flat on his back next to the shield carrier, but two more men replaced him, with half a dozen arms gripping Ordulf's upper body and finally overpowering him.

Ordulf was forced to his knees, and his hammer was stripped from his grasp. His roar turned to a mournful cry as these heathens toyed with him. His arms were pinned and then tied behind his back. He was left there kneeling at the edge of the river, head down, the fight gone from his body.

Ordulf took it all in. The bloody water swirling at his knees, the body of a Saxon soldier lying face down in front of him in the gentle waves. He raised his eyes across the river.

On the far bank, the rest of the Saxons were watching in silent rows, some sitting on their haunches, helpless, having watched their friends die. In the shallows, a single figure sat on his horse, sword still in hand, dark slits watching, shoulders slumped in defeat.

He couldn't meet that dark-eyed stare. He waited for death, terrified and angry, mind racing. He thought of Minden... his home...

An unseen blow hit the back of his head and his world snapped out.

Across the ford, Sir Hans slowly turned his horse to leave. He had forced himself to watch Ordulf kneeling in the sand. He had looked on as the blow fell and the smith died, falling to the sand among the bodies of his lost men. The men he had failed so bitterly. He could watch no more as the Norse started to strip them of their gear, careless, their laughter and jests audible from across the seething water. He left the faceless helm on as he passed back through his sullen men. It hid his face, and it hid his shame.

CHAPTER 13

SLAVERY AND SOLITUDE

'BY THE GODS, that big bastard was strong!' exclaimed Ulf. He was rubbing his back, which was sore from being thrown over the Christian's shoulder.

'Like a god,' mused Leif. He was sitting on the bank, nursing his left arm, which was numb from the elbow down, and staring at his shattered shield. 'I swear, that was like being used as an anvil by Thor himself.' He shook his head in amazement.

The Norse were collecting their dead and stripping the Christians of any valuable gear. They had lost seven men to the desperate enemy. The seven men were lined up along the bank, their swords and axes in their hands folded on their chests. One of the men was standing over them, intoning some words. A few others stood around watching or recounting to each other what they had seen of the dead men's last fights and the manner of their deaths.

The huge Saxon lad was lying motionless in the sand, hands and legs strongly bound, chest rising and falling weakly, blood trickling through his greasy hair.

'So why did we spare him?' asked the man who had tried to charge Ordulf down, fury still written on his face as he glared at the prisoner.

Ragnvald walked across the sand. 'Look at what he was using: a hammer. Look at the tools he is carrying. He is clearly a smith and thus valuable as a slave,' he replied. 'Judging by the way he hammered Leif flatter than a dried fish, I bet he is a good one too!' The men laughed and poked fun at the rueful Leif, sitting on his wet arse in the sand, still rubbing his arm back to life. 'I know I said no prisoners, but I make an exception for such a special one.'

Ragnvald was dressed head to toe for war. He was armoured in fine maille with a rich fur cloak, golden arm rings shone on his left arm and Bjóðr sat in its worn leather scabbard at his waist. His helmet was a steel-plated dome with four riveted strips culminating in a decorated, scaled bronze rib that ran from the crown of his head all the way down to the point of his nose and made his face look ridged, like a reptile. His eyes were recessed behind a steel eyepiece that came down to the level of his top lip. Hinged cheek pieces were tied under his chin, leaving only his mouth exposed. A thick maille curtain was attached all the way around the back of the helm, covering his neck while allowing him ease of movement. He looked like a lord of war striding across the sand, with the proud crest of a dragon's snout on his magnificent helm.

If the warriors' laughing and joking at Leif's expense made them seem unaffected by their companions' deaths it was because, largely, they were. These were experienced raiders, Vikings of the old ways who lived for battle and rejoiced in a good death. Their seven companions had fought worthy enemies and died well with their weapons in their hands. They would soon be drinking in the halls of Valhalla with Odin or be collected by the Valkyr to fight in the Fólkvangr with Freyja.

It was the wish of most men in that band to die thus. Their

deaths would be celebrated, not mourned. Only one man there was not sharing the celebration: Fenrir. He was a proud man. Being shoved to the ground and denied his kill in front of everyone grated on him bitterly, and his eyes burned on Leif like a noon-day sun.

Ragnvald looked across the river at the retreating Christians. He had set this ambush on the ford hoping to catch unwary scouting parties, but he had not had the men to take on this whole force. So he had waited until enough had crossed to allow an easy victory. Much as he and his men celebrated death in battle, that didn't mean he wanted to waste their lives. He was deeply impressed by the green-clad warrior in the steel-faced helm. He had seen that man take the lives of two of his men and force back others without a scratch in return and still fight his way clear to safety across the river.

A great warrior. A shame we did not face each other. His men had finished paying their respects to the dead. They would be given to the sea, to Ran's care; they would be in the hands of the fickle sea goddess now. Ragnvald gathered the men around their bodies. 'We will raise mead to our brothers when we return with tales of their victory,' he said, and men nodded and thumped their chests. 'Frangir, my huscarl, died fighting bravely, holding the ford and preventing the enemy escape. We honour his deeds.' The nine remaining huscarls hammered their swords on their shields and howled at the sky as the rest looked on in respect and anticipation. They all knew what would come next.

'Another must stand in Frangir's place, to be at my side in peace and in war, to bear my shield and guard my back in dark places, to stand with Frangir's brothers in the shield wall.' Ragnvald looked around the assembled men, saw the hunger in the faces of many of them. 'So many of you deserve it and have fought bravely here and in a dozen other places. But only one can be called.' His eyes settled on one of the men. A tall, slim warrior with long braids in his beard and a fine maille hauberk and long spear. 'Svend, step forward and take Frangir's body. You will bear him to the boat and forever bear his responsibilities.' The men, even those who were clearly disappointed, shouted their respect to Svend as the man gave his spear away and strained to take up the body of Frangir to carry him to the boats. It would be no easy task in the soft sand, but he would not dare fail.

'Take the rest of our brothers. We will give them to the sea. Let's go.' The men gathered the bodies, and everything of value, and made their way down to the riverbank, following Svend.

One of his men had gone upriver to signal to the boats hidden around the next bend to come and collect them. With the Christians now on the north bank heading overland to Aalborg and another force of them closing the road around the fortress of Fyrkat to the west, he was trapped against the coast with nowhere to go but the sea. He could not reach King Øystein, whose whereabouts he did not know for sure, but he suspected he was in Fyrkat. That alone was truly disappointing.

He could row upriver and die in the futile defence of the fortress trying to reach the new Norwegian king, but he considered that pointless. No. He and his men had fought three skirmishes, killed over fifty Christians and filled their boats with captured equipment. All at the cost of thirteen of their own. He decided this was enough. He would take his men home and prepare for whatever came next. When he returned to Uppsala, he would have to make new plans with King Eric, find another way to reach Øystein, if he even survived.

The Norsemen packed the bodies of their comrades, the looted maille, weapons and valuable possessions of the dead Christians into the two longboats and boarded them. It was around midday, and if the winds held fair they would reach the Scanian shore before nightfall and camp overnight before making the five-day voyage back to Uppsala. Although they could sail and row through the night, it was unnecessarily risky in these coastal waters. They would land the ships and make camp each night ashore.

They pushed the two longships out into the river current with oars and then settled into their benches as the river took them gently out towards the sea, which was just a handful of miles downstream, already visible. Their shields were lined along the sides, maille, leather armour and other heavy gear wrapped in greased covers and stowed under the benches. Each warrior now became an oarsman with seamless ease.

The benches were a little more sparsely occupied than they had been on the journey there, but this was of no concern. The boats were now merely lighter and rode higher in the water. Those fine-built ships could sail as well with six men aboard as sixty, unless the weather turned foul.

The rowers settled into the cadence of the oar master's sing-song voice as they pulled their way downstream. Once at the mouth of the river and clear of shallows and bends, they would raise the sail and ship the oars.

As the last sandbank passed the ship's side and the water started to get rougher, the shipmaster, Ulf, the oldest of his hus-carls and his best sailor, called the oars in. Four warriors sprang to the central mast and laid hands on the ropes that would raise the sail. Four more grabbed the long boom from which the sail hung, which was laid lengthwise along the centre of the boat. They lifted it to waist level while others untied most of the wraps holding the sail to the boom.

A well-practised series of movements followed. The four men on the ropes released them from their cleats and played out the slack. The men holding the boom walked forward with it and swung the front out and towards the side from which the wind was blowing. They swung hard, hard enough for the rear end of the boom to clear the vertical ropes that tied the top of the mast firmly to each side of the boat, holding it upright against the power of the wind.

As the back of the boom cleared those ropes, the men at the mast began hauling vigorously on their rope halyard, taking the weight of the boom off the men at the front and lifting the wooden spar into the air above their heads. As the boom swung up above them, the front men pulled on the loose end of the remaining sail ties, and the sail burst out of its tight folds, blooming and billowing into shape.

As the boom reached its point near the top of the mast, ropes attached to each corner of the sail were being pulled in and adjusted, allowing the sail to fill and pull on the boat in the stiff breeze. They all felt the shift in power as the sail filled and the ship surged forward.

The whole process had taken less time than a thirsty warrior takes to drink a horn of ale. Ragnvald smiled from his position near the steering oar, where Ulf played the great oar and watched the sail and water like a hawk. This was a fine crew of sailors and warriors, one of the best he had ever led. He was glad he had not decided to spend their lives in vain any further. They had done enough to return with some stories of victory, loot and, most importantly, no shame. That would have to be enough. Victory and revenge would wait for another day.

Turning to look at the quickly receding shore of Denmark, he wondered if he would ever see it again and how long it would be before the Christians turned their gaze across the narrow sea to his homeland. He suppressed a shiver at the thought. He had seen their numbers and witnessed the quality of their army. Above all, he had seen the awesome power of their armoured knights, and he felt a dread he had not felt for as long as he could remember.

Shaking the thought away, he turned back towards the bow and set his eyes, and his mind, on the way home.

Ordulf woke slowly, feeling confused. His limbs were numb, and his head felt as if a tiny hammer team were using it as an anvil. His body was swaying and moving most disconcertingly. Was he in a wagon? Was Orbert here? His groggy mind slowly kicked in, and his memory returned. *Oh God, the battle at the ford, kneeling in the sand.*

Why wasn't he dead?

Was he dead?

Why would death hurt this much?

He tried peeling one eye open. His body didn't want to respond to command. He got an eye half-open, but the image was blurred, unfocused. Whatever he was seeing was close and brown.

Wood. He was in a wagon, then. He was freezing. His body suddenly noticed this and started shivering uncontrollably. This had the unpleasant effect of waking him up very quickly, and the full pain of his frigid body and injured head suddenly hit him.

He moaned, long and low, and tried to lever himself up. His legs and arms still wouldn't respond. They felt dead. He wriggled and tried to bring his hands up to his face, but they wouldn't move.

Tied. He could remember it now; he had been tied up.

He rolled his head to the left to look around the wagon. The wagon was large and had water sloshing around in the bottom of it. Men were sitting chatting on benches, and a big white sail was hanging above them.

The wagon was a boat.

Oh God. Panic started to set in over his pain. He was in a Viking's boat, being taken captive to be eaten or sacrificed to the gods. He had heard stories about this, how Christian captives were taken by the Viking raiders, never to be heard of again. How the heathen Norse sacrificed them to their gods and ate the captives at great festivals and horrific gatherings.

He retched into the bottom of the boat. A voice near and above him made angry noises. Hands grabbed his arms, and he was lifted into a sitting position. A tall warrior with a braided beard crouched down in front of him, a huge knife in his right hand resting point down on the deck, a serious expression on his face.

The man looked over his shoulder and nodded. The command he gave, his air of authority, made it clear this older warrior was the leader. Someone behind Ordulf pulled his arms back; he closed his eyes so he wouldn't see that big blade coming for him. But the bonds on his arms loosened and fell away as the ropes were untied.

Ordulf opened his eyes after a moment, and still no one was trying to kill him. He gingerly brought his arms around in front of him. His hands were totally numb and useless; he shook them and tucked them under his armpits. The leader just stayed there, watching him. *Why?*

For a minute or so, the old warrior continued to watch. Then, very deliberately, he lifted his free hand into a clenched fist and shook it, then stopped and shook his head. He then indicated Ordulf with the point of his seax, mimicked slitting his throat and inclined his head and eyes towards the side of the boat.

The message was clear enough: any trouble and you go over the side with a hole in your neck.

The warrior continued to look at Ordulf and raised an eyebrow, so Ordulf nodded slowly. Whatever was going to happen to him, he decided he preferred that to going over the side with a second mouth.

They gave Ordulf a fur cloak to wrap around himself and pointed to a corner of the boat where he was to sit. It was above the sloshing water, so he was pretty satisfied with that, and he sat there and hugged his knees to his chest.

The first night camped on the shore he tried to run. Of course, they were ready and waiting for him to do just that. They caught him in less than ten paces and beat him bloody. He didn't try to run again. He had only done it out of panic and really had no idea where he would run to. He was in the lands of the Norse and had no hope of escape in any meaningful way.

For the rest of the voyage, which passed in a mixture of cold and despair for Ordulf, the Vikings watched him day and night, but thankfully they didn't throw him over the side, and he caused no more trouble.

On the sixth day, or rather, what he thought was the sixth day but couldn't be sure, they rowed up a wide river for about half a day, twisting and turning and passing side channels, sailing through wide lakes and seeing small villages and two large towns on the banks.

Eventually, they arrived at the head of a broad lake, and a forest of masts was visible in front. There was a wooden dock there, as big as the one at Bremen. Ordulf thought there must be fifty ships clustered on its many branches. They were mostly long-ships like the one he was carried in, but there were some barges too. Over the trees behind the dock, he could see a broad haze of light smoke rising. There was a settlement there. A big one.

The two ships sailed past the dock and up a narrow river hidden to the right of it, which couldn't be seen until you were right next to it. They rowed up this river, narrow enough that the ships were forced to row one behind the other, for a few more miles until they arrived at another dock along the bank. The dock was long, and eight or so longships, all richly decorated with pagan symbols and strange creatures were tied to it.

Fully armoured guards stood on the dock with shields and spears. They called out to the oncoming boats, and the old warrior called back. One of the guards turned and jogged across the flat, cleared space behind the dock, calling to someone. The space, maybe twice the size of the training square that had been in the Saxon camp, had various boxes, supplies and spare equipment piled along the sides and rear. Bundles of rope, spare sails and bits of boat were visible. A low wall surrounded the area, about high enough for a tall man to sit on comfortably.

The two boats slowed to a crawl and drifted into a space alongside the dock. The men secured them with ropes and started unhurriedly unloading their gear and loot. Ordulf saw his pack and tools being carried ashore and made to stand up and reach for them, but the man merely laughed and said something incomprehensible to him. Their language was very odd to him. It was rough but flowing, unlike the sing-song French he had heard or his own familiar, sharp German tongue.

The men finished unloading the boats and lounged around, some sitting on the wall, others examining their gear or rinsing it in the river water and drying it with bundles of the tall, tough grass lining the bank.

After some time had passed, Ordulf could hear wheels and the sound of voices approaching. A convoy arrived at the bank with a single cart drawn by a pathetic-looking pony and a number of very plainly dressed men around it. In front of them were some more fully armed warriors and a man in fine furs and boots. Despite all the armed men, no one looked remotely concerned.

The man in the furs and the old warrior from the ship walked towards each other and clasped hands, elbow to elbow, and talked in loud voices, interspersed with laughing and gesticulating. After their conversation was over, the old warrior started pointing at things and giving instructions, while the man in furs nodded.

As the old warrior pointed, men started getting up and picking things up. Boxes of loot were put into the little cart along with spare gear, captured equipment, shirts of maille and weapons. The men picked up their own gear and shields, and then they gathered in a loose group by the entrance and waited. Then the old warrior pointed at Ordulf. His heart began racing again. Was this it? What would happen now?

The man in the furs nodded and snapped his fingers at two of the plainly dressed men. They hurried over to Ordulf, who was sitting on the wall with two watchful Norsemen standing either side of him.

The first man to arrive asked him a question in what sounded like French, but Ordulf shook his head uncomprehendingly. The first man shrugged and turned away. The second man, a taller, thin man with a shock of curly black hair asked in perfect Low German, 'Where are you from?'

Shocked to hear his own language, Ordulf didn't immediately answer and just sat there with his mouth open. The man was about to turn and leave when he said, 'Minden.'

The man turned back, eyebrows raised. 'Minden, eh? Right then, come with me.' The man strode away, leaving no opportunity for questions or protest, so Ordulf stood and followed him, Norse guards following him closely. He didn't understand why this German speaker was here, seemingly free to walk around, wearing good quality – if plain – clothes and giving instructions. Was he a traitor? Was he a Norseman who had learned German? Ordulf didn't think so; the man seemed to have the dialect of northern Saxony.

He saw the German speaker talking to the man in furs, who nodded and signalled to the cart to get moving. Ordulf caught up with the German and opened his mouth to ask a string of questions. The man moved his hand to silence him. Ordulf noticed it was missing the little finger, a scarred stump left above the joint.

'Shut up – don't speak now. Don't cause trouble or they will whip you. I will explain later.' And with that, the whole little convoy started down the path towards the town that was now visible just a mile or so away.

The town they were heading towards was a walled town in the middle of an expanse of wide fields. The warmer weather was only just arriving here, but Ordulf could see the first evidence of crops growing in the otherwise bare fields.

The river continued alongside the road towards the town; in fact, it went right past the walls, but Ordulf could see it was shallow, and in places banks of stones broke the surface. They arrived at the city wall, a huge and well-maintained palisade with an imposing gatehouse built into it, and passed through.

The first thing that struck Ordulf was how odd the buildings were. Each stood alone in its own patch of ground, enclosures with a low fence attached to the side of many. The buildings were constructed from thick, wooden planks supported at the corners and along the side at intervals with angled logs. The buildings were long and low and varied in size. The bigger ones seemed to have some partial second storey, but most were a single floor with deeply sloping roofs of thatch or wooden tiles. The roads between the buildings were unpaved and uneven. As they wound their way into the centre of the town, the buildings became larger, better built and more richly decorated. Some were even made of stone, at least the lower walls. A wide central area came into view, a town square, Ordulf reckoned. On the far side was a huge wooden building. Ordulf gaped up at it. A broad flight of stairs led up to a huge set of double doors. The roof was tiled with something dark, and it sloped away on both sides from a pinnacle above the doors. It went as far back as he could see.

They passed this great building and went into a side street. There was a large horseshoe-shaped building there, formed of two long, steeply roofed buildings, the left one much larger than the right, connected at the back by a semi-open building with a simple, angled roof. The whole compound was maybe a hundred feet deep and just as broad across the prongs of the open end of the shoe, which was facing them. The central courtyard was open and unwalled at the street. The wagon ground to a halt in the yard, and men swarmed over it to unpack. Boxes, gear and people disappeared into different doorways; other men and women appeared from those doorways to loud greetings. Hands were clasped and hugs exchanged between the newcomers and the men from the boats. Ordulf watched as one woman, tall and beautiful and dressed in a flowing kirtle and woollen cloak, looked around the yard searching for someone, an excited look on her face.

One of the warriors saw her and walked over to her, putting a hand on her shoulder and pressing his forehead against hers. He said some words to her, and her shoulders slumped. She nodded to him and turned to walk away, one fist clenched at her side and the other hand held to her mouth. The warrior watched her go sadly and then returned to his work.

'Frangir's wife,' said the German.

Ordulf started; he had not noticed the man arrive. 'Who was Frangir?' he asked.

'A warrior. You probably saw him die. The others said he fell during the ambush on the riverbank, killed by a Christian with a steel face,' the German explained. 'Does that make sense to you?'

'Ah, Sir Hans,' Ordulf said quietly.

'Hmm,' said the German. 'Well. Come inside. I have a lot to explain to you and other work to do after.'

'Come inside? Where am I going? You seem so calm – are you a servant here?'

'Inside first, questions after,' said the man, trying to guide Ordulf towards the low building on the right of the courtyard but failing, like a man trying to push a stubborn cow when it is feeding.

Ordulf eventually relented and trudged across the courtyard. Again, he saw his possessions being carried by one of the warriors. 'Hey, that stuff is mine!' he cried in protest, pointing at the man, who ignored him.

'No it isn't. That stuff is his. You don't own anything anymore. You don't even own yourself,' said the German gently, perhaps more out of fear of his enormous charge rather than actual patience.

Ordulf turned to the German with sadness and anger in his eyes. 'So I am a slave?'

'Yes,' said the German flatly, meeting the bigger man's gaze and still trying to gently guide him towards the building.

'Will I be sacrificed?' Ordulf asked, his voice shaking.

'What? No, don't be absurd. You are here to work. Anyway, Christian slaves are not sacrificed, not often anyway. We are usually not worthy of it, and they think it would be an insult to their gods. So be grateful for that and come with me. Now!'

Ordulf wasn't sure if he believed the German, that he was safe, but he had little choice, so he trudged across the courtyard with him. The building they walked towards was low and long, lime-washed walls topped with a steep, thatched roof, all supported by thick trunk pillars along the sides and at the corners. The columns and the doorway were decorated with rough carvings; snakes and wild beasts snarled and wrestled, frozen in the timber surface.

They ducked through the low doorway, and Ordulf stopped to look around the dimly lit space. The building was open along its entire length, with a partial second floor of wooden boards at both ends. In the centre, opposite the doorway, was a pair of separated firepits with simple benches and tables around them. The whole central area was flat, beaten earth. Some areas with flat, wooden planks for a floor were arranged around the edges of the earthen area and at the ends of the room. Along the walls were all sorts of tables, shelves, piles of clothes and gear, firewood, sleeping rolls and countless other domestic items. It was clear that a number of people lived in this room. On the left, at the end of the room, was a door leading outside. On the right was a larder area with meat hanging from the roof, boxes of winter root vegetables, drying pelts and a number of jugs of water around a large basin. The whole room stank of smoke, burnt fat and rarely washed people.

The German let Ordulf take in his new surroundings and then set to work explaining.

'What is your name?'

'Ordulf.'

'Ordulf, I am Otto, a thrall of Jarl Ragnvald, who you also now belong to. This compound is his. The other long building is his hall and the home of his family and some of his huscarls; you are not allowed in there unless ordered inside. This house is for the lesser men, their women and the slaves. You sleep here, you eat here and you will work elsewhere during the day as commanded.'

'I sleep here?' Ordulf said, surprised.

'Yes, it is the Norse way. They don't have separate rooms to sleep in, and they sleep around the firepit. In the winter, you will understand. The freemen and women sleep closest to the fires, the slaves further out or up there on the second level. It's warmer up there, but smokier. You are free to try both and decide which you prefer.

'Let me run you through the rules as simply as possible. These aren't all of them, and you will learn more, but I beg you to pay attention. The Norse can be easy masters to those who behave well and utterly savage to those who do not. It is up to you to decide which you want. Trust me, you will want to behave well.' He held up his left hand, showing the little finger that was missing down to the last knuckle, his eyes conveying the meaning of that missing digit. Ordulf was shocked into silence.

'Main rule. You are regarded as a particularly smart animal. You are not seen as a person like them. If you are a good and useful animal, you will be fed, kept warm and not mistreated, perhaps even given a mate. You will be allowed to keep to yourself outside of the work you perform and even allowed to wander the streets once they trust you. Before that time comes, to leave this compound unaccompanied means death. You need to take this seriously. If you walk out of that courtyard without instructions, they will use you for sword practice. I've seen it before.'

Ordulf bridled and turned red with anger. The German was unfazed.

'Second rule. If you strike a Norseman, you will lose the hand you struck them with. Which for you would end your usefulness as a smith, and you will be sent into the fields to pull a cart or a plough until you die. You have no idea how lucky you are to be a slave here, in this hall, with your skills. Most slaves are kept as nothing more than farmhands and worked in the worst jobs until they die. If you try and touch a Norse woman, with her agreement or without it, you will lose something more precious than your hand. You understand me? They don't allow animals to lie with people, and you are an animal.'

Ordulf's red face drained at the dire warning, and he clenched his teeth.

'This hall may seem simple and strange, even disgusting, to you, but this is better than how most Norse families themselves live. You will have a better life here than almost any peasant. Even better than some of the lesser warriors. So you should feel blessed. They don't much care what the slaves get up to with each other. We can fight, fuck, sing, play, eat and sleep and do whatever else we want as long as we don't damage each other or fail to complete our duties. So wipe that look off your face. You hurt another slave and much worse will happen to you,' the German said, with a confidence he clearly didn't feel.

'Understood? That's the basics. When everyone is back tonight, you will see what is and isn't being used in terms of furs and clothes and beds. There is plenty to go round. That door at the back leads to the shit pit. Don't fall in it; it often takes a while for someone to hear you and come dig you out. Now, I have work to do.' With that, he turned to leave.

'Wait!' said Ordulf, looking confused. 'What do I do? Where do I work?'

'Do? You wait for instructions in here or in the yard. Someone will tell you to do something, and you do it. Between instructions, you do whatever you want as per the rules. Eat, sleep, abuse yourself in the corner. I don't care.' He abruptly turned and left through the door.

Ordulf sank onto one of the benches, alone in the hall, struggling to comprehend his situation. He wasn't wearing chains, and no one was beating him or telling him what to do. There was food sitting there that he could just eat, and no one would punish him, or that was how he understood it. But if he walked out of that door and crossed an invisible line, he would be brutally killed.

And that was it, for the rest of his life. The thought was too vast to comprehend. Thinking about food also made him realise he was intensely hungry. He saw that the massive pot hanging over the fireplace in front of him held some still-warm stew, and there was some sort of flatbread on the table at the end of the room. Looking around to check no one was watching – he still believed that he might be stealing or that Otto was playing a trick on him – he grabbed a bowl and a wooden spoon from a table and set about dealing with his hunger.

Ordulf was dozing on a pile of pelts when the door opened and a gaggle of people arrived in the hall. Most of them stopped to stare at him and a few asked him questions, but he understood none of it and just shook his head blankly. There were three men, two old women and two younger ones, one around his age and one a little older. The men he recognised as the men who had accompanied the wagon at the docks earlier that day. The whole lot of them were wearing simple woollen clothes and homemade tunics. They all scattered throughout the space and got on with various activities. One of the older women and one of the men started pulling logs out of a pile and rebuilt the fire underneath the pot containing the broth.

Ordulf looked guiltily at the half-empty bowl he had left near the fire and wondered whether it would cause trouble. An older woman picked it up and looked at him, holding it out with questioning eyes and pointing at her mouth. He nodded, and she brought it over with the spoon and gave it to him before wandering off. Ordulf finished the cooled and greasy remains. He had eaten much worse. Even cold the stew was much better than the slop that the tavern by the patch served.

A short time later, two armed men came through the door, and Ordulf stiffened, heart starting to hammer in his chest. However, the two men simply removed all their gear in a corner next to a stub wall on the far side of the fireplace and hung it up. A group of women and children arrived next, and the children went over to the two men who greeted them with smiles. One of them picked up a small child and lifted them onto his shoulders to squeals of joy.

Otto was the last to arrive. Some of the other slaves went over to him and asked him questions in their babbling language, looking over at Ordulf as they did. He answered their questions and they drifted away, apparently satisfied.

Otto got himself a jug of water and came to sit with Ordulf, offering him a drink.

'You speak their language?' Ordulf asked.

'Yes. I was a sailor. Sometimes we smuggled goods into Denmark; they pay good silver for iron and other things. I worked with some Danish, and I learned their language,' he said, shrugging his shoulders. 'Then my ship was captured leaving Hamburg by raiders led by Jarl Ragnvald four years ago. I have been a slave ever since. Now it's one of my jobs to turn our words into theirs.'

'How do you accept that?' said Ordulf, his eyes burning.

'Because there is no alternative. I cannot have any other life, so I accept this one. So now I am Otto the slave. A translator and servant to the jarl. Ordulf, everyone in here who was born free has gone through what you're thinking and feeling when they first were captured. They either learned to live with it or they didn't. It doesn't end well for the ones who don't. It's that simple.' He got up to go over to the firepit and said over his shoulder, 'Only time will tell whether you can live with it or not, so don't do anything stupid now.'

'So what if I can't live with it?' asked Ordulf, misery colouring his tone.

Otto sighed. 'Well, then you have no future here. Anyone who cannot accept this fate is destroyed by the loneliness and frustration of existing between two classes of people. You cannot join the freemen, and if you refuse to join the slaves...' Otto shrugged.

Ordulf thought about this for a moment and walked over to the firepit, leaning over to talk quietly and still be heard. 'Are slaves ever freed?' he asked.

Otto stopped his tending to the fire and sighed in frustration. 'Yes, it does happen. Usually after many years of loyal service. Other Norse captured in war can be freed sometimes. Norse born into slavery, rarely; foreigners captured in battle, never. Where would you go anyway? Non-Norse are banned from living here permanently as freemen, or from owning property.'

Ordulf was crestfallen. 'So we are to be slaves forever?'

Otto didn't reply. He just shrugged and strode off down the longhouse, leaving a miserable Ordulf in his wake.

The evening passed rapidly with Ordulf brooding in the corner. The only time anyone interacted with him was when the old lady came and tried to explain with sign gestures and grunts that he was sitting on her bed. He got to his feet and moved to a bench where he had more of the piping-hot reheated stew and enjoyed the heat of the fire.

When darkness fully fell, the freemen shooed the slaves away from the firepits as if they were shooing away a cat and set their beds down to sleep with their families. The stinking animal-fat candles were put out until only the glow of the dying fire lit the space. Ordulf found a flat area at the back just out of the fire's glow with a hide bed and some old furs to wrap himself up in and lay down. He didn't sleep much that night. He was too confused and shocked to even cry. He just stared blankly at the roof.

The morning came, and someone's toes nudged him in the ribs. He looked up and saw the old woman. She was offering him a steaming bowl, which he quickly accepted. He looked around and realised that everyone else was up and about. Some had already left the house. There was a freshly cooked stew on the fire, and Ordulf had to admit, it was pretty good. Hearty and with a good amount of something's meat in it. There was even a lump of fresh, warm bread. He was amazed.

Otto came in through the door and called over to Ordulf. 'You are wanted. Come with me.'

Ordulf got up and followed him across the yard towards the bigger longhouse. He hesitated before the carved doorway. *Was this a test?*

'It's fine, you have been ordered in,' said Otto, waiting impatiently.

Ordulf went through the door and was hit with that same smell of people and cooking, but the room was much larger and taller, the smell of smoke less overpowering. Huge vents at the peak let in the light and let out the bad air. At this end of the building, it was a great hall with groups of tables around a huge and well-built firepit. Towards the middle, a wall divided the building in two, and it had a full second floor from that point onwards. In the middle, before the wall, stood a raised platform with a few large and comfortable-looking chairs and a table to one side with fine metal jugs and cups on it. Torches burned on the posts supporting the ceiling, and men and women talked and ate at the tables. There were rich decorations and fantastical carvings everywhere, and along the walls stood shelves and racks full of looted items.

Ordulf's eyes bulged. There were crosses and silverware from churches, Christian shields and weapons, suits of chain maille and even a knight's saddle on a wooden beam. This whole room was a trophy collection. It was intended to impress, and Ordulf had to admit, it was very impressive. He saw that the old warrior from the boat was sitting in one of the big chairs on the dais, chatting to an elegant woman in the seat next to him. Otto gave him a nudge in that direction, and they walked towards the seats.

'Is that Lord Ragnvald?' he hissed at Otto.

'Jarl Ragnvald, yes. Your master.'

Two warriors detached themselves from the walls they had been resting against and stood on either side of the dais, short axes casually dangling in their hands.

The jarl said something to Otto at length, and Otto nodded and then turned to Ordulf.

'The jarl has some questions for you. You will answer me, and I will tell him. First, are you truly a smith? He has your tools here.'

Otto gestured to a shelf at the side. 'They do seem to be the tools of a smith. But are they yours?'

Ordulf nodded. The jarl grunted.

'What do you make?'

'I am a swordsmith,' Ordulf said, not able to keep the pride out of his voice.

Otto translated, and the jarl perked up. He rattled off some quick words at Otto.

'This is a big claim. Can you prove it? What have you made?'

'Yes, I can prove it. In fact, you might have some of my swords here.'

Otto and the jarl conversed for a while and looked confused. 'How can some of your swords be here?' Otto asked.

'The ones you took from the men at the ford.' Ordulf paused as the fear and anger of that memory filled him and then continued, 'I think some of them might have been ones I made.'

The jarl leaned over and said something to one of the guards. He went over to the trophy wall and rummaged around, bringing back an armful of swords.

'These were among those taken from the soldiers at the ford,' said Otto, indicating the blades. 'Did you make any of these?' Ordulf could easily see that three of them were from the batch made at Minden.

'The black-scabbarded sword with the cross in the pommel – that is my work or, at least, partly my work.'

Otto explained this to the guard who passed the sword to the jarl who drew it from the scabbard and inspected it and felt its balance. He looked at it thoughtfully for a while and then spoke again.

'He says this is an acceptable weapon, but he thinks it is not a warrior's sword. It is too narrow, and… I don't totally follow his meaning, but it has other deficiencies.' Ordulf flushed with hurt pride and nearly snapped an angry retort. His temper would get him killed one of these days. The jarl shrugged and looked unimpressed with the sword, which was taken away, then said something to Otto that required quite a bit of back-and-forth conversation.

Finally, Otto turned to Ordulf. 'You are to go and train with the city's swordsmith. He is old and very wise and knows everything about swordsmithing the proper Norse way. You will learn from him and help him in whatever way he requires, and if you are useful, the smith might keep you. If he does not, you will be sold to a lesser town smithy, or perhaps to a farm. The jarl thinks you would fetch a good price from a farm. You are young, and you look like you could do the work of two normal slaves.'

The jarl waved his hand in dismissal, and Otto took Ordulf's arm and guided him out of the door.

'Bastard,' said Ordulf, spitting into the dirt, eyes narrowed and fists clenched.

'What? That was a good meeting. You will be a smith. You have the chance not to become a farm animal – what is the problem?' said Otto.

'He said my work was only *acceptable*,' Ordulf raged, gesturing wildly with his hands. 'He doesn't understand the design and he just… dismisses it like that? Those swords helped cut Denmark in half! I was there – I saw it. What does he know?'

Otto laughed sharply at the pinked pride in the young man. 'What does he know? Ordulf, he has been fighting with swords since before you were born. He has fought hundreds of men, armed with every weapon you can imagine. If he says the thing, he is right. But if you go back into that room full of experienced men of war and explain that your sword is better than theirs, I am sure they will take you really, really seriously.' Otto sneered the last few words like a housewife scolding a child.

Ordulf blanched and shut his mouth. He cast his eyes down,

feeling stupid for his outburst. There was silence as they walked back across the yard and then, at the doorway, Otto said, 'Now, you will be collected tomorrow to be taken to the smithy. I suggest you keep your ears open and your mouth shut and try and learn something. Maybe, you never know, you might find that at your age you haven't reached the peak of human knowledge. Oh, and I am to teach you Norse. Until you can speak the language, you are not much use. So we will spend our evenings learning, which I will enjoy even less than you. Perhaps you will be able to point out to me some of the finer points of language while we are at it?' Otto's voice dripped with sarcasm.

With the biting lecture over, Otto turned and walked back to the great hall.

Ordulf lowered his head and trudged into the lower hall, dragging his wounded pride and his desolation with him.

CHAPTER 14

THE SLAVE AND THE SWORDSMITH

THE NORSE SMITHY was familiar, yet alien. All the basic tools were there: tongs, hammers, punches, engraving tools, various shaping tools, anvils. But the shapes were odd, the layout just... *wrong*. The forge itself was totally different. Ordulf was used to a broad, flat forge that they fed with charcoal. They built up, shaped and moved the charcoal around to move hotspots, and they managed the temperature with bellows feeding in below the fire. It was flexible but laborious and consumed charcoal like a cow consumes grass.

The forges here were shaped like open-ended pig troughs with the air from the bellows feeding in from the side. Ordulf was fascinated and confused by this design, although he could see how it would help to make long blades more easily and use less fuel, but it would give much less room to work in.

The Norse master smith was a surprisingly small and surprisingly old man called Dengir. He had wiry arms that were rippled with rope-like muscles. He spoke no words of Low German and mostly just grunted and pointed at things, even when directing the Norse slaves and junior smiths. The wiry little man couldn't have been more different to his old master in Minden. Ordulf started to doubt the smith was any good. Until he saw him work.

Dengir's hammer *flew*. He sang as he worked, and his hammer moved like the beats of a goose's wings. He seemed tireless. His small, wiry arms didn't deliver great dramatic strikes, but he had a fine eye, and his rapid, accurate blows massaged the metal into shape with astounding efficiency.

Ordulf found himself at the bottom of the workers at the forge, which he bitterly resented. He was given the simplest tasks and did the basic work. It was as if he was just an untrained boy again. It ate at him more than his captivity. He was a smith, a good one! And now he was reduced to the lowest apprentice, fit only to help as they made axes and spears and big knives. They weren't even making any swords.

In the longhouse one evening, tired and frustrated from a day swinging a hammer with men who did not respect him and whom he could not speak to, he sat brooding over his evening meal. His Norse lessons were too slow for his liking. It was infuriating having to learn a new language from scratch. Everything was infuriating at the moment. He slammed his bowl down and went outside for some air to get away from the cloying and smoky atmosphere in the hall. He paced back and forth in the yard, his mind racing. He felt trapped and useless. He was leaning up against a wall when someone started shouting. Ordulf looked up, confused. He suddenly realised that he was looking at the yard from across the street, and one of the men from his hall was coming towards him with a sword.

Oh God. I've left the courtyard.

He raised his arms in supplication as men started boiling out of the hall on the left, some armed, some not. He was quickly surrounded, and a sword was put to his throat. He couldn't even beg – he desperately tried to recall his brief Norse teaching but came up blank. He was picked up and carried to the yard before being dumped on the floor, flat on his back with a sword point in his throat. He shook and wildly swept his eyes from side to side.

The warrior above him was arguing with another, who was gesturing at the main hall. Otto arrived and stood to the side, looking around nervously.

'Otto!' Ordulf gasped. 'Help me!'

'What did you do, Ordulf? Why did you run?'

'I didn't run, Otto. I was just wandering through the yard and forgot about the line. Please, tell them it was just a mistake!' Ordulf was terrified; his life hung on a knife's edge.

Otto exchanged some quick words with the warriors and was clearly rebuffed. One of the warriors pushed him back.

'Ordulf, it's out of my hands. I'm sorry. They are waiting for the jarl to decide your fate. Everyone saw you had left; the rule is the rule.'

Ordulf shivered on the ground for what seemed like the whole night until finally the crowd parted and the jarl appeared. He stood over Ordulf. He looked furious. He snapped some words at Otto. Otto replied with his head bowed and voice low.

The jarl listened to Otto and then to the warrior with his sword at Ordulf's throat. Ordulf looked up and realised it was the warrior from the ford, the one who had charged him and been stopped by another man. This only deepened his panic. This warrior had never looked at him any other way than the way a wolf looks at a lamb.

The conversation abruptly ended when the jarl pointed at the hall.

'Otto, what is happening?' Ordulf cried.

'It's good news. They aren't going to kill you right now,' Otto said from somewhere at his side.

'*Right now?*' What do you mean *right now?*' Ordulf cried.

'I assumed they would kill you right here, but the jarl has decided to hear your case in the great hall. It's the best result you could have hoped for.'

Ordulf was dragged into the great hall and dumped unceremoniously on the ground in front of the dais. A warrior held him down with the point of a spear and didn't seem to mind if it drew blood.

The jarl sat above him and fired questions at Otto. Ordulf understood nothing of the rapid exchange, and Otto translated.

'Why did you run?' Otto asked.

'I told you, I didn't run. I just forgot the rule while I was outside thinking. I was just leaning against a building outside when they saw me,' Ordulf pleaded.

The jarl heard the explanation and scowled. 'The others saw you looking angry all evening and then slamming a bowl down before you left the longhouse. They say you were angry and you ran,' Otto relayed.

'No!' shouted Ordulf in Norse. 'I was only frustrated with the smithing and needed to think about it. The house was too hot and noisy!'

Otto spoke to the jarl back and forth at length, and the jarl nodded. Otto looked relieved. The jarl looked at the warrior from the ford, who was now speaking. The warrior then brought over Ordulf's old pack, which he dumped at the jarl's feet, giving Ordulf a sinister and triumphant look as he did. Rummaging through the bag, he brought out a number of small purses and packets. He emptied them out, dumping silver and copper coins all over the floor. He stood back triumphantly and glared at Ordulf. Some in the audience whispered and gestured to each other. The jarl spoke again to Otto.

Otto looked confused and worried. 'Fenrir says you are a thief and thus cannot be trusted under Norse law. The word of a thief means nothing in his own defence. Ordulf, why did you have so much money in so many different purses?' Otto pointed at the ground, littered with pouches and silver. 'Did you steal all this money from your comrades?' Otto looked confused, hurt even. 'Ordulf, this looks really bad. No junior smith would have this much money.'

Ordulf was stunned; he could not form words to defend himself.

'Ordulf, explain yourself or you will die here on this floor!' Otto hissed at him.

His hesitation was damning him, he could see it. 'The money was my share of the contract for that batch of swords,' he said, pointing vaguely at the side wall. 'I split it up to hide it from thieves and so I couldn't lose it all in one go!' He looked pleadingly at Otto and moved his eyes to the jarl who had his hands on the arms of his chair, his face a blank mask.

Otto relayed the explanation to the jarl, who raised his eyebrows and stroked his beard. He thought for a moment and spoke again to Otto. Others in the room muttered in sharp tones or made noises of scorn. The jarl spoke and everyone was silent.

'The jarl accepts your explanation. You are not a thief. Some of the warriors say a strong man does not hide his wealth, he displays it as a warning of his power. But the jarl said you are not a warrior and would not understand this.'

Ordulf breathed a deep sigh of relief. 'So what now?'

'Now they decide if you die for leaving the compound,' Otto said flatly.

Ordulf's relief withered on the vine. 'But I explained!'

'It does not matter. You broke the law by disobeying your

master's command. People saw you leave. If you are spared, others will be emboldened to break it too and use the same excuse,' Otto said, a sympathetic look on his face. 'You will be punished – they only debate what that punishment will be.'

Fenrir was standing in front of the dais, pointing down at Ordulf and gesticulating between himself and Ordulf. Many of those gathered grunted and nodded in agreement with what he was saying. Another warrior that Ordulf recognised, the one whose shield he had crushed with his hammer, appeared and stood next to the circle. He spoke, and the men fell silent. Fenrir turned with hatred and rage on his face. The two men stared at each other, fists clenched, veins throbbing at their temples. The men seemed on the verge of violence. The jarl held up his hand and spoke. The room broke into cheers when he was finished. The spear was removed from Ordulf's back and he looked around. Suddenly, everyone was ignoring him.

Otto walked over. 'The jarl said he was inclined to spare you because of your strength and skill and potential usefulness. They debated taking a foot to ensure you could not escape but decided it would hinder you too much.' Ordulf's mouth opened to speak, but he drew a blank. 'Fenrir suggested you fight to prove your worth. To cross swords with him, and if you live, be allowed to return to being a slave. Leif called him a coward for wanting to fight an untrained man. Fenrir called Leif a woman because you beat him down with just your hammer at the ford.'

Ordulf struggled to keep up with the conversation. The room was draining of men as they all headed outside, including the jarl.

'Both men insulted the other grievously and thus by law they can demand a fight to settle it. Sword and shield, in a square of their peers. It is called *hólmganga*, a duel, usually to the death.' Otto shook his head. 'They have hated each other for a long time. This is merely their excuse. Anyway, the jarl says the winner gets to decide your fate. Normally, they would hold the duel after five days, but both men insisted it be fought now. If Fenrir wins, you will also fight him to the death in turn. If Leif wins, you will fight him, both of you unarmed, so he can beat you with his fists and prove in public that you are not his superior, which will expunge the insult Fenrir made on him.'

'So... so, whatever happens I have to fight one of them to the death?' Ordulf was beyond confusion now.

'No,' said Otto with a wry smile. 'Leif won't necessarily kill you, just assert his dominance by beating you. So pray he wins this fight.'

'They are going to fight to the death for the right to fight me, and they want to fight me to retain their honour?' Ordulf said, losing his wits.

'Yes.'

'They are completely mad!'

'Perhaps to you, but for them, this is normal. Honour is everything. Fenrir was denied the chance to kill you, and he is embarrassed. Leif was humiliated by being beaten by you and called a woman for it by Fenrir. It is the worst of insults here. From the moment that was said, blood was always going to be spilled.'

Ordulf didn't have time to reply. He was picked up by two warriors and dragged into the yard. A square of men had formed already, torches in hand, shouting and jeering. Inside the firelit space, shields up with the top rims on their shoulders, faces slanted down across their fronts, swords low and forward, the two men faced each other. They were semi-crouched, bobbing slightly on their feet, eyes fixed on each other. Ordulf watched from his place on the floor sprawled between two guards, captivated despite the implications of the result.

Fenrir attacked first; he had been taunting the bigger Leif, provoking him and faking steps forward. Leif was unmoved.

Suddenly, Fenrir slid his front foot forward and tried to lever his shield rim under the rim of Leif's. Leif pushed down and deflected the serpent-like strike aimed at his legs. He countered with a thrust at Fenrir's head. Fenrir snapped his head back and dodged. The two fighters separated, watching each other warily.

Fenrir tried a double move to put Leif off balance with his great speed. He lunged off with his left foot, struck the rim of his shield into his opponent's and raised his sword as if to cut down over the top of Leif's shield. Leif raised his shield to cover and lunged under it into the line of the attack beneath the shields. But Fenrir had changed the direction of the blow as soon as Leif was unsighted by his own shield. Instead of passing his blade over both their shields, he pushed back hard off his right foot and whipped it back in a reverse cut. In that moment, Leif had his shield high, covering his head, his sword extended forward in the centre, missing the body of the dodging Fenrir, and was open on his left with Fenrir's blade cutting back towards him.

He dropped and rolled to his right, a desperate move. Fenrir's back-cut swung through open air, but his opponent was down and rolling to regain his feet. Fenrir pounced and rained blows down on his out-of-position foe. One knee still in the dirt, shield high warding off the rapid slashing attacks, Leif thrust forward under the shield, trying to find a leg, trying to create space to rise.

The crowd was roaring, each man shouting and pointing, pumping their fists. Leif missed his fouling attacks on Fenrir's legs. Fenrir tried pushing down on the upraised shield with his own, but he wasn't heavy or strong enough to press Leif into the dirt. Instead, he put his sword hand behind his shield and swung it back in from the right with the force of both his hands, trying to topple the defence sideways and create an opening. Leif was too fast; he pulled his disintegrating shield back into his body and shoved the lighter man, propelling him into the wall of the crowd, unharmed but furious.

Leif was bleeding from a nasty gash on his shoulder. His eyes were narrowed, his teeth set hard in his jaw. He threw down the ruined shield and called for another from a man in the circle, who passed it to him. The two men settled and faced each other again. Ordulf understood little of the tactics of the fight, but he could see that Leif had been in desperate trouble with one knee down and was hugely relieved to see him back on his feet, even if he was bleeding. It didn't look too serious, or so he hoped.

Fenrir was angry. Ordulf could see his mouth gaping, spit trailing from his teeth. His eyes were wild. He was slamming his shield with his sword and taunting the carefully moving and steadily bleeding Leif. Fenrir made an extravagant attack, sword flashing left and right and left again under his covering shield, which was held out in front of him. Leif covered himself, pulled out of range and fended off the attempts to get around his defence, blades clashing and scraping almost too fast to see. Men around the circle were jeering now and pointing at Leif. His eyes stayed narrow, his jaw set.

Fenrir attacked again, an overhead swing to bring Leif's shield up, then a low thrust to target the space beneath. Leif blocked the first and stepped around the second and didn't even return the blow. He just raised his shield again and readied himself. The mood in the crowd was getting ugly now. They were urging Fenrir to finish it. Ordulf couldn't understand Leif's passive approach; was his injury that bad?

Fenrir surged forward again, this time trying to force his opponent's shield down, hacking and pushing at it with the edge of his own. Splinters flew, and his sword clashed with the other shield's boss. In the increasingly wild attacks, Leif did nothing to counter, and Fenrir's shield started to drift. On one particularly hard swing, his shield opened out from the left side of his body as his right hand came down.

Leif struck like a bolt of lightning through the gap. Stepping hard in towards his opponent and pushing his shield up to take the oncoming swing, he thrust his sword, with his entire body weight behind it, down the open centre line.

Ordulf saw the point burst through Fenrir's back in a gush of blood, and the man dropped like a sack of wheat, eyes rolling, sword falling from his hand. His shaking body slammed into the dirt in a tangled heap as he gasped and gurgled through the hole in his chest for a few agonising seconds. Leif quickly grabbed the fallen sword and pushed it into the dying man's nerveless fingers and closed them around the hilt.

Fenrir stopped twitching; the last pulse of blood pumped out past the sword that still transfixed him. There was a mixed reaction around the circle. Some men were shocked into silence at the outcome and a few cheered. Friends of Fenrir shook their heads or cursed. One man howled in fury, like a wounded wolf. He tried to run into the circle, but he was slow, walking awkwardly, limping, and two of his fellows restrained him and pulled him back while he thrashed his arms and cursed in fury. Ordulf watched the raging man with detached curiosity as he was bodily dragged away.

Leif carefully placed the dead man's hands over his chest and pulled his own sword from the body. The crowd was stunned into silence, but then a cheer erupted from one man and the rest followed. They had been disappointed by the apparent lack of spirit Leif had shown, but it had just been a masterful display of defence and patience. Leif had only struck two hard blows in the entire fight.

Leif handed his gear to someone in the crowd and walked over to exchange an arm clasp with the jarl. The two men spoke briefly, and Leif gestured to his shoulder from which blood was still flowing, running down his side and staining his tunic red from shoulder to knee. The jarl raised his hand, and silence gradually fell around the group. He waved his hand first towards Leif and then towards Ordulf and said something. Whatever was said caused a lot of the men to laugh and cheer; most of them turned to look at Ordulf.

Even Otto was chuckling. Leif walked back out into the centre of the square and stood facing Ordulf in a relaxed pose.

'Leif says he cannot wrestle you with his arm injury, so he will let you off with a joke,' said Otto.

'A joke?' said Ordulf in confusion.

'Yes. Go out there, and he will tell you a joke. Then you will be considered cleansed of your crime. That is his decision, and he has earned the right to decide your punishment.' Otto shrugged as if such a thing wasn't mad.

A joke? Before, they were talking about killing me. Now a joke will suffice?

Someone pushed Ordulf, and he didn't resist. He walked out to face Leif, looking around him suspiciously, but saw no trap. He stopped and faced the stern and bleeding warrior. He was half a head taller and generally larger than the Norseman, so he looked down and waited, trying to appear much more relaxed than he felt.

Leif suddenly spoke over Ordulf's shoulder at Otto, who translated.

'He asks for a demonstration of how Christians worship. He has heard they hold their hands together. He wants to see this. Then he will show you how the Norse celebrate the god Loki.' Otto was suppressing a grin as he spoke, unseen behind Ordulf's back.

Ordulf was perplexed, but he placed his hands together, palm to palm, in front of his chin, fingers pointing up, and looked questioningly at Leif. Leif looked him up and down with great feigned seriousness. Men around the circle were jeering and laughing. Leif again addressed Otto.

'He believes you pray like this to get into heaven and asks where you believe heaven is?'

Ordulf sighed, split his hands and pointed up, raising his eyes to the sky and opening his mouth to reply.

His breath left his body through his open mouth like a storm wind as Leif's fist smashed into his stomach. The fist hit him so hard Ordulf briefly wondered if it might appear through his back, as the sword had done through Fenrir's. Then his legs gave way, and he dropped to the dirt as the pain reached him and became his whole world. He rolled and gasped, unable to breathe, hands clawing at the dirt, trying to raise an arm to ward off the next blows, but none came. He looked up. Leif had his arms raised in victory and was baying at the crowd, who were laughing and slapping each other on the back.

Ordulf's first breath came back as his vision was starting to go black. In all his time fighting on the patch, he had never been hit that hard or been caught that unawares. The pain was shocking. By the time he could breathe enough to speak, the crowd had started to melt away into the buildings, some still gesturing and mimicking his eyes-up, hands-raised posture before braying with laughter again. Ordulf lay on the ground and moaned as Otto walked over.

'How… was that… a joke…?' Ordulf gasped between searing breaths.

Otto shrugged. 'They seemed to find it pretty funny, so it must have been. I wouldn't complain too loudly – that man just saved your life… and he killed a fellow Norseman to do it.' Otto shook his head in wonder, unable to comprehend that Ordulf was still alive as he helped the whimpering smith to his feet and they started hobbling towards the longhouse.

'Just so you know, if anything like this ever happens again,

Loki is the trickster god, famous for deception and countering the work of the other gods out of malice or just for fun,' Otto said, struggling under about half of the bigger man's weight. 'Perhaps I should teach you about their gods. I expect it might be useful again in the future.'

Ordulf just groaned and stumbled towards his bed. His stomach felt *wrong*. His knees collapsed once more just before the door as his stomach gave up the fight. He vomited violently all over the ground, his knees and the unfortunate Otto's feet.

'Oh, for fuck's sake, Ordulf. Could you not have warned me?' Otto let go his grip on Ordulf, who nearly toppled completely over.

'Shit... I... I'm sorry, Otto,' Ordulf moaned, heaving and clutching his hands to his burning belly.

Otto walked off, disgusted, heading for the water basin to wash the muck from his shins and boots. Ordulf felt utterly miserable kneeling alone in the dirt. He was a plaything for a bunch of crazy Norsemen. He didn't understand what was happening at the smithy, a job that would apparently consume the rest of his life. He couldn't walk around without risking death nor talk to more than one other human in the whole world. A human who, he was pretty sure, hated him for some reason he couldn't fathom.

Ordulf managed to prise himself from the floor after a short time and hobbled to his bed. He had had enough of Norsemen for one day.

He didn't sleep that night. The pain in his stomach took a while to subside to a dull ache, but that wasn't it. His mind seethed more than his stomach. His pride and his frustration were taking over his existence. The strange ways of the smith with whom he could not communicate, the laws he was subject to that he had no way to understand, the restrictions of the house with a couple of handfuls of people he didn't even know the names of and who essentially ignored him – all of it weighed down on him, sapping his spirit.

His instinct was to fight it. But openly railing against the bonds that held him so tightly would do nothing, he could see that. That coward, Otto, spoke of accepting his condition or being destroyed by it. Clearly, he had given up on the idea of having any future outside of being a slave, but Ordulf furiously refused to do that himself. He would never give up that part of himself that had been a free man.

However, equally, he knew could not thrash like a wild animal against the bonds. That would only lead to more suffering and punishment and mental anguish. He was lucid enough to understand that he would have to bottle his pride. He remembered that day at the ford: eyes locking with Sir Hans across a gulf so wide, over a distance so short, that neither of them could ever hope to bridge it. That was the first and only time he had given up and was left without hope; the shame and weakness of it burned in him like a brand. He decided never to let go of that hope again. He had survived that moment of his certain death, and he would do so again. He would keep hope alive as a counter to his despair, no matter what. He swore that to himself in the cloying darkness.

His hope, the hope that he took to his chest that night, was that the crusaders were coming. It might take them years, it might take them half his life, but he believed they would never stop until they had captured the north, just as they had captured the Holy Land from the infidels of the desert in the year of his birth.

He took that hope, he held it tightly in his mind and he buried it like a shining jewel in the core of his being. He would *never* give in – but he would be smarter. He would show patience; he would stop raging against the world around him. He would be useful to the smith; he would be obedient and servile to the master. He would ensure that he survived until his rescue. He would not live his whole life as a slave.

Something changed deep inside Ordulf that night. The naïve boy, who wanted to understand everything, who resented every unfairness and who held his pride like a torch above him, died in that yard with Fenrir. Ordulf the man, the man who planned ahead, who would bide his time and be unassuming and patient, was brought into the world. His priorities shifted from wanting to prove himself and receive recognition for his skills to gaining the tools he would need for survival. The first thing he would need was the ability to speak, listen and – most importantly – understand. He needed to learn Norse, and so he needed Otto.

CHAPTER 15

A Song for a Sword

13th of July, year of our Lord 1116

My Lord Duke Lothair

The subjugation of the province is complete. Our forces have now crushed the last remnants of the pagan forces in the far north and west of the peninsula. Viking raids continue to be a problem on the east coast. Without sufficient ships to quell these attacks, or permission to cross the straits and clear the neighbouring islands, we will continue to experience this harassment. I can report that, of our own forces, I will soon have to send half our strength home for the winter. The land here will not produce as much food as we anticipated. The remaining Norse peasantry are more unruly and fewer in number than expected. We have not the manpower to enforce firm rule here to ensure the harvest is taken in and distributed according to our needs. The constant raids make moving supplies around difficult.

I implore again, while I have sufficient forces and good weather, that we be allowed to discreetly take control of the islands that lie a mere mile from our new province and which serve as a base for these raids. If I cannot act now, it will have to wait until spring, and our position for the next crusade will be greatly weakened in terms of time, bases for supporting the army and local supply.

I remain, as always, your faithful servant,

Count Adolf of Schauenburg, governor of Jutland

For the first time since he had arrived, despite his writhing guts and lack of sleep, Ordulf got up early and, much to her delight, helped the old woman to make the morning meal. She smiled affectionately at him and showed him how to chop the ingredients, how to prepare them, what order to feed them into the cauldron and how to brown the meat against the fire before it was added. He watched, he smiled, he learned. And he began to make an ally.

He filled a bowl and went over to Otto, who was dressing himself for the day. Otto reached mechanically to take the offered bowl, then started when he saw who offered it. Ordulf had become notorious for not getting up on time and not doing his share of the work in the house, something he had been apparently totally oblivious to. Ordulf smiled at Otto's raised eyebrows.

'Got to change my ways, eh?' he said, smiling at Otto sheepishly. 'Don't think I have any more luck left in me.'

Otto smiled broadly. He accepted the bowl and clasped the younger man's hand. 'So, Ordulf, you have decided to be one of the ones who accepts his fate?'

'I guess you could say that' he said, thinking carefully about what he was going to say next and how he was going to say it. 'I have decided I cannot continue the way I was going. It wasn't helping me. I need to settle into this, give myself an easier time.'

Otto nodded sagely. 'Yes, that is essential, Ordulf, and I must say, I am surprised and pleased to hear it. I thought your pride would be the end of you before the summer was done.'

Ordulf frowned and nodded. He added, as if an afterthought, 'Otto, if I am to settle in here, I must learn Norse as fast as I can. I will be a better student. Can you help me?' He affected his most pious and earnest face. Otto visibly wilted before Ordulf could worry whether he had laid it on a bit thick.

'Of course, I would be happy to. It's my job anyway, so I don't have a choice,' he said, smiling and tucking into his bowl.

Ordulf went to the smithy that day with his new attitude in tow. The weeks passed as he watched and learned. He stood where he was told; he held what he was asked to hold. He scrubbed, he swept, he tidied, and he polished. Yes, Ordulf, the lad who hated polishing so much, willingly and gratefully polished basic swords and axes and seaxes. He was grateful for it for two reasons: it earned him favour, and it wasn't all that hard. It turned out the Norse didn't care much for shiny weapons.

Finally, after many weeks, they started making a sword. But the process was so different that Ordulf did not recognise it at first. The Norse made steel quite differently. Their furnaces yielded small lumps of iron and steel, which they worked into bars of varying properties. These were fine for making a simple axe head or a knife, but a whole sword? How could a sword be made from these, when you could not know the quality of each piece? Again, he started to doubt the Norse sword-making skill.

Ordulf was made to stand at the back and observe as the smith went through the piles of rough forged bars, examining them, testing them with a saw blade, separating them into piles. Then, after a long time fussing over the material, he was satisfied.

Dengir took a pair of bars from different piles, and at his

direction the junior smiths heated those bars, forged them together and then folded them. They repeatedly heated and bent them double and forged them together again. This process was repeated four or five times as Ordulf watched in confusion. He had never in his life seen odd bars of steel being folded and forged together again in this way.

Some of the smaller bars were forged together in pairs and twisted instead of folded. Two smiths would take the heated bars in great, flat-headed tongs and twist them against each other's grip like men fighting over a shield, each trying to spin it the other way for advantage. The twisted bar was like decorative iron work that could adorn a lord's carriage, but it was most certainly some form of steel, not iron. Ordulf could not fathom the purpose, and nor could he form the words to ask. So, he just watched in rapt fascination and doubt. This was all now alien to him.

Once the smith had four different larger bars, three twisted and one larger and longer folded bar, his juniors pumped the bellows vigorously as Dengir piled charcoal high and brought the fire to its fullest heat. He carefully piled the three twisted bars together in a stack, one above the other. The smith watched the fire intently; Ordulf could feel the tension in the room. There was now a large amount of steel, in three bars, and joining them successfully without cracks or flaws would require immense skill. He could see that the heated portion of the stack was at the highest temperature that steel would allow before it spat fire and crumbled. He was concerned, but he kept silent and waited.

The master suddenly withdrew the pile of three bars from the fire, steel glowing the colour of the sun in that dark space and laid them on the anvil. Then he did something Ordulf had not seen before. He started singing. Gently, the song started, and the juniors struck the blazing bars firmly with their great hammers. Faster and higher his voice went, and the strikes became more forceful and the impacts more frequent. He stopped with a stamp of his foot as the metal went a deep red, and he inspected it for only a few heartbeats before grunting to himself and returning it to the forge fire.

The atmosphere in the room relaxed noticeably. Ordulf watched with interest; clearly that had been the most difficult part.

Then the glowing metal returned from the forge once more, and once more the smith started singing. This time it was a chant, deep and resonant. The hammers fell much slower, harder and with more spacing between hits. They worked the bar from the centre outwards, alternating blows seamlessly without a word, guided by the sound of the master's singing. Ordulf was deeply impressed. His master in Minden had used a language of grunts and whistles and foot tapping because it was faster than speaking, but it was also slightly inflexible and hard to predict, hard for the apprentices to get into the rhythm of.

This song, this chant that the old Norse smith used, was flowing and almost sensuous. Ordulf found himself anticipating the strength and speed of the hammer blows before they fell. He started to understand the sing-song direction, each note not only depicting the falling blow but also, with its tune and rhythm, helping direct the next one. This was the best hammer team he had ever seen. Ordulf watched, drinking in every detail of this alien skill until the smith set aside the bar and left the forge to cool.

Ordulf didn't want to go back to the longhouse that night. He wanted to see what would become of that strange, twisted metal billet next. He cornered Otto in the longhouse that evening and described what he had seen in the forge.

'It was remarkable the way the smith controlled the hammers with a song. I don't know how to describe it. Have you seen it being done? Do you know why they twist the steel in the blade, or why they use so many different parts of metal of different types?'

Ordulf asked, the questions that he had held simmering in his head gushing forth in a rapid torrent. Otto held up his hands to slow the onslaught.

'No, Ordulf. I know nothing about swordsmithing. I have never witnessed any sword making, and it's not part of my job to stand around watching a blacksmith. I will ask Dengir tomorrow when I take you to the forge in the morning, if you promise to calm down and let me eat.'

Ordulf ate his evening meal and slept, mind racing over the possibilities and purpose of the crazed patterns in the metal.

The next day, Ordulf was waiting in the yard for a good while before Otto emerged. He was desperate to go to the forge and get answers. He practically jogged to the smithy, with Otto struggling to keep up and snapping at him irritably to slow down. When they arrived at the forge, Dengir was not even there.

'Ordulf, I have to return,' said Otto. 'I cannot just stand here waiting. I have duties to perform.'

'Just wait a few more moments. I am sure he will be here soon.'

As he was speaking, Dengir walked into the yard and Ordulf practically shoved Otto into his path with a meaty hand on the smaller man's arm. Otto shook his hand off, his patience at the limit, and started talking to Dengir. Ordulf tried to catch what words he could understand from the flow. Dengir cut the Saxon slave off and spoke just a few words before walking off towards the forge.

Otto shrugged and turned around to face Ordulf. 'He says he will not explain it. You will either understand the song of steel or you will not, and you will learn by watching and doing, not talking. Sorry.' Otto shrugged, turned and left the yard, leaving the frustrated Ordulf standing alone in the morning light, deep in thought.

The song of steel? How can I understand without being told?

He remembered the rhythm and the flow of the song, how he had started to anticipate the strokes of the hammer team without explanation despite not knowing the words or understanding the rules. He sighed and followed Dengir into the forge building, hoping they would once again be working on the twisted billet.

He was not disappointed. Once the fire was set and the hammer team ready, the master smith brought the bigger, folded bar out and put the half-finished billet on the anvil with it. The large bar was stacked with the billet from the previous day, and the song started again. Ordulf watched enraptured as Dengir directed the forging of the billet into a rough sword blank. They forged the folded bar onto the outside of the twisted billet, wrapping it around the tip, and then forged it along the other side until it almost completely encased the one within.

The finished billet was then forged into a sword in much the same way as Ordulf was used to, except it was broader and flatter, and it had a less pronounced fuller. The work took all day and most of the next, then the song was finished for the last time. After a long period of inspection by the master, the rough blade was set aside to cool as another, simpler blade billet was brought out to be worked on.

Ordulf had hoped to be involved but was instead given a piece of what he recognised as plain iron the thickness of his thumb and the length of his hand. He was then given a small knife, which he thought was probably a skinning knife. The smith pointed at the small billet, then towards the other forge and then back to the skinning knife. The message was clear: make this from that.

A simple enough task. Ordulf was a little disappointed. He had not made such a simple thing as a test since he was a lowly apprentice. The Ordulf from a month ago would have bridled, been sullen and resented the banality of the task. But that Ordulf was gone. Instead, he decided to take the opportunity to learn about the forge and work out how best to maintain and move the heat around, how strongly to work the bellows and how long to heat the unfamiliar metal. He was glad to be finally doing his first piece of forging at the unfamiliar smithy.

In previous days, he might have tried to show off and make something more than asked, something better or more elaborate. Instead, he simply made the best copy he could, focusing on the fine details of the upcurve towards the tip of the blade, the way the profile varied along the length, the thicker spine and wickedly sharp edge. By the end of the day, it was forged, finished, sharpened and fitted with a simple wooden handle, burned onto the tang and held in place with an unfamiliar glue that an apprentice produced and that smelled sour and sickly. He inspected the finished knife at length, giving it more time than the simple item really deserved, noting whether its finish was correct, eyeing the profile and straightness of the edge, testing the firmness of the handle's fit before leaving the glue to set overnight.

The old master smith inspected his work in the morning, passing it back and forth between himself and the junior who had been watching Ordulf, grunting and talking in low tones. The conversation was short; the smith nodded approvingly at Ordulf. He found himself desperately hoping that the smith really was pleased; he desired approval of the old master. He tried to shut the feeling out as it had no utility to him or his goals, but it remained nonetheless. The smith beckoned Ordulf to follow him, and they went back through to the forge.

Inside, he saw the smith was preparing to work again on the strange sword blade. The fire burned low and hot between the walls of the forge. Two apprentices stood by, hammers in hand, eyes on the old master. The master settled himself on his little stool by the forge. Ordulf had found the forge heat unbearable that close for extended periods. It made the wool of his trousers singe and smoke, so he had worked the forge standing and leaning over, despite the uncomfortable low height of the anvil. But Dengir simply bore it, a resilience born of decades of exposure, his lower height and better position allowing him to crouch right down low over the anvil as he carefully directed the strikes and laid his own blows.

Dengir started the heating at the tip of the sword blank and began working in the central fuller. On this blade, which was already quite thin, the fuller was not made very deep. There was only a slight depression in the metal, and the process was quickly worked from tip to tang. Next, he carefully formed the bevels, sometimes hammering on his own when some detail needed correcting, other times merely singing the song of steel softly to the juniors as he let them work bigger sections with lustier blows.

Eventually he was satisfied, and he carefully set the nearly finished sword to one side. Ordulf recognised the next preparations. They let the fire between the forge walls die down to a medium heat, raking, covering and working the bellows more slowly until Dengir was satisfied. He started heating the front portion of the blade in the coals, moving it slowly back and forth, getting an even heat into the blade. He pulled it out when it had reached a warm, orange glow and let it cool, the ring of blackness moving down the steel to the point and then dissipating. Ordulf smiled to himself. Chasing the shadows. Some things were always the same.

Then, once the blade was cooled a second time, the smith rebuilt the temperature in the coals and went to work, sawing the blade back and forth through the heat, standing for this part, eyes never leaving the forge. He heated the entire length of the blade, ready for quenching.

Then, when Ordulf became sure that something must be horribly wrong, as the blade was glowing almost at the heat he would hammer it, Dengir whipped the blade from the forge and, twisting, plunged it into the water trough. Steam burst from the water and Ordulf waited, straining his ears for the telltale crack or clicking that would surely show the blade failing.

No such sound came to him. The forge died down in the background. Sweating, charcoal-stained apprentices stood back or mopped their brows on their aprons, bellows abandoned, glowing coals left to cool. Dengir withdrew the still-steaming blade from the water and looked it up and down. It had curved slightly to one side. He jammed the point into a wooden block embedded into the floor at his feet, wrapped his leather-clad leg around the still-sizzling blade and bore down on it with his own weight. For three or four heartbeats, he rapidly flexed the blade under his wiry thigh and then released it, raising it once more into the air to inspect. One more rapid flex under his thigh and he was satisfied. The blade was arrow-straight and uncracked.

Ordulf longed to inspect the blade, to test its hardness, but the smith did no such test, and Ordulf was sent to continue his work.

Days passed with Ordulf helping around the forge. The strange blade was ground and finished by one of the junior smiths on a grinding wheel, which he powered himself via a footplate and a cunning wooden mechanism.

His lessons with Otto were progressing much faster now that he regarded them as beneficial to him, not a chore. During the mornings and evenings, he tried as much as possible to speak to his fellows in the longhouse, pointing at things and making an inquisitive face. Some of them were not interested in this game and ignored him or brushed him off. Some of them, particularly the old woman and one of the young women, were delighted to help and found his brutalising of the words he tried to repeat hilarious. More and more, Ordulf started to notice the gaze and amused expressions of the young woman who, he learned with a stumbling attempt at asking, was called Brunhild.

Ordulf was tempted to explore this further, but he knew that the woman was the partner of one of the other slaves, a surly man whose name he did not remember. They usually slept together in the longhouse. It would not benefit him to make enemies, so he pushed that desire away and was merely polite and distant with Brunhild. It was not as though he could have a secret liaison with her. There was nowhere to go.

The longhouse offered very little privacy, and one of the things that Ordulf had become accustomed to was their almost complete lack of modesty or sense of shame. On the colder nights when he first arrived, no one was taking their clothes off in the open for practical reasons. The longhouse was never bitterly cold, but it wasn't warm either. People tended to change clothes infrequently and under the covers. Washing them was as hard as drying them. Space around the fire was limited.

The main indicator of their disinterest in modesty came at night. One evening, early in Ordulf's captivity, he was shocked when, before most of the occupants had returned from the day's work, he walked back from collecting food to find that the slaves in the bed next to him, the other young woman and her bed mate, were vigorously rutting. They paid him no attention whatsoever, and not knowing what to do, he went to the far side of the house and sat, wide-eyed, next to the old woman who appeared utterly oblivious to the goings-on just the other side of the house.

He soon learned that this was commonplace. The warriors were even more brazen, as befitted their station, he supposed. They would couple with their wives at night with the entire longhouse full, uncaring of the dozing or sleeping people around them.

One day when summer was in full bloom and the weather could be described as almost stifling, he came back from working at the smithy to the longhouse to find one of the warriors' wives stark naked, facing the door not two paces in front of him, working on a plait in her hair with the help of Brunhild, who was likewise free of her clothes, although hidden behind the freewoman. Even used as he was to the lack of modesty in the house, Ordulf was flustered and, for an agonising moment, wasn't sure if he should turn around and leave or just carry on as normal. His indecision left him simply standing there, eyes flicking around, looking flushed and nervous like a boy who has been caught stealing food.

The freewoman just gave him a confused look and carried on with her plait. Ordulf couldn't help looking her up and down. She was delicately built, fit and lithe with narrow hips and a slim chest. He suddenly saw Brunhild was locking eyes with him, an amused smile on her face. She had moved around slightly, her hands still helping the warrior's wife work her long brown hair into the thick plait. Moving around had exposed the whole left side of her body to Ordulf, who was still frozen to the spot, trying to maintain eye contact. Her smile became broader. She raised an eyebrow and glanced down, indicating her body with her eyes. Ordulf's restraint cracked, and he snuck a quick glance down as he started walking forward past the naked pair. His eyes lingered on the side of a full, round breast, half-hidden behind the end of her hair, before she laughed. He snapped his eyes back up to see her laughing at him, eyes full of mirth. The freewoman, exasperated, removed a hand from her hair to shoo him away. Chastened, he hurried off to busy himself with food.

The door opened again, and Otto walked in, barely even

glancing at the women. Brunhild spoke to him as he passed and laughed again, nodding her head at Ordulf. Otto shook his head and tutted as he walked over to Ordulf, who was still flushed with embarrassment.

'Brunhild doesn't think you have ever seen a naked woman before. She wants to know if she should come over so you can have a proper look.' Otto was washing his hands and face next to the basin as he spoke. Brunhild had finished plaiting the freewoman's hair and was now helping her dress, her body moving and swaying while she did it in a manner Ordulf found impossible to ignore. She spoke to Otto again over her shoulder. The freewoman had taken up her thin cloak and walked out of the door, leaving the three of them alone.

'She is now certain that you have never seen a real woman naked before,' said Otto, in a dry, almost bored, voice. Brunhild was now striding over to them, eyes still flashing with mirth. She hopped down from the raised side platform to the dry earth below, hair flowing, body lithe in motion.

Ordulf forced himself to look away. He scolded himself internally. He was here only to survive and not to cause trouble. He didn't need this. Brunhild came across and stood next to Otto, arms crossed beneath her breasts, and spoke to Ordulf, words full of teasing, half that he understood, half that did not cross the language barrier.

Otto rolled his eyes. 'She suggests you are too old to be so shy around a woman. She suggests you take her now so that your shyness is cured.' Otto finished drying his hands on the hem of his tunic and turned to leave. 'Whatever you want to call it, I think you two can take care of the rest. I've taught you enough words to deal with this alone – I have to go to the main hall.'

Otto strode away towards the door, leaving Ordulf standing in the corner, Brunhild looking at him with her mocking expression.

She slowly paced over to him, languidly, confidence and mirth radiating from her, bright eyes teasing him. His temper and caution overcame the other feelings that were stirring uncontrollably in his body. He wanted to neither cause trouble nor be mocked, but he wanted her more strongly than he could believe. She was a vision of beauty in that half-light, staring at him with her mocking eyes. He thought she was the most beautiful thing he had ever seen. *Perhaps I should…* He shook his head free of the thought and, pushing gently past her, walked off to the far end of the house and the promised seclusion of the latrines.

His intent to avoid causing problems backfired badly. That evening, he found himself the target of much mocking from the younger women, both slaves and wives, that he did not understand. Assuming they were merely making fun of his embarrassment from earlier, he tried to ignore it. What he couldn't ignore were the clouded looks and hostile glances from the men. He had done nothing to wrong them. He had resisted the temptation to cause trouble, yet as he sat by the fire eating, Brunhild's man was gazing at him with what looked like anger or contempt.

Ordulf walked over to the bench at the side of the hall, mind racing, trying to make sense of the situation. Otto crossed his path as he went and grabbed his arm forcefully.

'Otto, what is going on? What have I done?'

Otto stood tight-lipped and looked around out of the corner of his eye. 'Come outside in a moment. I will not explain it here; I have my own position to consider.'

Ordulf released the smaller man's arm, mouth open with unformed protest. Otto strode briskly for the door and left. Ordulf went to his bench and looked up at the old woman as she came around handing out bowls of food. She shuffled past him without giving him one.

Furious, he snapped to his feet and barged out of the door. Otto was sitting on a stool in the low, open-sided building at the back of the yard that was used for storage in summer and would have animals living in it during the late autumn and winter.

Ordulf strode over, fists clenched and temples throbbing. Otto stood and held out his hand placatingly.

'So tell me, what poison has spread in the group?' said Ordulf. 'Does that shit lie and say I stole his woman? I did nothing. I didn't touch her, despite her attempts to woo me.'

Otto sighed and rolled his eyes. 'Ah, that explains it,' he said, his whole posture relaxing and a look of sympathy crossing his face.

'*That explains it?* So it was him! By God, I will split his head for this!' Ordulf was raging now, barely able to keep his voice down, all notion of keeping a low profile lost in his swirling mind.

'No, you will not, and you misunderstand me. Look, just stay calm and listen. There is much you do not understand.'

This drew an angry glare from Ordulf, but the smith remained silent and waited.

'Brunhild told them you refused her and that you looked scared. She said you ran from her and went to hide in the latrines. The warrior's wife, Turid, told everyone that the sight of her nakedness seemed to shock you, to unman you, and said she believed you were indeed terrified.'

'What? I wasn't scared of them. I was just trying to avoid trouble with her man!' Ordulf said, raising his hands in exasperation. 'I wasn't scared of Turid – I thought that I might be punished for looking at her because you told me that to touch a freewoman was death!'

'Brunhild doesn't belong to Geir, her man. They are slaves. They couple together because she chooses to at the time. She is free to bed any other, and so is he. It means nothing if you had accepted her advances. What matters is that they think you are afraid of a woman! Now, listen. I should have explained this before, and I will remedy that now. To the Norse, the most important principle in a man's life is his honour – his lack of fear, his respect for others and his ability to do what is right despite danger or threat. It's a whole code of behaviour, and those who exemplify it are admired while those who don't are reviled.'

Otto lowered his voice and leaned in. 'The most important of those attributes by far is the lack of fear. A Norseman is supposed to be unmoved by danger, fear of failure, fear of death. He is especially supposed to be unafraid of standing up for himself, his family and friends and, above all, his lord. If a Norse warrior was said by any man to have run in fear from a woman, he would have to duel that man to the death to save his honour, and even then he might still be shunned.'

Otto put his hand flat on Ordulf's chest for emphasis. 'The only reason you are still allowed in that hall is that you are a slave and not bound by those rules in principle. However, those ideas are still deeply ingrained, and everyone is judged by them, no matter their status.'

Ordulf's anger turned to surprise and then incredulity.

'So I am damned for refusing to rut with her?'

'No, listen to me. Refusing her is fine. You are damned for *fearing* to rut with her. The reason doesn't matter. Whether it was out of fear of another man's anger or fear of her naked body, it doesn't matter. You. Showed. Fear. Of. A. Naked. Woman.' Otto poked Ordulf's chest with his finger to emphasise the words. 'And that is inexcusable to them.'

'Look!' he exclaimed, exasperated. 'You arrived here with a reputation. You were the big, wild Christian who beat Leif flat with nothing but a hammer and fought off two others while you did it. You are the bull it took four men to capture. They expected to see that strength in you. Instead, they saw you beg for your life in the yard, they saw you felled with a single blow by Leif and now they hear you run to hide from some tits.' Otto shook his head and tutted. 'Ordulf, your reputation hangs by a thread, even for a slave. I understand you not wanting to make trouble, but that fear will be your undoing. You cannot behave that way. You do not have to seek trouble, but you cannot hide from it. You cannot recklessly challenge others, but you cannot allow any challenge to go without reply. You *must* learn to think like the Norse, or you will be worse than nothing to them. You must stand up for yourself and show no fear of the world, or you will be branded a coward forever. The jarl will hear of it, and he will sell you to the farms rather than be associated with a coward or have one under his roof.'

Ordulf was silent, his eyes fixed on the ground. He chuckled, which surprised Otto.

'So I must not be the hot-tempered youth who causes conflict or the acquiescent slave who avoids trouble. I must walk a middle path?'

'That is not an inaccurate way of thinking of it,' Otto said, with a smile at last on his face. 'There is more subtlety than that, but I think you will find your way.'

'So how do I fix this now?'

'Well, the men think you a coward, so they will likely seek to humiliate you. Maybe tonight, maybe tomorrow, but they will seek to enforce their dominance over you while they are not afraid of you. You *must not* let that happen.'

'I never saw they were afraid of me before!'

Otto nodded smugly. 'Exactly! You never saw it because they acted as if you did not scare them.'

Ordulf rolled his eyes at the now-apparent obviousness of that and cursed his lack of perception.

'Ordulf, you arrived as the giant who could crush warriors,' Otto continued. 'Do you know that on the first night you set yourself to sleep on a pile of everyone's bedclothes and only the old woman had the courage to come and retrieve hers?' He laughed. 'Ordulf, half the slaves in the house would have gone cold that night because of you. They didn't dare do anything about it, but also they did not whinge or complain. They were outwardly unperturbed. They pretended it was nothing until the old woman shooed you off the pile.

Let me give you an example of how that works for the Norse. A couple of years ago, the jarl and his warriors had to settle a feud with a rival. The rival had insulted the jarl by not showing up when called for a feast and sending no apology. When confronted, the rival suggested that he should have sent his men's wives instead, as they were more suitable company – a grave insult, implicitly questioning the jarl's manhood. The jarl sent six of his men round to kill everyone on one of the rival's farms, including three warriors who were part of the rival's family.'

Ordulf's eyes widened. 'He committed a massacre of innocent people to avenge an insult? That's insane!'

'Yes he did, and no it's not,' said Otto, without a trace of agreement at the proposition. 'It's entirely normal, and the rival was merely testing the jarl's resolve. Here, if you insult another man or question his honour unfairly, he has many means of redress. He can appeal to the court or his lord for judgement, he can call the man to a duel or he can simply take revenge and hope the court later rules it fair. The revenge does not have to be on the perpetrator personally; it can be on his family or anyone under his care. The law is very clear on this. I think the idea is to dissuade the starting of conflicts as you cannot protect everyone you love from a powerful enemy.' Otto's face was stern.

Ordulf sat back. 'I cannot believe you would think it is normal to kill families over an insult. Such a thing would be unspeakable evil at home.'

'This is now your home, and this is the way here. So it simply is normal, and you need to understand it,' Otto said forcefully. 'Anyway, his warriors burned the longhouse with the enemy inside it. The three warriors who were inside burst out of one door together to try and fight free. They were all killed, but one of them had fouled one of the jarl's men with his own shield and twisted it violently, breaking his arm very badly between elbow and wrist, with the bone coming through the skin.' Otto indicated with his own arm the mechanism and manner of the gruesome injury.

'The jarl's command had been for the warriors to return immediately the farmers were dead to present their actions publicly as the law demands. The injured warrior decided it was more important to do this, and include his testimony, than to go and have his arm set. For three hours, they waited for the lawgiver to hear them, and they presented their testimony in full. The warrior simply ignored his broken arm, which was bent and twisted most horribly, until this duty was completed.'

Ordulf scoffed. 'I don't believe this nonsense. Why would he do that?'

'Believe it, I was there when he returned and saw it myself. He made sure he completed his duty just in case his testimony made the difference; he would not risk his lord being ruled against and have the act ruled as murder. By the time he went to have his arm set, it was too late to heal properly, and it had to be removed.'

'That's stupidity!' said Ordulf, pacing a small circle in front of Otto.

'No it isn't, it's *drengskapr*. It showed his honour and his lack of fear, and he is still very highly regarded for it. He is regarded as one of the jarl's most loyal and respected men, although he cannot now fight. He manages a village in the jarl's lands as the lawgiver.'

Ordulf shook his head in amazement. 'I would get my arm fixed.'

'And that is expected. You are a slave, not a Norseman,' Otto said with a tinge of contempt creeping into his voice.

'So how can I avoid humiliation? I am not allowed to harm another slave,' Ordulf said, arms spread and palms upturned.

'You are not allowed to harm them or damage them in a way that would interfere with their work, just as you are not allowed to damage any of the jarl's property, but no one said you are not allowed to stop them if they try and humiliate you,' Otto half whispered, cautiously. 'Now I must go to the hall and pretend to be busy. I don't want them to know I helped you. You are dangerously close to being untouchable.' And with that final needle, he walked away, leaving Ordulf exasperated and wondering what form the humiliation would take and how to defend against it.

He didn't have to wait long. He strode into the longhouse and did his best to ignore the stares and contempt. *Be imperturbable.* In truth, it wasn't that hard; he was so fed up and so physically unafraid that he barely had to act. He went to the pot over the low fire with a bowl and spooned himself some food. Brunhild's man walked over to him from the side of the room, shoulders set aggressively and eyes full of contempt.

The man stopped and slapped the edge of the bowl Ordulf was holding, knocking it from his grasp and spilling it all over the ground by his feet, splattering his leg with steaming broth. Ordulf ignored the pain; he didn't move. He felt... pleasure, he suddenly realised. He now had an outlet for his frustration and rage. And that outlet was standing glaring at him from half an arm's length away.

Ordulf slowly straightened from the pot, every move deliberate and economical, like a predator stalking its prey. He raised his eyes to lock with the man's. What was his name – Geir? He didn't much care. He drew himself up to his full height and looked down at the man.

And he slowly smiled. The smile held no joy. It was the smile of a wolf looking at a lamb. The lamb suddenly realised his error; the smugness and contempt dropped from his face like a falling veil. Ordulf watched, fascinated, as the man tried to maintain his composure. He could not back down from the provocation he had just made – everyone in the house was watching. Just as he saw the man's eyes flick to Ordulf's neck and his arm start to swing forward in a punch, Ordulf brought his hand up to block.

By luck more than skill, and with Ordulf's exceptional hand speed from all those years swinging a hammer – he could move his hands faster even than most small men – he caught Geir's punch in his own hand. Geir's eyes went wide; the mask slipped completely. Ordulf's smile grew. He whipped his other hand around and grabbed the back of the smaller man's head. Twisting the captured arm with his right hand, he pushed down on the back of Geir's head with his left, a move he had used on the patch a number of times. Then Geir was forced to bend over double, and he tangled the man's legs with his own and slammed him onto the dusty floor. He pulled the captured hand behind Geir's back and sat on him, completely trapping him.

Then, smiling, he picked up his bowl from the dust and raised it to another slave near him, gesturing to the pot. There was a moment of hesitation as the man faced the choice of either refusing or accepting the task. Accepting would mean publicly recognising Ordulf's superiority, refusing… well. He took another long look into Ordulf's predatory eyes, smiling up at him from on top of the still-wriggling Geir, and decided against refusing. He walked calmly over, filled Ordulf's bowl and handed it back to him.

Ordulf enjoyed that meal. He was sitting comfortably by the fire. He took his time over the hot broth, ignoring everyone in the room and whistling to himself between mouthfuls. His seat stopped wriggling after a while and apparently just concentrated on breathing. It must have been hard to breathe in that position. *Poor seat.*

When he was done, Ordulf casually stretched his legs and rose to his feet, ignoring the dusty and wheezing man who got up after him. He strode over towards his area, then paused and looked at the more comfortable and central position that Geir usually occupied. Casually throwing Geir's bedding to one side, he moved his own things over and arranged them on the wooden boards nearer the fire. He sat on a stool, back against one of the supporting posts, and sighed contentedly.

The rest of the longhouse occupants went back to their business. Geir shuffled over to his new bed's location sullenly, trying to maintain his own dignity, which was hard under the circumstances. Otto pulled up a small box next to Ordulf and sat on it.

'That was well done,' he said, trying to keep his face neutral but eyes brightly smiling. 'I was worried you would rip his head off, but you did it just right.'

They chatted for a while, and Otto continued his Norse lessons. Ordulf had progressed beyond individual words and was picking up simple sentences and constructs. He couldn't yet have a conversation, and following when someone spoke rapidly was still like trying to understand the wind howl, but he could now name most of the objects in the house and make and understand some simple requests related to them.

When the fire had died down and everyone had settled into bed, he lay on his back, perhaps as satisfied as he had been so far in captivity. Suddenly, someone arrived at his bed. In the very dim light, he realised it was Brunhild and then realised she was naked. She stood there, looking down on him, hands on hips, awaiting his response. Most of the house's occupants had only just settled into bed; he knew almost none of them would be asleep and everyone would be watching to see what happened. He knew he had only one choice, but as he felt a rapid stir under his sheets he realised it wasn't a difficult one to make. If swiving this slave was required of him, then, by God, he would carry out that duty earnestly and fully. It was too dark to see facial expressions, but Ordulf smiled anyway and pulled aside the furs, making space for her to lie next to him. She dropped down to her knees instead, one each side of his thighs, straddling him, and pressed her face into his. One of her hands took one of his and pressed it to her breast, while she kissed him fiercely, biting his lip hard enough to draw blood. Then the hand let go of his and disappeared down between them to pull his trousers roughly out of the way of what she sought.

Ordulf revelled in the freedom from modesty and worry about shaming himself. He cared not that everyone was awake and probably listening or even watching. *Damn their sleep.* They had thought him afraid to lie with a woman, and he decided he would make certain that no one thought that again. He was tired of the fear; he was tired of the helplessness; he was tired of feeling lost and alone and out of control. He put a hand in Brunhild's soft, flowing hair and let go of all his worries. *Let them know I am not afraid.*

CHAPTER 16

KILLING FOR A KING

Uppsala
Late autumn 1116

Imperial dispatch

*For Sir Hans Metel of Oldenburg, captain of the Lower
Saxon forces*

Sir Hans

*I have reported our success in the subjugation of this land and
received instructions that our efforts in God's name are complete
for the year. We are to return the bulk of the forces home and
retain only garrison forces.*

*You know my opinion on this matter, but our orders are clear.
My request to continue the offensive has been refused with
great finality. We cannot be seen to continue a campaign that
the emperor has decreed complete and the pope has blessed as
a great victory. We will, from now on, only receive supplies for
moderate garrison forces and so have no choice but to return the*

army home for autumn. We will suffer a hard winter up here with so few men. I have decided to remain myself, to ensure the good governance of the province. I regret that I will not be able to join you, but your orders are to gather the Lower Saxon forces and return home with them. They will not be part of the garrison.

I commend you for your successful command of the northern clearances. My last task for you this year is to return home and ensure my family and lands are secure and well managed. I will not return this winter, nor, if I have to plan the preparations for the next crusade, will I return in the spring. Look to my son; he will need to continue his training. Tell him to be diligent and look after his mother. For my wife, ensure she has a good steward to manage the estates in my absence. I enclose a private letter to her. Ensure she alone reads it.

I regret that I will not see you again until next year. I will send instructions for the preparations of next year's campaign as soon as it is clear what form it will take. You will need to raise and bring the men of Lower Saxony next year. I am sure that after your accomplishments during this great crusade they will flock to your side in my absence with no less vigour when called.

Count Adolf

Ragnvald was nervous. They were all nervous. Dark times were abroad for them to be discussing what they were discussing in the place they were discussing it. The sun was setting as he strode up the steps to the great hall in the centre of Uppsala and went through the vast and open doors, which were left locked open behind him. A king's hall, but standing empty without a king, the doors were never closed, and never would be until a king was once more inside. A Symbol that the hall would give no comfort, no warmth, no home to any man who was not the king. So the doors would remain open until a new king was chosen, the very matter they were here to discuss, a gathering of the most powerful lords of Sweden.

The hall of the king in Uppsala was the grandest structure in all of Sweden, besides the temple just a mile to the north. But there was no longer a king of all the Swedes and no sons to claim his place if they could. The new king would be decided at the Dísablót in the spring of the new year when the jarls gathered for the great spring festival, a king who would decide the course and fate of the Swedes against the crusader threat.

Jarl Ragnvald was determined that the new king of Sweden would be King Sigurd of Norway. King Eric had died shortly after returning from Denmark, but not before he had told others of his desire for Øystein to be offered the crown after he and Magnus died. And Magnus had died, somewhere in the ruin of Aarhus, but Øystein's kingship had been short-lived, he had been trapped at Fyrkat and slaughtered, leaving Magnus' second son, Sigurd, newly on the throne in Oslo.

And the Swedish jarls had been split. Some contended that Eric's instructions specifically meant Øystein, not Sigurd, and others that the command of a dead king meant nothing. The remainder believed it did not matter which king sat on the Norwegian throne and that the old king's wishes that the thrones should be joined should be respected. Ragnvald had called the lords of Sweden to this hall to decide the matter.

A Norwegian jarl, Jarl Steinar, had come to Uppsala at his invitation, quietly seeking support for King Sigurd and testing the strength of his claim. Jarl Steinar had waited for two weeks for the most powerful Swedish lords to arrive to discuss the proposed union. He had met privately with Ragnvald who, in the king's absence, ruled Uppsala. Ragnvald had found the man to be quiet and careful, quite unlike many of the Swedish warlords. That care had belied a fierce intelligence and blazing conviction in what he did. Steinar was not a great warrior, but Ragnvald could see why Sigurd had sent him; the man was cunning and ruthless. Ragnvald found him impossible to like but impossible not to respect.

'Is this all who would come?' asked Jarl Frode, who was standing impatiently by the empty dais and who looked around at Ragnvald entering the room. With no king to occupy it and the household disbanded, the hall was empty, eerie, the light from a small fire in the central hearth barely touching the corners of the vast space that so often contained so much life.

Ragnvald cast his gaze around the roughly two dozen men in the room and nodded sadly. 'It appears so. We have received lies, excuses and refusals from everyone else of note.' Frode scowled and kicked over a dusty bench.

'Our enemies gather even as we speak, and half the great lords of Sweden won't gather to even discuss this?' Frode asked bitterly.

'No,' replied Ragnvald flatly, disappointment edging into his voice.

'It should not be a surprise. What we have gathered to discuss is treason,' grumbled Jarl Erling, a stout, wild, bearded man from the north of Svealand.

'No!' shouted Ragnvald, slamming his fist onto the thick table. 'We discuss the last command of our king, his dying wish and the key to our people's future. Do not darken this hall by suggesting we plot treason. No. We are not gathered here to betray our country. We are gathered in this noble place to save it.'

Erling shuffled and looked at his feet, discomfort written clear on his face. 'Well, it would seem the rest disagree, so what do we do without them?'

'Keep calm heads, brothers,' a new voice spoke. 'We have, what, half the power of Sweden gathered here? None would come to hear this matter if they did not at least consider this Norwegian king's claim. So let us lay out the options and decide on a course.'

Ragnvald nodded, fixing his eyes on the speaker. Jarl Gustav was old, the oldest man in the room, he had rich lands on the coast south of Uppsala where the people called him jarl and he was widely respected for both his wisdom and his broad network of alliances. A long, steel-grey beard, tightly braided, lay over crossed arms that bore a network of scars white against knurled brown skin. Jarl Gustav, known as the Raven's Claw, was so named because his left hand was missing the forefinger, and his thumb was bent back towards his wrist, broken and scarred. He had taken the injury decades before, in a raid in the Baltics. Despite his injury, which left him unable to properly wield a shield, he had killed a man who challenged him for his lands and stayed in power for all the passing years. Only a fool would not listen while Jarl Gustav spoke, and there were not many fools in that gathering.

'Firstly, who among our people would have a claim to the crown? By power or by right?' Gustav asked the gathering, his clawed left hand sweeping around the group as he spoke. He answered his question before anyone else could. 'There is Jarl Harnsted, the cousin of Eric. Who else?' Gustav unfolded his arms and gestured around the assembled lords. 'Has anyone heard of another gathering support?'

Jarl Frode spoke up. 'Aye, there is another. One of Jarl Alf's men approached me, asking if I would support a claim.'

Ragnvald raised an eyebrow. Jarl Alf was a powerful lord from the border with Norway. He had not considered the man would seek the throne. Harnsted, on the other hand, had spent his entire life desperate for the power of the chair they gathered around, the hall they gathered in. Rumours suggested he had arranged a curse to be put on Eric to leave him childless. Widely despised outside his northern lands, he was nonetheless powerful and wealthy from the fur trade he controlled.

'Alf would try his hand? That might help; it would split the support with Harnsted,' said Gustav. Ragnvald stared at the table in deep thought.

'What is your position, Ragnvald? Many would have thought you would contest for this hall. You can spit on it from your lands, it is close to your home and you have a famous name and a powerful force at your call. Many lords here would support you.' Gustav was fixing him with a questioning gaze.

'I came here expecting you to declare yourself for the kingship. You would have my support over Harnsted,' called out one jarl, and several men murmured their assent.

Gustav nodded around the room. 'You could probably take the throne right here and now, cite the threat of the crusade. No one would be able to stop you. Why would you so readily give up the chance for a foreign king?'

A tense silence fell over the room as men waited to see Ragnvald's reaction. Ragnvald walked up to the dais and stared at the empty throne with its carved sides and magnificent headboard. The power that flowed from that wooden seat was almost tangible. He could feel the lure of it, its history and the presence of those who came before. He gently toyed with his neatly braided beard, deep in thought. He remembered the words of a dying king.

'There was a time,' he began finally, 'when Eric was ruling and disappointing so many of us that I considered challenging him for his cowardice and taking the throne for myself.' He paused, tapping his fingernail on the battered wood of that ancient seat before turning away and stepping back down into the circle. 'But that time is gone. We all saw the chaos of a divided army with many weak kings. The answer to the problem is not many new kings but one single, strong one. I hear Sigurd is a leader, a killer of men, a man to follow, worthy of the title Nordking.' He turned and fixed his gaze on Steinar. 'You know him. You have seen his worth. Should we entrust the future of our people to your king?'

Jarl Steinar smiled. 'I would say he was worthy in any case – he is my oath-sworn lord – but the task is made easier because it is nothing but the truth. King Sigurd is the best leader of men and the best warrior I know. He is young and impetuous and head-strong, but he takes advice when worthy men give it. He is no proud or greedy tyrant, and his men would follow him anywhere. He did not wish to be king – he did not expect to be king – but the moment it was his duty he never gave it a second thought. He cares about one thing and one thing only: saving his people from the fate of his father and brother. He would be a good king to Sweden, and a terrible one to our foes.' Steinar gazed around the room in silence as his words sunk in.

'We have no wish to be used on an expedition of revenge by a foreign king,' said Erling, eyes narrow with suspicion.

Steinar shrugged. 'It is not his intent. He wants to prevent more loss, not rage over that which is done. I cannot prove it but it is the truth.'

'To bring a foreign king to rule us, to sit in this hall our fathers built, in the country we fought to keep our own for so long? To give it away? The thought sickens me. I will vote against it,' said Erling with barely concealed disgust.

Steinar was unmoved. 'King Sigurd will not come here and be humiliated at the Dísablót by being rejected. I need to know he has support for this unification before I leave. If you choose one of your own to be king, Sigurd will not come to contest it and risk a pointless war between our nations. There will be no war between Norsemen. Not now. You must welcome him willingly. It is that simple.'

Gustav stepped forward into the centre of the loose circle.

'There was a time, when Eric was yet a boy, when men spoke of me as a challenger to the previous king. Truth be told, I wanted it! I wanted it more than women or battle glory or gold. I wanted to be the king of the Swedes.' He chuckled mirthfully and gazed around at his audience, his claw hand resting hooked into his sword belt. 'The foolishness of youth. Perhaps I would have been a better king, but I doubt it. I had no plans beyond the claiming of it, no great notion of duty. It was the ultimate prize for a vain young man.' Then he took his hand off his belt and turned it over, looking at it ruefully. 'Then I received a sharp lesson about unchecked ambition. Now, I see the kingship for what it is: a burden to be borne by a man who is driven by duty, not pride.'

He turned to face Steinar. 'I don't know if you speak the truth, but I have heard a thousand liars in my life, and you don't smell like one. Your king has my support.' He stepped back out of the circle, and men around nodded in agreement. Gradually, all gazes turned to Ragnvald, and the room fell to silence. Ragnvald looked around, seeing the decision on a knife point. The kingship was still there if he chose to seize it. A lifetime's ambition, the pinnacle of his worldly desire. If he but reached out for it, his name would live forever in the rune stones and the skald songs. His eyes caught Gustav's and the man raised an eyebrow at him, staring at him pointedly. Ragnvald understood. The older jarl's little speech had been for an audience of one. A warning and a message. He made his decision. It was an easy one, and he had sealed it with his promise to a dying man.

'And mine,' Ragnvald said simply. With those two words, he dropped his close-held ambition to the floor, and the tension in the room evaporated. Other men voiced their agreement, and the chorus of assent rolled around the small group. Truly, most of them had only come to hear Ragnvald's decision and to follow it. 'But it is not enough. We must end the claims of the other contenders,' Ragnvald said bitterly. He knew that he would receive little support from the jarls who had refused to come. They would all have other candidates they preferred or would simply join the strongest candidate when his victory was assured.

'I will speak to Alf. He is a good man and was a close friend of my son before his death,' Gustav said sadly, biting back more words left unsaid.

Ragnvald arched an eyebrow. 'You are sure? You can talk a man out of the chance to be king? We must be certain, or we must find another way.'

'What else do you suggest?' said Erling, bristling.

'You know what I suggest,' replied Ragnvald softly. 'You all know the alternative.'

Jarl Erling blustered in protest through his beard. 'You would countenance murder to deny a candidate for the kingship at Dísablót by treachery? By the gods, you go too far, Ragnvald. You condemn yourself with your words. First you vote to give our land to a foreign king, and now you wish to murder those who oppose him? There is nothing but dishonour in this.' The heavily bearded man was shaking with anger, stabbing his finger at Ragnvald.

The insult cut Ragnvald deeply, and he knitted his brows together and lowered his voice. 'What else is there, Erling? I know you live close to Harnsted's lands. I know you have sympathy for his claim. But we must unite, and we cannot afford a fight among ourselves. The Dísablót is too late to decide who will be king. Plans must already be set, forces already in motion, or it will be too late.' His voice was low, placating. 'It might already be too late,' he added then, with a smile just for himself. 'We must do whatever it takes.'

Jarl Erling looked around the room, seeking support. There was none to be had in the hard-set faces around him.

'You know Harnsted better than any of us. Would he ever relinquish his claim?' Ragnvald asked.

Erling started to protest, but he deflated and shook his head. 'He would never give in. He is already gathering supporters, taking oaths as if he were already king. He asked me for my word, and I delayed a reply. I wanted to hear you first. His lands border mine, and he is much more powerful than I am, but he would be a terrible king. He is nothing but ambition and petty spite.'

Ragnvald nodded. 'So we all know what must be done.' He looked around the gathering. There were grim faces and narrowed eyes but no disagreement. 'Who has already sworn to him? Who would back his claim if it came to the force of spear and sword?'

'Jarl Birkir is the strongest, and Jarl Halvar is also his ally,' said Frode, stroking his beard in thought.

'Jarl Birkir is my friend – he is a good and honourable man!' Erling said.

'Too honourable to betray his oath to Harnsted?' asked Gustav, voice full of ice.

Erling gaped, appalled. Then he forced his mouth shut and nodded. 'Aye, I suppose he is.' He shook his head vehemently. 'Has it really come to this, brothers? We stand in the hall of our kings and plan the deaths of our own people to allow a foreign lord to rule us?'

'No, Erling. We plan the survival of our people by whatever means necessary.' Ragnvald put his hand on his sword. 'I need the oath of every man present that he will keep this discussion secret, on pain of death.' He looked around, questioning. All but Erling put their hands on their hilts, faces resolute. Erling took one last look around the room and reluctantly joined them.

The oath was sworn, and a cold breeze from the open doors made the small fire flicker, causing men to shiver and touch their hammers at the omen. The air was black with the night and with the shame of the men inside.

'So, we are committed. Gustav, you will deal with Jarl Alf. Convince him one way or another. He must make known that he renounces his claim, or he must disappear.'

Gustav nodded grimly at Ragnvald. 'It will be done.'

'Jarl Frode, you will deal with Halvar and his key supporters; he is nearest to your lands. Twenty nights from tonight, we will strike together, and it will be over before anyone can react. I will deal with Birkir and Harnsted. Birkir's hall is on the river that leads to Harnsted's lands, so we will have to take them both together. Kill as few as possible. If men can be convinced, do so. If not, be ruthless. We must avoid a cycle of blood feud.' He turned to look at the silent Steinar. 'You will come with me. You will see with your own eyes what we do to bring your king here, and you will tell him of our commitment. You will stain your hands with the blood of this deed and be bound to us in it.'

Steinar walked slowly over to Ragnvald and clasped his arm at the elbow. 'I will, and may our paths never be separated again.'

'Everyone else, go out and speak in support of Sigurd. Spread word of his worthiness, convince doubters, give favours and quell doubts. At Dísablót, we must speak with one voice to support him or we risk catastrophe.' No one contested Ragnvald's orders. The men exchanged grim looks and went out into the night, leaving Ragnvald alone in the chilled hall with his fears and the ghost of a dead king at his shoulder.

'So where are we going, my lord?' Leif was standing with Ragnvald in the stern of the longship, working its way out of the river outside Uppsala.

'I told you, we are going hunting,' replied Ragnvald gruffly.

'And I accepted that lie while we were in the hall and men

were listening, but we have never been hunting at sea before. I do not believe there are many deer in the cold waves. We are too many to hunt and too few to raid.' Leif returned the fixed stare of his lord unflinchingly.

'I did not say what we hunted,' Ragnvald replied, no hint of a smile on his face. And then he turned back to look down the river, signalling that the conversation was over.

The longship carried twenty of Ragnvald's warriors, unarmoured, with no shields. Swords, spears and bows were their only weapons. The ship was filled with supplies of food and ale, tents and camping gear. Ragnvald had left his precious helm behind and only carried his father's old sword, Bjóðr. Just a jarl going out with a large hunting party in autumn, or so he hoped people would think. A boat laden and slow, with too few men to man all the oars, no war vessel, for sure.

Ragnvald had not told anyone the plan, not even his closest *hirdmen* – his huscarls – and they were annoyed at the lack of trust. But too much was in the balance to risk word escaping to the ears of his targets. He would tell them when they were away from the land, when he knew they could not be stopped or called back by some misfortune.

It would be two days' sail to the mouth of the river that led to Jarl Harnsted's hall in the town of Ulfhafen. And to reach it they would have to pass by the riverside hall of Jarl Birkir at Fljótsode, the brother of Harnsted's wife and his most powerful and loyal supporter. And Ragnvald's friend.

The men of those lands would never let a longship pass their river unnoticed or unchallenged. Birkir would have to die first. They would take him at night, creeping through the darkness like wolves, before moving on to strike at Harnsted in the dim light of the dawn.

Birkir had stood with Ragnvald in the storm of swords, had

drunk with him in victory and sworn that the next time Ragnvald visited his hall he would welcome him like a brother. Ragnvald winced at those words that he remembered so clearly. He had not visited Birkir's hall since that day, and now he brought nothing but betrayal and his sword.

Whatever it takes, thought Ragnvald bitterly, his foul mood lying heavily on him like a wet cloak.

The men rowed in silence, the light wind helping them along the coast, the creak of wood and the cries of gulls the only noise penetrating the gloom of that usually boisterous group. Ulf stood silent at the steering oar. The only evidence he was not carved from the same wood as the ship he rode was the gentle corrections he made to keep the ship on course. Finally, Ragnvald could bear it no longer, and he stood up in the stern to address his men who shipped their oars to listen.

'I have pledged myself to King Sigurd of Norway to vote to make him our king at the Dísablót. He is the best hope we have of saving our people from the crusaders. You were all with me in Denmark, and you all saw their power.' The benches of hardened men stayed silent, watching their lord in the gentle swell.

'Jarl Harnsted would challenge for the crown. Half the north would back him. The country would be torn by war or, worse, given over to his control. He is a weak man, a coward who refused to come to Denmark, a raven starver who has never left a body in his wake for Odin's messengers to feast on. He plots and schemes like a woman. He does not fight in the shield wall or risk himself for his people. He would be the end of us.' He let this sink in as he looked around.

'We go to put an end to his claim, and we will end it the old way, with steel and blood. Not for him the struggle of politics or weasel words of compromise. For this, I have no regret. To get to him we must go through an honourable man, Jarl Birkir. Many of you will remember him from a raid we shared four summers ago.' Some men grumbled and looked around at each other with narrowed eyes. Remember him they did, and an air of shock and discomfort took over the watching men. 'He is oath sworn to uphold Harnsted's claim to the throne, and his sister is wedded to him. We cannot go around him, and if we did, he would wage war on us in revenge for his family. So he must also meet his end.' Ragnvald spat over the side in disgust.

Sebbi muttered darkly at this. 'We are not armed for an honourable fight with our skjaldborg against his. How will we take Birkir? Like cowards in the night? With a hall burning? He has done nothing to deserve such a fate. How can we do this thing right in the eyes of the gods and of men?'

'You are right. There will be no hall burning, no murder in his sleep. We will surround his hall and call him out to decide his fate like a man.'

Jarl Steinar unfolded his arms and spoke up. 'But we risk everything for our honour, and we give his men time to gather and repulse us! Surely we must strike fast and silent. The gods will understand.' He was clearly alarmed, fearing the plan would unravel as they tried to bring a sheen of honour to the act.

'No, the country will hear of this one way or another. And if they hear we acted so poorly, we will never get support. How this is done is as important as ensuring that it is done. We will not kill his family. His sons are too young to revenge him, not soon enough to matter anyway. We will take only him and those of his men who are there to defend him.'

'But his wife and others will tell who did this! The whole plan will be lost. You will make Sigurd a murderer!' protested Steinar.

'No.' Ragnvald frowned at the interruption. 'I will make Sigurd a king. He will not be the first king to kill for his crown, and the people will care more than it was done with honour and good intent than with the murder of women and boys. No, my word is final.'

Steinar sat down on his bench, brows furrowed, but he voiced no more dissent. He was a guest on those benches and had no choice but to concede.

'When we land, two men will hurry on upriver and scout out Ulfhafen. Find out where Harnsted is and, when we join you, lead us to him. We must be fast. If he gets warning from Birkir's village, we will be undone. Hjalmar, Inge, you will be our scouts.' The men nodded silently.

'Good. When this is done, none will speak of it again until I permit it.' Silence was his answer, the silence of men and the cry of the gulls. Ulf cast his steady gaze on Ragnvald and gave his jarl a slight and simple nod, then returned his eyes to the cold, dark sea.

The longship scraped gently against the bank in the darkness. Men sprung quietly out of the bow, taking ropes to secure it to the riverbank. Hjalmar and Inge got onto the bank and, with a nod, loped off into the darkness to the west, bows in hand and seaxes on their belts.

The rest of the men assembled in silence, crouched low to the bank, listening. The village was just past a copse of small trees. No sound could be heard, no light seen, the half-moon the only illumination on the clear summer's night.

Ragnvald motioned with his hand, and as one the group started a low walk through the trees. With buckles muffled by cloth, swords and seaxes snugly in sheaths and scabbards lest they be dropped or scraped on a rock, the men slipped like wraiths into the sleeping village, unlit torches in hand. The village had just five houses; most of Birkir's men lived in other villages in the land around, or on their own farms. Spread out as they were, it would take them until after dawn to assemble. No more than ten warriors lived in the small collection of buildings, the jarl's closest *hirdmen*.

Two of Ragnvald's men crept silently to each door in the village and waited. The rest moved towards the hall. No light shone from within, but somewhere inside, a dog started barking. The men froze, and then voices rang out from inside the hall, a man shouting a challenge into the darkness. Ragnvald, all need for silence gone, ordered some of his men to the back of the hall to stop any escape and then stood in front of the main door. One of the men lit a torch and passed the flame around to light the others until fire surrounded the hall, bathing them all in its glow and forcing them to shield their eyes as they adjusted to it.

'Jarl Birkir!' he shouted. 'Come outside with your sword. Your family will not be harmed.' Men started shouting in some of the buildings, confused voices woken from slumber. A handful of doors slammed open and half-naked men staggered out into the night, weapons in hand, eyes squinting at the glare, all to be instantly killed or seized by Ragnvald's waiting men.

'Who comes here to my hall in the night like a coward? Announce yourself, whoreson!' thundered a furious voice from the flame-lit hall, sounding as if Thor himself had been disturbed.

'Come out and see. I am no coward. Come forth and know me, or I will burn you out,' Ragnvald shouted back.

There was silence for a time, and then the doors burst open. Three armed men came out, weapons up. A large man was in the centre, naked from the waist, a long axe held on his shoulder, a war cry in his throat, muscles rippling in the torchlight. He planted his feet ten paces from the door and scanned his opponents, growling at them. On each side of him, two other men, clothed in wool and with shields and axes in hand, guarded his flanks.

Jarl Birkir stepped out into the light behind them. He wore a magnificent shirt of maille, gold braided into the links at his neck and sleeves. He wore a fine new helm that covered his eyes, and he carried his sword, unsheathed and glowing with reflected torch fire. The two sides stared at each other. More of Ragnvald's men assembled, their prisoners from the houses bound and gathered or the bodies left dead where they had fallen. Birkir saw this and growled with furious anger.

'Who are you? What evil have you brought to my hall in this time of peace? How dare you!' he thundered at the circle of armed men. Then his eyes fixed on Ragnvald, and he froze in disbelief.

'Ragnvald, is that you?' Birkir almost whispered, stepping forward for a better look in the torchlight. He was speechless with shock and rage for a moment. 'By what outrage would you, a man who fought with me, who called me brother, bring murder to my hall? I have not wronged you. I thought you a man of honour! I thought you *drengskapr*, but now I see you are only a snake!' His eyes narrowed, and he stepped towards the half-naked huscarl at his front. 'Do you come here to kill Jarl Harnsted, to take the crown for yourself by blades in the night? I would never have believed this possible.' He spat on the ground.

'Not for myself, Jarl Birkir, but for King Sigurd. I am sorry, friend. Harnsted would be the end of our people. I take no pleasure in this, but he must die. He cannot be king.'

They were interrupted by shouting and cries from the rear of the hall. Birkir visibly deflated at the noise. Ragnvald's men appeared from the gloom at the back of the hall, two defiant young boys, a fiercely struggling woman and an unconscious warrior dragged with them, bleeding badly from the back of his head.

'Caught this lot sneaking out the back. There are no others with them, or in the hall, apart from some thralls,' said one of Ragnvald's men.

'Your family, Jarl Birkir?' Ragnvald asked.

'Do not harm them!' Birkir shouted in desperate fury, spittle frothing from his mouth. 'You coward, you dog! The gods will piss on your honour, you who stood with me in the skjaldborg now brought low with this outrage!' He was almost incomprehensible with rage.

Ragnvald shook his head sadly. 'I said no harm would come to them and I meant it, Birkir, I swear it. They will be held here until we escape and then released unharmed. I assure you they will be protected once you are gone. No harm will come to your boys, and they will inherit your land, if we are able to defend it from the Christians.'

Birkir slowly calmed his voice, controlled his shaking fists and nodded, lowering his sword. 'So it is decided, then? The Norns cut my thread tonight?'

Ragnvald nodded. 'It is done, brother. There is no other way. I would not dishonour you by asking you to betray your kin and turn on Harnsted.'

'Nor would I offer it,' Birkir snarled in reply. 'What of my men, those who still live? These are good men who would carry their swords against the Christians.'

'They will come with us as prisoners. We cannot leave them here to spread word of who we are.'

Birkir nodded wearily. 'That will do. Let me speak to my family, then we will end this.'

'Birkir, do not tell them who we are.' He gave Birkir a stony look. Birkir nodded solemnly. They both understood the implications. No one could be left behind who could reveal the identity of the raiders.

Ragnvald nodded to the men holding the two boys and the wife, who was weeping freely even as she still struggled against her captors. The three of them rushed over to the jarl, who opened his arms to embrace them all tightly. He kissed his wife and then leaned down to press his face to his boys' ears, saying something to them as they shook their heads and protested.

Steinar slipped over to Ragnvald and whispered in his ear. 'We don't have time for this. We must move or risk a warning reaching Harnsted. Who knows if some man was pissing when we arrived and is even now running to raise the alarm? The dawn will be upon us soon.'

'We will do this right or not at all, as I told you,' Ragnvald replied curtly, the shame and anger of what was happening burning in the back of his throat. But he did nod to Birkir and called over with a hoarse voice, 'Jarl Birkir, it is time. Have your men put down their weapons and take up your sword. A warrior you are, and a warrior's death you shall have.'

Birkir nodded. Blinking as he forced back tears, he stepped to the side of the small square with his family, gently pushing them out of the circle of armed men, ignoring their protests as they were led away out of sight. He returned to face Ragnvald and spoke softly, fighting for control of his voice. 'I had hoped for a different death, Ragnvald. To die fighting the Christians or in defence of my family. Not like this.' He shook his head bitterly.

'This is an honourable end. Dying for your lord, true to your oath and in the service of your people to secure their future. I will make sure that story is known – the skalds will sing of it one day. I swear it.' He gave the man a brusque nod, barely able to meet his eye.

Birkir straightened his spine at this encouragement, head raised in defiance, and adjusted his grip on his sword. 'Then let us end this. Lads, put down your weapons. There is no need for you to die here. It is my last command.'

'Pardon me, my lord, but go fuck yourself,' said the big axeman. 'I ain't gonna be the one in those songs who left you to die alone, killed by these tiny little pricks. Not this man, not this day. I reckon I'm gonna take a couple of them with me to piss on outside the doors of Valhalla.'

Birkir nodded sadly. 'Thank you, brother. We will be drinking tonight in Odin's hall. You others, you see I am dying in good company, so put down your weapons and live.' The two other men looked at each other and nodded, reluctantly dropping their axes and surrendering to the waiting men in the circle of torches.

'Leif,' said Ragnvald.

Leif stepped forward with his sword drawn and the big axeman roared and charged, winding up with a devastating swing at the smaller man. Leif waited until the swing was committed, deftly sidestepped and, reversing his sword with a twist of his wrist, passed the edge of his blade along the axeman's bearded neck as the charging man passed, unbalanced by his swing and unable to avoid the torch-gleaming sword. The big man coughed as his battle cry was cut off, and he staggered to a stop, axe held in one hand as he clutched the other to his neck, blood frothing between his fingers, a look of complete surprise on his face. And then he collapsed, twitching to the ground, and was still.

Birkir watched in distaste at his huscarl's poor death. 'So you are to end me, boy?' he said, looking at Leif.

'No.' Ragnvald put a hand on Leif's shoulder and stepped past him. 'This I have to do myself.' He put his hand on the hilt of Bjóðr and drew it, shining in the flickering light, from its scabbard.

Birkir smiled and nodded. 'Then let us fight, brother, and be warned, I will try and kill you. No man will say I did not earn my place at Odin's table.'

'I would be disappointed with less.'

Ragnvald stepped forward and set his feet apart, knees bent, sword flat and held forward as he advanced. Birkir spread his arms and roared, teeth bared under wide eyes, and then stepped forward with an overhead swing. Lacking a shield or Leif's speed, Ragnvald deflected the blow on his blade and shoulder-charged the other jarl. Snarling, Birkir shrugged off the thumping blow to his chest, reversed his wrist and struck again. Again, Ragnvald deflected it. For a few dozen heartbeats, Birkir landed blow after blow on Ragnvald's defence. Ragnvald blocked and covered, countering with lunges to gain time and balance. His father's sword jumped and shook and cried out as the two swords repeatedly clashed. It was saving Ragnvald's life, but in the hacking and chipping of sword edge on sword edge, it was giving its own.

But Ragnvald did not yet attempt a killing blow as his friend roared and slashed at him. He was letting Birkir make a show, a fight that men would talk of, a defiance for the skalds to sing about. He was giving the man an honourable death. They were both tiring, but Birkir more so. Ragnvald scored several thrusts and cuts to his opponent's chest as his attacks slowed and became more predictable, but Birkir's maille stopped the blade. Ragnvald felt the heat of battle beginning to weaken his arms, saw the ragged edge of his sword and could hear the roar of his own breath in his ears.

It was time.

He stepped back a half pace further than normal, drawing his tired opponent into an over-extended lunge, and parried him on the outside, driving the sword out and past himself, locked with his own blade. He used that momentum to start a reverse cut, down at Birkir's sword arm. The cut caught the other man below the cuff of his maille, and the ragged sword bit deeply through muscle and into the bone below the elbow.

Birkir roared in pain and staggered away, his other hand clutching at his ruined arm. He was panting in shock as he shuddered to a stop and stood facing Ragnvald. He let out a soft moan of pain and raised his narrowed eyes to meet his killer's. His friend.

His betrayer. His sword was slipping from the blood-slicked grip of his injured arm.

'I have done my duty. I have died for my lord,' he said through gritted teeth, pausing to take a few ragged breaths, visibly swaying. 'Harnsted would have been a shit king. Make my death mean something and kill him.'

Ragnvald nodded solemnly, tears cutting unbidden at the corners of his eyes, panting from the exertion and suddenly unable to do what was required. To take his father's sword and strike down his friend.

Birkir was shaking now, blood pouring onto the ground and down his leg, knees struggling to remain locked. 'Finish it! Before I can no longer stand or hold my sword,' he implored, his voice shaking. Birkir let go of his ruined arm and transferred his sword to his good hand. Clasping his sword to his chest, he closed his eyes and raised his chin. Ragnvald took a deep breath and moved in.

Bjóðr's still-sharp tip swung round and sliced through Birkir's throat. The jarl gasped once before falling to the ground and finally becoming still, nerveless fingers letting go of his sword.

Ragnvald walked to his side as the sword fell to the ground and stooped to return it to the dying man's grip, face grim and flushed, tears falling unchecked from his face to Birkir's 'I'm sorry, brother.'

He waited until the last signs of life were gone and then stood and turned to his men. He looked bitterly at the huddle of prisoners. He was dreading what came next and nodded to the men guarding them. The men turned their weapons on the horrified prisoners, bound and defenceless as the steel tore into them. In a matter of moments, it was over. Sebbi spat on the ground in disgust, touching his hammer, a hopeless gesture to ward off the shame of what he had just done.

Ragnvald saw the disgust written clearly on the faces of his men, only the strength of their bonds forged over years of kinship keeping their loyalty intact. 'We couldn't afford to fight them, not so few and with no armour or shields. And we couldn't take them with us or leave them to arrange an ambush or plot revenge. It had to be done.' He said this softly, to no one in particular, perhaps mostly to himself. Leif nodded, and Ulf turned away, muttering through his wiry grey beard.

'It was an ill thing to deprive them of an honourable end. But they had the choice. They should have fought to the death for their lord like him.' Leif nodded his head at the cooling body of the half-naked axeman. 'He earned a warrior's death. The others took the coward's way out. Don't let it concern you.'

Ragnvald nodded with no conviction, and Steinar walked over to him urgently, brows furrowed. 'You will kill the family?'

'No. I gave my word. No women or children will be harmed. You know this.'

'You also said those men would live.'

'I didn't swear it.'

'A minor difference, some might say.'

'Not to me – I made no promise. I let them hear what they wanted. They had weapons in their hands and breath in their lungs. They could have fought, but they made their choice. Leave me what is left of my honour, and don't question it. Let's be gone. We have a long way to go, and I can see the dawn coming in the east.'

'The woman has seen you – you cannot leave her alive!' Steinar pleaded, anger and worry reducing his words to a hiss.

'It is dark, and she has never met me. She cannot know who we are. I will not kill a family I gave my oath to spare, and I will discuss it no further,' Ragnvald hissed angrily, turning his blood-shot eyes on the Norwegian. Steinar exhaled in frustration but bit his tongue. He could see further words would do nothing.

The men quickly staved in the bottom planks of the two ships and a number of smaller boats that were moored at the small dock on the riverbank near the hall, the proud wooden ships gurgling and sloshing as they settled into the mud of the river bottom, masts and figureheads still above the surface, painted white eyes glaring in anger in the darkness.

Then they left the site of the massacre, torches burned out, striding west in single file along the path to Ulfhafen, the first tinges of dawn chasing them as they melded into the forest and were gone. A village of wailing widows left in their wake.

CHAPTER 17

THE FEAR IN THE FOREST

'HARNSTED IS OUT hunting.'

'What? Shit. Where?'

'Out further west. He left with about a dozen of his men yesterday, and he is expected back tomorrow,' Hjalmar reported when Ragnvald met the scouts outside the town, the first rays of dawn breaking the horizon.

'Hmm, perhaps this is a blessing. We can take him alone and far from help.'

'If we find him. If we miss him in the woods, he will surely return to news of our attack and we will be done,' Steinar added grimly.

'Indeed. Hjalmar, how do you know where he went?'

'We took a man outside the hall, a slave, and questioned him.'

'And where is this slave?'

Hjalmar shifted uncomfortably. 'In a ditch in the woods.'

Ragnvald bared his teeth in frustration. 'By the gods man, we needed to know where exactly he went,' Ragnvald chided him. 'He is no use to us dead.'

'He didn't know any more.' Hjalmar shrugged.

'This isn't good,' said Leif. 'A missing slave will be searched for.'

'Yes, and dawn is here. People will be rising. Fuck, we will have to go into the woods and hope the gods are with us. We will search out Harnsted's camp and work out a plan when we find it.'

'This could go very badly, very quickly. This is an armed, alert group of men searching the woods for prey, and we have no idea where they are,' Steinar mused.

Ragnvald looked at him, a grim smile on his face. 'We risk much, but it is for everything. Are you afraid of a little challenge? Let us go and hunt these hunters.'

Dawn was fully upon them by the time they had circled around the small town and were out of sight of it. Behind them, the folk would be rising for the day's labours, going out to their fields and collecting water and a hundred other tasks. The dead slave would be missed, and perhaps found. Ragnvald could only hope they looked for the killer within the town, not without.

The woods were different in that gently undulating land to the ones in his own lands further south. The trees were taller, with bare trunks twice the height of a man, and there was less undergrowth of small trees. You could see further and be seen from further. His men loped along behind as they followed one game trail after another, seeing signs of recent passage by people often, but nothing they could be sure was their quarry.

Ragnvald grew increasingly worried. The hunting party could have already returned to the town via a different path, discovered the attack on Birkir and even now be arming for war. He would be trapped, cut off from his ship. He considered spreading out his men into multiple groups to search, but it was a desperate plan; they would be impossible to find again in these broad and unfamiliar woodlands. He gathered his men together to quickly discuss their options.

As they gathered quietly in a low depression between two large pine trees, quiet men with strained faces, they all understood the danger they were in. One of the scouts hissed for silence and listened to the wind, slowly turning his head.

There. They all heard it this time. Faint but unmistakable: a horn sounding to their west, away from the town.

Ragnvald smiled, the first time he had done so for days. 'The gods favour us at last. That is a hunting horn, is it not? They are driving deer, perhaps.' The scout nodded.

'Aye, that is no war horn. And it is not close to Ulfhafen.' He looked up at the sun, filtering as it was through the dark-green canopy of needles. 'If they are hunting now, they do not mean to return to town before dark. They will return to their camp for the night.'

'I agree, so we must find it. Let's go, and hope they keep blowing that bloody horn.'

Ragnvald was lying behind the tree, silent, and listening to the sounds of merriment in the camp hidden below them in a dell by a stream. For half the day, they had carefully tracked the hunting party by the sound of its horns, the bark of its dogs and the voices of men shouting at each other. Now, having carefully followed the trail of drying blood left by the men taking the slaughtered deer back to their camp, the manhunters had gathered together to plan the attack.

Ragnvald crept back from the edge of the small rise that overlooked the camp and quietly returned to his hidden men some hundred paces further down the slope.

'The report was accurate. There are fourteen of them, including Harnsted. They are eating and drinking and celebrating their success in the hunt. No sentries, no watch. Only men frequently leaving to piss that might spoil an attack. They are completely relaxed.'

His men strained to hear his whispers.

'Here is what we will do. We have to ensure that none escape. Leif, you will go up over this small hill behind us, cross the stream and cover the camp on the far side. Make sure no one runs across the stream. Take five men. Steinar, take another five and go left, down to where the stream leaves the camp. When the signal comes, you will attack from there. I will attack from here. Questions?'

'What will be the signal?' asked Steinar.

'A lot of shouting,' replied Ragnvald, grinning. 'They have bows and spears, and we don't have shields, so we go in fast and hard and don't give them time to react, or this will get very messy. No noise until they raise the alarm, and then make them think Ragnarök is upon them. Shock them into inaction. Every moment counts.'

The men quietly split up into groups and moved off. Ragnvald allowed a lot of time. He had to be sure everyone was in position and had no way of checking except giving them all the time they could need. He was nervous. Everyone was nervous. This was the worst part of battle. Waiting, worrying, hoping to suffer neither humiliation nor an agonising and helpless death. Men checked and rechecked weapons. Swords were kept out of the damp tree litter by men who were searching the trees for danger, wide-eyed and alert.

Finally, when he couldn't take the tension any more, he motioned to the men around him and signalled the attack. They broke into a loping run through the trees, seven of them, swords and spears held out in front. Their mouths were open as they exhaled like men who had run all day, the nerves taking their breath as much as any exercise.

Ragnvald's shoes swept through the soft litter of needles and the small plants that called the ground their home. They quickly reached the rise and dropped over it, slithering and sliding down the slope leading into the open dell. In front of him, a confused man was pissing onto the last tree, mouth moving like a landed fish as seven armed men, silent as forest spirits, burst out of the woods in front of him with death in their hands. The man desperately tried to fumble his trousers back up as he turned to run, screamed for help and then died with Sebbi's sword in his back.

Ragnvald's men started screaming like demons as they burst from the tree cover and crossed the dozen or so paces of open ground to the camp. Ale-fuddled men gaped at them or scattered, running for weapons, for their tents, for the pair of horses. The attackers swept into the camp like a fell wind, running down everyone regardless whether they fought or not. Steinar's men burst out of the trees on the left, yelling like fiends as they fell on the backs of the terrified men in the camp.

Ragnvald swung his sword at a man who was desperately trying to nock an arrow onto his bow. The man fumbled it and cried out as Bjóðr cut through the bow and through his arm, gashing his chest from breastbone to armpit, the tip scoring off ribs. Ragnvald kicked the man to the ground and speared his sword at his chest, while he twisted and tried to scurry away with his one good arm. His attempt to crawl away and his twisting meant the sword went between the man's buttocks and sliced into his groin. The wretched man screamed like a wounded deer and scrabbled at the cold blade, ripping his fingers to shreds in his pain and panic. Ragnvald finally managed to free the blade and thrust it again into the wounded man's throat, ending the horrible screams at last. Ragnvald grimaced with displeasure. It had been a messy death, undeserved. He looked up from the ruined man and saw Sebbi hacking a boar spear to one side and killing the wielder with a perfect thrust to the heart. The clean kill only angered him more.

It was over as fast as it had begun. Men who had been drinking ale and eating in relaxed safety just heartbeats ago were dying on the ground, spitted with sudden steel, merriment still warm on their gasping lips.

Within fifty heartbeats of the first man at the tree dying, the camp was clear, and no enemy was left alive in it.

'Where is Harnsted? Where is his body? Who killed him?' Ragnvald asked, looking around at the bodies, bending down to turn over one that lay face down.

'Eleven!' cried Sebbi.

'What?' shouted Ragnvald, turning around, counting the bodies himself. It was true. There were only eleven bodies on the ground.

'Leif! What of the stream – did you see anyone cross it?'

'No, my lord, I did not but… Shit. Askund is missing. On the left, he was on the left!'

Ragnvald cursed and started towards the area where the man had been.

'Askund!' shouted Leif, crashing through the low branches along the far side of the stream. Ragnvald ran to the stream, crossing it with a single splashing step, his foot struggling for grip on the smooth and jumbled stones on the riverbed. Men were following him.

He caught up with Leif as he found Askund. The young man was lying against a tree, a deep wound in his chest, sucking with his breathing, which was ragged and weak.

'Three men,' he forced out, though blood bubbled in his mouth. 'I hit one. I'm sorry.' He gasped and started choking. A man rolled him over onto his side, but it was too late for him. He went into the death shakes and then lay still, blood spilling from his open mouth.

Ragnvald let out a string of curses, which would have made any drunkard blush, then calmed himself. 'Gather half the men and follow me. We must chase them down. It is half a day's walk to the nearest village we passed. They could run it in less than half of that. Go!'

With that, Ragnvald got up and started running through the trees eastwards with the men who were there with him, following a bright trail of blood. Soon, they came upon the source of the blood: a man sitting against a tree, breathing heavily and bleeding from a gut wound. Ragnvald ignored him and carried on past. Men were spreading out left and right, trying to pick up the trail through the trees.

Their quarry had been in a hurry and was not careful. Despite the end of the trail of blood, the way they had gone was often clear, scuff marks in the dry pine needles showing damp earth underneath, cracks of breaking twigs and snagging branches heard in front of them.

The scout, Inge, passed Ragnvald as he started to slow, age taking its toll on his endurance and his legs as the slight young man hared on. It saved his life. Inge passed a large pine trunk on the trail, and an axe swung out from behind it, catching Inge square in the neck and nearly beheading him. Ragnvald was a few paces behind and swung his sword wildly at the revealed foe, who was still drawing his axe back from the body of the falling scout. Ragnvald made contact with the wild swing, felt the edge bite flesh and then he was past. He kept going. Someone behind would deal with the wounded ambusher.

On and on he went, the trail still clear in the otherwise undisturbed leaf litter. His breath was starting to fail him, throat burning, legs burning with the exertion, sweat running down his face and stinging his eyes.

His quarry, who had been eating and drinking when he was surprised, reached his limit first. Ragnvald stumbled into a small clearing to find Harnsted leaning against a tree on the far side, gasping, vomit dribbling from his chin into a splatter at the base of the tree. He looked up in alarm at Ragnvald's appearance and started off again, launching his exhausted legs into another effort as his feet struggled for purchase on the soft forest floor.

As his prey disappeared around the tree, Ragnvald wearily started after him, only to hear a shout of triumph from ahead. Reaching the tree, he saw that Harnsted was lying on his back on the forest floor, backed up against another tree, a spear at his throat and terror in his eyes.

Steinar appeared at Ragnvald's shoulder, and the two jarls caught their breath as they strode over to the prostrate and whimpering man. Hjalmar spoke without taking his eyes off Jarl Harnsted. 'I got around in front of him. He doesn't have a weapon.'

'Doesn't have a weapon?' Ragnvald exclaimed in surprise.

'Who are you?' blurted out Harnsted. 'Spare me, and you will be greatly rewarded. I will be the king next year, and I will make you wealthy men.'

'Silence!' grated out Ragnvald with a deep growl. 'We know who you are, coward. Do not disgrace yourself with begging. You will be nothing next year but mud. Your life ends here. Try to die like a man.'

'You know who I am?' stammered Harnsted. 'Who are you? Why do you come for me? I am no coward! I am the rightful king of Sweden!'

'You are nothing. You lie there unarmed and beg for your life? I am ashamed to even be near you. Where were you in Jutland? Where were you when your king went to fight the crusaders?

Where were you when we stood against the Christians and our brothers bled into the damp earth? Where were you when your men died in the forest this day?' Ragnvald was furious now, and Harnsted tried to shrink from this, the tall old warrior who towered over him with blood all over his sword and arms.

'Someone had to stay and defend the king's lands while he was gone!' protested Harnsted.

'And of course it was you who volunteered. I wouldn't leave you to guard a chicken coop.' Ragnvald shook his head violently. 'How did we allow the royal line to grow so weak? You and your cousin the king disgraced us. Our people have grown weak since the end of the old ways when a king had to earn his position with blood and iron, not the bleating of old men at the Dísablót and silver quietly filling open hands. No! Enough excuses. Your whimpering embarrasses me.' Ragnvald cut off Harnsted's attempt to reply with a foot on his neck.

'You didn't even pick up a weapon in your haste to flee, so you can die like a thrall without one, barred forever from Odin's hall.' Ragnvald abruptly plunged his sword into the open mouth of his captive, pushing down as it crunched through gristle and then bone, and the man's wide and desperate eyes glazed over and stilled.

Ragnvald stepped away in disgust, wiping his sword on the dead man's tunic. 'And that would have been our king? How did it come to this? Perhaps we have earned this calamity. How the gods must look with despair on our people.' Men touched their hammer amulets or just stared at the dead jarl, a dark stain spreading on his trousers in a last act of cowardice. 'Let us head back to the boats before better men than this come to find us.'

The party retraced their path to the site of the massacre. The men who had stayed there had collected the bodies and laid them out in a row, what weapons the dead had with them pressed into cooling hands. Ragnvald looked at the scene and sighed at the next outrage he must commit. His men gathered around him. The bodies of the two who had fallen, Askund and Inge, were being wrapped in blankets. They would return with them to the ships.

'Loot the camp, spread the bodies around and take everything of value,' he said bitterly.

'What?' said Leif, mouth agape. No one wanted to take the spoils of this dishonourable massacre. They would be a curse to whoever owned them.

Ragnvald could feel the loyalty of his men on a knife edge, see the anger in their eyes as he asked them to lay another stain on their honour.

'No bandits would lay them out like that, and they would not leave them their weapons. We must take everything of value and leave nothing but their bodies for the crows. We will cast all of it in the sea when we leave.'

None of his men moved, and some would not even meet his eye. But Steinar snapped his fingers at his two men and then took them over to the line of bodies, starting to strip them of all that they carried. Slowly, the rest of the men joined in, pulling sword belts from bodies and ripping rings from arms, fingers and beards. Ragnvald watched and fretted. The sun was starting to sink in the sky, and they had to return to the boats before they were discovered. Already, the alarm would have been raised, and the surrounding villages would be full of men arming and organising themselves to defend their land. It was only a matter of time before they were out searching the woods and rivers.

Once the camp had reluctantly been looted, the party set out, carrying the spoils and the bodies of their two fallen brothers. The solemn band pushed hard, covering the miles back out of the forest as fast as they could, not encountering a soul, not sharing a word. Finally, they reached the edge of the forest and the edge of the first large clearing, a broad meadow beside a small stream, a stream that would take them back to the river and their ship.

After following the stream for a few miles, Ragnvald started to believe they might get clear unseen, but then their luck ran out. As they rounded a corner of tall bushes beside a bend in the stream, they came face to face with a party of four warriors armed with spears, shields and surprised expressions. Both sides hesitated for a moment, unsure what to do, but the four strangers took in the tired, blood-spattered armed party with two bodies slung on poles of cut branches, and their guilt was inescapable.

'Skjaldborg!' shouted one of the men, and his fellows brought their shields up and formed a small wall that blocked the narrow path, spears protruding, eyes settling in behind the shields. Only one of them was wearing maille, and none had steel helms, but still they were clearly men accustomed to violence and weapons.

Fuck. Ragnvald knew that where there were four men searching, others would not be far away. He considered the options for a moment. The enemy was only four, but they could not easily be flanked on that narrow path, and men with shields and spears who cannot be flanked are almost impervious to men with swords and no shields. His men could break that wall, but the cost would be horrendous.

They could turn back and find another path, but the enemy could move to block them, and all the while he risked a larger party finding them. Even ten fully armed warriors would mean death for them all and the failure of all they hoped to achieve.

He grabbed Leif and whispered in his ear. 'Take three men. When we start the attack, go around them, and be quick.' Then he drew his sword and pointed at the enemy. 'With me!' he said, keeping his voice low, like a man talking in a hall. There would be screaming and shouting soon, but the longer it waited, the better. His men dropped the loads they were carrying, and axes and swords were put into hand. The men formed a loose line and advanced on the tiny skjaldborg, eyes focused and heads lowered, half crouching as they closed.

As they were just about to reach spear range, one of his men threw an axe. An enemy jerked his shield up and deflected it harmlessly over the line, but the momentary distraction and the break in the wall were enough for several men to try attacking. One of Steinar's men jumped forward, hacking a spearhead aside and making a lunge for the man wielding it. Another enemy tried to turn his spear enough to thrust at the charging Norwegian but missed, the point brushing past his side. With two of the four spearmen engaged, another man rushed into the gap and received a stab in the thigh for his trouble, cursing and pulling back, fouling the next man along.

Ragnvald stepped forward and cut at the spear as it lunged for another attack at the wounded man, managing to push it aside and then skipping back himself as another thrust came for him.

The Norwegian was hacking furiously at the wall, inside the range of their spears, trying to shove his way through as the two men he faced braced their feet and held him back with their shields. Another man tried to reach him but was driven back again by the spears of the others. The Norwegian was clinging to the top of a shield with his hand, trying to pull it down to hack at the man behind it. The leader of the enemy shouted a command, and the whole wall suddenly took two paces back. The man whose shield was being wrestled grunted and pulled to the side, throwing the Norwegian in front of the rest of his fellows.

Ragnvald called a warning that came a lifetime too late as two spears lashed out and sank deep into the Norwegian's side. He gasped and fell to his knees, still clinging to the shield as he stared in shock at the man who stood above him. Then the shield was wrenched free, and he fell to the ground. The shield wall instantly re-formed, and four spear tips once again fell down into line, some now dripping with blood.

Steinar's other man howled in impotent rage. Nothing but death awaited any who advanced down that narrow path onto those blood-slicked stones. But the man's death had allowed Leif and a couple of others to slip away around the bushes. Ragnvald had no idea how long it would take them to get around the thick, impenetrable bushes that lay to their side, clinging to the shallow slope of the small gully in which the stream lay. They could extend merely to the top, twenty paces away, or they could be the start of a thick field margin half a mile long.

He just set his teeth and stepped forward again, fixing his eyes on the dancing spear point in front of him, trying to find a way past it. He took another half step forward, and the spear sliced out towards him. He hacked at it, shearing splinters off the shaft, but it sliced through the side of his tunic, scoring a shallow line along the skin on his side. He dropped the sword and grabbed the spear with both hands, trapping it between his arm and his injured side and yanking on it with all his strength.

The spearman was taken completely by surprise, and for a moment he tried to cling on, almost overbalancing and being pulled out of the line, but then he either let go or lost his grip, stumbling back as the spear left his grasp. Ragnvald staggered back and reversed the spear, now facing the wall on even terms. He growled and lunged at the eyes of the man whose weapon he had stolen, a man who now only had a long seax, but the man kept his jabbing attacks at bay with his shield. Again, another man tried to get inside the range of the spears on Ragnvald's right, and again, the spears lashed out and pinked him, catching him across the forearm and sending him reeling back with a string of curses.

Ragnvald hammered at the shield wall with the spearhead, trying to lunge for someone's legs, but he could not reach them without exposing himself to a deadly return. He cursed in impotent rage as his spearhead rattled uselessly off the shields once again.

He drew back from another attack, and for a moment the two sides just stared at each other. Then there was a rush of footsteps, and the wall dissolved as three men bowled into it from behind, steel and fists and feet pummelling into the surprised men, who had no time to turn their spears. One moment it was an impenetrable barrier and the next, a mess of screaming, brawling, dying men.

The man with the seax managed to turn his shield and deflect the first attack, but Ragnvald put his spear into its previous owner's spine, and he arched and went down. Two enemies went down with swords in their bellies, but the third managed to skip aside and then run. He splashed into the river, Leif's desperate swipe with a sword only nicking his arm, and then he was gone, across the narrow stream and powering up the other bank.

'After him!' shouted Leif, leaping half the stream to follow, sword hanging from his hand.

'No!' shouted Ragnvald. 'He is gone, and we must leave. Now!'

Leif carried on for a moment, watching the enemy as he disappeared over the top of the bank, then he howled in frustration and turned back.

'We must run. Carry only your weapons. Take their shields and spears, but leave the loot behind.'

'What of the dead?' asked Steinar, looking at his dead man in dismay.

'I'm sorry, friend. We cannot take them.'

'And if they are recognised?'

'So be it. We have no choice. There are miles to go, and we cannot carry them and hope to stay ahead of our pursuers.'

Steinar nodded. He knew the stakes.

The men set off at a jog down the path, the dead and anything they didn't need to carry left dumped on the path. Ragnvald took one last, regretful look at the wrapped bodies of Askund and Inge, men whom he had pledged to honour and protect, and turned to follow them. Askund would have been next to be made huscarl, but now his body lay deserted for his enemies. Ragnvald howled internally at the shame of it all.

They carried on down the riverbank, Ragnvald driving the pace from the back, lungs burning, legs weak from exhaustion. The man with the wounded leg was his new huscarl Svend, and he was gasping and limping, struggling to keep up. Ragnvald physically pushed him, cajoled him and tried to half carry him along. Finally, he was forced to call a stop as more of the exhausted men started to fall behind. The river was running wide now, deeper and probably uncrossable without swimming. Ragnvald was nervous about following it, trapped as he was against the bank, but in unfamiliar land it was the only thing leading him back to his ship.

Svend groaned and stumbled. Ragnvald caught him under one arm and felt his own tired muscles flag as the man's weight bore down on his shoulder. 'We must continue. We will walk, but we will not stop for anything. Perhaps we have got far enough ahead,' he said between strained breaths.

Leif was standing there, perhaps the least affected of the men, and he nodded, turning to urge others who had slumped to the ground to rise and continue.

Ragnvald set off, supporting the injured Svend, and men staggered to their feet to follow him. None were willing to be shamed by an old jarl supporting a wounded man. For a few hundred paces they continued, Ragnvald not recognising the river they were travelling along but feeling certain they must be nearing their destination.

Suddenly, he heard a shout of excitement from the other bank and, dreading what he would see, turned and looked. A single man had appeared on the far side, looking over his shoulder and pointing with his spear at Ragnvald's bedraggled band. Within moments, a line of warriors, probably a dozen, jogged into view to join him. They were all armed and ready for war.

'Go!' shouted Ragnvald, shoving one of his men in the direction they were going. The leading men broke into a jog again, a wave of fear overriding their tiredness. Svend cursed as Sebbi, the man now supporting him, half dragged and half carried him along. Ragnvald watched the enemy as he followed his men, half walking and half sidestepping as he tried to see what they would do. *Would they try and swim it?* A river could be swum with weapons by those few who had the strength and the skill, but not many did. Then he saw one of the enemy point back along the way they had come, and the whole band surged into a run along the riverbank.

Ragnvald stopped to watch, confused, then he followed the direction of their travel with his eyes and saw something in the water, not two hundred paces away, a broad line of ripples stretching from one side of the river to the other. A ford.

His heart sank. The enemy would reach the ford, cross it and be chasing back after them, only four hundred paces behind.

He turned and ran after his men, catching Svend within moments. The man was sweating, red in the face and moaning, barely able to move his injured leg, from which blood was streaming to the ground, his wound ripped open again by the desperate run.

'We must go. They will be on us in moments!' said Ragnvald, grabbing Svend's other arm and starting to run again with the wounded man supported between him and Sebbi. Svend gritted his teeth and cried out, trying to pump his injured leg to keep up, but it would not respond, most of the feeling gone. He tripped on it, and the three men all went down. Ragnvald rolled to his feet and reached out to pull Svend roughly up, Sebbi giving him a wordless look across the back of the injured man. Silently telling him what they both knew. *We have to leave him.* And Ragnvald's eyes shouted back, *I will not.*

Two men came back to them: Leif, and a man carrying a captured shield and spear. Leif looked back along the river. He saw the enemy splashing across the ford, and his face set in a grim frown. 'They are coming.'

Ragnvald reached forward, helped them get Svend to his feet and then started to try and drag him back into movement. 'Enough!' growled Svend, pulling his hand from Ragnvald's grasp.

'We have to go now!' shouted Leif angrily.

'So do it. Give me that shield and spear and go!' He looked at Ragnvald once and then grabbed the offered shield. 'No time for your pretty words – they are coming. Run Jarl Ragnvald, and if you live, take care of my family. I will await your thanks in Valhol, if I have enough honour left to get in.' The rebuke cut Ragnvald more deeply than any sword could.

Svend straightened his injured leg and turned around, using the spear like a staff, turning to face the oncoming enemy. He didn't look back at them. Sebbi slapped the man on the back and gruffly mumbled his thanks. Ragnvald had no reply; there was no time, and he was too ashamed. Leif was already tugging on his arm.

He turned and ran without a word, leaving the lone warrior to guard the path.

Svend sighed and let the fear and pain flow from him. He gripped the shaft of the spear that he was bracing against the ground and shifted his hand on the shield. He heard the running footsteps recede behind him and could not yet hear the rush of the oncoming enemy, who would be approaching him unseen before his closed eyes. For a moment, he could hear only the river gently lapping the bank nearby, the gentle whisper of the breeze in the reeds. He felt the sun on his skin and the thump of his pulse in his temple. He felt alive, and he made his peace with death.

Ragnvald caught up with his men as the river broadened and they went around a corner. Ragnvald finally saw what he had been waiting for on the other bank: Birkir's village and hall. It was teeming with men. At the same time as he saw them, they saw him. Men who had been trying to raise the sunken ships looked up and shouted in alarm, but there was nothing they could do to cross over. He urged his men on, ducking as an arrow flicked across the river and disappeared in the reeds beyond them.

He suddenly heard the unmistakable sound of a spear shaft beating on a shield boss from behind him, a shout of defiance and a curse promising death to Svend's enemies. He managed a bitter smile as he faintly heard Svend suggest what the hunters following them should do to each other with the hafts of their axes, then there was a howling war cry and the sound of steel on shield, a rain of blows that reverberated across the calm river for a few moments. Then nothing.

Ragnvald offered a breathless prayer to Odin to take Svend into his care and pushed his legs to give their last. The copse of trees they had passed before they reached the village finally came into view. Ragnvald turned and saw the enemy, closer than he expected, perhaps two hundred paces behind them, running after him in a strung-out column.

He tried to shout at his men to hurry but couldn't. His mind was starting to fog from exhaustion. They rounded the bend where they would finally be able to see the place they had left Ulf and three others with the ship, but to his horror it was gone, and some of the enemy were on the bank at the landing site, shouting and pointing both at him and downstream. His weary eyes flicked right and saw the slim mast of his ship above the reeds. It was downriver to his right. Another five hundred paces, another impossible distance with the hunters on his heels.

Leif was urging men on. Even his face was flushed red, and his arms were limply swinging by his sides. They pounded down the riverbank, barely even running now, until finally they came to where the ship was. Ulf, bless his ancient soul, had launched the ship and was holding it on an anchor stone near the bank. The man himself was standing in the stern waving and gesturing, the other three men rushing around the ship setting oars and clearing benches. Ragnvald realised that if the ship had been beached, they would all have died before they launched it. He hadn't even thought about it.

The first men reached the bank by the ship and ran into the river, water spraying as they jumped up and pulled themselves into the wooden hull. Men too tired to lift themselves in were pushed and dragged over the wooden side. Ragnvald and the last of his men arrived, and hands reached down to meet them. Behind him, the first enemy came around the corner, and there was a shout of triumph as they saw their quarry with men still struggling to get aboard, just a few paces from the bank.

There was a twang and then a scream of surprise, then another twang. Ragnvald looked up as he was bodily dragged into the boat to see that Ulf, that beautiful old seabird, was launching arrow after arrow at the hunters from a bow he had acquired from somewhere. 'Cut the anchor! Get on the fucking oars!' he yelled as he nocked another arrow and sent it lancing out towards the enemy, who had regained their composure and were rushing towards the riverbank with raised shields.

Exhausted men dragged themselves onto benches and grabbed oars with quivering arms. Ragnvald staggered to the stern and brought Bjóðr down on the rope that held them to an unseen anchor stone on the riverbed. Behind him, Leif shouted an order to pull on the oars, and a bedraggled wave of oar blades rose and splashed back into the river, the ship jerking lazily as current and oars started propelling them downstream, achingly slowly.

The first enemy splashed into the river, Ulf's arrows not able to stop the flood of shielded warriors. One man nearly reached them as the ship started moving faster than he could manage in the waist-deep water, and as he was left behind he launched his spear with a howl of anger. The spear arced towards the rowers, and Leif threw out a hand and caught it, plucking it from the air like a hawk snatching a sparrow. The man's howl of rage died in his throat at the remarkable sight, and then he ducked behind his shield as Leif returned his spear. But for all the skill of his catch, his throw, propelled by tired arms as it was, merely rattled off the side of the shield and splashed into the river.

And then they were gone. As suddenly as the enemy had arrived, they were left behind, shouting and cursing and calling them cowards from the receding riverbank. Ragnvald sat down heavily in the bottom of the boat as Ulf growled at the men to keep rowing lest they lose control and careen into a bank, dooming them all. But Ragnvald couldn't move. He just sat in the bottom and tried to breathe. Leif took half the men off the oars to rest and then slumped down next to him.

'Did you really catch that fucking spear?' asked Ragnvald, looking at him incredulously. 'Or am I so tired I am losing my mind?'

Leif laughed. 'I am as surprised as you. I didn't intend to – it just happened. One moment I saw the spear coming, and the next it was in my hand. I don't think I made any decisions in between.'

'Well, it was a feat for a skald song.' Ragnvald closed his eyes and lay back against the hull of the boat, his entire body relaxing and a dozen burning aches flaring up in his mind.

'Well, I hope the throw doesn't make it into a song. A ten-year-old child could have done better.'

'I have often thought that about you,' quipped Ragnvald weakly.

Leif smiled, and they sat there for a while in silence. 'So what do we do now, return home?' Leif asked.

But Ragnvald had no reply. He had passed out, open mouth resting on his chest. Leif smiled to himself and looked out as the bank slid past them, river and reeds giving way to mudflats and, finally, the wide, cold sea.

CHAPTER 18

A SERPENT IN THE STEEL

AFTER WEEKS OF repetitive and simple work on basic axes and spearheads, at last Ordulf was called in by Dengir at the smithy to watch the final stage of the making of the mystery sword that had lain aside while other work was completed. The blade was sitting on a cloth in a cradle. It had been ground to shape and smoothed with stones but not yet fully sharpened or polished. One of the other smiths had cast a thick bronze cross guard and pommel, which he had spent weeks carving with wild shapes and figures, then inlaying with silver patterns, burnished to a high polish until they were utterly magnificent to behold and quite unlike anything Ordulf had seen before. They lay next to the sword, along with a dark, wooden hilt and its bronze bands, waiting to be fitted.

There was a stone trough in the corner of the room that Ordulf had never seen used before. Now, an apprentice was stirring a strange mixture in the trough, taking some crushed dark berries and a brown-grey powder and mixing them into the liquid. It smelled earthy and tangy. He stared at it in fascination; he had never seen such a thing before in a forge. The master smith took up the blade and washed it down with some sort of soap, carefully scrubbing it and then removing the mess with a clean cloth under clear running water from a jug. When the blade was clean, and touching only the tang, he carried it over to the trough and carefully placed the point at one end on the smooth stone under the liquid's surface. He then laid the rest of the blade down into the mixture. Removing his fingers, he licked one and rolled the flavour around on his tongue, deep in concentration.

He grunted and held up four fingers to the apprentice who nodded and sat down beside the trough, arms crossed. Ordulf wondered at the purpose but still didn't have the language to ask such a complex question. Not that Dengir would answer a question – he almost never did. In fact, Ordulf had rarely seen the man speak at all, even to the other smiths. The master smith left and Ordulf sat there, watching and waiting for something to happen. The apprentice was watching the trough intently, occasionally stirring it but being careful not to disturb or touch the blade. After a short time, the master smith returned with another apprentice carrying a jug of water and a clean sheepskin. Dengir went over to the dark trough, which the apprentice was still carefully stirring every now and then. He reached into the liquid and brought out the blade. Carrying it over to the apprentice, they cleaned it with the wool and the water while Ordulf craned his neck to get a better look.

The smith finally turned around, the blade wrapped in the purple-stained wool, and ushered Ordulf outside into the dying light of the day. He held up the wrapped blade for Ordulf's attention and then carefully peeled back the wool. Ordulf's heart caught in his mouth. His eyes opened in wonder at the sight of the blade.

He had seen that blade go into the liquid with his own eyes, and it had been plain shining steel, stoned smooth but not polished. The blade now before him in the pale evening light, sparkling in the light of the setting sun, looked like one of the carved wooden arms of the jarl's chair, but subtler, deeper, more convoluted, and yet breathtakingly beautiful.

In the centre of the blade, running down towards the tip, two alternating shades of metal twisted and writhed and wrapped around each other in three distinct strips, their paired strands crossing, re-crossing, splitting and entwining. It looked like twisted rope, but more complex, more alive, like a roiling mass of serpents frozen in time, wrestling in the heart of the steel. The edge was different. For two finger widths along each side of the blade, the steel looked like water rippling at a river's edge. Lines and waves of dark and light steel ran along the sides, piling into each other, rising, falling, disappearing under new ones, before appearing again further down. Pools of circles like raindrops on water were scattered through these waves. It reminded Ordulf of wood grain in the way the lines flowed around these ringed areas.

It was utterly the most beautiful blade he had ever seen. He brought his gaze up to the Norse smith, who was smiling coyly. 'Why?' Ordulf asked, pointing at the patterns. Dengir cocked his head at Ordulf's and for nearly the first time replied briefly, before dismissing Ordulf for the night. Ordulf couldn't catch the whole meaning of the short reply, but he thought that the smith said it was for strength, and to give the blade 'spirit'. He was puzzled by the meaning of both. He thought back to the repeated fold-ing of the different metals and pondered the pattern it had left. He realised the cunning of the process. His own swords back in Minden were variable in quality simply because the material varied. This meant that, for anything but the best proved steel, they sometimes cracked or failed at weak points. It was something he had never really questioned. Some swords failed. He didn't even see it as a problem; it was simply the way of it.

Dengir's method was so simple. By mixing the metals the way a tailor might mix dyes for cloth, he was getting a more consistent result in the final blade. In the central twisted sections, any small failures or impurities in the steel would be limited in size and would not travel through the softer metal entwined around the harder, making bad cracks less likely. It was genius. Ordulf suddenly felt very ignorant. How could he not have known about this method? How could they not have used it back home? He thought through the process of making this serpent blade and realised that it had probably taken them two or three times as long to make as the fine blade he had made for the count's son. Probably ten times as long as it took to make one from the batch of simple swords for the count's men. And it wasn't even finished yet. Perhaps this was simply too labour-intensive. Perhaps the art was lost?

Dengir rewrapped the blade and handed it to one of the junior smiths to store before dismissing them all for the day. Ordulf returned to the house with only one thought in his mind. He needed to make one of those blades. He lay awake for much of the night, imagining what he could do with those bands of steel now that the secret was opened to him.

The next day, he asked to make his own sword in a mixture of gestures and basic Norse. Dengir flatly refused to let Ordulf make his own serpent blade. Ordulf was frustrated and miserable. Instead, Dengir let him work as part of the hammer team on a new blade he was starting, effectively making him a junior smith rather than simply an apprentice. Ordulf accepted this small advance with as little sulking as he could manage.

They forged the steel bars into a billet, and Ordulf and the junior smiths hammered it into shape at the direction of Dengir. Ordulf could see it was a lot less complex than the serpent blade, with fewer folds and twists and a core of pure iron, much like the swords he had made at home. Perhaps that was why he was

trusted to help. He made a few mishits when he didn't fully understand the sung forging directions, which earned him curses and
scowls from the wizened master smith, but in general he thought it
went well. The blade was finished, and they started another. These
blades were clearly of lower quality and simpler design, but Ordulf
revelled in it, finally hammering hot steel into the swords.

When the serpent-patterned blade was fitted and finished with
its glorious inlaid guard and hilt, the master smith brought it out
into the courtyard to inspect one final time in the light. He spent
a long time going over the edges and inspecting the fit of the
handle and the detail and integrity of the fabulous inlay work in
the fittings. The lobed bronze pommel burst with lines of silver,
twisting and writhing around and across the domed surfaces and
then collecting down into the valleys between them until all were
combined at the tip of the pommel where a large bronze cap hid
the peened head of the tang. The silver was worked in so that
it looked like a landscape of rivers or the roots of a tree. It was
breathtakingly beautiful.

The cross guard held a runic inscription that Ordulf could not
read. He had not learned Norse script at all, as Otto said he had no
need of it as a slave and a smith. However, the pattern was quite
beautiful and drew the eye further into its intricacies the more
you looked at it. The dark, wooden hilt was uncovered except for
bronze ribbing laid into grooves cut into the wooden surface.

The edges of the blade had been sharpened at a shallow angle,
which removed the very outside of the rippled pattern but also
smoothed the edge so that it did not have the slight peaks and
troughs of the patterned surface. This made the outside line of
the blade shine like a rim of light around the darker etched flats.
The body of the sword itself had been lightly polished so that the
lighter areas shone more brightly and the darker areas were slightly

more pronounced. It was entrancing, and Ordulf could not take his eyes off it.

Ordulf had seen the scabbard being made. It was constructed from two shaped wooden halves, coated on the inside with wool, trimmed short and snugly holding the blade. The wooden shell was coated in tough leather on the outside, dark brown and reinforced with engraved bronze fittings at the tip and throat. Ordulf had been curious about the sheepskin inner surface and asked the smith why it was there. In Minden, they had used linen linings or no lining at all. The smith had taken part of the sheepskin and wiped it on the blade, leaving an oily smear. Ordulf nodded in understanding. The wool was naturally slightly oily but had also been impregnated with some sort of plant oil; the sword would be well protected from rust in that scabbard. On the side of the scabbard, on the side facing outwards as it was worn, a carved bone dragon lay. The tail started half way down the scabbard and it thickened as it reached the body of the beast, which sat snarling with its open mouth at the throat of the scabbard, a single blazing eye of red gemstone meeting his gaze.

All in all, it was quite the most beautiful sword Ordulf had ever seen, and he was spellbound. 'Who is it for?' he asked Dengir.

'It's for me,' said a voice behind him. Ordulf turned and saw that Jarl Ragnvald was behind him, standing in the entrance to the forge with a pair of his huscarls, Leif and Sebbi, and Otto alongside them. He was dressed in fine clothes, and his men were wearing their swords with shields slung over their backs. He was smiling at Dengir, who slid the sword into its elaborate scabbard and placed it on a trestle table for the jarl to inspect.

Jarl Ragnvald strode across the packed earth of the yard to the table. He removed his own sword from its scabbard, drab and tattered by comparison. He examined it with a strange expression, running his thumb over some jagged, unrepaired damage along the centre of one edge of the blade. Ordulf almost winced at the state of it. No wonder the jarl needed a new sword – that one was ruined.

Ragnvald laid the old sword down on the table and then moved his hands to the new one. He picked up the scabbarded blade, holding it out in one hand, running the other over the tight, dark-brown leather, fingers moving up to explore the shape of the beautiful dragon's head. The dragon with a sword sheathed in its throat.

He brought the hilt up to inspect it in the light, eyes wondering at the inlay of silver and the carved runes in the bronze cross guard and the pommel. His eyes were alight with pleasure, and he finally seized the hilt and slowly drew the blade from the serpent's throat, the rippled, twisted steel coming out into the sunlight with the quietest rustling of wool, the deathly whisper of a sword being freed from a scabbard.

Ragnvald pulled the tip of the sword free with an uncontrolled sigh of pure delight and raised it into the air, watching how the light played over the pattern. Finally, coming out of his personal trance, he looked over at Dengir. 'Magnificent.'

The stone-faced Dengir gave the slightest hint of a smile and a faint nod of his head. 'What will you name it, my lord?' asked Leif, standing at Ragnvald's side, marvelling at the blade along with the rest of them.

Ragnvald looked thoughtful for a moment and then brought the tip of the blade back to the scabbard, pushing it gently back into the dragon's mouth, then sheathing it, running it all the way home. 'Drekitunga,' he said, rubbing the white horn teeth of the fantastical beast that had swallowed the sword.

Ordulf looked around, puzzled. Otto tried to mouth something at him from across the yard, but Ordulf couldn't make it out. Ragnvald caught the look and smiled, saying something to Otto, who nodded.

'It means "dragon tongue",' he said, not needing to explain it further. Ordulf smiled. It was a good name. The idea of naming a sword was alien to him, but seeing the gleaming red eye of the dragon on the scabbard made it seem almost alive. It seemed right that it should have a name. Ragnvald was speaking to Otto again, and Ordulf was trying to follow, picking out words he knew but missing the flow of meaning.

'The jarl wants to know what you think of his sword,' said Otto with disinterest. He was the only one in the yard who had not been captivated by the sword's unveiling.

Ordulf smiled unashamedly. 'It is the finest sword I have ever seen.'

Ragnvald laughed heartily at the translation. Then he said something that made Dengir grunt and give Ordulf a filthy look. 'So do you still think your pointy swords are better?' Otto asked. Ordulf winced, trying not to meet the eye of his incredulous master smith. *Why had Otto told Ragnvald of that conversation?*

'I don't know,' he finally replied, honestly.

Ragnvald put the magnificent sword on the table and spoke briefly to Leif, who nodded and left the smithy at a jog. The jarl picked up his old sword and twirled it around in his wrist, loosening and stretching. The remaining warrior took up his shield and moved into the empty space in the centre of the yard, facing the jarl.

'The jarl says we should find out,' drawled Otto, who was failing to disguise his boredom but still working his way through the back-and-forth translation.

'This was my father's sword, Bjóðr. The best sword I have ever owned.' Ragnvald picked it up and gazed at it reverently for a moment. 'But its days of fighting are over. This last damage…'

Ragnvald paused, and for a moment his face held a deep sadness. 'This last damage cannot be repaired.' The fleeting look passed, and he looked up again at Ordulf, regaining his composure. 'So I have brought it here so that Dengir can cut it down, remake it as a seax and forge a spearhead from the tip.' Otto shrugged under Ordulf's curious gaze and did not elaborate further.

As he was looking at the old sword, Leif came back, breathing hard and carrying one of the captured Minden blades and a Saxon shield. 'Ah, good,' said Ragnvald, and he directed Sebbi, who was standing in the centre of the yard, to take the Christian weapons. Then Ragnvald took up Bjóðr and his own shield, and the two men faced each other in the slight crouch of a combat stance.

They faced each other for a few moments, exchanging words, and then the huscarl attacked, slowly and deliberately. He closed to striking range with a step and thrust, Ragnvald easily fouling the attack with his outstretched shield, knocking it to one side. Again, the man attacked, trying to bash Ragnvald's shield out of the way with a charge to get into position to thrust at the body. Ragnvald fended the charge off and danced to the side, the thrust clattering harmlessly from the edge of the shield.

Ordulf could see clearly what the problem was. Ragnvald's outstretched shield was making it impossible for Sebbi to get control, or get close enough for a thrust, not without exposing himself to a counter. His own shield, strapped to his forearm, could not reach out nearly as far from his body to cover himself. As soon as Ordulf saw it, it seemed obvious.

Sebbi became frustrated and started swinging at the jarl's shield, hoping to force it out of position with rapid cuts. Ragnvald bounced and moved, shield recoiling from the blows without much damage. Then, as one heavy swing came in, he turned the top of the shield into the swing and let the sword bite into the edge of it. The sword stuck fast in the end of the grain and Ragnvald twisted violently, ripping the sword from his opponent's grip. He had never even made an attack.

Ragnvald nodded to Sebbi and stepped back with a smile. 'So, my little Christian, now he has no sword, and I still have my old blade. Would you care to see what it can do?'

Again, Ordulf simply nodded. He could already see where this was going, but the jarl was clearly enjoying himself.

After his opponent recovered his sword from the ground and made ready, the jarl snapped his sword back and threw it into a series of fast probes, sword flicking out like a snake's tongue, aiming to go around the other man's shield. The warrior grunted and took half steps backwards as he blocked and covered and parried, but with his shield much less mobile, he was having to do much of the work with his feet and his sword. One crunching blow from Ragnvald hit the shield while it was braced against the man's arm, causing splinters to fly and Sebbi to stumble back with a grunt of pain. Finally, the jarl stopped his attack.

The jarl stepped back to face Ordulf, his face triumphant. Ordulf noticed that the shield warrior was bleeding from a deep slice on his upper arm. He also noticed that Sebbi was ignoring it, even ignoring the splinter protruding from the wound. Ordulf's eyes widened. He was shocked at how much more effective the Norse weapons had been.

'It is true that my sword cannot be thrust easily through maille, but in a fight such as this it does not matter; you can attack where the maille does not cover.' He twirled and cut at the air with his sword as he spoke and waited for Otto to relay his words.

'You see, our shields are light, designed for moving, deflecting blows, gaining dominance over another warrior in attack. Our swords are mostly broad, balanced for cutting, and thin so that the cuts are deep.' Otto was struggling to keep up, but Ordulf managed to fill in the gaps. 'Our swords and shields are perfect for fighting lightly armoured enemies in the open, for attacking swiftly and with deadly effect. So, as you see, for fighting with sword and shield one-on-one, our way is better. Even with my ruined sword, a sword older than I am, I still beat your new one with ease.'

Ordulf nodded, trying and failing to hide his embarrassment. His pride had once again made him look foolish.

The jarl signalled to the injured warrior and snapped an order. Sebbi nodded and handed his weapons to his fellow before turning to leave.

'I have to actually order my men to treat their own wounds,' he said with a sigh of frustration. 'One of them ignored a serious wound for so long in the name of honour that it became unhealable, and I lost one of my best warriors. They now compete ever harder to impress me with their bravery.'

Ordulf nodded. 'So I heard,' he said.

The jarl raised his eyebrows, surprised. 'Oh, did you?' He barked a single, short laugh. 'Otto is teaching you well. I shall have to reward him.' He paused, smiling at the flustered, nine-fingered slave, who was busy translating his own praise.

Ragnvald turned back to Ordulf. 'But now we are fighting Christians in large battles, and we are losing. Our weapons aren't as good in packed formations. Some of these Christians wear maille from head to toe, which makes our swords near useless in the press of battle. The battles in Denmark showed us this.'

He rolled his shoulder, stretching out the soreness from the sword demonstration as he continued his musings.

'So it is my opinion that we must learn from your Christians and adapt to their ways in order to fight them better.' He picked up the Minden blade and inspected it thoughtfully. 'This is why you are interesting. You are the only Frankish smith in the Norselands, the only one who has made these Christian swords, the ones that can punch through maille.' He looked at Ordulf and studied him carefully. 'I wonder what would happen if you combined your Frankish design with our steel.'

Dengir was standing beside them, his eyes turned upwards, chewing a black fingernail and thinking it over. 'It can be done,' Dengir said, after a short while. He nodded to himself as he spoke.

'Excellent. Then, Ordulf, I wish for you to make me such a sword, so that I or one of my men can test it against the Christians, to see if my idea is correct. Use Dengir's skill with steel and your knowledge of Christian swords and what I have just shown you. Perhaps, if this works, you will prove yourself worthy of staying in my household.' The veiled threat, delivered with such careless ease, unnerved Ordulf, who nodded furiously and tried to thank the jarl in Norse and, from Ragnvald's amused expression, clearly made a mess of it.

The jarl took his new serpent sword from the table and swept out of the yard to take the path back to the hall. The remaining warrior followed close behind with Otto. Ordulf was left examining the damaged swords they left behind, deep in thought while Dengir directed the rest of the workers to clear up the yard and get back to work.

Ordulf didn't even consider the implications of the request, that he was being asked to create a weapon to kill his countrymen, even to help the Norse against the crusade. His mind passed entirely over that without notice as he bubbled inside with the excitement of the only piece of information that he cared about, the only thing that mattered to him in that moment. He was a swordsmith again.

Prove my worth? I'll do that. I'll show them who I can be. He whistled brightly as he carried the two blades into the forge and laid them down to begin trying to work out how he would design the new blade. The invisible chains of his slavery slipped away unnoticed from his mind as he savoured the task and the responsibility laid out for him.

Ragnvald walked back to the hall with Leif, scabbarded sword still in hand, turning it over and admiring its detail.

'Do you really think the boy can make a better sword than that?' asked Leif, his doubt evident in his tone.

'Perhaps not,' said Ragnvald with a shrug. 'But it costs very little to try, and we must try everything possible to gain an advantage over the Christians, to defeat them.'

'You think we will retake Jutland by copying their swords?' said Leif with unconcealed amusement.

Ragnvald stopped and turned to look at his young huscarl with a cold expression. 'I doubt we will ever see Jutland again. No, I am talking about saving the land that is still ours. Protecting our people from this gathering storm. Is there anything you would not try?'

Leif was taken aback. 'You cannot think they will invade Scania, Gotland, even Svealand?'

'I cannot believe anything else. They will not be content with what they have, and you saw them – you saw what they are capable of. We must assume they will come for us, even here, and plan accordingly. Why else do you think I would do what we just did? What wouldn't you do to save our people?' Ragnvald's tone was bitter.

Leif looked away, uncomfortable at the raw memory of their hunt. 'What will we truly save if we kill our own kin and trust a foreign king, if we put our trust in foreign swords? What else will we sacrifice to stop them?'

Ragnvald put his hand on the man's shoulder and smiled bitterly. 'Let me share the wisdom of a dead man with you, Leif.' The huscarl turned his head to meet the jarl's eye. 'We will do whatever it takes.'

Jarl Ragnvald Ivarsson, warlord of Sweden, faces Sebbi with Bjóðr in hand

Epilogue

Røros, Nordland
Summer 2015

TWO WEEKS AFTER the discovery of the sword and the excavation at Bjørsjøen lake had been completed, a team of archaeology students from the University of Lundjen had methodically explored the lake bed around the original finds, recovered all the artefacts they uncovered and taken them back to Lundjen for analysis and conservation. Professor Hallsson had told Halfar they were receiving X-ray results from the sword that afternoon and compiling a review of the recovered artefacts and that he would call to tell him what they had found.

Halfar was nervous and fidgety, unable to concentrate on anything else while he awaited the review later that day. But then there was a shrill noise.

His phone. Caller ID said it was Professor Hallsson. He answered and was launching into a cheery greeting when he was stopped by the torrent of words coming the other way.

'What? Sorry, say that again. I couldn't make it out,' he interrupted.

A terse pause.

'Halfar, check your email. We have made some very significant finds among the artefacts, and you need to see it. We can go over the rest another time.'

The bemused Halfar tucked his phone under his cheek and opened his email. He found the message. There were two photo attachments. He opened the first one.

It was an image of a magnificent gold arm band, now cleaned and laid out with measuring sticks alongside. A printed label sat on the bench beneath it:

Gold arm torc, 11th–12th century Norse
Outer runic inscription: 'Born under the cross, live under the hammer.'
Inner inscription: 'Bjorn – Vidar – Leif – Gunnar'

Halfar sat back and rubbed his face with his free hand. Those were the names of the four mythical companions of Gjaldir from the Icelandic saga *Ljós ór Norðan*. Mighty warriors whose names had lived on alongside the mythical hero. He had never seen their names on any artefact found outside of Iceland.

'That is remarkable, to see a torc with those names on in the highlands of the old kingdom of Sweden. How on earth did that get there?'

'I think the second photograph would answer that question,' said the professor.

Bemused, Halfar clicked on the second image and opened it. Immediately, he jolted bolt upright. He stared open-mouthed at the screen for what seemed an eternity, unable to mentally process what he was seeing.

The image was split and showed both a colour photo and an X-ray of the cleaned sword. The X-ray showed that, indeed, the sword was made from pattern-welded steel. Clearly visible was a uniform central core with a twisted pattern surrounding it all the way around and down towards the tip. The pattern resembled flames eating at the core. Outside that, in the outer parts and at the edge, a roiling, swirling pattern was embedded in the steel.

But none of that was what really caused Halfar such a shock.

They had cleaned up the blade and the runic inscription was more visible, although still illegible. But that didn't matter; the runes were laid out vividly in the X-ray.

'No, it can't be,' whispered Halfar in shock.

'I think it might!' said Hallsson with a burst of excitement.

'It's impossible. It's just a story. This must be a fake.'

'The period and design is correct, and all the artefacts found with it are from the correct period too. This cache is from before the saga was written; it predates it.'

Halfar sat in shocked silence as he went over the implications.

'Hello?' came the voice from the other end of the line.

'Yes, I'm still here. I just don't believe it. I always thought it was just a myth.'

'Amazing, isn't it? When can you get down here?'

'Get down there? What do you mean?' Halfar answered, befuddled by the idea.

'What do you mean, *What do you mean?* There will be a public statement, a press conference. They will want to hear from the people who discovered it, and you are an expert on Norse mythology, perhaps the leading one in the country. Of course you should be there!'

'I see, yes, I suppose so. I don't much like the idea of facing the media,' said Halfar, nervously.

'Don't be ridiculous. Isn't the whole purpose of your museum to teach people about Norse history? You have a whole display on this saga!'

'Yes, but that is only for a few people at a time.'

'Exactly! Now you have the chance to show thousands, maybe

hundreds of thousands. Halfar, this story needs to be told. Come down and be the one who tells it.'

'Okay,' mumbled Halfar uncertainly.

'Excellent! Now, I have the deputy minister of culture on the other line. I'll let you know when the plans are made.'

Halfar muttered his goodbyes and hung up, putting the phone down and staring once more at the photographs of the artefacts in wonder. He could barely believe it as he stared at the X-ray of the sword and the words engraved into it. The myth he had known for his entire life, studied and taught to generations of students was sitting there in corroded steel, staring back at him in runic script: *Ljós a Norðan.*

Afterword and Historical Note

Writing an alternate reality gives a writer a lot of latitude with events and background but can lead to confusion and blurring as to what is real and what is fantasy. I will try and clear some of that up here. I have tried to maintain a solid level of realism based on the known and implied knowledge of the time. Everything that happens differently in that world is something that I believe makes sense and could have happened. Since the main separation from reality is the rejection of the path to Christianity, the vast majority of historical detail remains unchanged.

For example, because this alternate reality is separated so narrowly from reality, almost all the high-ranking characters are real. These are men unknown to popular history but who lived fascinating lives that had huge consequences for the Europe we live in today. I have changed details of their lives to match the alternate history, but Adolf, Count of Schauenburg (and later of Holstein and Stormarn), was a real military leader of Saxony who raised himself from obscurity and became a major part of the Germanisation of the northern parts of that land in the 1100s, a campaign that had historical repercussions that last to this day.

He participated in large parts of the conquest of the base of the Jutland peninsula and the German Baltic shore, changing the face of Europe forever. He would have been a natural choice for this crusade. His son Hartung is also real, although he did not live a life noteworthy enough for us to be left with more than a mere mention of his name. He is a footnote to the history of his father.

Adolf's feudal lord, Lothair, the Duke of Saxony, was a skilled and able politician and leader who became emperor after Henry. The Norwegian kings are all historical figures, although the Danish and Swedish are made up, since the real kings were Christian appointments who would not have gained the crown in a Norse society.

Most of the other great crusader lords are also real, all with lives altered by the differing events of this book but all in ways that I think are realistic. The various jarls are all fictional, sadly, because there just isn't a lot of information preserved about the Norse lords of this age. So Ragnvald is a work of pure fiction.

The finding of the sword in the lake is also a fictionalisation of a real event. In 2018, a young Swedish girl called Saga Vanecek pulled a Viking-era sword from a lake near Jonkoping in Sweden. When I read about that sword, I wondered what its story was, where it had been and what it had seen. I decided that story needed to be written, and not knowing what it was, I made it up. The girl's name being Saga. It was too perfect, a message from the gods, and so the saga of the sword Ljós a Norðan was born.

I have also paid close attention to and done a great deal of research into the details of Norse life: combat, culture, religion, craft and mythology. I do not pretend to be a historian on these subjects and will characterise my portrayal as 'reasonable' but not accurate. Some scholars would no doubt cringe at a few of my simplifications or oversights, but this is a work of fiction and some things did need to be 'adjusted' to make a better story. Some inaccuracies are deliberate; others are ignorance. I hope those who notice them forgive me.

It is pretty clear that pattern-welded swords fell out of fashion around AD 1000. Probably this was because of access to better, more consistent steels that allowed mono-steel blades to be as good or better than pattern-welded ones. However, if the Norse were prevented from trading with western Europe, it is conceivable they would have continued making pattern-welded steel for longer. So this is the kind of logical adjustment to history I have made. If you absolutely have to put me right on something, or just want to discuss something of interest, poke me on Twitter (@ JCDuncan7). I welcome the debate.

One of the things I love about this period of history is the 'old' forms of record keeping, legends and storytelling. The preservation and embellishment of stories by word of mouth, visual art and folklore, a lot of it preserved by local people, is so much more interesting to me than much of the sanitised, sometimes falsified, politically and religiously motivated 'history' recorded in the Christian kingdoms of medieval western Europe by the elite.

I love the fuzziness and artistic nature of 'pagan' Norse and Saxon stories where fantasy and reality freely mixed and was deeply culturally significant during its own time. The Norse way of telling and recording history is truly fascinating and heavily misunderstood. I want to represent the creation, propagation and evolution of a story over 1000 years. I am trying to bring to life one fictional example in this book series (much more of which will be explored in the sequels), but anyone wanting to know how the Norse lived and told their stories should look to the Icelandic sagas which provide a rich portrayal of Norse life. I am incorporating aspects of those stories into these books: ways of war and ways of life.

Most people only know of Norse storytelling and beliefs through sensationalised and frankly silly myths and legends. I will try to show in this series why those stories were so exaggerated, and I will delve into my opinion that it is not because they were simply believed but because those stories held deeper meaning or were just outright entertaining. And outright entertaining they were. Films and TV shows are still being made about Thor, Loki, Beowulf, Ragnar Lothbrok, Ivar the Boneless and his brothers, and many other mythical or semi-mythical figures today.

I have also been studying the historical swordsmithing and weapon-making of the era in great detail. Swordsmithing forms another key theme of this book. There is a fascinating history of different types of bladesmithing in Europe. The internet and common knowledge is full of misinformation about swords: what was good, what was bad, what steel was like in different times. Falsehoods like the idea that Damascus steel was better than anything today, or that Katanas are so sharp and hard that they can cut through (insert improbable object here). There is now a dedicated and growing community of craftsmen and women recreating these lost arts, studying the historical records and conducting forensic recreations, so there is no excuse for these inaccuracies. The truth is that the best smiths in Europe and the Middle East were making steel as good as or better than the steel in a mythologised Katana before the first Samurai ever swung a sword. It was a very advanced craft. There is so much to learn about European swordsmithing. It was a fine and deep art, making some superb weapons (and a lot of basic ones), and I attempt to scratch the surface for the casual reader in this book.

As part of both the research and inspiration for this book series, I have gone as far as training to become an amateur bladesmith. I have forged my own recreation seax from pattern-welded steel I folded and forge welded myself. I have swung a hammer in a few hot forges, tempered, hardened and ground my own blades and, yes, I have spent many, many hours hand-sanding and polishing blades, a process that our protagonist hated so much when he did it for others he didn't care about and loved so much when he did it for those he did care for. Many smiths will recognise that duality of the hand-finishing process – the frustration and the satisfaction. Some things you have to do to understand. You know nothing of polishing until you have taken a blade from a rough piece of steel to a mirror finish in dozens of hours of repetitive, aching manual labour. It's one of the best and worst things you can do in all my broad experience of handcrafts.

For those who want to, I highly recommend going on a taster course to forge a Viking-style knife or similar blade. I have swung hammers and forged steel in half a dozen forges and never met a person I didn't like there; smiths are as friendly and interesting a bunch as any I have met.

These courses are available all over the USA and Europe, and if you are in England like me, you can sign up to learn with Owen Bush. Owen is a renowned teacher who I started my bladesmithing journey with and who is as bearded and mad a smith as you could hope to swing a hammer with. As well as being a world-renowned expert on pattern welding and weapons such as the Dane axe, Owen has also forged the 'real' Ljós a Norðan. The day I typed this sentence, he was smelting iron ore in a bloomery furnace to make steel for the blade in the same way the Norse smiths once did. Getting Ljós a Norðan made alongside the book is a fantastic and exciting event for me. It will be a prop and a source of inspiration. The sword will be as close as possible to the real thing, a hardened, pattern-welded, battle-ready Norse sword. Some of you may have found this book because of a video or article about the sword.

If you want to know more about Viking life and culture, I highly recommend Hurstwic. This group of re-enactors and historians have a website that is the best resource for a casual history buff like me that you could hope to find. They cover every aspect of Norse life and culture and have spent decades painstakingly recreating Norse combat from the archaeological evidence, descriptions in the sagas and their own practice sparring to find out what does and doesn't work with those weapons. I have taken heavily from what I learned from their website and their wonderful series of videos recreating famous fights from the Icelandic sagas.

I would also thank the people who inspired me to start writing: the authors of historical and fantasy fiction I have been reading for over twenty-five years. I started with the megastar Bernard Cornwell, perhaps the most successful and the cheerleader of historical fiction and fantasy authors, by reading his *Sharpe* series starting when I was about seven. I have since moved on to other superb writers: Conn Iggulden, Ben Kane, Giles Kristian, Angus Donald, Joe Abercrombie, Daniel Kelly (who was my first beta reader and cheerleader in the business, a thousand thank-yous), Matthew Harffy, John Gwynne, Jonathan French, Griff Hosker, Ken Follett, David Gilman, Dan Davis… (I read a lot of books, as all authors should) and others who don't spring to mind right now. It was enjoying their books so much that made me so interested in this genre and made me start thinking about writing myself, but it was the work of Christian Cameron that finally tipped me over the edge into writing my first series. He brings a level of detail, excitement, political background, culture and first-hand knowledge into his writing that just blew me away. He writes about fighting in armour, and he does train and fight in armour himself. He writes about living with and using ancient equipment, and he does re-enactments and long marches in replica gear. That kind of knowledge just doesn't come from reading about it on Wikipedia. It shows in his work and elevates it hugely, which is why I had to go and actually make a pattern-welded blade before I wrote about one. That lesson I owe to Christian.

I met Christian shortly before I finished this book, and we spent three hours discussing the finer points of sword and shield combat and writing style, which was a perfect evening for a budding author and fan. If you liked my book, go and read his, if you haven't already. If you see a little of his style in my writing, it is deliberate. I borrowed some of my favourite aspects of his style, his marking of time for example, and I am not ashamed.

Finally, I have to thank my wife, who put up with me semi-disappearing from her life to hammer steel and write books and was still gracious and supportive enough to beta read and help edit this book for me.

The saga of *Ljós a Norðan* will continue. The eyes of
the Christian lords will be set across the narrow sea,
and the Norse will face a war for their very survival.
Book two will be published in winter 2021.

If you have made it this far, I thank and congratulate you.
As a debut self-published author writing in my spare time in
the age of Amazon and social media, my publishing career
will live and die on reviews, tweets, facebook recommends,
goodreads write ups and 'likes'. So if this tale entertained you
and you wish to see more, go to the nearest internet portal
and let the world know. Each review makes it more likely I
will be able to continue to write. Thank you all so much.

You can also sign up to my reader's club, 'The Warband'
(https://jcduncan.co.uk/warband-signup). My reader's club
will give you a vaguely monthly newsletter (no spam, no
referrals), information on upcoming releases, my bladesmithing,
and most importantly – discounts, sales, signings, freebies
and giveaways. All my giveaways will be solely to list
members. So join the warband today, it's completely free!

James C. Duncan. December 2020

GLOSSARY

Named Characters

Adolf, Count of Schauenburg and lord of Holstein and Stormarn: A Saxon lord of Duke Lothair's patronage, Commander of the Saxon contingent in the first Northern Crusade

Aurick: Father of Ingrid, discoverer of the sword Ljós a Norðan

Brunhild: A Norse slave girl in the service of Jarl Ragnvald

Dengir: The Norse master smith at Uppsala

Eric Silverfist of Sweden: King of Sweden from 1105 to 1116

Gjaldir: Legendary Norse warrior

Professor Hallsson: Dean of the Archaeology Department at the University of Lundjen.

Halfar Asleson: Curator of the Røros Museum of Norse History and Culture

Hildewa: Wife of Ragnvald

Harald Bluetooth: Danish king who made the decision to ban Christianity after a Christian missionary failed a trial by fire and then tried to kill him in the 970s

Henry V: Emperor of the HRE at the time of the first Northern Crusade

Herman: Master smith of the Minden forge

Ingrid: Eleven-year-old girl who likes history and hates fishing. Discoverer of the sword Ljós a Norðan

Jarl Alf: Swedish jarl, a one-time contender for the throne after Eric's death

Jarl Birkir: Ally of Jarl Harnsted

Jarl Erling: Swedish jarl

Jarl Frode: Swedish jarl, ally of Ragnvald

Jarl Gustav: Swedish jarl

Jarl Halvar: Swedish jarl, ally of Harnsted

Jarl Harnsted: Swedish jarl, cousin of King Eric and one of the contenders for the throne

Jarl Ragnvald Ivarsson: Important jarl of the kingdom of Sweden

Jarl Steinar: Norwegian jarl, close associate of King Sigurd

Leuter: Farmhand, fist fighter and soldier of the crusade

Leif Leifson: Huscarl of Jarl Ragnvald

Lothair, Duke of Saxony: Contender to be the next Holy Roman emperor, crusade leader

Magnus 'Barefoot' Olafsson: king of Norway from 1073 to 1116

Orbert: Saxon camp master and lover of lists

Ordulf: German smith from Minden in Lower Saxony

Otto: A German slave in the service of Jarl Ragnvald

Sebbi: Huscarl of Jarl Rangvald

Sigurd Magnusson: Son of Magnus, the king of Norway

Sir Hans Metel of Oldenburg: A leading knight of the Saxon contingent. Revered as a great swordsman

Ulf: Huscarl of Jarl Ragnvald and his shipmaster

ABOUT THE AUTHOR

Hi there! I'm James Duncan. As an author I am fascinated with history and fantasy. I write historical fantasy/fiction based on our world, but in an alternate timeline, past, present, or future. Each book or series asks and tries to answer a question of 'What if?' This series asks the question 'What if the Norse didn't convert to Christianity, and instead the Viking raids continued.' And posits the answer, which you will have to read the rest of the series to find out! I do not create new worlds, I mess with the history and future of ours, grounded in our own past and the laws of our universe, but tweaked in events and often adding a soft sprinkling of the divine or fantastical, resulting in relatable historical and future fantasy.

Upcoming books include the questions:

'What if the black death was actually a coverup of something much, much worse.' - 'The Black' -An alternate history of the time of the black death, based in southern and eastern Europe, coming out in 2022.

'What if the human race develops a race of gene engineered worker drones, but they are turned against us.' - 'Outriders' - A post-apocalyptic fiction set in the 22nd century in Poland and Hungary, est. release date late 2023.

Outside of authoring I am a professional engineer, and splits his spare time writing, reading, and being an amateur bladesmith. My bladesmithing work, and more information about my life and authoring, and the ability to contact me and talk to me directly, are available on my website.

www.Jcduncan.co.uk